ALL THE GOLD BETWEEN US

JADE LE BRIS

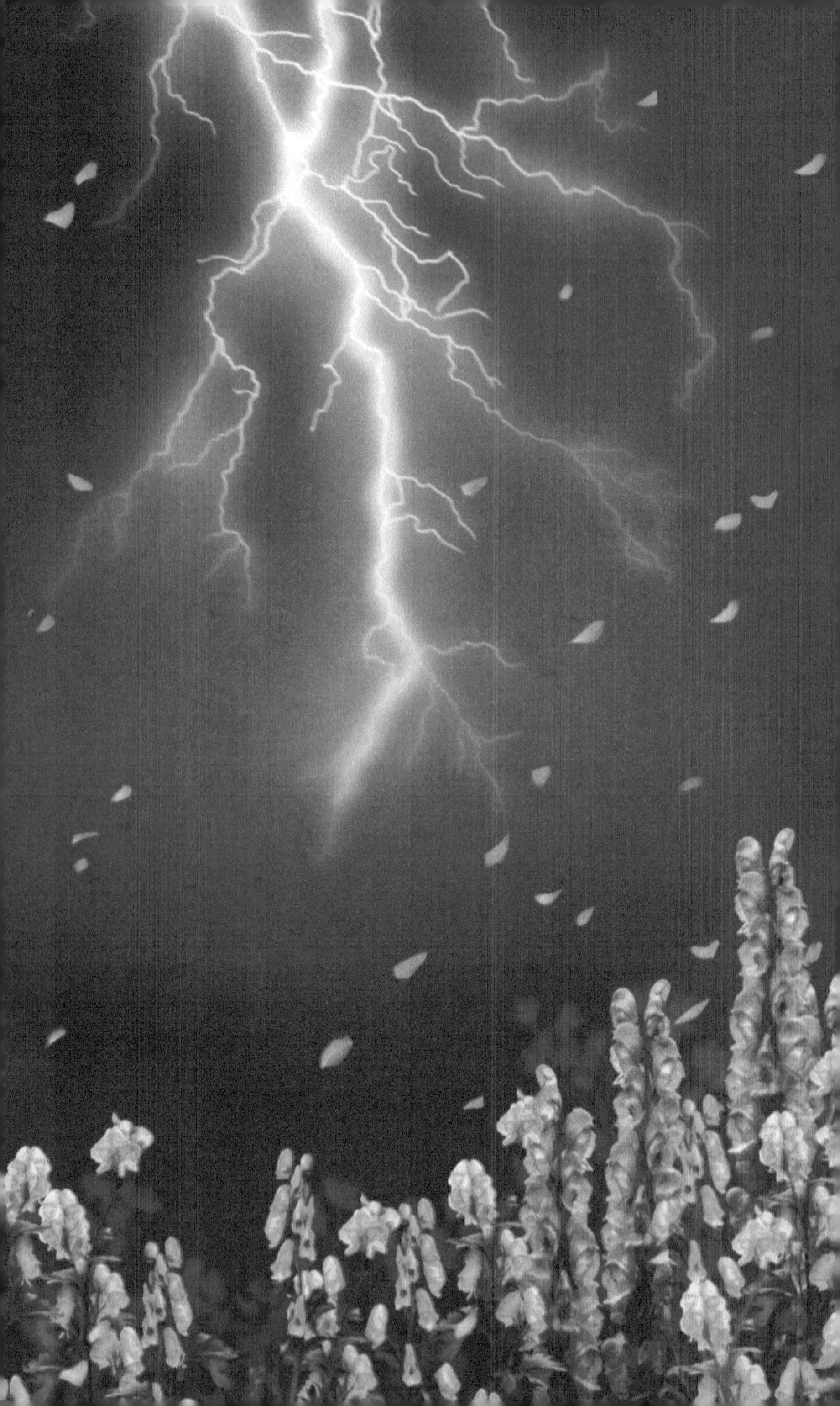

JADE LE BRIS

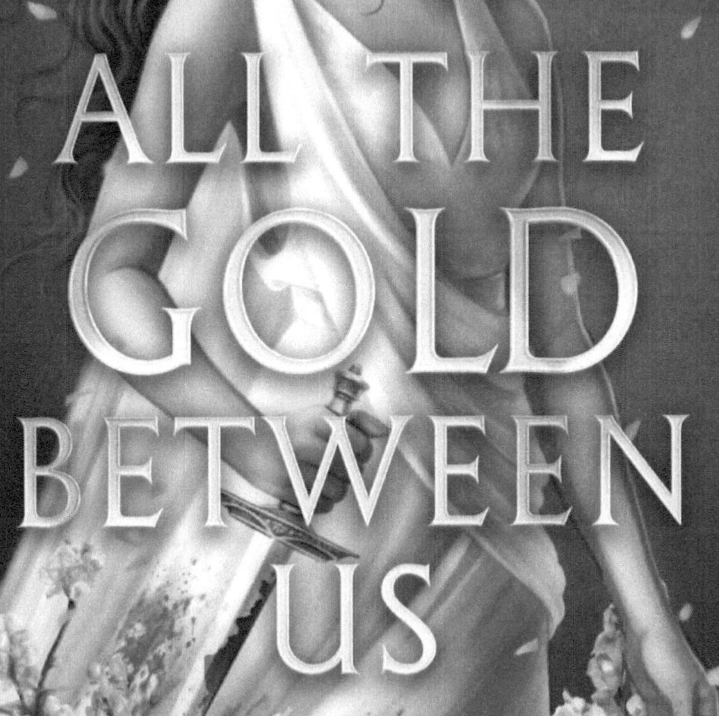

ALL THE GOLD BETWEEN US

First published in 2023 by Jade Le Bris.

Paperback IBSN: 979-8-9884041-0-1
eBook ISBN: 979-8-9884041-1-8

Content Warnings

'All the Gold Between Us' is a New Adult fantasy book about a young woman who is mistakenly enrolled in a deadly Tournament with the descendants of Greek Gods. While fun, this story also contains elements that might not be suited to some readers. Swearing, hate speech, attempted sexual assault, fighting, violence, and graphic death are present on-page in the book. Readers who may be sensitive to these elements, please take note.

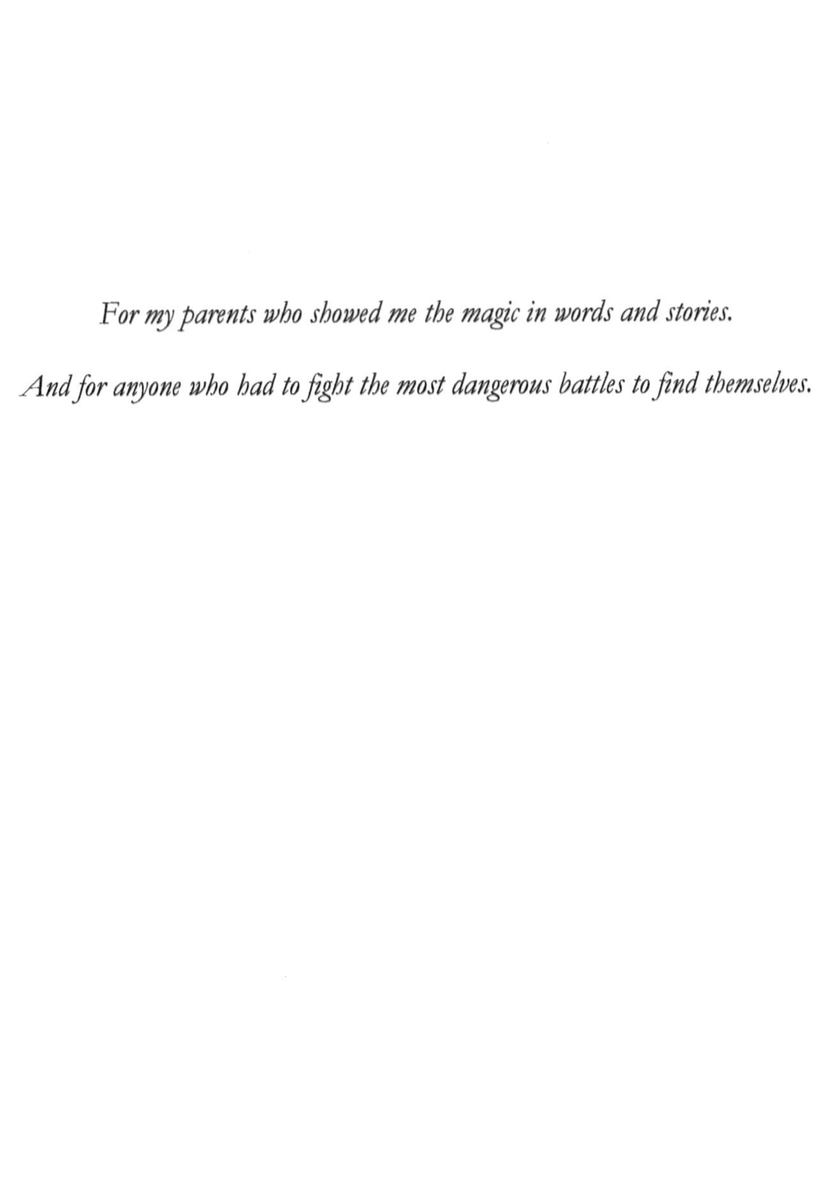

For my parents who showed me the magic in words and stories.

And for anyone who had to fight the most dangerous battles to find themselves.

Prologue

To be clear, I had no plan at all.

I ran until I came face to face with the girl who had taken Charlie's life. The only thing I could think to do was ram into her. I had accumulated a lot of momentum, and we both went flying. I landed on her, far enough away from Charlie's body that she couldn't reach for the weapon in his back. And then I punched her. Straight in the face. Based on the crunch and her yell, I broke her nose.

Then I punched her again. And again. She took a few seconds to recover from the shock of my attack before she started fighting back. She punched me in the ribs from below, ripping the air out of my lungs. Fighting to breathe, I pressed my left forearm on her throat and moved my weight up and to the left so that my body prevented her from using her right arm to hit me. With my right hand, I grabbed her free wrist and immobilized it to the ground. She buckled, trying to breathe and escape. But I held as strong as I could.

I had no idea how far I was ready to take this. But I knew I had to knock her out fast if I wanted to avoid meeting her power. Now that I was heading on this path, I might as well go for it.

Except the girl wasn't going to take it lying down. Because, of course, that would be way too easy. Instead, she shimmied her hands out of mine and put them on either side of me. She pushed and thrust her hips up, which made me lose my balance. I had to put my hands out to catch myself, which allowed the cold-blooded killer to escape my hold.

Suddenly I was on my back, and she was on top of me, punching me straight in the jaw. I raised my hands to protect my face, leaving my ribs open for her to hit me again. I groaned as I was forced to exhale with force. Shit. That was a terrible situation to be stuck in.

But if I had thought that it couldn't be worse, I was wrong. Because I quickly discovered that Charlie's killer had a nifty trick up her sleeve. She had freezing hands. Quite literally. Ice Queen girl put one of her hands on my chest, and it was so cold that it *burned*. In seconds, my respiratory muscles slowed down until breathing became a struggle. Panic crept in because the air I could force into my lungs was becoming so small that I was getting dizzy.

I had to fight back. I couldn't just give up now. My first instincts were to fight dirty, so I went for the eyes. It must have been painful because Ice Queen screamed and released me. The cold let up just long enough for me to get her into a desperate chokehold.

And I squeezed.

I felt the moment her body became loose and unresponsive. I didn't know how long I held on, but I was terrified of letting her go, only for her to attack me again. I didn't want to kill her. But I knew damn well that if I gave her the opening to hurt me again, I wouldn't be able to defend myself anymore. By that point, pure survival instincts helped me hold on.

Chapter One

Six weeks earlier

Life was filled with good and bad days. Bad days were vital because they enabled us to appreciate the good ones more. Or so everyone said. The issue was that I'd have a succession of particularly terrible days lately.

Today was no exception.

The first piece of evidence was my complete lack of patience. You would think kids would be exhausted after almost an hour of intense gymnastic practice. Well, no. My students were always so full of energy, especially during practice. It was as if coming here, training with their friends, having rules, expectations, a purpose, and people who cared gave them an extra push.

And they all became replicas of the Energizer Bunny.

Usually, I loved seeing them so happy, so full of life. I loved this job. Teaching them gymnastics and seeing how I could help these kids forget their crappy reality, even for an hour, filled me with a deep sense of pride and purpose. And making them smile and laugh was the best part of the job.

Not today, though.

Today was a shitty day. Again. Most of my days weren't exactly fun and giggles, but today had been especially bad. My *Animal Physiology* test didn't go well this morning, which sucked after studying for it all week. My boyfriend, Brad, broke up with me over lunch break. Admittedly, I wasn't very attached. But still. It stung. So, *obviously*, my now ex-boyfriend ruined my lunch, partly because of the whole break-up thing but mostly because he got angry that I wasn't balling my eyes out. Trust me. It was the longest and worst lunch break I'd had in a long time.

I thought it was it for the day, that my day couldn't get worse that easily. But it did because it wouldn't be fun otherwise, right? During my first afternoon class, I had to spend the whole hour and a half doing all the work for our *group* project – worth twenty-five percent of our grade, mind you – while my partners chilled on Netflix. Awesome. And, to end the day beautifully, I got a flat tire without any spare in my trunk, and I had to walk the whole three miles to the gym.

So, yeah, I didn't have much patience left today.

"Coach Kalani! I made it!" Sierra came over, clapping her hands, a smile over half of her face. She was so cute and probably one of my favorite kids to teach. And at just nine years old, she was already doing some pretty impressive tricks.

"Awesome job, little one, that dismount was perfect! I am really proud of you!" I smiled at her and tapped her head lightly, making her beam. That kid lived to please others – I guess it was fair when you had five siblings, your parents worked three jobs each, and you lived in the shittiest neighborhood in the city – you wanted people to notice you, to *care*.

"Great job, everyone!" I announced to the others after playfully flicking Sierra's cheek. "We are done for today! I will see all of you on Wednesday at four o'clock," I emphasized with a look to three girls who always chatted in the locker room until they were late.

A few minutes later, the gym was empty and quiet again. Thank goodness. Looking at my phone, I was relieved to find no new messages from either Mom or Makaio, my nine-year-old little brother. It meant I didn't have to return to the apartment in a rush to make food for Makaio because Mom forgot. Again.

Sighing, I removed my sweatpants and sweatshirt, leaving only my shorts and sports bra. I had two hours before I had to leave to go to work – just enough time to practice, eat, and get over there for my evening shift. Thankfully I had the eight to two shift; I didn't want to deal with the flood of black-out drunk people that crowded the bar afterward.

Putting my favorite playlist on my speaker – I had to have a different one for the kids – I went to the mat to warm up.

Practicing was my favorite part of the day. I had three loves: Makaio, gymnastics, and surfing. So, even though it wasn't the same as before, getting to practice was good for me. Good for my soul.

I poured my heart, soul, and energy into old routines for the next hour or so. I turned, leaped, bounced, tumbled, spun, and flipped. And for a few minutes, I felt like seventeen-year-old me again.

All too soon, I was at the bar, ready for my shift. This was much less fun.

Pulling my hair up in my usual ponytail, I got behind the bar, smiling at Maria. The girl was nice, way too much to work as a barmaid in this hell hole. Somehow though, she survived the past three months here without getting chewed to death by either our boss or customers.

"Hey there, Kalani!" Maria said with her signature smile, the one many guys came for every night. "It's pretty busy tonight, and there is a bachelor party, so I hope you're ready for a long night!" She even looked genuinely happy saying it.

Great.

Bachelor parties were the worst.

Never mind. I lied. *Bachelorette* parties were the worst. Bachelor parties were a close second.

I didn't have time to think about it or complain, because the first people shouted over the music to get my attention. Then, it was a long stream of making drinks and trying to stop the headache starting from the loud music and bright color LED lights.

Four hours later, after serving countless drinks, calling security twice on men harassing me, and fending off at least twenty demands for my number and future dates – the groom's friends were pretty insistent and drunk – I was finally done.

Callie, a thirty-year-old biker lady with sass and curves to die for, relieved me of my spot, and I couldn't wait to get out of there. "Have a great rest of your night, darling. I'm taking it from here!"

Answering with a smile and a wave – I didn't have the strength to shout anymore - I left toward the staff lockers. I put on my leather jacket - because nights in North California could be chilly in April – and got my keys ready. I didn't want to search for them when I got to my building; my neighborhood wasn't the safest and I didn't want to test my luck with drunk and potentially violent people.

The walk to my apartment was short and as uneventful as possible. With my car stuck on campus with a flat tire, I had never been so happy before that I worked so close to home.

Everything was dark in the apartment, and both Makaio and Mom's shoes were at the entrance. Good. It meant Mom didn't forget to come home and care for Makaio – a first this week.

I knew she did her best. She was a single mom with two kids, working two jobs to make ends meet, and still half depressed from my father's death. She did what she could, even though it wasn't enough at times.

My dad had been the love of her life. Dad, aka Keanu Hale, had moved from Hawaii, where he had lived all his life, to California to become a surf and scuba diving instructor. They had met at the beach, where my mom had taken a surf lesson with some friends. It was instant love. Soon, they had an apartment, were engaged, and had me on the way.

Then he died in a car accident the week before their wedding. Two months before I was born.

The few of Mom's friends she still had from before told me that she was never the same afterward. The thing was, I'd only known the *after-dad* version of my mom, with the depression going on and off every year and the pain she felt every time she saw me.

Because I looked so much like *him*.

I was pretty sure she felt the tearing pain of his death over and over again every time she saw my face. That might be why I had never had a remarkably loving and caring mother.

At least she loved Makaio. He was a mistake, born from a one-night stand and a pierced condom, but he didn't look like her long-lost soulmate. And she cared about him in her own way.

He was the reason why I was still here, though. He was my little light in this dark world.

I ate the rest of the pasta with red sauce and cleaned my brother's mess on the kitchen table – he always made a mess while eating.

Suddenly, small steps resonated behind me. Smiling softly, I could already tell who it was before I turned around.

"Hey, big guy, what are you still doing up this late?"

"I just wanted to wait for you, Lani," Makaio looked at me with his big brown eyes wide, arms crossed over his chest. It was cute how hard he tried to pretend he was a man. Nine years old, and he was growing so fast.

"Did you have a nightmare?" Because that was usually why he waited for me this late, not just for fun.

"I'm not a baby anymore, and I don't have nightmares!" Makaio said, buffing his chest and widening his eyes, trying to impress me. I had to bite my bottom lip to refrain from smiling.

"Sure, big guy. Come on, let's go to bed."

Tomorrow couldn't be worse than today.

It could get worse.

When the doorbell rang, I was washing the dishes and dancing to Queen B's *Single Ladies*. I hadn't heard the doorbell in so long that it took me a few seconds to recognize it.

Mom was at work, Makaio was at his friend's house for the whole day, none of my friends knew my address, and we hadn't ordered anything online in years. So, when the doorbell rang again, I thought someone had gone to the wrong door.

Turning down the music, I opened the door slightly, keeping the chain on. A guy, tall and super muscular, with some weird-looking leather outfit – a cosplay player, maybe – was standing there.

"Hi?" I asked, raising an eyebrow. No idea who this man was. And he didn't seem like an Amazon delivery guy or someone from our neighborhood either. Strange.

"Are you Miss Mayfield?" he asked with a gruff voice and an accent I couldn't quite place. European maybe?

"Yes, I am. Who is asking?"

"I am going to need you to come with me." I almost choked on air; I was so surprised. Who the fuck was this guy?

"I don't think so. I don't know what you want with me, but I will ask you to leave. I don't want anything to do with whatever this is. Thanks." And then I closed the door.

Or I attempted to.

Because, suddenly, the door was open, he was inside, and everything went blindingly white.

When I opened my eyes, I wasn't at home anymore.

Chapter Two

For some reason, I first noticed how green the grass was beyond the white rock patio. We didn't have green and lush grass in my part of California, even during the spring. Wherever I was, they must have had fantastic gardeners.

Then, I realized I was on an open patio, Greek style, in front of twelve thrones. Like, actual thrones, with gold paintings and incrusted precious stones. Who the fuck had thrones nowadays?

Maybe this was a cult. Oh, jeez, just my luck.

How had I even gotten here anyways? Five seconds ago, I was in my apartment and obviously wasn't anymore. Was that a science-fiction thing? Like a teleporter or some shit? The second option was that leather guy somehow drugged me, and I was so high I was hallucinating.

I was leaning toward option two.

After the grass and the thrones, I paid attention to the people sitting on said thrones. Only three were occupied out of twelve, two women and one man. All three looked like models, their bodies shining a soft golden light. The lighting must be excellent.

The man was in the middle, with golden blond hair, bright blue eyes, and a body chiseled from stone. He wore a white toga and looked decently young, but I couldn't pinpoint his age precisely. On his right sat a beautiful dark-haired woman with high cheekbones, dark eyes, the longest eyelashes, and the fullest lips. She had curves for days, but her body still looked toned under her light blue toga held by a gold pin. She seemed in her twenties, but her eyes were those of a wise and calculating woman. Finally, the other woman was all golden: skin, hair, and eyes, all in different tones. She was turning an arrow in her hands, looking bored as hell. And she was also wearing a light gold toga.

I sensed a theme here.

Finally, I noticed the half dozen armed guards standing at attention in a circle around the patio. That meant I probably could not make a run for it.

I was going to ask what was happening when Leather Guy suddenly fell on one knee, bowing his head like these people were royalty. *Definitely a cult.*

"Zeus, Artemis, Athena, I am honored to serve you. I am bringing a new Copper to you for the Tournament." I gave a puzzled look to Leather Guy. A Copper? What did that even mean? And why did these people have Greek God names?

"Thank you, Hunter," the man on the middle throne declares with a strong voice. The guy had a crazy strong presence. "Hecate!"

A few seconds ticked in an awkward silence before a white light blinded me – again – and yet another strikingly beautiful lady stood here. This drug was strong.

She had white hair, light chocolate skin, endless legs, and eyes a fluorescent white-blue. Did they get group prices on colored contacts?

Surprisingly, she was not wearing a toga, but a really short and tight black dress, with red high heels. I liked it, to be honest, even though it wasn't my usual style.

"Zeus, what did I already tell you? I am not a dog you can call at will." Hands on her hips, she was all attitude. I liked her.

"Hecate," Zeus sighed, "I won't even start on this. You know very well that your contract says you have to respond to my call regarding Coppers."

The black-haired woman stood and walked two steps closer to us. She fixed her eyes on me, seemingly trying to open me up to find my deepest secrets. "Hecate, we need you to test this young woman. She intrigues me."

Leather Guy, still bowing next to me, tensed up. Yep, man, I didn't know why he had brought me here, but there was obviously a mistake. I had no interest in joining a cult. Not that any of this was real. Because people appearing from thin air were not real. I was just under a powerful drug. Obviously.

Hecate turned to look at me, and her gaze was so intense that a shiver ran through me. A lavender light emanated from her hands, and after a few seconds, her lips curled up. I crossed my arms over my chest, feeling scrutinized by everyone around me.

A small laugh left Hecate's mouth, her eyes never leaving mine. "I am sorry for you, Hunter, but it seems like you severely messed up." She waited a few seconds, and I hoped she would announce that I had no place there. "She is pure human, not Copper."

Silence stretched, and Leather Guy – Hunter? I wasn't sure – was still as stone next to me. Yep, you messed up, little guy. I gave him a little smirk until I realized the Hecate lady had said I was *human*. That didn't mean anything: we were all humans, right?

Weird-ass cult.

"Hum," I finally said, feeling extremely uncomfortable about this whole situation. "Now that we established that I am not fitting material for whatever you guys are doing here, can I go?"

Yet another stunned silence followed my words, and all eyes fell on me. O-kay. The Zeus guy raised an eyebrow, seemingly shocked by my words. Did he expect me to worship him?

This was such a bad trip.

Admittedly I had never been high before, so maybe it was typical that one's imagination was exacerbated while on drugs.

"I like you, little human. It is regretful that you will soon be dead," Hecate said with a smile.

"Wow! Excuse me? Am I going to die? What does that even mean? Why the fuck would I die? And who are you, people? Just so you know, this, right here," I glared at them, pointing around me, "this is kidnapping. And I will press charges with the police if you don't flash me back to my apartment right now!"

I sounded stressed, and I started to freak out. On the off chance that this was actually happening and not just in my head, it began to sound like a dangerous situation.

Walking back a few steps, I started looking more clearly for options. The guards were still waiting, hands on what looked like swords, and I could tell that I couldn't go through them. They all wore similar outfits to Leather Guy on my right, and I wondered once more who they were.

"How dare you speak to your gods this way?" Zeus bellowed, standing up in one smooth motion. Suddenly, lightning shattered the sky into a million pieces, and the thunder was so loud I could feel the vibrations in my bones. The man was glowing, and tiny sparks of electricity were jumping from his hands.

I was so shocked that I froze for a second. My brain slowly realized that this didn't feel like a hallucination, and it seemed too complicated of special effects for a cult.

This felt real. Too real for my sanity.

"Dad, you should calm down. The girl doesn't know who we are or what is happening. She is just a human. She should have never been taken away from her home." The black-haired woman had a calm voice, and she effectively managed to calm the man next to her. However, she still looked like she was analyzing the situation from all angles, searching for potential outcomes.

"Athena is right," the other woman with golden *everything* declared, still looking bored as hell. "I think we should deal with this situation quickly; I want to return to Dionysus's party. It's not complicated anyways. She is human, so she has nothing to do on Mount Olympus. Either she becomes one of our servants, or she dies. Do we even need more servants?"

Golden girl and Lightning Guy then started arguing about what to do with me, but it all fell into the background because Athena's gaze was fixed on me so intently it made me shiver.

"What I am intrigued about is why this human was taken. The order should have been explicit, with the name and address of the Copper to retrieve."

Athena kept her eyes on me, but she wasn't addressing me at all. Leather Guy, who had been bowing this whole time – man, his knee must hurt – stood up and put both fists on his chest in a similar gesture to *Wakanda Forever.*

"Goddess Athena, I don't know how to express how sorry I am. The retrieval order said Lena Mayfield, twenty years old, female. And I checked twice that I was in the right apartment building."

"My name is Kalani Mayfield, though."

It was only a murmur, but Leather Guy heard me because he turned toward me faster than I could blink. "What was that? You're not Lena Mayfield?"

"Well, you asked for Miss Mayfield. But no, I'm not Lena. I think another Mayfield family is in my building, but their daughter died last month. A real tragedy."

His fists closed, joints turning white. Well, he was angry. And I got it: this misunderstanding could cost him his job. How could I have known, though? I thought it was just some weird guy at my door.

"How could you, little b…" He stopped before finishing his sentence, but I didn't need it to guess his thoughts. I almost snapped back at him but narrowly decided against it – I didn't need to attract more attention to myself than I already had.

"Well, this explains it. You must've retrieved the wrong Mayfield. And unfortunately, this one cannot participate in the Tournament. This situation is regretful for both of you." And Athena did look pained by this. She was not even the one who was threatened with death!

"Excuse me? Why can't I go back to my home? I promise that I won't say anything about all of this. I just want to go back to my family."

"I'm sorry little human, but I'm afraid that won't be possible. When Hunters retrieve Coppers from Earth, they also erase them from everyone's memory. It's standard protocol."

Oh. My. Gosh. I was so shocked that I didn't even know how to react. This… this was ridiculous. Did I land in a remake of *Harry Potter* as Hermione after she obliviated her parents?

"Can't… can't you reverse it?"

"It's irreversible, stupid human." There was disdain in Leather Guy's voice and a sick satisfaction at seeing me hurt. As if all of this was retribution to him.

And my heart cracked. All I could think about was my little brother, all by himself, with a mom who couldn't keep it together long enough to parent him correctly. How was he going to do without me? How was I going to do without him? Makaio was my reason to keep going in this life.

I guess I wouldn't have that problem: my old life was truly over.

The realization almost crushed me. How could someone move forward knowing that their whole life had disappeared? That their loved ones had no idea who they were anymore? How could one survive this loss?

But I still had hope. It was a tiny flicker in my chest, fighting against the darkness of hopelessness that overwhelmed me. No one could completely erase one's love from one's heart, right?

"… you will be sentenced to two years of correctional facility for your incompetence, and your title of Hunter for the Throne is revoked as of right now," Zeus announced, sitting back down on his massive throne. I had probably zoned out during a part of the scolding because Leather Guy was fuming and not even trying to hide it.

Oh well. Too bad for you.

"And, unfortunately, we don't need more servants. Thus, we will be taking you, human, to termination."

Zeus hadn't even finished his statement that Artemis was standing up, clapping her hands, and exclaimed: "Great! Time to party!"

Was that it? What this how my life was going to end? Like it had no value at all?

"Wait! Isn't there another solution?" I sounded desperate, but I didn't even care.

"Well… There is the option of joining the Tournament since you were retrieved for it in the first place."

"Hecate! Don't be dense! She is human. She can't compete with the other Coppers."

Ignoring Artemis, Hecate continued. "The Tournament is where the other Coppers – second descendants to the Olympian gods – fight against each other to earn their freedom and right to live in Olympus." Then turning to Athena. "She could fight. I know you can see that she has something special. She has potential."

Artemis tried to talk again, but Athena raised a hand to stop her. Silence fell on the patio. My heart was pounding so fast and hard that I could barely hear anything else. This was my chance to live and get my life back.

"She will fight."

Chapter Three

"So, um, what does this Tournament entail exactly?" My voice was higher pitched than usual, but I blamed it on the craziness of the situation. On top of that, Hecate was an intimidating woman to be around.

"Every Copper is retrieved from Earth and brought here. Every year, the Tournament takes place, and they fight for their right to live. The Tournament consists of physical battles, sometimes to the death, as well as trials that test the participants' intelligence, courage, and magic. It is a complete assessment of the Coppers' potential," Hecate said with a proud smile.

Swallowing, I tried to calm myself. This Tournament seemed extremely dangerous, especially for a human with no powers and no training in martial arts. But at least I had a chance. And some part of me still hoped that this was all caused by a hallucinating drug.

"And who exactly are these Coppers?"

The goddess – because yeah, it was becoming hard to deny it anymore – moved her hand, and the massive doors leading inside the training-center-slash-dormitory-building for Coppers opened without a sound. Impressive.

"Gods and goddesses have had kids with humans throughout history: we call them Goldens because they bleed gold, like the gods. It comes from the high quantity of ichor mixed with red blood cells. However, even though the Goldens were supposed to be brought back to Mount Olympus so that their powers wouldn't impact Earth, either we didn't retrieve some of them in time, or they snuck out to have sex with humans. The babies between Goldens and humans are called Coppers. Here again, it reflects the color of their blood. And they weren't supposed to exist. Thus, the gods initially decided to retrieve them as soon as they were discovered and bring them back here. The issue is that Goldens had many children, and Mount Olympus isn't big enough to house everyone comfortably." The goddess paused briefly to indicate that I had to turn right down a white marble hallway. "The first option was to kill all of the new Coppers. However, their Golden parents protested quite violently. Which is why Zeus created the Tournament."

Hecate shrugged like this history lesson was the most commonplace thing ever. Not for me. This was a whole new world, and I had to master it – or at least understand it well enough – to survive the Tournament.

Nodding, I tried assimilating all the information Hecate had just given me. This whole situation felt surreal, but I had to gather as much knowledge as possible. I was figuring out the following question to ask when a girl with the most stunning red hair came to us.

"Mayfield?" she asked with a voice smooth as honey.

"Kalani, yes. And you are?"

"The welcoming committee. Unfortunately. Follow me."

And she was already on her way down the hallway. O-kay. Enthusiastic it was then.

"Well?" Hecate asked, raising an eyebrow at me. "What are you waiting for?"

Patting my back, she gave me a reassuring smile. I was terrified, and we both knew it. But I still put on my best smile, nodded, and left down the hall.

After sprinting down the hallway, I finally caught up to the *welcoming committee*. Damn, she had long legs.

"So, uh, are you part of the Tournament?"

Fire Hair turned her head my way, giving me a glacial look. "Yes, I am. We all are."

One more look back, and then she was leaving. Again. Wow, what a warm welcome.

Sighing, I picked back up the speed – because she had endless legs and I certainly did not – following her without even taking the time to observe what was around me. This place was massive, though, and I knew with certainty that I would get lost, especially with how helpful this tour was.

It took us forever to get to our destination: a huge room that looked like one of those arenas from ancient Roman times, the ones in which the gladiators used to fight. Well, it was similar, except that the people fighting on the sand weren't half-naked and wielding swords. I mean, some were fighting with swords. But the important part here was that these people – Coppers? – were fighting with fireballs and tornados and changing into freaking animals. I had to pinch myself to ensure I was not having yet another dream about one of my fantasy books I liked to read for fun occasionally.

Sadly, this seemed real.

"Welcome to the Pit," Fire Hair declared with a little wave of her hand. She looked annoyed, but I couldn't tell if it because she had to show me around or because she didn't want to be there. Either way, looking at the Pit, I quickly realized that I was already dead. There was no way I could fight against people who had magic powers.

Death by fire or a werewolf might be worse than whatever 'termination' by the gods would've been.

Before I had time to wallow in self-pity and wonder how someone could be this unlucky, Fire Hair dragged me through the Pit toward a guy standing against the wall. Could he even be classified as a guy, though? He was at least seven feet tall, if not more – it could be difficult to judge when you were five-two like me – and wider than a tree trunk. An *old* tree trunk. And last but not least, he was rocking this menacing air with his beard, long black hair tied in a bun, and silver eyes that looked like they could kill. They probably could, seeing as everyone in this arena was deadly.

The guy didn't want company; he was leaning against the wall, arms crossed, seemingly assessing everything happening in front of him.

I wanted to ask Fire Hair why we were heading toward him, but seeing as she never answered my questions, it seemed pointless.

"Xander, here is the last recruit," Fire Hair announced with a touch of fear in her voice. I rapidly understood why when he – Xander – turned his silver gaze on me. It was terrifying, like seeing death in person. I was instantly frozen, my heart pounding so hard I half wondered if the other people surrounding us could hear it.

Xander didn't say anything. He pushed off the wall and walked over until he was so close that I could feel the heat coming off his body. His gaze swiped over my body – he was assessing, looking for my strengths and weaknesses.

Xander finally spoke after what seemed like hours – but was probably more like minutes.

"I am one of the trainers here, I coach half of the Tournament participants before they go in, and you were assigned to me. Training sessions are not required, but they are highly encouraged, especially if you hope to survive this Tournament." He looked over my body once more before going back to propping up the wall and nodding toward the center of the Pit. "Now, go. Show me what I am working with. Elena! Spar with the new girl!"

Turning slightly to see who Xander was talking to, I discovered a woman over six-foot tall walking over to the center of the sand arena. The other Coppers had stopped training, moving to form a large circle around the Elena girl.

Shocked, I turned back towards the trainer, unsure what this meant. Was I supposed to go there and… what? Fight this woman? She was twice my height, with boulders instead of arms and legs, and probably years of experience fighting people. I was still in my baggy t-shirt and spandex shorts, for fuck's sake! I didn't even have proper shoes on!

"I… what?" I stuttered, flushing from both embarrassment and terror slowly creeping in. I was going to die within the first hour of being here. "I can't."

Fire Hair scoffed on my left, and Xander crossed his arms across his chest, raising an eyebrow. The Pit was suddenly eerily quiet as if everyone had stopped breathing, waiting for Xander's reaction.

"If you don't train, if you don't fight, you die. As simple as that. Choose."

That's how I fought Elena, this giant of a lady who could probably crush me in her sleep. I mean, fighting was a bit of an over-exaggeration. We had started for thirty seconds, and my jaw was already in pain, my ribs were hurting, and I was slightly light-headed.

This was going *great*.

"Are you going to fight back, New Girl?" Elena taunted with a smirk and a slight German accent.

I wanted to say yes. I wanted to attack, fight, and show all of these Coppers that I wasn't the weak girl they were all seeing right now. And I tried. I did. After circling with Elena for a few seconds, I tried punching her, but she evaded easily enough, my fist barely grazing her arm. Moving back, she seemed amused by the situation. She was playing with me as if I were her toy. And I could do nothing about it because I was too weak, with no idea how to survive here.

And I knew it then, as Elena circled me and continued to tease, punching and kicking me, but never staying in one place long enough for me to retaliate. I knew it when she kicked my legs from behind me, and I fell to the ground. I knew it when she pressed her boot against my throat, pressing just hard enough to cut off my air supply. I knew it when she laughed at me, when the other Coppers left, and when she gave me a pitying look.

I knew it from deep within my bones. I was going to die. I was never going to see Makaio again. Or my mom. I would never coach my kids, go to class, or practice gymnastics anymore. My life would stop before I even reached the golden age of twenty-one.

And I wasn't the only one who knew it. All these Coppers could already tell that I was no competition to them. One less person to fight against. One less person between them and their right to live on Mount Olympus.

Even Xander knew it. Once Elena left me lying on the ground, still trying to catch my breath, he took long seconds to come over. Crouching next to me, he shook his head, looking utterly disappointed.

"You're already dead, new girl."

I had gotten plenty of injuries being a gymnast. Most people didn't realize how brutal the sport was – the impact of tumbling on the articulations; the strength needed to hold onto a bar while flying around it; the strain of constant stretching, and always *more*; how landing on a beam could destroy your shoulders. Gymnastics practices were brutal, especially at the level I used to train at. I got hurt, and went to practices with sprained ankles, partially torn tendons, and bruised ribs.

I did all of that because I loved it with all my heart.

Having to stop because of my knee injury during my junior year of high school was the hardest thing I had to do. It was like a part of my soul had been torn away. The pain had been terrible, but I knew that if my doctor had let me, I would've done anything, *anything*, to keep going.

It's wild the pain one can endure when it is for something one loves.

My pain tolerance levels were significantly different now, probably because I did not enjoy being here, surrounded by predators who would kill me soon without hesitation or remorse. It was everyone for themselves here. All of them were fighting for their right to live, just like I was.

Except I had no hope. Undoubtedly, I could not find the energy to search for the – slim – positives of this situation.

Wincing from the pain in my ribs, I sat down at one of the tables in the dining hall. After a few seconds of trying to breathe through the pain, I cut through the steak on my plate. Usually, I would enjoy the nice meal – it wasn't every day that I got to eat red meat, and this was *good* meat – but everything tasted like ash.

Focusing on my meal, I tried my best to ignore the looks and the whispers from the other people around. The room was full of Coppers eating dinner, and, thankfully, I had managed to find an empty table. This meal felt surprisingly like this first day of high school when I didn't know anyone and had to sit by myself during lunch break. I did not like this feeling then, and I still did not now.

Great. This was great.

Scoffing, I shook my head at my thoughts. I was getting ready to participate in a Tournament to fight for my life, and all I could think about was how this felt like the socially awkward first day of high school. No wonder even the coaching staff didn't think I could last more than a day.

I was focused on eating my food and trying to zone out the whispers of all the Coppers sitting at tables around when someone slumped into the chair right in front of me. The someone in question was a stunning girl that looked about my age. She had long honey-blond hair and the bluest of eyes. Surprisingly, she was also smiling – and not in a way that said she wanted to eat me. Or kill me. Or both.

"So, you are the new girl, then! That was quite the show you put out there earlier!" Her smile widened, eyes twinkling. She was joking, but not in a mean way. At least, I didn't think so. "Name's Sadie. Nice to meet you!"

A little stunned by this whirlwind of a girl, I took the hand she offered and shook it slowly. This girl – Sadie – was the first person who was remotely nice or welcoming to me since I got here. Instantly, I put my walls up. This was too good to be true.

These people were here to kill each other, not make friends.

"Kalani."

Sadie bobbed her head, and I couldn't ignore how inhumanely pretty she was. She looked like a goddess of beauty. She did have god blood in her, I guessed. And under this pale skin, blue eyes, high cheekbones, and long honey hair, she could probably kill me instantly. *Like everybody else in this room.*

"Well, Kalani, you definitely made a grand entrance," she adds with a wink. "Also, I couldn't help but notice that you don't seem to have any change of clothes. I have extras that will probably be slightly too big, but better than nothing, right? Just come to my room tonight after you are done eating and getting settled in. You should be in the room right next to mine, too, since it is the only one still open, and you are the last competitor to arrive."

She was about to continue her monologue when someone shouted her name from the other side of the hall. We both turned toward the man who was waving at us –waving at *Sadie*. She winced apologetically and stood up.

"Well, anyway, I should go. The guys get impatient. You know how it is!"

And then she was gone. And I was left wondering what had just happened. This girl was a whirlwind of words, and I was still trying to process our conversation. Well… mostly *her* conversation.

I was still determining whether or not Sadie was genuinely offering help. We were all in the Tournament to fight for our lives, not make friends. This whole conversation might have been a way for her to test me and detect my weaknesses. To lure me into a false sense of safety.

At the same time, it wasn't like I was any threat to any of them. I was the cute baby bunny surrounded by thirty hungry dragons. The metaphor might even be literal, for all I knew.

A shiver ran through my body because all the eyes on me suddenly felt like the eyes of predators watching their bleeding prey.

Watching me.

I was the bleeding prey.

Chapter Four

I was sweating. My palms especially. I kept wiping them on my shirt while pacing before the door. If I were in a movie or a book, this would be a good idea – befriending the nice girl that came up to me on the first day. It was always best friend material.

But this wasn't a movie.

This was real life and not the first day of high school. This was *the Hunger Games* if the competitors had god-like powers. And we all knew how friendships ended there.

However, even knowing that this was a bad idea, I couldn't not knock on this door. First, I had no clothes or shoes, and fighting in this Tournament would probably require more tactical clothing than my baggy t-shirt and spandex shorts. And second of all, I needed intel. I needed to understand what was happening around me and how life here worked. I needed to survive, at least until the actual Tournament started.

So here I was, pacing in front of Sadie's dorm, trying to compose myself so I didn't look as freaked out as I felt inside. I felt so out of my element here; everything in my life had changed so fast. I needed to get some control back on the situation, and that started with controlling my emotions.

This was like gymnastics meets. I just had to imagine I was going up on the beam. *You got this, Kalani. Just keep breathing and focus.*

Finally, after what felt like forever, I knocked. When Sadie's voice answered for me to come in, I released a breath I hadn't realized I had been holding. I could do this.

Her room was very similar to mine, except hers had pictures on the wall, and her closet was overflowing with clothes. She had been living there for a while. How long were they keeping the Coppers in there for?

"Kalani! I'm so glad you came! Did you get settled in well?" Sadie smiled again, sitting up from her bed and putting her book on the covers.

I nodded and smiled, but it felt forced even to me. If she saw it, though, she didn't comment on it, and she walked to her closet. Jeez, even her walk and posture were super graceful. She picked up a box sitting next to her mountain of clothes and turned back towards me.

"Here it is! I hope it mostly fits, even though you are petite so…" Then she assessed me from head to toe very clinically, frowning. "I guess we'll see. We can figure something else out if it doesn't work."

After she gave me the box, I suddenly felt extremely uncomfortable. She looked pleased. She was genuinely trying to help. And my gut was telling me that this was not a trap. What would I even have to lose at somewhat trusting Sadie? I needed information, and, for some reason, she seemed like she wanted to help me.

"Thank you, Sadie. The clothes will be helpful. Staying in mine for the foreseeable future would not have been enjoyable," I ended with a small smile, trying to show I was truly grateful.

Because I was. I had nothing, and this girl gave me some of her clothes without asking for anything in return. At least, not yet.

"No worries, I am happy to help." Patting the bed next to her, she smiled warmly. She was good at this smiling, friendly thing. "Do you want to stay for a while? You must have questions about all of this. We all did at the beginning."

Nodding, I sat down on the soft covers. Sadie's bedding was way nicer than the one in my bedroom next door. With a little wave, she encouraged me to ask her something. There were so many things I needed clarification on, though, that I had a hard time deciding what to ask first. I needed to start with the basics.

"Everyone here is a Copper, right?"

"Everyone is supposed to be, yes," Sadie answered with a slight frown. I waited for her to explain more, but she didn't. Maybe she knew I was an anomaly and should not have been here. It made me a little uncomfortable.

"What is your power?"

"That's a pretty bold question for a first time, Kalani." I immediately tensed. Had I fucked up already? Was asking someone's power super rude?

Then the corner of her mouth moved up, and her eyes crinkled. "Relax, I was just kidding. I have control over the dead. It's necromancy. I can control dead bodies and skeletons, and make them do what I want. These kinds of things. It's decently useful."

I remained motionless, stuck on the words coming out of her mouth. "Dead bodies?" I asked with a cracked voice, suddenly overly aware I was in an empty room with a deity's grandchild who could control cadavers.

"What were you expecting? Sunflowers and butterflies?" Sadie smirked at my discomfort. As discretely as I could, I stole a glance at the door. How fast could I reach the door if something happened? Why was I even entertaining that thought? Descendants of gods and goddesses surrounded me – if they wanted to, they could kill me in half a second.

"Relax Kalani, I am non-violent. Mostly. I only get power-happy when some asshole annoys me. And I like you," she added with a light tap on my knee.

Heart beating pretty hard, I nodded slowly. These people – Coppers – were intense. I did not know how I was going to survive here. At the rate I was going, I would die from a heart attack before the first Tournament fight even started.

I debated whether or not I should leave right then. I did not know how to navigate this conversation. Sadie was friendly, but I was having trouble deciphering where all of this was going. Why was she helping me? Could I even trust that this was real help?

But then, Makaio's face appeared in my mind. This little boy was the love of my life. He was full of joyful and energetic, and I only wanted to return to him. This Tournament was the only way back. I had to try, and even if Sadie had unknown motivations, she offered me more than anyone had.

"Yes, I guess I was not expecting this... sort of power," I chuckled uncomfortably. "I just would have expected someone with the power over dead people to look, uhm..."

"More like the dark and mysterious type? Well, that's the look my granddad sports. Suits him well. He's Thanatos, the one and only Death God," she said ironically. "Thankfully, I got my mom's good physical genes. Bless Tyche!"

She laughed softly, and I somewhat relaxed. This girl was weird, but she didn't seem malicious. I was opening my mouth to ask her how the Tournament would work when the bedroom door opened quite violently.

"Why didn't you come to the freaking training arena Sadie? You left me with Søren and his latest fling for an hour and-"

And I was face to face with the most beautiful man I'd ever seen. And that was saying something since I had been surrounded by Gods and Coppers all afternoon. But this man... He had jet-black hair that was short on the sides but long enough on top to brush his forehead and eyes. High cheekbones rested below eyes that were dark blue around the pupil and lighter on the outer ring. His jaw looked cut from marble, and he had the fullest lips I had seen on a man before. He was tall, and I could tell that he was ripped without being overly muscled even with him wearing a black t-shirt. He was so attractive that my brain froze for a second, long enough that I missed part of Sadie's answer.

"... told you that I would be busy. I am making a new friend right now. And stop whining. I am always the one who has to endure Søren's feminine company. Good deal that it's you for once!"

The man glared at Sadie for a second before rolling his eyes at her self-satisfied face. And then he shifted his gaze to me, taking in my shocked face. Why was I acting like I'd never seen a man before?

He moved his eyes up and down my body so very slowly. "Nice outfit, new girl," he said with a smirk.

And like a prepubescent schoolgirl, I blushed. Oh. My. Gosh. I needed to get a grip on myself.

"Stop being an ass, Archer. The poor girl was not allowed to get any luggage before they brought her in." Sadie stood up and turned so she could face both of us. "And be more polite, you didn't even say hi. Kalani, this is Archer, one of my best friends. And Archer, this is Kalani, my new neighbor!"

Archer – what even was that name? – smirked and nodded. "Nice to meet you, new girl."

It sounded like a tease, not necessarily mean but not pleasant either. This guy was hard to understand. And my body was having extremely unusual reactions to him. I answered with a nod, not trusting my voice to sound natural. This day was too much for my mind and body, and I was losing it. It was the only plausible explanation for the serial blushing and body shutdown that was going on.

After a few seconds of awkward silence, Archer turned to face Sadie. "Do you mind if I chill here? I don't want to know what Søren and his flavor of the week are doing in our room right now."

Sadie laughed like she knew all too well what this Søren and his lady were doing – who even was Søren? Then she looked at me and raised an eyebrow, seemingly asking if I was okay with that. I was the odd one out here, so I couldn't see how to answer any other way than with a nod. Again. Because nodding seemed to be the only thing I could do lately.

The god of a man – literally, since he was a Copper – sat down on a cute pink chair in the corner of the room and whipped out a book from thin air.

"Do you have any other questions, Kalani? I bet this is very strange to you. Did you get to meet your Golden parent?"

"Not really, no."

"Oh, that's weird," Sadie frowned. "Usually, that's how they welcome you here. With the genitor that shouldn't have conceived you. Who is it? Did they give you any information?"

That conversation was getting dicey. I wasn't sure what to say because there had been a colossal mistake, and I did not have any god ancestry whatsoever.

"You know, that meeting was quick. I think a party was going on, and everyone was excited to leave, so I didn't get much information on anything. Not even on how the Tournament works."

There. That was a nice answer, wasn't it? Remaining vague and rerouting the conversation onto something safer for me was a great plan. No one had told me what I should tell the other Coppers, and I did not want to spread the word that I wasn't like them.

"I bet it's Ron. That guy has like sixty kids all over the Earth, if not more," Archer chimed in.

"Yeah, or it could be Lee. You could make three Tournament editions with just his kids." Then Sadie turns back to me. "What's your power? That can help narrow it down."

And that was the elephant in the room, wasn't it? Cause I did not have any power. None. Except maybe that I could make some mean pancakes. But that wasn't going to save me in the Tournament.

And now I had to choose what I would do about it. I could either fake it and hope I could survive without help or trust these two people and hope it didn't kill me any faster than the Tournament would. Tough choice, right? At this point, though, I wasn't sure I had much to lose trusting them. Plus, Sadie seemed to genuinely want to help, so maybe she would still feel inclined to do so even when she discovered I was plain old human me. And, although Archer was intimidating the hell out of me, something deep inside me was pushing me to trust them.

"I... I don't have one, actually," I murmured, looking everywhere but at either of the two Coppers.

"What do you mean? You haven't found it yet?" asked Sadie.

"No, I mean that I don't have a power. And I never will. Because…" I stopped to wet my lips anxiously. This was the moment. The big reveal that could either save or destroy my life. "I am not a Copper. I am human. Someone made a big mistake, and my only chance to go home is to survive the Tournament."

No one answered, and the silence stretched, hanging over me and threatening to drown me. This was it. I had given my biggest secret to these two strangers, and now they could use it to harm me if they desired. Why had I even done it? For all I knew, they had a considerable prejudice against humans and were going to kill me with a smile on their faces. Or maybe they would denounce me to everyone else, and I would get expelled from the Tournament, also resulting in my death. Hecate hadn't said anything about whether or not my being human was a secret. I probably should have checked before spilling it to these two random people. What an idiot. I wasn't going to make it past my first night here.

Minutes passed by – it could have been less, but it felt unbelievably long – and my heart was beating so fast that I felt like I would throw up. Sadie and Archer were staring at each other, completely ignoring me. When I felt like I was going to pass out, and still neither of them had uttered a word, I grabbed the box of clothes with my shaky hands. "It's fine. I'll go. Thanks for the clothes."

I was ready to open the door and flee for my life when a hand caught my arm. I half turned, then froze on the spot, images of my death flashing through my mind. This was it. I was fucked.

"Sorry about that. Sadie and I had to discuss the situation in private." I could not even fully process that Archer was talking about having a conversation with Sadie when no words had left their lips – could they mind speak or something? – because he was so close that I felt like the air had been sucked from my lungs. Being so close to Archer was way too much for my poor body.

"Archer can manipulate the brain," Sadie explained. "He is mostly known for making people feel immense pain or have terrifying hallucinations, but it is also pretty useful for sensitive conversations."

That made sense. Right? But I couldn't think straight because all I could think about was Archer's eyes on mine, his hand on my bicep, and how much I wanted it to stay there. It would also be nice if he added his other hand to my cheek and pushed me against the door, and kissed m-

Wait.

Hold up.

What was happening to me? Was he playing with my brain? Making me fantasize about things?

"She really is human. She has no mental blocks at all against my power."

"Archer, stop it! The girl is terrified," Sadie scolded him with a frown, getting up from her bed. He released me from his hold, and I had to swallow a protest. This was insane. I had never felt anything like that for a guy.

Sadie came to stand in front of me and put her hands on my shoulders, grounding me back in reality. "We are going to help you, Kalani. Everything is going to be okay, alright?"

I frowned. Really? Was it going to be that easy?

"Why?"

"Because I feel this kinship to you, and I think you are what we have been waiting for. Plus, as outcasts, we have to stick together, right?"

Chapter Five

I woke up feeling like I had been run over by a freight train before being left for dead on the side of a road in the cold. My eyes were crusty from crying myself to sleep thinking of Makaio, and I hadn't been able to sleep more than two hours straight, too scared that someone would break in and kill me in my sleep. So yeah, not the best night of my life.

Even now, after showering, finding clothes that sort of fit me in Sadie's box, and halfway through eating my breakfast, I still felt terrible – mainly because this situation had finally sunk in. No doubt now, I was not drugged, and this was not a trip. I was here, for real. Somehow, I had ended up in the middle of a fantasy book, and I would have to find some way to survive the Tournament to get back to my brother.

So here I was, eating an admittedly delicious pancake and watching the thirty or so Coppers in the dining room. I did not know any of them since Sadie and Archer were absent, and I still had yet to learn what we were supposed to do during the day. Did we have a set schedule? Or some list of things to do? No idea – partly because the red-haired girl had done the worst ever job as the welcoming committee. But I did know three things. One, I had revealed my secret, and nothing terrible had happened – I was still alive, and no one was staring at me strangely. So, I could probably trust both Sadie and Archer, at least for now. Two, from what I had gleaned from my short conversation with Sadie after the big revelation, I had eight weeks before the Tournament started. Eight weeks to train. Eight weeks to learn all I needed to survive. And three, I might not have any magic or powers, and I might not be one of the best gymnasts anymore, but I was still strong physically and damn smart. So, I was going to use that. I was going to train day and night, make sure I had all the information I needed, and then I was going to outsmart all of them. That was the plan.

Now, I just had to get all that life-saving information. The only people who seemed friendly to me were Sadie and, somewhat, Archer. And they weren't here. It seemed already pretty late in the morning – no one had given me a watch, so I couldn't be sure – and I had been sitting here for at least an hour. If they never showed up, I wasn't sure what to do or where to go.

While observing a group of Coppers talking animatedly about some game, I couldn't stop my thoughts from wandering back to the night before. And, specifically, to Archer. So far, all of the Coppers I had seen were winners in the genetic lottery. Archer was no exception. He was probably the prettiest man I had ever met. But more than that, his presence made my body react in a way it never had before. The heart palpitations, staring at him like I had never seen a man before, losing my voice and part of my sanity… I had never – and I meant it, *never* – reacted that way to a guy! And I wasn't sure how much of that was due to him using his gift on my poor human brain. Hopefully, all of it, so I wouldn't have to feel as embarrassed. At least I hadn't had such an extreme physical reaction to anyone else here – silver lining.

I was going to bite on yet another piece of this delicious fruit halfway between a pineapple and a cantaloupe when someone called for the new girl. I guessed that was me.

It was a girl with long black hair, slanted dark eyes, and a cute, innocent look. Plus, she was short. Like short, short. I might even have been taller than her. And that was pretty rare here – I had only seen incredibly tall people so far. She probably had a terrifying power, and her appearance was all a disguise to trick people into feeling safe.

Anyways, she was walking energetically towards me, and I was unsure why. I didn't know her at all, and so far, except for Sadie and maybe Archer, I hadn't met the most welcoming people here.

"Here you are! I have been searching for you for hours." she exclaimed as she reached my table.

"Uhm… hi?" I asked, raising an eyebrow in question.

"My bad, that was kind of rude of me," she giggled. "I'm Mei. Nice to meet you! My baby asked me to come and get you. So, here I am!" She ended with a hand in the air like a cheerleader, and I was just full of questions. Why was she so nice to me? And who was her *baby*?

"I am still confused here, *Mei*. Why were you looking for me?"

She stared at me like I was the craziest person she had ever met and crossed her arms on her chest before answering. "Søren, my boyfriend, asked me to come and get you because his sister wants to play with her new toy. And in case you hadn't realized, you are the shiny new toy."

Suddenly, her tone wasn't so friendly anymore, especially while talking about who I guessed was Sadie. Mean girl alert? Already? Jeez, this really started to feel like high school all over again. Just a tiny bit deadlier.

I was unsure about that girl, but if she could take me to Sadie, who happened to be the only person I semi-trusted here, then I would take my chances on her.

I could feel many eyes on me as I followed Mei out the cafeteria door. The other competitors were wondering what was happening. And, judging by a few laughs and snide comments I overheard, many thought that I was going to be 'used and thrown away by the Kings,' whoever they might be.

Mei started walking, and I followed blindly because, let's be honest here, I got lost three times this morning and had no idea where I was in this building. The trip was only a few minutes long, and then we were at the entrance of the Pit.

Suddenly I very much wanted to turn around and run away.

But Mei must've sensed my unease because she positioned herself to block my exit and nodded for me to go through the entrance. I hesitated for a second – I got my ass handed to me *hard* the last time I was here – but still walked through. What other choice did I have anyway? I didn't know what power Mei had, and I preferred not to give her a reason to use whatever it was on me.

There was a short, dark, stone hallway and then the opening to the sand arena. The Pit was even bigger under the blinding sun of the mid-morning. It looks like the Coliseum, or at least the images I had seen online. The Pit was much bigger than a football field, and the bleachers were so high I could barely see the details at the top.

The Pit was empty. Almost, at least. There were just three people in the whole stadium – Sadie, Archer, and, after making a wild guess, Søren. They were on the other side of the arena, but I could still see from here that they were fighting. They didn't seem to be using their powers – although I couldn't have known for sure with Archer – but I could see swords or something similar. And they were going at it. Even from where I stood, I could hear the clangs of metal against metal. After a couple of minutes, it seemed clear that the twins were teaming up against Archer, and watching their intricate dance made me realize, once again, just how out of my league I was.

They were *lethal*.

All I knew how to do was flip in the air gracefully.

I was fucked. So, so fucked. And my earlier surge of empowerment was dwindling to dying embers. Watching Archer hit Sadie's blade so hard that she stumbled, I winced and stepped back. I already knew from my fantastic time in the Pit yesterday that fighting against the Coppers' powers was going to be hard, but this? Did I not even have a fighting chance against them *without* their powers? What was I supposed to do then? Fight them in their sleep?

"Baby! I'm back!" Mei chanted with a high-pitched sing-song voice that already grated on my nerves. From the corner of my eyes, I estimated I only needed a few more steps to get to the hallway and out of the-

"Kalani!" Sadie interrupted my short-lived hopes of leaving unnoticed. I turned back towards her and forced the corners of my lips to go up, hoping I looked happy to be there. She was jogging toward us, looking like a model as she did it. "It's good to see you! Sorry, I couldn't come and get you myself, but I had promised to train with those two over there," she said nodding toward the two men. "But I am glad you could attend our first training session!"

"Our first training session?" I asked, my eyebrows shooting upwards. I hoped she didn't expect me to go and join their sword fight because it would be a massacre. No one in their right mind wanted to see that.

"Archer, Søren, and I talked last night, and we decided to help train you so you can be better prepared for the start of the Tournament. We are all very excited to start!" She put her hands on her hips as she finished, looking proud and genuinely happy to be helping me. The two men walking behind her seemed a lot less *excited to start*. Archer was staring at me like he was trying to decipher my deepest secrets, and Søren was sizing me up, looking distrustful. And Mei… well, Mei was only here to see her *baby*.

My mouth was suddenly drier than the desert because I could see the swords up close, and, boy, they were even bigger and more dangerous looking than I had thought from afar. I did not want to be anywhere close to those things. And, for that matter, I did not want to "train" with them if it involved the same beat-down I had gotten the day before.

"You know, I am not sure that it's necessary. I can probably just…" I gestured broadly around the Pit, "watch?"

"Are you kidding? This is going to be so much fun!" And Sadie took my hand, dragging me toward the center of the Pit.

The two men had stopped in the center of the arena and seemed to be on the verge of boredom already. I was trying very hard not to look at Archer for too long because he was very distracting – even more so than the night before, if that was even possible. He was not wearing any shirt, and his chest was gleaming with sweat under the hot sun. I couldn't tell what the tattoo on his left pectoral represented – I refused to look at it long enough, but it gave him a bad boy look that I liked. A lot. Too much.

I seriously needed to remind myself that I wasn't here to ogle at a pretty boy. I was here to survive so I could return to Makaio. I closed my eyes to center myself, and his sweet little face popped behind my eyelids. He was why I was fighting to get back, and I needed to ensure I didn't get distracted. Particularly by a guy I had barely met.

That was why I decided to focus on Søren. Even without knowing that he and Sadie were fraternal twins, I could have guessed they were related. They had the same light golden skin, piercing blue eyes, and blond hair. Søren wore his hair in a man bun and a faint shadow of a beard on his cheeks, which gave him a modern Viking look. He could have probably passed as a fourth Hemsworth brother, and I understood why Mei was so proud to be with him – he certainly looked like a catch, even among all the beautiful Coppers.

I was still dragging my feet behind Sadie when someone bumped into my shoulder. Unsurprisingly, Mei strode past, and almost jumped into Søren's arms. She basically assaulted him by vacuuming his face and he started full-on fondling her butt. Trust me. I could not hold back a shudder from the amount of PDA happening right there.

"Ignore them. My brother has clear exhibitionist tendencies." Sadie shook her head at him and turned back to me with one of her signature smiles. "How are you feeling about hand-to-hand combat?"

Well, I wasn't expecting such a sudden change in topic. Thinking back on the debacle from the day before, I winced. I didn't need to answer because Archer did for me.

"I think yesterday's terrible fight answers the question. We wouldn't be here otherwise, would we?"

And, while he was right, him saying it *really* annoyed me.

"Don't be mean, Arch. We all started somewhere, haven't we?"

Archer rolled his eyes at Sadie before turning back to me. "All right, I'm guessing we are starting from pretty low, but let's see how bad it is."

Okay, that was insulting. Yes, I hadn't landed a single punch the day before. Sure. But no need to be mean about it. But I didn't say anything because… well, he wasn't entirely wrong either.

Archer turned around and started walking towards a circle of red paint on the sand. Without looking back at us, he barked, "Søren, stop sucking her face like it's a straw and come here. I am going to need all the help I can get."

I stifled a laugh because that was such a great analogy. Søren moved his face away from Mei's and dropped his hold on her butt. She got back on the ground with more grace than I would have been capable of and whined. "Baby, come on, we were having fun!"

"Sorry, Bubba, duty calls." He sounded everything but sorry. I wondered how this relationship worked. And how long they had been together – did they meet here or before? And by the way, how long had all of those Coppers been here for?

Ignoring Mei's sad puppy face as she slowly walked away, trying to grab Søren's attention back, I turned to Sadie.

"Are you sure this is fine? I am going to slow you guys down. I can probably figure out some stuff on my own."

"Don't worry about it," she smiled. "Archer likes to be a grump, but he's the one who suggested we train you."

That made me pause, and, weirdly enough, my chest warmed. I ignored it. Obviously. Because I wasn't here to have a crush on a stranger. I was here to survive.

Archer positioned himself in the circle, leaving his sword outside – thank goodness. I still refrained from looking directly at his face, but I could feel his gaze burning on the side of my head. And while I didn't want to get my ass handed to me again, I knew that training with them would give me my best chance to survive.

I entered the circle. After several deep breaths, I finally dragged my eyes up until they met Archer's. His gaze was so intense that it gave me chills. For some reason, this instant felt like a decisive moment in my life.

Up until Archer tackled me to the ground.

Chapter Six

"**Y**ou need to use your feet more. Don't stand there waiting for me to attack. I asked you to stop being a coward, not to stand there and take it."

Archer had spent the past thirty minutes trying to teach me how to have a proper fighting stance and be quick on my feet. Let's say that grace came to me easier in gymnastics than fighting.

He threw a punch – a jab, I thought – and I ducked, desperate to escape from yet another bruise. Between yesterday's beat down and today's "learning session," I was going to sport a rainbow of bruises. How exciting.

Sweat was dripping down my whole body, burning my eyes. The sun was at its zenith, and its reflection on the sandy ground was almost blinding. Breathing harder than I would have liked after only thirty minutes, I circled outside the makeshift ring, trying to keep as much distance as possible between Archer and me. I knew I wouldn't I couldn't run forever, though – Archer was insanely fast.

Sure enough, I did not have time to catch my breath before he was right before me. He started moving his chest and right arm. I dodged to the right, and sure enough, his left fist caught me in the shoulder.

I fell.

Hard.

And I decided it was a good idea to lie down there, lying on the hot sand. Felt like the beach. If I closed my eyes, I could almost hear the waves. I could practically feel the salt in the air. I could almost imagine that I would soon be riding the waves.

"Maybe we should take a break."

Bless you, Sadie.

Eyes still closed, I heard Archer stomp all the way to his water bottle. He was annoyed with my inability to fight. That made me want to punch him – his attitude would get old really fast. The issue was that it would require me to both stand up and somehow manage to land a hit on him, neither of which was currently possible.

"Do you need help getting back up?"

I cracked an eye open to see Søren looking down at me from his giant height. He had a big smile, as if watching me get thrown around had made his day. Probably had, seeing as all these people here seemed to enjoy fighting each other.

Søren's voice was surprisingly melodic. Maybe his power was singing? Doubtful, but hey, one could hope.

"I should be good, thanks," I mumbled as I got up under his amused gaze.

"You know, I heard about the good time you had with Elena, and Sadie told me about the whole human issue, but I didn't think it was this bad. Don't they teach you anything anymore at your human schools?"

"I guess they focus more on math nowadays, but it's not really helpful to me, is it?"

"No, I don't think algebra will help you right now, sadly." He smiled ruefully, then put his hand on my shoulder. "Good thing we are here, though, right? We will mold you into the most lethal little human this Tournament has ever seen."

The way Søren said it, while looking at me up and down slowly, made it seem very sexual. And he was suddenly much closer to me, his hand moving slightly lower down my shoulder blades. "You know what they say about Hellfire wielders like me," he murmured seductively.

I actually didn't – here again, one more failing of the public -chool system – but now, at least, I knew his power was over Hellfire, whatever that was.

"I could teach you more things if you wanted. Things that Sadie and Archer can't help you with."

I sidled closer to him and got up on my tip toes to bring my mouth close to his ear, putting a hand on his chest to steady myself. "Thanks for the offer Søren. I'm not sure your *Bubba* would love that, would she?" Then, with a smile, I moved one step back, patted his chest, and added, "Plus, you're not my type."

He choked in surprise, and I turned on my heels to face a laughing Sadie. "I think it is the first time a girl has put him in his place. This has just made my year!" she added, wiping a stray tear from her eye.

Søren punched her playfully – I think? – in the arm, and they started fighting like kids. Like siblings. It reminded me of playing around with Makaio, pretending to wrestle with him until we had cramps because we laughed so hard.

God, I missed him so much.

Maybe I needed to say 'gods' now, seeing as there were a lot of very much alive Greek deities around.

I was trying so hard not to think of him and his smiles and big brown eyes that looked at me with so much love and pride. I hoped Mom was taking care of him. I hoped he was doing well and being his usual bubbly self. And I hoped that, somewhere in his heart, he still remembered some part of me.

I would make it back to him, though. I would.

Sadie was holding Søren in a headlock, trash-talking him, when Archer, being his usual grumpy self, sighed. "Kids, can we get back to work, or are we going to continue fucking around until the Tournament begins?"

Sadie and Søren did not seem bothered by their friend's shitty attitude because, while they released each other, they kept on joking around. And I could tell by Archer's soft gaze in the twins' direction that he wasn't mad.

Honestly, I was still wary of all three of them. They knew too many of my secrets already, and I wasn't sure I trusted them with more. After all, I had barely met them, and we were on very different planes of existence. But still, watching them like this, seeing their beautiful friendship… it hurt a little. It tasted bittersweet like I'd always be on the outside of a truly incredible relationship.

Five minutes later, I was sitting cross-legged on the sand in front of the three Coppers. Sadie had proposed that, now that it was widely known that I had no fighting skills whatsoever, it would be an excellent idea to… how did she put it?

Explore other horizons.

"Just so we are clear, are you certain you don't have any powers?"

"Søren, we went over this. Archer checked, and she is a full-blooded human. No doubt on that."

"Just saying that it wouldn't be such as hassle in that case."

Sadie rolled her eyes at her brother. He had already asked multiple times if we were absolutely, a hundred percent, entirely sure that I was powerless. We were. And the more we talked about it, the more uncomfortable I felt. I barely knew them, and I already felt like a burden.

They were respected in this place – some people had come into the Pit since we had started, but they had taken one look at our group and left. I was tempted to think they were intimidated by the three Coppers I was with, not me. Someone had called them the Kings in the cafeteria. I didn't know how they had gotten this nickname, and I wasn't sure I wanted to know.

"Okay, so what are your talents, Kalani?" Archer's voice brought me back to reality, and I winced.

"I do gymnastics, so I can flip in the air and balance on the beam, I guess. Not sure if that's going to be of any help, though. Otherwise, I can surf and make mean cocktails. And I am getting my associate's in marine biology, so I know a lot about fish and corals?"

My words were met with a long silence. It was probably not what they were hoping for. Even I was starting to think that my mom should have put me into fencing or boxing instead of gymnastics. Oh well.

Archer was the first to recover from the shock. "Alright, well, if we end up having to do a balance and agility trial, you might have an advantage over many of the idiots here. For the logic and intelligence trials, you should also probably be fine. But for the strength, combat, and magic trials," his voice trailed off, and I almost wished he didn't continue. "Well, you better start praying to Tyche, Goddess of Luck."

"Archer." Sadie raised her eyebrows at her friend, her glare a clear warning.

He sighed, and added, "We will find something. Don't worry about it."

I nodded, but I didn't feel very comforted. Archer didn't feel confident about his words either. And Sadie and Søren were still silent.

"We should figure out something you can say when people ask for your power and ancestry." Archer was all business, and, honestly, I liked that. It helped to focus on what I could control.

"I can't fake having powers. I can't do anything remotely magical."

"You could. Not all powers are visible to other people. Look at Archer's. His pain is noticeable, but most people can't tell that he's controlling their thoughts. He can give you hallucinations that seem so real that you would think it was real life."

Søren's explanations gave me a shiver. What world had I landed in? How could I feel comfortable next to someone who could make me see or feel whatever he wanted, someone who could raise the dead, and someone who could set ablaze this whole arena with a thought – as I had discovered minutes ago, was Søren's power. How was I supposed to compare?

"You don't have to worry. I wouldn't do that to you," Archer said softly, looking at me like he meant something more. I wasn't sure what, though.

"Sure. I'm not worried." I was, though. But hopefully, saying it would make it come true. Fake it till you make it, right?

"Anyway, what Søren meant is that we could come up with something that the others wouldn't be able to test out easily," Sadie said with a frown. "Something that would also be unthreatening so no one will want to ask questions."

"Empath."

"An empath? Like for emotions?" I asked Archer.

"Yeah, an empath can feel someone else's emotions. I don't think any of the other competitors are empaths, and the only mind reader is Sarah, but she doesn't care much about gossip. No one would be the wiser."

Søren nodded at Archer and added, "As long as she says that she can only feel emotions and not manipulate them, she should be fine."

"It's a good idea," Sadie said, a calculating look on her face. "The others will be too busy pitying her to ask questions. How do you feel about it, Kalani?"

Why not? I did not want to advertise that I was a human. Pretending to have a power like this was the next best thing. I had done drama club in middle school; I could probably act like a Copper for a few weeks. An empath shouldn't be too hard to fake. Right?

"Sure, that works," I shrugged, hoping that I looked much more confident than I felt.

The three Coppers then argued which Golden I should pretend was my long-lost dad. I soon stopped listening because I did not know anyone they were talking about. This whole lineage thing was much more complicated than I had thought initially. There was an entire hierarchy of power at play here.

I knew the basics already from Hecate. The gods had too many grandchildren, and while their powers were too dangerous for them to be allowed to remain on Earth, there also wasn't enough space for all of them on Mount Olympus.

I got all of that. And even though it felt like straight out of a book, it still made sense.

What I now discovered was how important power and lineage were for the people living on Olympus. Which god or goddess one was descended from led to how much respect one received from others. Grandchildren from one of the twelve main Olympians were revered, superior to descendants from lesser deities. The power level was also critical, but from what I understood, power strength was also mainly related to which god you descended from.

This hierarchy controlled everything in this society, including how high your chances were to get a place on Olympus after the Tournament.

"I don't know that I will know enough about this world to be a convincing liar. I have a basic understanding of the Olympians, but I have no idea who all the Goldens are."

Sadie hummed in agreement. "That's fair. Plus, the Coppers here are from varied origins, so it would be tough to find a Golden that no one knows."

"Apollo had a lot of affairs with humans and had tons of Goldens. You could say that your parentage is unknown, and Hecate was only able to detect that you were a descendant from Apollo."

Sadie and Archer were deep in thought, pondering Søren's idea. It seemed like a decent idea to me. I knew the basics about Apollo – one of the Olympians, son of Zeus, twin to Artemis, and God of light, music, and prophecy. I wished I was able to do some internet digging on this.

"I think it should work. And if someone gets too nosy, we will deal with it," Archer announced.

Sadie agreed, and, just like that, I had a whole new identity – an empath, granddaughter of Apollo. I would have laughed if someone had told me this would be my new reality a week ago.

"Why are you helping me?" The question popped out of me before I could stop it. "I'm grateful, I really am," I explained, wanting to ensure they didn't take it the wrong way. "I am just wondering why you would decide to help me. A human."

I felt weirdly vulnerable asking this. I had always been independent. The one that would make my own way in the world because what else could I do? And it was okay; I was used to being more alone than most. But this was a whole new world where I knew and had nothing. These three people were the only ones who had offered to help me. And, while I wanted their friendship and support more than anything, a part of my brain kept whispering that this was too good to be true.

"You know, Kalani, I don't have Archer's power for brain electrical signals, but I have good intuition. And I could tell from the moment I met you that we would be great friends," Sadie said softly as she squeezed my hand reassuringly.

"Plus, Archer hates when defenseless little cubs like you are bullied. He has a serious case of savior complex," Søren added jokingly with a smirk in his friend's direction. "And I am just here for the ride."

They all laughed. Even Archer shrugged his grumpy coat off for a second. I chuckled too because I was getting a feel for Søren's playful personality.

And when we started training again, I felt like a weight had been lifted off my shoulders.

I wasn't alone anymore.

Chapter Seven

"I don't know how I feel about this."

Søren scoffed and put his hands on his hips, looking offended that I didn't trust his plan. "Come on. I have perfect control over my flames; you'll be just fine!"

"Do you realize that you are asking me to play dodgeball with literal fire? And I should have total faith in you not harming me? I don't have super speed or healing powers, Søren!"

He started massaging his ear, wincing as if I had just screamed in his ear. Sure, my voice was high-pitched toward the end. But, in my defense, this idea was utterly terrifying. And, yeah, I was freaking out. But who would want to see how fast they could run away from a fireball? Not me, that was for sure.

"We have done it thousands of times with Sadie and Archer, and they're still good and alive! You'll see. It's fun."

"And remind me again, are Sadie and Archer humans?"

"No, but-"

"And how long would it take for them to heal after a severe burn?"

"I mean, it depends. Probably around four or five hours. I don't see how-"

"And how long do you think it would take me to recover from a severe burn, Søren?"

He squinted his eyes and crossed his arms. "I see your point."

"Great. Now, let's put this idea in the 'maybe-some-other-time' bin and work on more standard training techniques, okay?"

Søren huffed and puffed stopped suggesting we had a barbecue with me as the main dish. I might have started to like the guy, but I still didn't want to play with his fire-from-Hell power – small victories. Instead, we started working on my hand-to-hand combat skills. Again.

It had been five days since I'd started training with my new friends. I was decently sure that I could call them friends now. We had spent the past five days training and getting to know each other. I was sore and bruised. But I felt more in control as the days passed by. I could see my progress every day. The guys and Sadie were incredible teachers because, as Archer so beautifully put it, I wasn't "a hopeless case everyone should pray for" anymore.

Always the poet.

Anyways, I had graduated from running around the Pit, trying desperately to avoid my three teachers, to kind of fighting back. I had yet to land on punch on any of them, but I had gotten pretty damn close to that morning. I was hoping for a light graze by the end of the week.

Today had been a long day. We had trained for three hours in the morning, working on the basics of fighting with a sword. And now Søren and I were finishing up after two more hours of learning helpful jabs, crosses, and hooks combinations. I would return to my life and be a true fighter, so much so that the customers at the bar would not dare to annoy me anymore. What a dream.

"Maybe, we could just call it a day?" I meant it as a statement, but it sounded more like a question. I had gotten much more comfortable around all three Coppers, but they took training – both mine and theirs – very seriously. I knew not to mess with their schedule, even when I would give my left kidney to stop training early.

I was expecting Søren to say that we needed to continue for at least half an hour – because, and I quote, "you gotta work hard to look this good" – but he smiled, raising an eyebrow at me. "Are you in a hurry to go to dinner?"

"I mean… I heard there is cake tonight."

He laughed, then took my arm and started walking toward the door. Relief bubbled up because today – hell, this week – had been a lot. "Let's go eat cake."

I'd grown to love Søren primarily because he was laid back and made the most grueling training sessions fun.

I had learned a lot about all three of my protectors-slash-trainers that week. I had learned that Søren played on his whole player persona – he liked to make others laugh and be the cool guy everyone wanted to be friends with. He also liked to flirt with everyone that was alive and looked vaguely like a woman. Poor Mei wouldn't last long. Besides that, though, Søren was a good friend and an even better brother. He always put a smile on our faces, and while his ideas weren't always the safest, he tried his hardest to help me better adapt to my new world.

Sadie was the sweetest person I had ever met – even though the whole 'bring-the-dead-back-alive' thing was everything but sweet. She longed for friendship and connections. She loved her brother and Archer but wanted a female friend. She loved to gossip and give gifts. She loved chocolate and enjoyed partying – I did not witness it, but I heard she could go hard on ambrosia. I hadn't gotten a chance to see her using her power, but I could tell how fearless she was during training. Sadie was a mother hen. But she was also a real badass. I wanted to be like her when I became older.

I already knew that the twins were descendants of Thanatos, the God of Death. Thanatos wasn't one of the main Olympians, but he was one of the Primordial Gods. Other than being one scary grandfather, Thanatos was so powerful that it gave the twins with one hell of a street cred. I did learn, though, that their mom was named Emma Aska and lived in Denmark. She was a chef. The twins always got sad when they talked about her, so I mostly restrained myself from asking much more.

On the other hand, Archer still felt like a mystery to me most of the time. He had started calling me Mayfield, and I didn't think it came with much affection. He was usually exasperated with my performances when he said it. I learned his last name was Vasilias, but I didn't dare return the nickname favor. On the bright side, I had gotten over my weird physical reaction toward him (mostly), but I was still somewhat intimidated to ask him personal questions. Through his interactions with the twins, I discovered he used his grumpiness as a shield against everyone except his two most trusted friends. And even though he kept his dark and mysterious air around me, I noticed small things that slightly changed my perception of him.

Archer always smiled at Søren's jokes, even the bad ones – often, it was just a slight smirk or the corners of his lips that barely went upwards, but it was a smile. He took training exceptionally seriously, and I guessed it had something to do with the five nasty scars on his shoulder blades. I hadn't mustered up the courage to ask about them, though. I hadn't asked about the tattoo either – the tattoo of a flying bird of prey that I had kept ogling a little too long in the past few days. He was also fiercely protective of Sadie – I guessed that was because he could tell how alone she sometimes felt, even with Archer and Søren there. And finally, I discovered that Archer was descended from Zeus, which made a lot of sense, seeing as he could control the brain's electrical waves.

I didn't quite get why, but the three of them did not blend with the other Coppers. They had more in common with them than with me, that was for sure. But over the past five days, it had become clear that they were a unit – it was them and everyone else. It wasn't so much that there was animosity between them and the other Coppers. No, this invisible barrier separated the two groups, and the other Coppers treated my protectors like the kings and queens of the place.

"Am I not interesting enough, sweetheart?"

"What did I tell you, Søren? I am not and will never be your sweetheart," I smiled at his antics.

"You break my heart," he pouted, making me laugh. Søren liked to pretend my rejections were heartbreaking, but we both knew it was a joke. I didn't go for players anyway. And he liked sucking on Mei's neck too much.

We arrived at the cafeteria, which was already crowded. Most of the Coppers had finished their training session with their trainers a while back. The twins, Archer, and I had gone after everyone had left the Pit. That suited me just fine because I did not particularly want to see Xander, my ex-trainer – if he could even claim that title after only seeing me for twenty minutes. He had mentioned practicing with our assigned trainer was optional, so I hadn't returned after the first sessions. The embarrassment of my fight with Elena was still too fresh.

Archer and Sadie had left our training session a little early, which was weird, but they had mentioned a personal matter. Søren had gotten the short straw of babysitting me. When we walked into the crowded room, Archer and Sadie were already there.

Søren and I got food from the stations and sat besides the others as quickly as possible. Training had made me terribly hungry. Seeing the beautiful chocolate cake on my dessert plate was not helping either. I couldn't usually tell what I was eating – most of the ingredients were not things I had ever seen, and I doubted they even existed on Earth – but this cake resembled something I could have found at home.

To fend off any more thoughts of home – of Makaio – I turned to Sadie, sitting in front of me. "How did it go? Was everything all right?"

She nodded a little too fast, then replied flippantly, "Yep. All good. Just some family stuff to figure out." Then the three of them shared a look, and Archer nodded to Søren before eating another piece of his meat. There was something there. I could feel it. But I didn't ask anything more because it wasn't my place. I had met them five days ago. There were plenty of things they had done together before they met me. And that was fine.

Plus, while I mostly trusted them now, I still didn't feel like sharing my deepest and darkest secrets with them yet. It was fine if they didn't trust me entirely, either.

After all, trusting the wrong person could mean a death sentence in a place like this.

"How did the rest of training go?" Archer asked, clearly changing the subject. I thought he had asked Søren, but when the blond Copper didn't answer, I looked up, and Archer's deep blue eyes stared straight into mine. I was so shocked by our eye contact – we had both avoided doing so as much as possible for the past five days – that it took me a second to gather my thoughts.

"It was… it was good. I think I am getting better at doing combinations without losing my footing."

"Good. You've been doing well."

I almost choked on air at Archer's compliment. He wasn't a mean teacher per se, but he didn't throw out compliments. Especially while sitting next to me and staring at me so intently; I felt like he was looking straight into my soul.

Why was it so hot suddenly?

"Uh… ye- yeah, thanks." Gods. What a mess. Could it even be possible to sound like more of a flustering teenager? I thought not. I could feel a blush rise on my cheeks, and I hoped that my tan skin would hide it.

Because Sadie was the best, she asked Archer a question, a knowing smile on her face. I was so busy staring at my food that I didn't even notice what the question was about. But all that mattered was that my three friends started talking, and I could attempt to regain my composure, which was damn hard because Archer's body heat was a fire branding the left side of my body.

Why was I even reacting like this? Archer did not like me – he called me "annoyingly human" daily and almost never looked at me or touched me if he didn't have to. If my mom had taught me anything useful in twenty years, it was that men didn't play hard to get.

I finally managed to get my heart rate back close enough to normal to listen when Sadie leaned closer over the table. "There is a rumor going around that the first trial is going to be a team one."

"Why is everyone getting their panties in a twist about that?" Søren asked, putting a weird green fry in his mouth.

"Whoever is spreading that information said that the losing team will get eliminated immediately." We all knew what getting 'eliminated' meant, so I could understand why everyone was freaking out. *I* was suddenly freaking out.

"Do we have any intel on that?"

"Not specifically," Archer answered Søren's question thoughtfully, "but mom told me they wanted to shorten the Tournament, make it last two weeks top. Eliminating a big chunk of us right away would do the trick."

I wiped my sweaty palms on my gym shorts. Was it getting harder to breathe suddenly?

"Anyway, that rumor is spreading like wildfire, and I haven't figured out who started it yet." Sadie sighed and tightened her ponytail. "What worries me is that we are still five weeks out from the first trial, and tensions are already increasing."

No one answered immediately because a fight broke out three tables down from us. Elena, the mountain of a woman I had fought against almost a week ago, was arguing with a young boy who didn't seem older than fifteen. I hadn't even realized there were participants so young here. He was standing up to Elena, but I could tell from here that he was far from confident.

"You don't have to do this, Elena, please," the boy pleaded, his voice cracking under his emotions. "I promise I am not a burden."

"You haven't won a single fight in weeks of training," Elena spat at him with disdain. "I am not risking having a weakling on my team. I am here to survive. I won't die because someone can't pull their weight."

The warrior started walking towards the boy while he shuffled back, his eyes wide. Soon enough, he was going to be stopped by the wall. Everyone was openly staring at them, but no one moved or said anything. It was like watching a morbid show. This was the real beginning of the Tournament – when the participants started turning on each other before anyone had to force them to.

The boy bumped on the wall. Elena continued, stopping only when she was so close that they almost touched. "I refuse to lose because of frail little twigs like you who don't know how to use their magic. So, if I have to kill you beforehand to make sure that doesn't happen, I will. And maybe I should do it now, get this purge started."

It was so quiet in the room that I could hear the boy's heavy breathing so clearly it felt like I was next to him. Was she really going to go through with this? Was she going to kill him? And was no one going to stop this cold-blooded murder?

It felt like a dream when I saw Elena's hand turn into a gigantic white paw with the longest claws I had ever seen. She brought a claw to the boy's neck, and I wanted to stand up and scream at her to stop. I wanted to be the strong girl who could stop a bully. But what could I even do? I had no power, and Elena had already kicked my ass once. And the fear that she would come for me instead kept me sitting on the hardwood bench. So, instead of helping the boy, I kept staring, my mind frozen on everything I couldn't do.

A bead of weirdly coppery blood appeared on the boy's neck. Not quite red. Not quite human. Somehow, I kept on staring at that drop of blood. It felt like the whole world had stopped turning. My heart pounded so hard I could feel it in my arms, head, and ears.

The boy whimpered in fear. Elena's hand moved toward the boy's neck. She was going to cut his throat. I wanted to close my eyes, but I couldn't. Instead, a gasp fell out.

The spell broke.

Then everything happened too fast.

Archer's hand fell on my upper arm. Elena's claw stopped. The boy fell to the ground. And, suddenly, Elena was coming towards me.

"Maybe instead of dear little Charlie, I should deal with our new girl first. After all, if there is one person I really don't want to risk having on my team, it's you."

Panic started creeping in. She was going to hurt me. Or kill me. And no one was going to move. No one was going to stop her. Just like no one had stopped her from hurting the boy – Charlie.

And I was going to be the very first death of this Tournament.

Except Sadie and Søren stood up. Elena faltered slightly. But she was determined – desperate enough for survival and too far down in her power trip – to keep going. One step. Two steps.

"One more step, and you die, Elena." Archer's voice was almost too calm, but the hall was so quiet that it resonated. "Mayfield is with us. And if you or anyone crosses us, you'll regret it."

Elena froze. She was right to take the threat seriously – my three Copper friends could be scary. Even to me, sometimes. The woman took a step back. Then she stopped, seemingly wanting to pretend like she wasn't afraid.

"The three of you can't take on all of us," she spat with venom in her voice.

Archer raised a single eyebrow, as if the angry Copper-who-could-turn-into-a-polar-bear was only a fly on his radar – barely an annoyance.

"I don't see anyone else ready to take the Askas and me on right now. Do you?"

If I weren't happily on his side, I would have smacked his arrogant grin off his face. Instead, Elena looked at her minions and deflated when she saw none of them looking anywhere close to coming to support her.

"You know, you won't be able to protect her forever, Archer. The Tournament starts in five weeks. A lot can happen during the trials. Mistakes happen. People die."

"You better make sure you don't make a mistake that costs Mayfield her life then." Then, Archer turned around and resumed eating.

Chapter Eight

I was still turning Archer's words in my head an hour later while sitting on Sadic's bed. Sadie was next to me, Søren on the desk chair, and Archer leaning against the wall. Sadie called this crisis reunion after the whole dinner debacle. I was still shaken from almost getting attacked – and almost seeing a cold-blooded murder. But what stuck out the most to me was how my friends reacted. I hadn't quite believed that they genuinely cared until then. Sure, they liked me in an acquaintance-going-on-friends way, but I hadn't been sure that they cared enough to have my back in a tough situation.

"We need to figure out how to deal with this situation," Sadie said after a long silence.

"I'm sure we'll be fine. Stop stressing about this," Søren answered with a nonchalant hand wave.

"Are you kidding?" Sadie scoffed. "Elena's breakdown was just the start. When she was with Charlie, I looked around, and many people did not look appalled. The Coppers are scared, desperate for survival, and the pressure is going up. The closer we get to the first trial, the tenser everyone will become. And other people will get the same idea as Elena's and start getting rid of the competition early while they are still in control of the situation."

That was a fair assessment of the situation. I had never been in a situation like this one, but I could easily imagine how high tensions could run. Everyone here was fighting for their lives. And when survival was involved, people could do crazy things.

"You don't think Archer's warning will be enough?" I asked tentatively, not looking at him. I had avoided his gaze since the grand declaration because it was too confusing for my poor heart.

"I think it will work for a few days, maybe. But when the next rumor starts or people start getting on each other's nerves, things will escalate. We can defend you but can't be with you all day."

Archer nodded. "I agree. We need something permanent. The others need to understand that Mayfield is off-limits."

"What exactly are you thinking about, then?" Søren asked, one eyebrow rising in question.

Archer shrugged and crossed his arms. "I don't know yet. That's why we're brainstorming, isn't it?"

While the guys were talking, I could tell Sadie had an idea. She had this look on her face like she was debating saying something. She was also fidgeting. From what I had seen so far, Sadie wasn't the anxious type. She liked to be in control but also enjoyed the freedom and possibilities of the unknown. So fidgeting was something that arrested my attention.

While the boys were bickering about using brute force to bring the other contestants to leave me alone, I caught Sadie's gaze. I raised my eyebrows inquisitively. A small smile appeared on her lips, and she nodded. I wasn't sure exactly what she was nodding for, but I hoped she would talk about her idea. It couldn't be worse than Søren's proposal of breaking the arm of everyone that would look at me in an unfriendly way. Although, her smile was widening by the second and she was getting a little scary.

"Boys!" Sadie exclaimed loud enough to get Søren and Archer to stop talking. "I know exactly what we are going to do."

"And?" Archer asked.

"You're going to date her. Fake date, to be specific."

"Date whom?"

"Who do you think, dummy?" Sadie bent her head toward me. "Kalani."

"How would that solve anything?"

"It's quite simple, really. Relationships mean commitment. Commitment means loyalty, which means you attack both if you attack one. Fake dating will provide a layer of protection she didn't have until now. Friendships can be temporary and fleeting. But a committed, loving relationship? It will show everyone that Kalani is a true part of our group and here to stay."

Archer blinked a few times as if slightly overwhelmed with the idea.

"But- I don't- *Who* is going to date her? Søren?"

"Obviously, no. Everybody knows that my brother is a player. His relationships don't last long. People would not take this new relationship any more seriously than they take the one he currently has with Mei."

"I mean, fair, but-"

"It has to be you, Archer."

That left him speechless. Søren was almost snickering at his friend. Sadie looked like she was enjoying this conversation very much. And I? Well, I was stunned at both Sadie's suggestion and Archer's reaction.

First of all, what was this idea? Was Sadie a lover of those steamy romance books where the bad boy and the good girl pretend to date? Did she not realize that Archer and I were not the characters of a romance novel and would not turn a shitty fake-dating situation into the love story of a lifetime?

And second of all, was the idea of dating me that disgusting? Sure, the Coppers in this Tournament were all beautiful — even Elena, in a way. Being a descendant of the Greek gods and goddesses seemed to have some perks, genes for great physiques being one. And yes, I wasn't the tall model or petite cute type. Being a gymnast, I was too muscular for the usual occidental beauty standards. But still. Could he not even fake it for a minute? The whole aghast expression on his face was starting to be really insulting.

"I don't think that's a good idea." Archer finally said after a lifetime of silence.

"And why is that?" I didn't even know why I asked that. I didn't want to do this anymore than him. I was starting to think that Søren's arm-breaking idea had some charm.

"I don't date. I don't do commitment or relationships."

"We are not asking you to marry me, lover boy. Just to fake date me."

"I got that part. And no."

"Are you afraid or something?"

"Why would I be afraid?"

"You tell me." I challenged him with my gaze. This was becoming a personal argument. His rejection was hitting a little too close to issues with my mom that I had tried to avoid for years.

He didn't say anything for a long time, just staring at me. He had a strange look, like he was internally fighting something. The silence was so long that I thought he wouldn't say anything at all. But he dropped my gaze first and looked at Sadie. "How do you think it would work?"

I blinked in surprise at Archer's words. Was this really going to happen? Did I want it to happen? Did it even matter if this was the only way to ensure I remained alive and mostly safe? Søren had a shit-eating grin on his face, clearly enjoying the show. And Sadie… well, I could tell that Sadie was trying her hardest to keep a straight face after our argument.

"Like a real relationship. You would hold hands, smile at each other, do some light cuddles together, and kiss a few times in public. Pretend like you're in love."

Somehow, my mind got stuck on the word "kiss," and my eyes flew to Archer's mouth. His lips were so plump, so pink. What would it be like to kiss him? What would it *feel* like? It would probably be better than it had been with Brad, my ex. Anything could be better than Brad, though. And Archer… I had a feeling that kissing him would be a whole-body experience. Something I would never forget and probably ruin me for the next Brads in my life. Because, let's be honest here, I would probably end up with a Brad, not an Archer.

"Kalani?" Sadie's voice brought me back out of my thoughts. She and her twin were looking expectantly at me. On the other hand, Archer was staring at the ground, deep in thought. I hadn't heard her question, but I knew what she wanted.

"I… um, sure. I mean, I will do anything that will keep me alive. Even…" I cleared my throat and waved in Archer's general direction, "fake-date him."

Sadie nodded, visibly satisfied. Søren now had a full-on Cheshire cat grin – he was too excited about this. I was almost tempted to look around for a hidden camera prank.

"We're all waiting on you now, big man." Søren almost sing-sang.

Archer's deep blue eyes flew to mine. He was usually very guarded with his emotions, but I could almost see fear in his eyes right then. That couldn't be right because why would this super powerful Copper, who could control the mind, be afraid of fake-dating little old me? Was it some desire to protect his reputation? Or was something deeper linked to his scars and how he never showed any vulnerability?

"I'll do it."

Chapter Nine

I had slept in. It didn't happen often. In the past six days, I had trained early every morning. And at home, I often had to get up early either for classes, to give gym lessons, or to reward myself with a surfing session. And the few off days I had, I needed to take care of Makaio for breakfast. Gods, I missed that little guy. I gave myself thirty seconds to think of him – remember his sweet smiles, how he always pretended to be a tough guy, and loved to cuddle when he had bad dreams – before I put everything from *before* behind a heavy-duty locked door.

Anyways. I had slept in, which meant that Sadie hadn't been in her room when I'd left. I wish I could have walked to breakfast with her – she would have probably helped me calm down. But now, I was alone, standing in the hallway outside of the cafeteria, giving myself a pep talk to enter. "You can do this, Kalani," I murmured, eyes closed, shaking my arms at my sides. "Imagine it's Brad. Nothing more than Brad."

Some guy walked past and gave me a weird look. Oh well. I was already the girl who couldn't fight to save her life. I could also become the crazy girl who gave herself a stern talk-to before breakfast. Whatever.

After taking a couple of deep breaths, I finally turned the corner and walked in. Most of the Coppers were already eating breakfast and talking loudly, probably replaying the events from the night before. I purposefully avoided looking at my friends' table. I knew they were there already. And I knew I would have to deal with my decision from the night before. I had tossed and turned all night over it. I was getting exponentially more nervous as the night went on, to the point that when I finally fell asleep, it had been a dreamless slumber for way too long.

And here I was, taking my sweet time choosing between some purple apple I had been debating trying for a few days and a sweet carrot I knew I liked. Decisions, decisions.

"I didn't think fruit could be so interesting. Should I leave so you have more time to lovingly stare at your future meal?" Archer's voice came from right behind me, so close that I got goosebumps.

"These fruits are definitely more interesting than some people I know," I answered with a small smile. I took a few more seconds to ground myself and get my emotions under control before turning to face Archer.

"Good morning, boo."

Archer winced and shook his head. "Let's not do sweet nicknames."

"Oh, come on, you're no fun!" I pretended to pout just because he seemed to be in an unusually good mood. It felt like a good day to push his buttons, if just a little.

"Stop playing around, Mayfield. We have a show to put on, people to impress, and places to be very soon. Let's roll."

I didn't have time to prepare myself because he put both fruits on my plate, took the tray in one hand, and put his other arm on my shoulders. I immediately tensed up. I could feel people staring at us, wondering what was happening. This was way too weird, and I suddenly wanted to run away.

"Calm down, Mayfield," Archer murmured at my ear, his breath tickling the side of my neck. "Relax and walk. Let me do the rest."

What did that even mean? Let him do what? How far were we taking this? Sadie had mentioned kissing the night before. Was it going to happen? That morning? My heart started beating faster and faster. And it was because I didn't want to kiss Archer. Not because I wanted to know what it would feel like in real life. Not at all.

That would be ridiculous.

I was still thinking of the maybe-potential kiss when we arrived at the table. Sadie and Søren were already here, and, to my dismay, Mei was also present. She was so close to Søren's side that I was almost worried we would need all three of us to rip them apart. I still didn't get why Søren was with her. From what I had seen so far, she was neither nice nor interesting. Her power – control over birds – was cool but not particularly powerful. She was gorgeous, sure, but I wanted to believe that men wanted more than an empty body.

Sadie did a cute little wave as I sat down. She was too giddy about this – I didn't like it. Søren said hi, but Mei almost immediately grabbed his face to kiss him or suck his lifeforce from him. Was she a closeted vampire? Did vampires exist?

Focus, Kalani.

Archer sat next to me, close enough that I could feel the heat coming off of him. He took the weird apple and took a bite. Then he put his hand on mine, right on the table, and started playing absentmindedly with my fingers.

"How are you doing this morning, Kalani?" Sadie asked, seeing my uneasiness. I had never been big on PDA, probably because I had only been with Brads before. You didn't fall head over heels in love with Brads.

"Good. Great." I nodded to try to emphasize my words. "Slept so well."

"Was your dream of me so good that you didn't hear the alarm, sweetheart?" Søren asked, moving his eyebrows in a weirdly impressive wave.

"You wish, Søren." He gave me a look full of innuendos, and I rolled my eyes at him. Mei didn't seem to care about her boyfriend flirting with me because she kept making sexy eyes at him.

"I am sure she was dreaming of her new boyfriend," Sadie said slightly too loudly to be natural.

Mei suddenly stopped trying to molest her boyfriend and frowned at me. "Who is the boyfriend?" The way she asked made it seem like this was a question she never thought she'd ask.

"Him," I said with a strange pride, looking purposefully at Archer's hand on mine.

Mei did a double take on Archer's hand, then started laughing, to the point that she had tears in her eyes, and people started turning around. I wasn't sure how to react to this, nor did the others, it seemed. Only after almost a minute of hysterical laughter did Søren say to his girlfriend, "It's not a joke babe." That did the trick.

She stopped short and blinked a few times to get her thoughts in order. "Wait, for real? *She* is with Archer?" She looked around at us before fixing her gaze on my pretend boyfriend. "Are you okay? Did she…"

She didn't finish her sentence, but I knew what she meant. I hid a laugh. She was seriously worried about Archer. What did she think I had done? Threaten him into being in a relationship with me? Hilarious.

"Mei, you should know that he begged me, not the other way around." I leaned in closer to her and continued in a stage whisper. "It broke my heart, you know. He was so hopeful. I had to say yes."

Mei gasped, a hand going to cover her mouth. She was so invested; I loved it. "No way! Really?"

Archer's hand squeezed mine in a way that told me I should stop what I was doing. The thing was, this was the most fun I'd had in days. Before he could say anything, I answered Mei. "Yes! Archer is a big softie at heart, you know. I love that about him."

"Oh, and I bet you can feel it with your empath power, can't you? Oh, I want to know more! Are you guys going to start living together? Oh, wait!" She started flapping her hands around in excitement. "Did you guys do it already? You have to tell me how it is, Kalani! All the girls are wondering how he is in the sheets, and I want all the gossip!"

Damn, that girl was going right for the jugular, wasn't she? And also, when had we become best friends? She was suddenly super friendly after ignoring me for the past week. I could also see that many people were not so subtly listening to our conversation. Interesting to see how fast Sadie's plan was working.

"Honey, come on! That's not something you ask over the breakfast table." Søren said with a playful push to her shoulder. "Plus, we all know Archer learned everything from me."

I opened my mouth to answer, but Archer beat me to it. "Look, Mei, Mayfield and I appreciate that you care so much about this, but we want to keep our relationship as private as possible. And our physical love too. But I will say that Mayfield is more than satisfied. Aren't you, baby?" His voice turned seductive, and he turned to stare into my eyes as he asked the question. His gaze was so intense that all of my amusement fled. And then, to my surprise, he leaned in and kissed my neck, right below my ear. Warmth spread through my whole body, and I shivered. I barely heard Mei's gasp of excitement because all I could think of was Archer's lips on my skin. How could I feel such a small touch *everywhere*?

"Are you doing all right there, Mayfield?" Archer's voice was so low that I was sure I was the only one who could hear. His voice was rough and… was that amusement? I leaned away, and sure enough, his arrogant smirk was there. This was payback for earlier. He knew what he was doing. He knew very well the effect it had on me. And that annoyed me – his little game and my reaction made me mad. At myself, mostly. This was all pretend, and I needed to remind myself of that.

Still, I gave him a look that I hoped conveyed that I didn't appreciate this little game. He raised an eyebrow, challenging me without a word. He knew I couldn't say anything because we had to keep this pretense up.

"So," Sadie said after a long silence. "What are we working on today?"

Sadie was always coming through when I needed her. That girl was an angel.

"I think it's time we do some magic training," Archer said before taking another bite of the apple.

"Hell, yes!" Søren exclaimed, pumping his fist in victory. "That's my favorite part!" He was so excited; it was cute in a little-boy-gets-his-favorite-toy kind of way. Seeing as he had wanted to play dodgeball with fireballs the day before, I wasn't sure I wanted to play the same games as Søren. Or even the others, for that matter. I didn't think Archer had used his power on me since that very first night, but I could still remember how he had manipulated everything I thought. If this was only the top part of the iceberg, I did not want to experience any more of his gift.

"Don't make this face, Kalani. We're not going to eat you alive," Sadie winked at me.

"And it's not like we Coppers can be easily killed, right?" Mei added with a laugh.

Right. Good thing I wasn't one.

Chapter Ten

"*A*re you ready?"

I looked up to see Sadie staring at me with worry in her eyes. Ever the mother hen, she was making sure I was okay with the plan. Was I? Not really. But would I do it? Sure.

I nodded, and she smiled slightly before retreating a few steps. The three of us were in Sadie's room – Søren had gone to the Pit to train with Mei and a few others. And I was sitting on Sadie's bed, facing Archer, ready to get my mind invaded.

He was sitting on Sadie's desk chair, looking cool as a cucumber.

I was not.

I had always tried to be brave for my brother, especially when Mom wasn't the most present. But I wasn't the reckless or daringly courageous type. I knew my strengths and weaknesses, and knew damn well that I wasn't invincible. My knee injury during high school was a stark reminder of that. My point was that I wasn't the type of girl to willingly do something I knew I had no control over. And, let's be honest, I had no control over anything when it came to the Coppers' powers. Especially Archer's.

"Can we go over it again?"

Archer sighed, clearly annoyed with me. Oh well. "I will put you in an illusion, and I want you to get out of it. It's all about your strength of will and mental barriers against my power. Not anything complicated."

Nothing complicated. Right. It was clear as day that he had never been the prey in a room full of predators that had magical powers.

"Okay." I took a deep breath and imagined Makaio's little face and his bright smile. I was doing all this to get back to him. "I'm ready."

Archer leaned back in the chair without a word. I stared back at him, desperately trying to steel my nerves. I was almost positive that he wouldn't hurt me. But still. Someone invading my mind was both terrifying and way too intimate. My mind had always been my refuge, and I didn't want anyone to see all of my private thoughts.

Seconds passed, and nothing happened. Anticipation built up, and I couldn't stare into Archer's eyes anymore. I shifted my gaze to look at Sadie. She gave me a small reencouraging smile. I couldn't answer, though, because suddenly I was in a desert.

There was sand everywhere. Miles and miles of dunes and endless solitude. The sun was at its zenith, so hot that I could feel sweat gliding down my neck and back already. There was a very light breeze – just enough to blow the sand but not nearly enough to cool me down. It smelled like the beach – fresh and earthy – except without the salty scent of the ocean. And no matter how far I tried to look, all I could see was the sun reflecting off the golden sand.

A part of me knew this wasn't real – that was the only reason I didn't completely freak out. But it seemed so *real*. I could see, hear, feel, and smell the desert! It reminded me of the sensation I had after being teleported to Mount Olympus – except that day, I thought everything was a drug-induced trip. Turns out it was all too real.

Some corner of my mind kept reminding me that I had to get out, that the whole point of this was to escape back to reality. I sat down on the hot sand, deciding that maybe I needed to meditate back to the real world. I closed my eyes, trying to feel the bed or Archer's judgmental glare. But the more time when by, the more real the desert felt. Soon enough, I couldn't even remember what I was supposed to think about.

All that existed was the desert.

The sand burned my calves and thighs while the sun did its part on my face and arms. The whistle of the wind between the dunes was hypnotic and almost lulled me to sleep, only broken by the tingling of the sand carried by the breeze and hitting my skin. And I was getting so, so thirsty.

I had to move.

So, I started to walk. I needed to find out which direction was the right one to find water. I began walking away from the sun – it was too bright to have ahead of me continuously. Step after step, I kept on walking. My sneakers, which were slightly too big, kept on rubbing uncomfortably against my skin. The irritation was accentuated by the sand pooling in my shoes the farther I went.

The walk was endless. It felt like hours had passed, but the sun was just as high as when it started. How long ago was that? My legs were getting shaky from exhaustion. My eyes were burning from the sun and the sand battering them. My vision was starting to get blurry. And my throat… My throat felt like sandpaper. Swallowing was extremely painful because I had almost no saliva left. I did not know that it was possible to be so thirsty.

And through the haze of my brain, I had no idea where I was coming from or where I was supposed to go. My only thought was water.

My whole body was shutting down, though. I could feel it coming. My vision was so blurry from the sand that had gotten into my eyes. My skin was in terrible pain from the sun burning it. And my legs were so tired that I was more staggering forward than walking. It was a wonder I hadn't fallen already.

But I kept on walking. One step. One more. One foot in front of the other. Until a shimmer caught my eye. There. To my right. I could almost see water, just beyond a small dune. I felt a small surge of energy coming through me, and I almost ran toward the water. All my energy was spent climbing in the sand, desperate for just a sip of liquid. Getting to the top of the dune took everything out of me.

And there was nothing.

My gaze met only sand. Endless sand. And not a drop of water.

I fell down, laying there, feeling my body give up. My mind gave up too.

This was the end. I was going to die here, in a desert, all alone. And I didn't even have the strength or water to cry anymore.

"How disappointing."

The voice was so jarring that I almost jumped. Or, at least, I would have if I still had the strength to move. Instead, my reaction looked like a jerk.

Archer was here in the desert. Arms crossed like all of this was an inconvenience to him. Me included.

"What-" I tried to talk, but my throat was so dry that I could only get out a croak.

"I don't know why I was expecting better results," Archer mumbled just loud enough for me to hear. His gaze was clinical in assessing my crumpled body on the sand. And I felt shame. Because, I had vague memories of us in Sadie's room. Of me agreeing to go through mental resistance training.

And then the desert started to disappear around me. It was like peeling back wallpaper. Whole strips of the desert were gone to reveal Sadie's room. And soon enough, I was back on her bed, lying on my side on a soft duvet instead of harsh and burning sand. Could all of this have been a hallucination? But it had felt so *real*. The thirst had been a visceral, all-consuming sensation. And now? Now my throat was back to normal as if nothing had happened.

And it made me fear Archer's powers to a whole new level. Because it wasn't just reading my thoughts or playing with emotions anymore. No, this experience was a real eye-opener on how dangerous his powers were. I could easily imagine that someone could become insane from staying in such a hallucination for too long.

It took me a few seconds to regain my bearings before I could sit up. Instinctively, I scooted a little farther away from Archer. He was still staring at me with his assessing gaze. I could tell he was looking at this – at me – as if it were a failed experiment.

"Are you okay, Kalani?" Sadie's voice brought me out of my worried cycle of thoughts, and my eyes jumped to meet hers. She was frowning, clearly concerned.

"I'm…" I stopped because I had expected my voice to be gone as it had been in the desert. But it was back, without even the slightest sign that I had felt like I was dying of dehydration seconds before. "I don't know." And that was the most honest response I could give her because this experience had been jarring. I didn't know if it was even worth it to keep going. How could I hope to survive against someone who could manipulate my brain so thoroughly that I didn't understand what was real anymore? How could I compete against someone who could make me feel like I was dying without even touching me?

I couldn't.

I moved my hands to push my hair away from my eyes and realized they were shaking. Actually, my whole body was shaking. I couldn't tell if it was from the temperature change compared to the desert or if I was going into shock.

"I don't think I can do it again." My voice broke at the end, and some part of me was annoyed at myself for being so weak. At some point, though, there was a difference between having hope and being unrealistic and stubborn.

Sadie and Archer said nothing for a long time. At least aloud. I could tell they were having a mental conversation by how their facial expressions changed. These usually annoyed me to no end, but today I only felt a mild irritation. I didn't have the mental space for stronger emotions.

I was about to get up from the bed – my legs had finally stopped shaking – when Archer cleared his throat. "I'm sorry, Mayfield. I should have started with something easier." He seemed to search for his words, and I wondered how often he had apologized before. "I want you to know that I would never use my powers on you without your consent. Ever."

I nodded because I appreciated his words but wasn't sure what to answer. Was I ready to do this again? No. I wasn't.

"Listen, we can stop if you want, but you should know that Archer is not the only one with powers on the mind." Sadie walked closer and sat next to me on the bed. "Amara can make your worst fears come alive, Sarah can read your immediate thoughts, and Alexei is a seduction master – he can make you fall in love with him and kill yourself to please him. They won't hesitate to use their powers during the trials. Archer and I believe it would be the smartest thing for you to develop the mental barricades to fight their powers. It could save your life in the Pit. But we won't force it on you either." She squeezed the top of my hand reassuringly. "I can only imagine how scary it must be for you to be here. But I *know* you can do this."

"Sadie and I have a theory that she could act as an anchor for you, to help you fight my power and come back to reality easier."

"An anchor?"

"If she holds your hand while I put you in a vision, it should act as a tether and help you remember that it is not reality."

I stared at Archer a few seconds after his explanation. Did I trust this? Did I trust *him*? I knew that Sadie was right – I needed to prepare myself to fight against the Coppers that could control the mind. I had no way to fight against fire, larger-than-life animals, or undead zombies that some Coppers could control. But the mind was the one place where I had a chance. Potentially. If I kept on going.

At that moment, I had to decide if I wanted to fight. This moment felt like a decisive turn because it was the first time I was truly experiencing how dangerous this Tournament could be. But I could still see Makaio's little dimples and the love that shone in his eyes when we spent time together. I was fighting for him. That hadn't changed. And what was giving up going to give me? Nothing except for death. I had no choice.

It may be time to start being braver instead of being scared.

I took a deep breath. I squeezed Sadie's hand. I might not fully trust Archer, but I had gotten to trust Sadie in the past week. I knew we hadn't known each other for a long time, and I was usually very slow at allowing myself to trust others. But everything felt like it went faster here, as if the promise of an imminent fight to the death made us want to form deep connections.

"Okay. I'll try it again. But I don't want any desert." I was proud of how steady and sure my voice sounded. I was entirely in a 'fake it till you make it' mode.

"I know just the thing," Archer said with a smirk that promised mischief.

I could feel my heartbeat picking up from the anticipation, and my palm got sweaty in Sadie's hold. She touched my upper arm lightly, and I turned to look at her. She had a reassuring smile on, trying to convey with her eyes that everything would be fine. "Focus on my hand, alright? Everything will look different and overwhelming; you won't see me, but I promise you'll feel my hand holding yours. And I won't let go."

I nodded, not answering for fear of throwing up. God, I was stressed. Fully freaking out. Archer asked if I was ready, and I nodded. Deep breath in. Archer's eyes glowed for a second.

And I was underwater.

How ironic. I had felt like I was going to die from dehydration minutes ago, and now I was underwater and without an oxygen bottle. I hadn't planned on drowning today, but I guessed you couldn't always prepare for the day ahead.

For a second, I started to panic. But then Sadie's voice echoed in my head. *Focus on my hand. I won't let go.* So, I did. I closed my eyes, ignoring the fish swimming around me, and focused on my left hand.

At first, it felt empty, the water the only thing I could touch. But I concentrated on it, and little by little, I started to feel it – the ghost shape of a slender hand in mine. My lungs were burning. But it wasn't my first time stuck underwater – as a surfer, I had experienced tumbling below a wave for so long that I had worried I would never manage to come up. Even as my lungs started to constrict, I knew I still had time. Concentrating on my hand, I let out small bursts of air, tricking my body into thinking everything was fine. After a while,

Sadie's hand felt so real in mine that I squeezed back. And then I pulled. I pulled on her hand so hard I worried I would hurt her. I continued to pull even as I had no air left to exhale. I continued to pull even as I started to feel lightheaded.

As a last survival instinct, I opened my mouth. Inhaled.

Air. I inhaled air. Shocked, I opened my eyes and I was back on Sadie's bed, crushing her hand. "Holy shit, I did it!" A surprised laugh escaped me. Archer looked surprised before me, his eyes slowly returning to normal. And Sadie… I turned to face her and surprised myself by pulling her in for a hug.

Goodness, who was I turning into? A hugger?

Sadie didn't make it weird, though. She squeezed me into her arms, and I could tell she was happy too. This was a team achievement; I would not have been able to do it without her. But even knowing that, it felt so *good* to be capable. To not be completely helpless anymore.

As I moved back, I caught Archer crossing his arms over his chest. I couldn't tell how he felt – he always kept his emotions and thoughts close to his chest. "Good job, Mayfield," he said. Was I really going to get praise from Archer? "I guess you're not as incapable as I thought." Never mind.

"Don't rain on her parade, Arch," Sadie interrupted him. Then to me: "You did great, and I am very proud of you. We will just have to keep practicing until you can do it without me!"

Fantastic. I couldn't wait for that. I was sure Archer would find plenty of ways to make me suffer until I could finally stop him.

"By the way, Archer, when I said 'no desert,' I didn't mean that I wanted to end up almost drowning in the middle of the ocean." I challenged him with my gaze, defying him to apologize. Why couldn't the hallucinations be cute walks through the forest?

"Don't be a baby, Mayfield. I knew it would work. It did. End of story." He shrugged like it was all fine and I was the crazy one.

Right.

Somehow, I'd find a way to get back at him.

Chapter Eleven

"How are you really feeling?"

I turned to Sadie and found her looking at me more seriously than before. We hadn't had the opportunity to talk just the two of us in a while – it was constantly training, eating, training, sleeping, and repeat.

"It's, huh… it's not easy. I hope being here will feel less overwhelming every day, but it doesn't." I didn't know why it was so easy to be honest with Sadie. I could tell that she wouldn't judge me. "And I miss home. It's funny how you don't realize something is good until you lose it. I wish I could see my brother, just for one second. To make sure he's okay."

Sadie didn't say anything for a while. The silence didn't feel heavy at all. It was comfortable to be next to her.

"Wanna see something cool?"

I frowned, wondering if a Copper's definition of cool was the same as mine. "Sure?"

Sadie almost jumped off the bed and signaled for me to follow. We walked through the empty halls of the building. I was almost certain everyone was training at the Pit or one of the other gym spaces. Had I mentioned how glad I was that Sadie and the others had taken me under their wing so I didn't have to go through team training?

Soon enough, I was lost again, per usual. A week in, and I still couldn't find my way when it came to something other than my room, the cafeteria, or the Pit. However, Sadie seemed to know this place like the back of her hand. She kept taking turns after turns until we reached a part of the complex where the torches were few and far between, the hallways darker than before. Then after what felt like an eternity, we reached a steep staircase. Sadie started climbing, and I followed suit, curious about where this would lead us.

We arrived on the roof of the building as the sun was starting to go down. The whole day had gone by without me even realizing it. The fresh air was great on my face, especially after all of the day's emotions. And the view. The view was gorgeous. On one side, I could see the face of a mountain. It was beautiful, with Greek-style mansions that jutted from the side of the mountain. The buildings looked like a mix between the new contemporary villas in Hollywood and the old Greek temples you'd see in Athens. I could see vineyards and gardens full of trees with the prettiest flowers I had ever seen. It was just so… otherworldly. Magical. If I had to imagine a modern Eden garden, that is what I would have come up with.

But the most beautiful part appeared once I turned around. A sea of clouds. We were above the clouds, looking down at a sea of puffy white. It was incredible, like a dream.

"We are not supposed to come up here, but I thought it would be nice for you to get some air. And some context."

"I can't believe how pretty it is."

"I know, right? The gods and goddesses are very proud of their piece of rock." She shook her head while watching the horizon above the clouds. "It puts everything into perspective, you know? To see the place everyone is fighting to get a piece of."

I knew what she meant. I knew the Coppers were fighting at the Tournament for their lives. I got that. But I had yet to fully grasp what they were hoping for. Mount Olympus was the most beautiful place I had ever been to, at least from afar. And I knew very well that you shouldn't judge a book by its cover – beautiful places could be full of terrible people. But still. I could imagine how Mount Olympus, with its heaven-like look, was attractive to all of these Coppers. Winning the Tournament meant not only surviving but also earning the right to live in possibly the most beautiful place on Earth.

Could it even be considered Earth?

"Where even are we? Compared to Earth, I mean."

"Mount Olympus is not on the same place of existence as Earth. Do you know those movies that talk about parallel universes? It's similar to that. Earth is a plane of existence, and Mount Olympus is another. A few bridges link them, which is how full-fledged gods can cross between realms."

It was hard to imagine. How had I ended up in a parallel universe from Earth? It felt like a science fiction scenario.

"Have you always dreamed of living here? In Mount Olympus?"

Sadie didn't answer right away, seeming to contemplate her answer. "It's not so much that I dreamed of living in Mount Olympus. I just knew it was the only place I would be allowed to live in for the rest of my life." She waited a few seconds before continuing. "You might not realize it, but it can be very dangerous to have Coppers or Goldens living in the human world. Strong emotions can trigger our powers, and Goldens or Coppers have caused many natural disasters. We know from the time we are born that living on Earth is not sustainable. It's not a choice so much as a known consequence of our births."

It was hard for me to imagine, knowing from the time I was born, that, one day, I would have to fight to earn the right to remain alive. It seemed so terrible to submit all of those children to that knowledge. None of them had asked to be born. And yet, they were all getting ready to fight and die for something they had no control over.

I looked at the compound splayed at our feet. We could see the Pit where a few Coppers were still training – I wouldn't be surprised if Archer had gone to train with Søren there. The man seemed to love training more than life itself. But everyone looked so small from up here. After spending the past week feeling like I was the insignificant one, it was strange.

There was a small lake too that I hadn't seen before. It looked like something out of a dream, with a small island in the middle and lush bushes all around. What drew my eye were the bright splotches of purple – they looked like small fields of flowers.

"If I were you, I wouldn't go and take a swim there. I heard merpersons are living there. Trust me, they don't look like Ariel and tend to drown and eat visitors."

"Merpersons?"

"Yeah, people used to call them mermaids and mermen, but then there was this huge thing about being inclusive of non-binary and gender-fluid people, so here we are."

"And what about the purple flowers? They look so pretty!"

"Don't go near those either. They are aconite flowers – real pretty but real poisonous too. Rumors say that Athena poisoned Arachne using aconite and changed her into a spider. All because Arachne was a better weaver than her. Gods and goddesses can be so proud, you know? Anyway, no one got changed into spiders since then, but aconite has killed many people."

"Thanks for the advice."

The more you knew. I felt like every time I asked about something in this world, it was always something that could kill me. Or drown me. Or eat me. Or any other variation of a terrible death. This world was as beautiful as it was deadly.

"But anyway, we were here to talk about you. I can only try to imagine what it's like for you, to be thrown here against your will. But I want you to know that you impress me every day. I don't think many humans would adapt as well as you do."

I scoffed at that. It didn't feel like I was adapting well at all. Most days, I was barely getting by. "I don't know Sadie. I feel so overwhelmed all the time. And I feel like no matter how hard I train and learn these next few weeks, it won't make a difference during the trials."

"It will, though. First off, the boys and I will help because, honestly, you deserve it more than a lot of them. And you're smart. The trials aren't always one-on-one fights. Many of them can actually be won with brains instead of brawn."

I nodded and remained silent for a second, looking at the incredible spectacle before me. The clouds were painted with beautiful shades of orange and pink as the sun went down. Gods, I wished Makaio could have been here to see it.

"What are you going to do once you win this Tournament?"

"I want to get a place close by from the guys but not so close that they feel the need to continue coddling me. As if I need coddling," Sadie said with a laugh, and I couldn't agree more. That girl was a warrior and could raise the dead. She didn't need help from men, thank you very much. "And then, I don't know. My mom was a chef in Denmark. Maybe I'll follow in her footsteps and open a restaurant on Olympus."

"Do you miss it? Denmark?"

Sadie stayed silent for a few beats, staring ahead at the never-ending sea of clouds. "Every day." Her eyes were shiny, and I wondered if she would cry. I would have understood if she did – being away from home was awful. Instead, she took a deep breath and gave me a small smile. "I'll make Danish food and bring a piece of home here."

"That sounds nice. Maybe I'll come to try your food sometimes."

"Yeah, you will. You will." And the look Sadie and I exchanged meant more than promises about eating at a restaurant; it meant I would still be alive to do it.

The silence stretched between us, but neither of us felt the need to fill it up. It was nice to have someone I could sit with and just *be*. I liked to think that if we had met on Earth, Sadie and I would have also been great friends. She would have been the extraverted to my introverted, the Nairobi to my Tokyo, the Max to my Eleven. I wished she could have met my brother and my gymnastics kids. I wished we could have been two normal friends living a regular life.

As the sun disappeared beneath the clouds, Sadie started talking again. "I could tell that you were scared of Archer earlier."

She went right for the jugular, didn't she? And she was right, per usual. I hummed noncommittally and waited. We both knew she had something else to say.

"He is not so bad, you know. He's just… life hasn't been kind to him, and he doesn't trust easily. And I know he has a gift that can seem very scary. But he would never use it to hurt an innocent. That is part of why he hasn't had an easy life too." She stared blankly ahead for a few seconds before turning toward me. She was dead serious when she continued. "He is the best friend I have. He's a good guy. And he cares, even if he doesn't know how to show it sometimes. Just give him a chance. Alright?"

I took a deep breath, debating what to say. I got it. She had known Archer for so long that she knew him on a level that I never would. And I could imagine that the scars on his back were a part of this troubled past. So, I understood why Sadie wanted to protect Archer. But their relationship did not have the power imbalance that ours had. I would never be on an equal footing with any of them.

"Sure. I'll stay open-minded."

She nodded, seeming to understand that this was the best I could do.

Hours later, when I was back in my room after eating with Sadie – Søren and Archer were gone by the time we went down – I was still thinking of Sadie's words. Laying in my bed, staring at the ceiling in the dark, I kept replaying her words in my head. About Archer. And gods, I was so pissed at myself for not being able to stop thinking about it. But here I was, imagining what could have happened in his past. Imagining him as a child, hurting. And imagining him caring. About me.

Chapter Twelve

The next few days passed in a blur. My days were full to the brim between sparring, learning all I could on the Tournament, and practicing my mental blocks with Sadie and Archer. It was good because it prevented me from worrying too much. And I had lots of things to worry about. The first of which was the mounting tension between the participants of the Tournament. Groups had started forming, and some had extreme ideologies. There was a case study on group polarization happening in this place. Elena's clique was becoming more and more prone to violence as the days went on. It was a ticking time bomb, and we were just waiting for the explosion to happen.

The latest exhibit for this ticking-time-bomb theory had been during breakfast yesterday. Two people started hitting each other, soon followed by a few others. Why? Because they disagreed on whether being a werewolf was more deadly than being a water elemental. A stupid debate. But one that, under the current circumstances, had escalated out of proportion.

The one good thing was that Sadie's fake-dating plan worked so far. No one had dared threaten me since that night in the cafeteria. I could see the looks I was receiving, though. Many people were unhappy with how close I was to three of the most powerful Coppers here. But pretending to be head-over-heels in love with Archer kept everyone at bay. I just hoped that it would continue to be that way for the four weeks we had left before the start of the Tournament.

Today had been a stressful day. The morning sparring practice had been good – I was getting much better at hand-on-hand combat and could somewhat hold my own against the twins. But I had gotten my butt kicked during fencing practice. I had also managed to get pretty good at stopping Archer's hallucinations in the past few days, so we had tried without Sadie acting as an anchor in the afternoon. I had failed miserably and panicked when I couldn't find Sadie's hand anymore. I was two seconds away from losing consciousness when Archer brought me back. Then I left the room without a word after Archer remarked that I was "annoyingly slow at learning" and "should try harder." Good times.

Therefore, I decided to take some time for myself to try and relax. That was why I was in the Pit at night, on my own. The torches on the sides of the arena lit the space just enough that I could see around while keeping a very subdued ambiance. I didn't particularly enjoy being in this space, but it was the only place I could think of where I could have some fun.

I hadn't done any gymnastics in my two weeks here. To say that I missed it was an understatement. Gymnastics was my way of expressing myself, of breathing in a life that often felt suffocating. And I was in dire need of a breath of fresh air.

It was strange to warm up for something that didn't involve fighting. Habits came back quickly, though, and soon enough, I was doing dynamic stretches as if I never left my old life. It felt damn good.

The first tumble pass felt awkward. I hadn't realized it, but my body had changed since I arrived on Mount Olympus. I had always been muscular because of gymnastics, but the constant training of the past two weeks had honed my muscles differently. And it felt strange while flying in the air. Like I wasn't balanced anymore.

But I kept on going. Tumbling pass after tumbling pass, jump after jump, I found myself again. Soon enough, I could almost imagine that I was back at my gym, training on my own after coaching my kids. It felt like being home again. It was freeing.

Breathless, I stopped and put my hands on my hips. I had no idea how long I had trained, but I was exhausted in a refreshing way.

"Impressive work Mayfield."

I jumped at the voice and turned around to find Archer leaning against the entrance to the Pit. He looked handsome as always, in a black T-shirt and dark pants. He knew he was good on the eyes too.

"How long have you been stalking me?"

He scoffed before pushing off the wall and walking towards me. "I wouldn't go as far as to say stalking. That would imply a lot more interest than I have."

Raising an eyebrow, I stared him down. He wanted to see if I would rise to the bait. He always tried to rile me up. "How is sulking in the shadows, without any interest in me, of course, treating you then?"

"Great. The dark suits my mysterious aura."

I shook my head. He seemed to be in a semi-good mood tonight. That could be either very good or very bad for me.

"I didn't realize you were actually a gymnast."

"What did you think I was, huh?"

"You didn't seem like the greatest athlete when we first started your training. Hard to imagine you doing more than a few flips."

I was speechless for a few seconds. I knew I should be annoyed at him. But I could tell he didn't mean it in a mean way. He was just... too honest. And too used to being surrounded by supernatural people. It was a good reminder of how ordinary I was here.

"Thanks for the pep talk. You really know how to make people feel special."

Archer smiled, not bothered in the slightest, and kept walking until we were a few feet apart. Hands in his pockets, he seemed relaxed. Where was the brooding Archer?

"Are you feeling better now?"

I was surprised that he had noticed my earlier state of mind. I probably shouldn't have, though. Archer was quiet but usually the most observant of us all.

"Can't you read my mind to figure it out?" It came out before I could rein it in, and I immediately regretted it – both the words and my harsh tone. I didn't want to fight with him. But I couldn't pretend I wasn't still a little uncomfortable with his power after the debacle of that afternoon.

"You know I wouldn't do that." For the first time since I met him, Archer looked uncomfortable. "I came here to say sorry about earlier. I tend to forget that you are human and much more fragile than us. I am sorry for what I said. It was insensitive and unnecessary." He stopped briefly before adding: "And false, of course."

"Of course," I drawled with a slow nod. "You're not very good at apologies, are you?"

He winced. "Yeah, not my specialty, we'll say."

We stayed silent for a little while. I was unsure what to say. It was strange to be here, alone with him. There was no buffer between us. Nothing to stop us from bickering. Or me from being weirdly attracted to him.

"Do you want to practice?"

"Practice what?" I asked, confused if he was talking about gymnastics or something else.

"Sparring. Obviously."

"It's probably midnight."

"Yes, and?"

"We already trained a lot today."

"We could train some more. It's not like you don't need it." Damn. Always so nice.

"Why?"

"Why do you need it? Do I really have to spell it out?"

"No, *Archer*, why do you want to train with me in the middle of the night?"

He stopped briefly, seeming to restrain himself from saying something. I also realized it was the longest conversation I had ever had with Archer. Ever. How strange that it was happening in the Pit in the middle of the night.

"I'm feeling generous tonight." And after a beat. "Neither of us is going to sleep anytime soon anyway. We might as well be productive."

That was how we ended up sparring together. I had gotten significantly better at sparring, but Archer was a beast. I did not come close to even grazing him. But still, you know, I tried my hardest and all that. I tried to apply everything I had learned over the past two weeks which had somewhat worked on Søren or Sadie. There were a few combos I was particularly proud of, with feints in the middle that usually worked well. I had also gotten much better at kicks and tried a few of those. But to no avail. After the fifth time I fell miserably on my butt, Archer offered me his hand to get back up. "Your stance turns to shit as soon as we get started."

"Thanks for the constructive feedback." I puffed to blow a strand of hair out of my eyes. Sweat was dripping down my whole body, and I felt gross. Hopefully, I would become so sweaty in the next few minutes that Archer would lose any grip on me.

"Get into your stance. We'll do the next one in slow motion."

I raised an eyebrow in a silent question, but I did get into position – left foot forward, right foot backward, hands close to my face. He did, too, and raised his chin to let me know to start. I blew a breath – hoping it would give me some courage – and searched for a way to *finally* land a hit on the Copper. I got closer, keeping my gaze firmly on Archer's face. I threw a left jab, but he dodged – per usual – and moved in a semi-circle to my right. He didn't attack, just observing me and waiting for my next move. Deciding to try a classic jab and hook combo, I feinted right and went with a left-handed jab. He saw right through me and dodged, bringing him closer to my right hook. Leaning backward, the hook went well over his torso. He came back up, and I tried to move back, but he reached over, grabbed my shoulder, and hooked my front ankle with his. He didn't pull, but we both knew he had me.

"Here. See? You put your weight on your front foot for the hook, but then you don't return to putting most of your weight on your back leg. That makes it very easy for me to use your lack of balance to bring you to the ground."

I nodded, incapable of uttering anything. First, because he was right, and I had nothing to say about that. And second, because his body was very close to mine and his eyes... his eyes were staring into mine like they were searching for my deepest secrets and desires. My mouth was suddenly parched.

"Okay, so now don't move. I am going to come around and help you adjust your stance."

I obeyed without a word. I didn't breathe as Archer moved around me, his hand still on my shoulder. His breath was hot on my neck, giving me chills. His second hand landed on my waist. Low on my waist. Then his other hand slowly trailed from my shoulder down to my hip. I was acutely aware of the two points of contact between our bodies. They almost burned.

"Move your pelvis back a little. Good." Archer's fingers tightened on my waist, dragging it back inch by inch. Sadie's workout clothes were so thin that they felt almost nonexistent. Did it feel... sensual? Definitely not a 'teaching' type of touch. My mind was spinning with the potential implications of this moment.

"Now, slightly bend your back knee..." His knee touched the back of mine, and my leg almost buckled. He had to shift closer to me to connect my leg with his, and I could practically feel the electricity in the thin layer of air between us.

"This is the position you want to return to after each forward movement. Does that make sense?" Archer's voice was thick and husky, so close to my ear that I shivered. I could smell him. Sweat and the ocean and the air right before a storm.

"Yeah. I..." I swallowed a lump in my throat. "I get it."

Archer made a sound deep in his throat that sounded like an agreement. I felt my hair stand on my arms. I couldn't see him, still staring ahead, but I thought he was so close to my back that it would be impossible to pass a hand between us.

I had the insane thought of shifting back ever so slightly until my back hit his front. Until there was no space left between our bodies. What would it feel like? I imagined that his torso and thighs would be hard and strong. His body radiated heat even from here, so being flushed on his body would feel like having my personal heater.

Then suddenly, he was gone. The air felt cold – freezing, really – against my waist and the hollow of my knee. My legs felt weak, and I almost fell to the ground. What the-

"Great. Now let's do it again."

Archer's voice was cold and professional again. Like nothing had happened at all. Like I had imagined it all.

Chapter Thirteen

Søren was explaining something about fire swords or maybe fire katanas. Something sharp and deadly. He was passionate about it. I wasn't paying attention; I was hyper-focused on Archer's presence next to me. To be clear, I wasn't staring at him like a lovestruck teenager on her first crush. No. I stared very hard at my food, sometimes looking up to smile and nod at Søren's story. But I could feel his presence next to me, close enough that if I moved my left elbow just a little bit out, I would graze his.

I was still extremely confused about the night before. After the whole… *moment*, we continued sparring for ten more minutes. Then, after I had ended up lying in the sand again, Archer called it quits and left me in the dust. Quite literally.

Lying in my bed hours later, I could still feel the imprints of his hands on my skin. And as I fell asleep, I felt like they roamed my body. Everywhere. And then, the dreams… Gods, the dreams I had last night were not dreams I should have had about a guy I barely knew. And a guy who clearly did not have the same attraction for me. I was slowly losing my mind.

"Kalani, we need you to settle this," Søren exclaimed, shooting a look at his sister.

Shit. I was back in high school, getting called on after I spent the whole class doodling. "What exactly am I settling?"

Søren gasped as if I had kicked a puppy right in front of him. "Dude! How could you not listen to me? It was super important and a well-thought-out argument." He passed his hands through his air, acting extra dramatic. "Stars, I feel so unloved sometimes."

"Stop it, Søren, you're being ridiculous," Sadie sighed at her brother's antics. She turned to look at me. "Søren thinks using flaming weapons is super-efficient. I believe they're inconvenient – you could get burned as easily as your opponent. I think it is a stupid idea. And Archer thinks this debate is beneath him, so he didn't grace us with his opinion."

Søren took a bite of his meat – for once it looked and tasted remarkably similar to Earth's chicken – and looked at me expectantly. "So?"

Who would have thought I would have to settle a debate between two god-like twins on whether flaming swords were practical? Not me, that was for sure.

"On a general basis, I try to stay away from fire. So, I would go against flaming things on this one."

Sadie pumped a fist in the air in victory while Søren shook his dead. "I guess I will have to show you how sexy fire can be." He gave me a suggestive look, his eyebrows doing a little wave.

"Is that supposed to turn me on?"

Sadie almost choked on her water before laughing at her brother. Before we could add anything, Mei slid onto the bench right next to her boyfriend. She wore a very cute pink crop top with pink shorts, her long dark hair in a high ponytail, looking every bit like she was going to do some deadlifts at the neighborhood gym in front of all the gym bros instead of training for a deadly Tournament. However, Søren was undressing her with his gaze, so I guessed it was efficient at something.

The next minute was filled with Mei and Søren giving us the best PDA show they could, filled with tongues and way too many moans for breakfast time. After they *finally* stopped inhaling each other, Mei deigned to say hi to the rest of us.

"How's my favorite couple doing?" she asked with a knowing smile in both my and Archer's direction.

"You know us, just living our best lives!" Archer said with too much pep in his voice to be truthful. He put his arm around me, his hand landing on my hip, and brought me closer until my left side was flushed with his. He then kissed my temple, and I felt like something melted inside of me.

Kalani, get a grip. This is all for show. You guys are fake dating. Emphasis on the fake!

This was too much, especially after everything that had happened last night. It wasn't like I could move away, though. We had a pretense to keep, and I, for one, did not want to give some of the Coppers here ammunition to come and attack me.

So, I stayed there, in Archer's one-armed embrace, breathing through my mouth to prevent myself from scenting him. I focused all my attention on my food, Sadie and the couple, even the other Coppers sitting at tables beside us – basically anything except for *him*.

"Are you okay, Lane? You look a little… off." Mei reached across the table to pat my hand. I held back a wince at the nickname – she had gotten to calling me Lane, and even though I had told her multiple times that my name was Kalani, she didn't get the hint.

"Yep," I answered, emphasizing the p. "All good. Just peachy."

As I nodded – perhaps a little too enthusiastically – I looked past Mei, and my gaze met Alexei's. Like most Coppers were, he was a good-looking guy and was one of Aphrodite's grandsons. He was one of the Coppers with a mind-related gift; he could use seduction to mind-wash and control his prey into doing anything for him, including dying if it pleased him. Alexei was one of Elena's followers, part of a group of Coppers that wanted to eliminate the competition before the first trial. They claimed it was because they didn't want dead weights during the first team trial, but we all knew it came down to it being easier to kill people when they least expected it. They hadn't done anything yet, but I could tell their hateful speeches would soon turn into acts. And Alexei was staring straight at me, looking extremely pissed. What was his deal? I had never talked to him before, not even in passing. And I hadn't had an issue with his little extremist group since the whole incident last week.

Alexei and I had this weird staring match until Archer whispered in my ear to ask what was wrong. Surprised, I turned his way and found him frowning. "Nothing, I think. Alexei was staring at me. But I'm sure it's nothing."

Archer nodded slowly but didn't say anything. Instead, he shifted and looked in Alexei's direction. Following his gaze, I found the seduction Copper still staring and Elena, sitting beside him, looking in our direction too. I could feel their hatred coming off them in waves, and I was delighted I was seated next to three of the most powerful Coppers here – strength in numbers and all that.

"I think they need a little reminder of the hierarchy here." Archer wasn't looking at me when he said it, but the twins and Mei were deep in their conversation, so I assumed it was directed at me.

"What exactly are we talking about? Are you going to go and hit them just because they are looking at us? I don't think that's warranted. You can't physically assault someone because of a look – no matter how long the look is. That would look very much like a dictatorship; we don't want that. Plus, this is such a nice morning. We should go and enjoy the sun." I was babbling. Why was I babbling? And to Archer, too?

I looked at Archer, wanting to see if he was open to the idea of not hitting anyone, and found him already looking at me. He had a raised eyebrow and his mocking smirk on. "Are you done?"

How rude. It made it seem like I was some hysterical girl who had been talking his ear off. I didn't have time to answer with a witty remark because, suddenly, his face was *right there*. Like, really close. His hand was on my jaw, his eyes bore into mine, and his breath was on my lips. Then his lips were on my skin. They were not fully on my lips but more at the corner of my mouth. And I was shocked, completely and utterly shocked. So shocked that I kept my eyes wide open like a dear in headlights.

"Relax, Mayfield." He murmured against my skin, and it acted like he flipped a switch. My eyes closed, and my head bent to make it less awkward. And I felt like this was the first time someone kissed me. Not that it was the first time – Brad and I had kissed plenty of times, and I had had other boyfriends before that. Plus, this was not even a proper kiss, more a peck on the cheek. But the way my body responded? It was like a scene out of those romance books I read sometimes. Electricity fired between our bodies. My heart rate sped up; blood pulsed *everywhere*. And everything faded away except for him and his lips and hand cupping my jaw.

It could have been seconds or minutes before Archer moved back slowly. I opened my eyes to find him looking at my mouth, a small smile on his.

"Stars, get a room!" Søren exclaimed dramatically, covering his eyes with his hand. Mei was smiling big, her eyes ping-ponging between Archer and me. I avoided Sadie's eyes because I didn't want her to see in my eyes how confused I was. Instead, I focused on Alexei and Elena in the background between Mei and Søren's heads. They were still staring, but they looked cautious instead of hateful.

Archer had started a conversation with the twins by the time I tuned back to the present. He was laughing at one of Søren's jokes, not bothered by what had just happened and not confused about the almost-kiss. But I was.

I kept on replaying it in my head. His words, his looks, his smile, his kiss – or half kiss. It was like a broken record in my mind. And I didn't know why I was obsessing over it. Because I knew, I *knew* that it had been a way for Archer to send a message to Elena and her clique. This kiss had been a way for him to tell her I was under his protection. It was all part of the plan, part of fake dating him. My heart had better catch up on this fact because I was the only one who couldn't keep my feelings separate from our pretense. Part of myself – call it my heart or the part of my brain that had always dreamt of life-changing romance – kept hoping it was more.

So, when his knee touched mine – probably by accident – I wondered. When his pinky grazed mine, I wondered. When he looked my way after lightly laughing at something Sadie said, I wondered. I wondered if there would ever be something more.

Twenty minutes later, we left the cafeteria, trailing after the twins who were playfully pushing each other. Archer had his arm over my shoulders. Probably a part of the game. To remind the other Coppers I was a part of a strong group. But my heart still thumped painfully in my chest. Because as the days went by, I was learning more and more about him. Not straightforward information about his past or his deepest desires. But I learned what made him tick and what made him laugh. I learned what he preferred for breakfast and his favorite fighting style. I learned about his facial expressions – his smirk when he was amused but didn't want to show it or those dimples that appeared when he had a genuine smile, starting with the left one. I learned to differentiate between when he was mean and just being brutally honest. I learned to appreciate the rare moments when he let his guard down and had fun with the twins – or when he made fun of me because I thought he was starting to like me. And I learned to see the vulnerability in his eyes, like when he apologized last night.

I had gotten to know him on some level. He wasn't a stranger anymore. He also wasn't just the monster with the terrifying powers. Sure, he still had those powers. And I was still scared of what they could do to me. But I was starting to see the many levels of him. And it made it damn hard not to react when he was touching and smiling at me and acting… like he liked me.

We walked through the doors, down the hallway, and turned at the corner. We kept on walking towards Sadie's room, down and down hallways. And then there were only us four left. Archer dropped his arm. He moved two steps away, then sped up until he was walking ahead at the twins' level. He turned around at the last moment, throwing a "Good job, by the way! Really convincing!" before turning back towards his friends.

And I was alone.

Chapter Fourteen

After a few weeks on Olympus, I could confidently say that having godly genes did not stop men from being dumbasses. My initial thoughts were that since having ichor in their blood made Coppers prettier and stronger, it might have also made them smarter and nicer beings overall. Well, it wasn't quite true.

I had gotten plenty of examples to support my claim that 'boys will be boys' was, unfortunately, true everywhere. The latest was happening right under my eyes.

As Sadie put another one of her cards down – this one with a smiling Aphrodite in the center, below a pink spade – she gave me a look full of annoyance. At the same time, a groan sounded to my right, and my friend rolled her eyes so high I worried they might get stuck.

"Stars, I want to push him off the mountain's edge."

"Don't tempt me. I might just help."

For a second, I thought Sadie would take me up on my offer to help her kill our unwanted neighbor. To be honest, I was only half joking.

Just as we both decided that resorting to murder might be a little too drastic, Gym Bro beside us groaned again, and I had to hold in a frustrated scream. Maybe murder was the best answer here.

See, Sadie and I had decided to finish up our productive day of sparring and training with a lovely, relaxing afternoon of sunbathing and card games. So, here we were, laying on fluffy towels on the grassy hillside, trying to relax together, when Gym Bro showed up.

I had no idea what his name was, but I'd seen him before in the mess hall. The Copper wasn't that tall – probably around Sadie's height – but he was built like a brick wall. I wasn't sure who his godly ancestor was, but I would have put money on Ares or Hephaestus. Either way, the guy was crazy muscular, and he knew it.

So, now, picture this. Sadie and I were lying there, trying to enjoy ourselves in comfortable, companionable silence. The space around us was blessedly empty of anyone. And here came Gym Bro, who chose to do a bodyweight workout right next to us. He was so damn close that we could count in heavy breaths and see the sweat on his forehead.

Rude.

So, now, we were subjected to his presence, his groans every few reps, and the flirty looks he kept throwing our way. I wasn't sure if the guy hoped to be subtle or sexy, but he was neither.

The man was a walking red flag with an ego as big as Olympus itself. Wonder how I could tell? Easily enough – Gym Bro was currently going on his twelfth set of clapped push-ups while ensuring he flexed every muscle group after each set.

Sadie and I had decided to start a card game – because sunbathing required silence and relative peace of mind – but even Sadie's explanations about the rules couldn't drown out the noises Gym Bro kept throwing our way.

Another grunt followed by a loud clap of his hands, and Sadie put her cards down on the table. She was done – it was written all over her face.

Just as Gym Bro finished his last push-up, she turned his way.

"Did that set feel good, James?" she asked with a concerned look on her face.

I had to bite the inside of my cheek to stop a smile when Gym Bro – James – gave her a weird look. I could almost see the wheels turning in his mind about whether he had done a weird rep or had terrible form. The panic was evident in his eyes.

"Uh, yeah?"

"Oh, okay, never mind then. Great job, sweetie."

Then, with a thumbs up and a sweet smile, she returned to our game. Her smile had turned into a satisfied smirk, and I had a front-row seat to the moment Gym Bro's – he deserved his nickname – confidence completely crumbled. Seeing his cheeks turn pink and how he got up and left like someone was chasing him was glorious.

As soon as he was out of earshot, I let out the laugh I'd been holding in. I had never seen a grown man rethink his entire existence and sex appeal with only two sentences.

"Stars, that felt amazing!"

"I know, it was incredible! I wish I could be a fly on the wall when he gets back to his room. To see how long he spends in front of the mirror to convince himself he is still strong and good-looking." I even had to wipe down a stray tear from how hard I'd laughed.

"That one works every time."

"Do you do that often? Smile and drop a bomb on men's egos?"

Sadie smiled ruefully, and I honestly loved seeing this side of her. "Yeah, I enjoy antagonizing men too much for my own good. Depending on the context, I have dozens of lines ready, but my absolute favorite is to ask if they need me to open or carry something for them – something small, like a bottle or a book. Then, when they get mad, I like to follow with a nice 'You seem to have a lot of feelings right now. Take a deep breath, honey.' Works beautifully."

"You're savage, Sadie."

"Proud of it."

We high-fived, and feeling like two ordinary girls laughing about some weird guy's antics was refreshing.

Then Sadie started on a story of Søren and her growing up – how he always wanted to hang out with the weirdest guys who acted like they were the gods' gifts to women. The rest of the late afternoon was filled with laughter as we exchanged stories about our teenage years and how annoying boys – and men – could be.

By the time I was back in my room, I felt refreshed. It was nice to have a friend here.

Chapter Fifteen

I was on a tightrope. High in the sky. So high that the ground seemed tiny. So, so tiny.

The tightrope was long. A hundred feet. Maybe more. And I was right smack in the middle. The rope was unsafe, primarily because of the wind. And the wind was damn strong as if it were purposefully trying to make me lose my balance. And fall. And die.

I had no idea how I had gotten there. I was no tightrope walker. Sure, I was great at the beam. But a tightrope? So high above the ground? And without any rope securing me either. No, there was no way I would have willingly gotten on this thing. My survival instincts were way too strong for that.

Something scratched at the back of my mind. There was something I had to remember. Something I needed to remind myself of. Something important.

A powerful gust of wind made the rope sway to the right. Only quick reflexes and years of balance training saved me from falling to my death. My heart pounded as I stood there, knees bent, eyes trained on the horizon, and arms flung wide to regain my balance. There was no way I was going to be able to stay there. And I was unlikely to make it to the other side of the rope. But there were more chances of me making it out alive if I started walking, so I did.

Step after step, I started forward. Left foot first, right foot second. Again, and again, and again. I kept going, praying to the luck god – was there a luck god? Or a luck goddess? – that I would survive this.

Except, the luck deity didn't seem to want to help because the next gust of wind shook the rope so hard that there was nothing that I could do to stop it. I fell. And the fall seemed endless, like I would never reach the ground. The panic crept in, fast and hard. I had to do something. I couldn't just let myself splatter on the ground and die. I couldn't give up. I couldn't-

Focus on my hand. I won't let go.

Focus on my hand. I won't let go.

Focus on my hand. I won't let go.

Focus on my hand.

I could hear Sadie's voice echoing on repeat in my head. I had somewhere to return to – someone waiting for me. I focused on my hand, trying to feel something. There was nothing. Nothing at all. But I didn't panic because I knew, deep in my heart, that Sadie was still waiting on me.

As the wind was screaming in my ears and the ground was getting closer and closer, my mind latched onto a memory of Archer telling me to build a wall. This was not real. This was just a hallucination. No matter how real it felt, nothing would happen to me.

Closing my eyes, I blocked it all out – the wind, the sensation of falling, the fear. I blocked everything out and put all those emotions and physical sensations behind a wall. I built the wall like a full-on fortress, so high and thick that nothing could come through. I pushed everything I had seen and felt in the past few minutes behind the wall, and then, in the emptiness that was left, I searched for what my body actually felt. The softness of Sadie's sheets under my crossed legs. The sweet fruity scent of her perfume that she wore every day. The distant sound of someone slamming the door down the hall.

I opened my eyes and was back on the bed, facing three very surprised Coppers. And I? Well, I was pretty damn proud of myself. I had made it. I had managed to remove myself from Archer's hallucination without any tether. All on my own.

"That was badass!" Søren jumped forward and raised his hand for a high five. I clapped his hand with a laugh, still feeling high on adrenaline. And I would lie if I said I didn't appreciate Søren's explosion of joy. It felt good to be the one who did something impressive for once.

"Congrats Kalani! That's a big accomplishment." Sadie gave me a warm smile and a hand on my shoulder.

I thanked the twins, feeling warmth spreading in my chest. After weeks of feeling like a failure, winning at something felt liberating. And seeing the pride on my friends' faces was amazing.

Somehow, my eyes slipped from my control and moved to meet Archer's. I didn't need his reassurance or approval. I knew I had done good. What he thought didn't matter. At all.

"You played with fire; I was about to bring you back. But… yeah, it was decent." I could tell he tried to remain impassive, but one corner of his mouth tugged up ever so slightly.

"How does it feel to be bested by a human, huh, big man?" Søren teased before playfully pushing him around until they both started wrestling.

Sadie sighed affectuously at the two guys play-fighting on the ground and sat next to me. "You can be proud of yourself. That was almost a grand declaration of success coming from Archer."

"Sure," I laughed. We all knew Archer didn't give out compliments lightly. 'Decent' from him was often equivalent to 'awesome' from most people. "It was thanks to you, though. I knew you were with me even though I couldn't feel your hand. It helped a lot."

Her eyes softened. A smile came over her whole face, eyes crinkling and cheeks raising. That was the beauty of Sadie – she felt and showed her emotions fully. She never held back. It made me want to show how happy and relieved I was too. So, I relaxed my tense shoulders, took a deep breath, and let myself truly feel that win.

A clang resonated as the swords hit against each other so hard that I felt the vibrations through my whole arm. But I held on. The blade was still in my hand, and I hadn't fallen to the ground. That was a win in and of itself.

Søren gave me a rueful grin, clearly enjoying that I was becoming a little bit more of a competition. I gave him a challenging look in return. He wasn't backing down, but neither was I.

Arm still tingly from the shock, I got back into position right in time to ward off another of Søren's strikes. I stopped his assault and leaped away, trying to finally take a full breath. The Copper didn't let me have a second to rest, though. He pressed me, advancing step by step, forcing me to retreat and remain on the defensive. I knew I needed to get out of this defensive streak. Seeing that Søren was getting too comfortable with our pattern, I faked to the left before sliding to the right and advancing in for a hit. The end of my blade grazed Søren's side, cutting through his shirt. The blond-haired Copper pivoted forward and advanced to hit me. I bounced back into my guard, barely managing to counter his hit with my blade.

"Are you feeling tired already, baby girl?"

"What have I told you already, Søren? Your flirting doesn't work. You're not my type." I blew a kiss at him right as I lunged forward and went for a slice at his forward thigh. He pared it, but I let it shed, letting his sword slide down mine without changing its direction, and saw an opening for a neat trick Sadie had taught me – the empty fade. I leaped backward, pretending to fade into a defensive stance, but immediately lunged forward instead, extending my sword arm and hitting Søren in the arm. A thin rivulet of gold-like blood dripped down his arm.

Holy shit.

"And the winner is Kalani... Mayfield!" Sadie exclaimed, imitating an announcer at an MMA match. I almost expected her to hold my arm up, a half-naked girl coming up with a big ass belt for me to wear. The only thing that happened was a group of Coppers on the other side of the Pit that turned to glare at us.

"Damn, K." Søren quickly wiped the blood from his triceps. "My masculinity is hurt." With the way he pouted, though, I could tell he was fine. I knew he had fought well but hadn't given his everything. I had put my everything in. And then some more.

I put my sword beside my towel and grabbed my water bottle. It was always a nice late spring or early summer weather here – only the best for the deity – but today, the breeze had felt slightly too hot. It was one of those things that always surprised me here – two and a half weeks on Mount Olympus and not a drop of rain in sight. And still, the flowers, the trees, and grass were green, lush, and always looking magazine perfect. They probably had to thank Demeter or the goddess of flowers – Antheia, if I remember correctly – for that. It wasn't like I loved the rain or anything, but how could someone appreciate the sunny days without ever getting the clouds?

A shadow came over me, and I looked up to find Archer looking at me. Arms crossed on his chest, wide stance, he looked immovable like an ancient Greek statue. "So?"

"So what?" I put my hands on my hips, still trying to catch my breath but wanting to remain at my full height. I was already short enough; I wouldn't make myself even smaller.

"So, what are your thoughts on your performance?"

I felt like I was back in front of my gymnastics coach in high school and club. "I mean, I think I did good enough. I reacted faster than usual to stop Søren's attacks and managed to see when he left openings in his defense. But I think there is still much to work on. I wasn't always fast enough on my footwork and almost fell multiple times."

Archer nodded slowly. "Good."

"That's it? 'Good'? That's what you have to say about my fight?"

"No, that's what I have to say about your analysis."

A laugh escaped me because, of course, Archer would say that. And I shouldn't have expected anything less.

"But I have to say…" he raised an eyebrow, his eyes slowly going up and down my body. "You did okay." Then he turned around, and went to see Søren.

"Archer!" I yelled to grab his attention. He turned around and I crossed my arms over my chest in defiance. "One day, I will do so well that you will have to tell me I was awesome."

"Can't wait, Mayfield. Can't wait."

Chapter Sixteen

I was dreaming. I knew I was dreaming because of two things. First, I wasn't sore. That was a dead giveaway – I was always sore these days. And second, Archer was smiling at me. Not a mocking grin or an arrogant smirk. No, it was a full-on smile, with both dimples out and his shiny white teeth on display. There was no one else around – just us two. And I had never seen that smile directed at me.

This had to be a dream.

But I didn't pinch myself. I didn't want to wake up. I didn't want to be back in a reality where Archer barely looked at me outside of times when we were pretending to be in love. I knew it was stupid to have hopes for more, but this dream fed all the desires I was developing and couldn't contain.

"Are you coming, Mayfield?" His voice sounded sexy, and the way he said my last name… Gods, it should be illegal to sound so sensual.

I had no idea where we were going, but I did not even hesitate before putting my hand in his. His fingers intertwined with mine gently. He squeezed once. I squeezed back. And then we walked together.

I looked around for the first time and saw that we were in a beautiful garden. We were on a path made of flat white stones, surrounded on both sides by lush bushes filled with fresh pink, white, and golden flowers. A few yards away, there were trees full of plump fruits. Tiny lights were flying around the garden, the only light outside of the moon.

"These are faeries," Archer explained after seeing my fascination for the moving lights. "They are small but mighty, but if you don't bother them, they won't do anything to you."

"It's so beautiful here."

"It really is." Except he was staring at me instead of the garden. Usually, I would have laughed at the cheesy line. But it felt nice, alone with him in a magical place. It felt sincere.

"Why are we here, Archer?"

He kept tugging me toward a cute gazebo, looking similar to the one where Edward and Bella had their first dance in that one vampire movie. We went up the stairs slowly until we reached the pavilion's center. There were garlands of flowers all around the place, and the silver light from the moon made it look ethereal.

Archer made me twirl around several times, stealing a laugh from me. I liked this free and relaxed side of him. Then he brought me closer. Close enough that my chest brushed his when I breathed too deeply. One hand landed on my hip, the other around my neck. Feeling bolder than usual around Archer, I looped my arms around his waist – he was way too tall for me to reach behind his neck comfortably.

"I wanted to spend some quality time with you." He kissed my forehead. "Why do you seem so surprised?"

Why was I surprised? Because he usually didn't seem to want to spend any extra time with me. And I knew my mind was playing games, creating something I secretly hoped for. Something that I had been trying to deny for a while.

I was attracted to Archer – more than I should have. More than was healthy, seeing as there would never be anything between us. He was the king of the gods' grandson, and I was a regular girl.

But even knowing all that, I wasn't above letting myself dream. Just once. Just that night. Then I would be back to burying all those unwanted feelings beneath the ever-growing mountain of reasons why entertaining those thoughts was a terrible idea.

"Nothing. I'm just happy to be here. With you." I looked up to find Archer's eyes. They were a darker blue than usual, probably due to the low light. It was like staring at the blue of the deep ocean – I could have drowned in them.

He gave me a soft smile with so much affection that my heart bled. I had to stop looking directly at his face to stop myself from feeling so much. Instead, I got closer and laid my head on his chest. His heartbeat – calm and steady, like him – was soothing in my ear.

"You're all right, Mayfield. We are here together. Nothing can reach you here."

I wished this was true. I wished I could stay here, in this dream, forever. But even here, I could remember all the worries plaguing me while awake.

"Dance with me," Archer murmured in my ear. I nodded, even though I had no idea how to dance. I had never been a big partier – gymnastics, schoolwork, my jobs, and taking care of Makaio never left me much time to party all night. And I also had never had boyfriends who liked to slow dance. But it seemed fitting. We were in a dream, in a magnificent garden. What could be better to live out my fantasy of being with Archer than slow dancing under the moonlight with him?

"There's no music, though."

"I know." I could hear the amusement in his voice. "That's fine. We can make up our own rhythm. I got you."

And then he started leading me. We twirled around the gazebo slowly. After a while, I could almost hear a slow tune in the background. But then the music turned into whispers. I couldn't quite grasp them initially but could hear them as we twisted and turned. It was my name. Repeated over and over. And it sounded like my brother.

Surprised, I jerked away from my dancing partner and turned around to stare at the forest. Suddenly, it didn't seem like a beautiful and restful space anymore. The faeries had disappeared, and the light from the moon seemed duller, incapable of piercing through the shadows. And now the whispers were getting louder and louder as if hundreds of people were hiding in the forest's shadows. A shudder ran through me. This was starting to feel like the beginning of a nightmare, and I was getting more and more tempted to try and leave this place.

"Lani! Help!"

My head snapped to the right toward what sounded like my little brother. And he was there, in the middle of the path. A tall and muscular person was behind him, holding a knife to my brother's throat, their other hand across his little chest. I couldn't see their face or any defining characteristic – they were shrouded in shadows – but I could see the terror on Makaio's face very well. And it mirrored the one gripping my heart.

"Lani, please! Save me!" I could see tears glittering on his face, down his chubby cheeks. And I started moving, desperate to reach him. Desperate to make it all better.

"Take one more step, and I will kill him." The voice was unrecognizable. I couldn't even tell if it was a man's or a woman's. But I could easily tell that they were serious. I stopped dead in my tracks, only ten yards away from my brother. His little hand moved just a little as if to reach for me.

"It's okay, big guy. I'm here. Nothing is going to happen to you." I tried to sound confident and reassuring. I could tell from the panic in Makaio's eyes that I wasn't fooling him, though.

"What do you want?" I asked the aggressor. My eyes did a rapid take of the situation. We were in an unknown place. I had no weapons and no idea if they were alone or not. And the person holding my brother hostage was both taller and probably stronger than me. I had no leverage, no knowledge of which buttons to push to gain an advantage.

I had nothing.

Absolutely nothing.

And my brother's life was on the line.

"You have nothing to do among us. You are a dirty, undeserving human. And you should have never gotten the right to step foot on the land of the gods. You deserve to pay for your hubris." The person was angry. I could hear it in the way they almost spat the word 'human.' And I knew all too well how hate could lead people to commit terrible acts. Makaio could not become collateral damage from one of those hate crimes. I would not allow it.

The knife pressed on my brother's neck. A drop of blood dripped down his skin. He cried out.

"Please, don't hurt my brother. He's only nine; he hasn't done anything wrong. I'll do whatever you want. But please, release him." My voice broke at the end. I hated seeing my brother so distressed. I had already failed him by not being able to come back to him weeks ago. I could not fail him again.

"Someone has to die. If it's not him, then it has to be you." The voice came from behind me. I turned around, ready to fight the new attacker. The view of his face completely took me aback. Archer. His eyes were completely black and displayed none of their earlier affection. He looked at me as if I were an enemy on the battlefield.

"Arch-" I had no time to try to talk to him because he moved, and a knife sank into my abdomen. It was his knife. His face was above mine as the pain hit like a tsunami. His body was above mine as I fell to the ground. His eyes burned with hate as I lost consciousness.

I gasped, opening my eyes to complete darkness. Panic swept in, and my hands flew to my stomach, trying to stop the hemorrhage. Except there was no knife. No wound. No blood.

It was all a dream. Just a dream.

My body hadn't quite gotten the memo. My heart rate was sky high, and I had sweated through the t-shirt I had put on to sleep. It had felt so real. I had known it was a dream at first, but when Makaio had appeared, all knowledge that it wasn't the real world had disappeared.

I wished I had a way to talk to Makaio. A way to see his face and hear his voice – without the terror in it. I just wanted to hug him again. Just once.

Tears were pooling in my eyes due to the emotions I had just experienced and the loss I had tried my best to ignore for the past three weeks. I reached for the bedside table to get my phone without turning on the light. I had turned it off that first day because there was no reception here, and I wanted to save the battery for a day when I desperately needed to have a link with my normal life. Today was the day.

I turned on my phone, anxiously waiting for the home screen to appear. Opening the photo app, I had to scroll through several pictures of class notes before finding a selfie of Makaio and me. He was wearing his whole skateboard paraphernalia, his scrappy board under the arm. I had taken him to a bigger skateboard park, almost half an hour away from our house. He had been so happy that day. I had cheered him up as he practiced his tricks, and we had eaten sandwiches with Cokes, seated at the top of a ramp. I could still remember the huge grin on my brother's face – it had remained stuck on his face the whole day.

It felt like a lifetime ago.

The next picture was of Makaio with flour all over his little face. It took me a second to replace the moment. He had been asking for a chocolate cake for a while, so I had bought everything so we could bake it together. It had been a crap ton of work compared to premade packages, but we had so much fun. Of course, we had finished with a small flour fight and spent the next hour trying to clean everything up before Mom came back. It had been such a good afternoon.

I spent the next however-long scrolling through pictures of Makaio. Some brought a smile to my face; others made me almost burst into tears. I missed him so much. Little brothers could be incredibly annoying but losing them was like losing a limb. However, seeing him smiling in those pictures and remembering the good times helped me stop thinking of him with a knife to his throat.

When a notification that my phone only had 20% battery left popped up, I forced myself to turn off my phone. I had to save the little battery I had left – unfortunately, Mount Olympus did not have Earth technology, which meant no charging cables. I needed that battery life in case I needed emotional support again. Which I probably would.

Instead of overthinking in my bed, I decided to go to the Pit and flip around. It helped the last time; maybe it would again today.

I changed, hunting for one of the pairs of shorts relatively close to my size – Sadie was much taller than me. Then I was out, walking through the silent, dark hallways towards the Pit. The training compound was a little creepy at night, especially after the nightmare I had just had. I walked a little faster than usual, listening intently to detect unusual sounds. But I got to the Pit, and nothing had happened to me, no weird sounds or strange shadows to report.

There was magic in the Pit – like in most places here – because as soon as I stepped into the arena, the torches on the walls started burning and lighting the space. The sky was ink black above, with countless stars twinkling. I had never seen so many stars before I came here. Busy cities in California were not the best places for stargazing. If not for everything else, I had to admit that I had never seen somewhere more beautiful than Mount Olympus. It would be a fantastic vacation spot if not for its murderous Coppers and deities.

I started my warm-up routine, trying to get in the zone. Tonight was harder than usual. My mind kept circling back to my dream. Or nightmare. Whatever. My lab partner for my *Anatomy* class last year, Sammy, had been big into theories on the subconscious and dream interpretation. She always said that our dreams revealed our deepest desires and fears. If you had a nightmare about drowning, you were probably terrified of water or losing control over your surroundings, whether you acknowledged it or not. The point was, if I did decide to believe her, then I was in deep shit. Sammy would say that I both desperately wanted Archer and was terrified that he would stab me in the back and kill me, on top of being terrified of hurting my brother.

Yeah, way to have an internal dichotomy.

I tried to clear my head during my stretches but still felt off. I couldn't get my brother's desperate pleas or Archer's murderous look out of my head. And I couldn't stop overthinking whether my decision to trust Archer and the twins had been right. Was I heading right into the wall? Was I just a game for them, a little laugh that they could share before stabbing me in the back and getting rid of me right before the start of the Tournament? Was I a plaything?

And once the seed of doubt was in, there was no way to remove it. Minutes passed, hours maybe, and the doubts grew and grew until I started rethinking everything. Every single interaction I had had with the three Coppers who had offered to help me. Every single time we had laughed or joked together – was it real? Had I been so naïve and clueless that I had had no idea they were playing me?

But then, it had all been a dream, right? I had no proof whatsoever that they had done anything wrong or would do anything to me in the future. This was all in my head. And I was getting crazy because a stupid dream was getting out of proportion. Me usually so logical and down-to-earth. And now I was turning crazy over a dream.

I got annoyed with myself and the endless cycle of my dark thoughts, so I drew a line in the sand with my shoe. I didn't have a beam, so a line would have to do. The beam was tough, but it had always helped to center me. So, here was everything.

I positioned myself at one end of the "beam" and closed my eyes. I had to imagine I was at a meet. I took a few deep breaths, grounding myself in the present moment. It took a while, but I only opened my eyes when I felt in the zone. Ready to give all of me over to my sport.

I did the first routine that came to mind. It was one from high school when I was still hopeful that gymnastics would take me far. Before the knee injury that would leave me stuck in physical therapy for so long that everyone had moved on without me.

I still remembered it by heart. I went through it like you sang an old song by heart. It was good for my soul. Jumps, tricks, flips in the air. It made me feel alive, like the old me.

When I stopped, I felt better. Not fully good. But okay. Better. A little less distressed over the potential implications of my nightmare.

So, I did it again. And again. And again. Until my legs were shaking from exhaustion, and my breath was short. Until I felt like myself again. Or as close as I could get to it. Sometimes, it felt like I had changed too much over the past few weeks to truly know who I was anymore.

"Would that be the little sheep without her big bad bodyguards?"

I turned around, surprised to hear something other than myself and the rustle of the wind. A woman stood at the entrance of the Pit, with two other people in the shadows at her back. Elena. And I guessed from their corpulence that the two shadows were Alexei and Nathan, both followers of Elena's extremist motto.

Elena had a grin on. Not a nice one. More of a murderous, sadistic grin. "No one to protect you right now, is there?"

I was fucked.

Chapter Seventeen

I had to find a way around the catastrophe coming my way. I was alone, with three Coppers who had spent the past two weeks talking themselves up to hurting the less powerful participants of the Tournament. Fake-dating Archer had protected me so far by putting me under the protection of people more powerful than Elena and her clique. But the night and being virtually alone could make people feel invincible and untouchable.

The dark made people braver than usual.

Or, at least, it made *them* braver than usual. The dark had never been my friend. And I was very much aware of the power imbalance at play and how slim my chances were of getting out of this unscathed.

"You know what, guys? I'm just going to go back to my room, leave you to your workout and everything," I declared in a way-too-cheerful manner. I grabbed my water bottle and started walking toward the exit. Sadly, it also meant walking toward them. But I hoped that offering to leave would stop any violent acts from happening.

The two goons came out of the shadowed hallway, and sure enough, I was face to face with Alexei and Nathan. I wasn't sure what Nathan could do, but I knew Alexei's seduction wouldn't be fun. On top of Elena being able to turn into a fucking polar bear, I wasn't feeling very confident about my odds here.

How loud would I have to scream for help before someone came?

"I don't think that's gonna happen, sweetie," Alexei drawled with false niceness. He gave me the creeps. I repressed a shiver at how his eyes slowly covered my body from head to toe and back.

"Look, I don't want any trouble." I held my hands slightly up, aiming for a calming gesture. That's what they did in true crime shows when they tried to stop the serial killer from killing their last victim. Except there were usually other police officers at their backs, holding a gun up at the bad guy.

"Thing is, little empath, just you being here is enough. You are almost as powerless as a mortal. You deserve to remain in the dirt with them." Elena spat at me with so much disdain I could almost taste it.

It looked like senseless hate and racism – speciesm? Were humans and Coppers considered two different species or not? – was present in all the worlds.

Alright, so they seemed to want to hurt me. Make me pay for just being here. It was probably time to get out the only guns I had.

"Do you want to risk upsetting Archer Vasilias? Or the Aska twins? 'Cause I don't think they will appreciate this little game you're playing right now." I tried to sound confident. I didn't know how well that went. Nathan seemed to pause at my words, hesitating. Elena still looked like a trigger-happy little psycho. And Alexei? Well, I was starting to think he was in this more because he wanted to use my body for his pleasure. How amazing.

Elena did a dramatic 360, making a show of looking around. "Where are they, though? Not here, that's for sure. There is just you and us. No one will know it was us if we kill you right now. Not even your beloved protectors."

Fair point.

I really needed to stop coming here in the middle of the night. I was not as safe as we had thought. Archer and the twins did not scare the other Coppers as much as they had thought either. Some misconceptions had been cleared, at least. Good to know for next time, if there was ever one.

"Can't we make a deal or something? I am sure there is something you want more than me dead. I have important friends; I could get you many things." I was grasping at straws, and I knew it. But what else could I do?

"Thanks, but no. I want to survive this. It's time we started getting rid of those who don't deserve to survive. Boys!" Both guys started walking forward, rapidly decreasing the distance between us. Suddenly, I was walking backward, wondering how I would even be able to escape this death trap.

From the corner of my eyes, I analyzed the seats around the arena. There was a wall to climb before I could even reach the seats. And I had never been up there, so I didn't know where the exits were. But going in there blindly was probably better than staying on the ground where I had no way to defend myself.

Keeping an eye on the three extremist Coppers, I waited until I had backed up enough and was near the middle of the arena before I sprang into action. I dropped everything I held – towel, water bottle – and sprinted toward the nearest wall. It took me a few seconds to get there – I had never run this fast before – and I immediately jumped to grab the top of the wall. Pushing my shoulder blades back, I pulled as hard I could on my lats and back muscles to bring me up. It took me longer than usual because of my weird hold and the uneven stones under my fingers. But I made it just as the two men reached the wall themselves. I slung myself over and ran as soon as my feet touched the ground next to the first row of seats.

I could hear the two Coppers starting to give chase. Their footsteps resonated behind me. They had much longer legs than me and were pretty fast runners. But they were also bigger, heavier. I was small but agile. So, I started going up, too, weaving between the rows. My plan of suddenly changing directions worked for a while, but I was tired. I had just spent over an hour practicing; my whole body was burned out. I would not be able to continue to hold this pace for long.

I could see what looked like an empty door frame at the end of the arena I was running toward. This could be it. I just had to get there. That's all I needed to do.

Except suddenly, a giant polar bear was climbing the wall and coming to stand in my way. Elena was between me and the door – my potential salvation.

If I kept on going, I'd run right into her. If I stopped, I would collide with her two friends behind me. This was the best example of being stuck between a rock and a hard place.

In a desperate move, I climbed up the dozens and dozens of rows.

"Where are you going, honey? There's nothing for you up there! You should just come down," Alexei called from behind me. "I promise you'll have a great time."

I did not want to see what a "great time" was, especially with him.

Soon enough, I was in the third to last row. Then the second to last. Then the last one. I could hear their footsteps getting closer and closer behind me, coming from both the right and the left. There was nowhere else to go to. Nowhere to hide.

I was screwed.

There was a small wall surrounding the outside perimeter. Waist-high. Low enough that I could see the drop below. It was way too high for me to survive the fall. A voice inside my head murmured that it would be better to fall than to see what the three Coppers had in store for me.

A low voice came from behind, sounding like a deformed version of Elena's. "Alexei! Use your power, dammit! Make yourself useful!"

Shit. Shit, shit, shit. Panic crept in, and I tried to build the wall in my mind. I tried remembering Archer's advice and closed my mind off from external control. But my concentration was frayed; I was terrified and so exhausted. The wall was more of a fence full of holes.

And Alexei went right through. I could *feel* him in my mind, his oily presence making me want to puke for a second. Then everything changed.

I turned around because I wanted to see him. I needed to see him. And when my eyes landed on his face, I felt relief. He was so beautiful. So charming. The most perfect man I had ever met.

I instantly moved away from the enclosure wall, wondering why I had tried so hard to escape. There was no reason to. I wanted to get as close as possible to Alexei. He was like the sun: big, radiantly glowing, and pulling on me like the most intense gravitational force in the universe.

Almost running toward him, I cried out his name. Blinding smile, perfect teeth, glowing golden eyes – I couldn't get close enough. Suddenly I was pressed against him. I was vaguely aware of a polar bear and another random guy next to us, but my whole focus was on Alexei. I was so lucky that he was looking at me. I would do anything for him.

"There you are, sweetheart. I was worried for a second," he purred at me.

I looked up, and our eyes met. How he looked at me, like he wanted to eat me whole, made my heart beat faster. I could feel a blush coming to my cheeks. He must have seen it because he chuckled lightly.

"I am going to take very good care of you, little girl." His voice gave me shivers. And I wanted to be the best girl for him. I would do anything he asked because I loved him. And I really, *really* wanted to please him.

I vaguely heard someone tell Alexei to hurry up and get it over with. My gaze remained stuck on him. My body was attracted to his like we were opposite magnets – two halves of a whole.

Alexei took my hand and led me all the way down back to the arena. He said we would be more comfortable down there. I wasn't sure what he meant, but I wasn't about to ask questions. He would tell me whatever I needed to know. I trusted him. I would do anything for him.

"Do you know what I want right now, sweet little girl?"

"What is it? What can I do for you?" I was hyperaware of how close our bodies were. And I was waiting with bated breath for him to tell me what he wanted. I needed to do whatever it took to please him.

Alexei stroked a hand down my cheek, down my neck, all the way to the top of my sports bra, peaking from my tank top. "I want you."

I didn't need more to know what he meant. And relief came through me because I could give him that. I wanted to give myself to him. He could have all of me if he wanted.

As I started removing my tank top, I heard a male voice mumble, "For fuck's sake, do we really need to go through this? Can't we just get rid of her?" and a female voice answered that it was okay for Alexei to play for a little while, that it would only add to the final result. I wasn't sure what they meant exactly. I didn't care much, though. I just wanted to satisfy my personal sun.

Alexei made an approving sound after my tank top hit the sand, and I beamed with joy. I was doing this right. Failing to suppress a smile, I bent to remove my shorts. As I straightened, Alexei put a hand on my butt and squeezed. "Good girl," he praised. And that made me happy.

Before I could start removing my sports bra, he pulled me into his arms and kissed me. I felt honored that he had chosen me for a kiss and more. And I did my best to satisfy him by opening my mouth and letting his tongue enter my mouth. He seemed to like it because a low growl rumbled in his chest.

His hand on my butt moved until his fingers started going below my panties, caressing my bare skin. I should have removed them already. I should have made it easier for him. I was about the start removing them when a voice boomed in the arena.

"What in the Hell is going on here?"

Immediately, Alexei stopped touching me altogether. I cried out, desperate for more touch, for more of him. But then, a beat later, my desperation for the Copper disappeared – snuffed like blowing on a candle. And, suddenly, the horror of what was happening gripped me. I was in my panties and sports bra, and I had been seconds away from getting raped and then killed by three Coppers.

I moved back several steps, my whole body shaking uncontrollably. I needed to distance myself from the man who had almost assaulted me. I wished I could have disappeared from the shame of failing to protect myself from his power and everything that happened afterward.

Needing to determine if the new voice was also a threat, I shifted slightly to look toward the newcomer. I didn't know who exactly I had been expecting, but it wasn't Hecate. Standing in a black leather dress and red high platform heels, she looked like she was on her way to the club.

"Nothing was wrong, Mistress Hecate," Alexei declared with a slight tremble. "Kalani and I were just having a little bit of fun."

"Really? Because, from where I stand, it looks like you were using your powers to sexually assault someone." Hecate had a dark look on her perfect-looking face. Her voice was frozen-cold. She was pissed. And I was currently thanking the stars that she was. She advanced, passing by me before stopping once she was standing right in front of Alexei. "I do *not* tolerate rapists here, no matter who your parents and grandparents are. Is it understood?"

Alexei nodded a little too fast. I could tell he was trying to look confident but failing miserably. His hands were shaky, his face had lost all color, and his eyes were wide from fear. I had a sick satisfaction watching him scared. He deserved to feel every bit of the terror I had felt at his and his friends' hands.

"Good. So, now, you are going to apologize to the lady here. And then you are going to swear on your life that you will never sexually assault anyone ever again."

Alexei opened his mouth, probably to protest, but closed it right away under Hecate's frigid glare. Instead, he turned his head toward me. His Adam's apple bobbed as he swallowed nervously. "I am sorry, Kalani. I shouldn't have taken advantage of you like this. It won't happen again."

Hecate scoffed at Alexei's words. She and I both knew this apology was as much a lie as Santa Klaus. Before Alexei could say or do anything else, Hecate drew a dagger from thin air and sliced Alexei's forearm. Coppery blood trickled down his arm. Hand visibly shaking, he coated his fingers in blood and held his hand out. Hecate clasped it.

"I swear on my blood and my life that I will never again sexually assault another woman."

"Or any other living being," Hecate corrected him.

"Or any other living being." Sweat was dripping down his forehead from the stress of it all. I wished I could hit him for what he had done and tried to do. But I also did not want to come any closer to him. If I could never cross his path anymore, that would still be too soon.

"And if you sexually assault someone, you will die in horrible pain. Am I clear?"

Alexei nodded so fast that it must have hurt his neck.

It felt like the stars moved above our heads. They aligned in a symbol I had never seen before, and an ethereal light shone down from the sky on Alexei. It looked almost like a caress to me. But based on how Alexei's stupid face contorted, it must have been painful. Good for him.

"Now, leave. I don't want to see your face ever again." Alexei nodded emphatically at Hecate's words, and she shooed for him to leave. He didn't need to be told twice because he full-on ran from the arena. Elena and Nathan were about to follow their friend, but Hecate called out to them. "Did both of you think you'd get out of this without consequences?"

Both Coppers stopped dead in their tracks, knowing that there was no way they would be able to escape a Titan.

Hecate started muttering under her breath, her eyes glowing a fluorescent purple. Lavender smoke left her hands and floated to the two Coppers. Their eyes tracked the progress of the smoke, widening as it got closer and closer until it reached their skin. It moved to their faces and got into their noses and mouths. They choked on it, gasping and struggling for air. It took nearly a minute for all of it to enter their lungs. By then, they were on the floor, convulsing in pain. I would lie if I said I wasn't a little glad to see them in pain.

After observing them crushed with pain, Hecate nodded satisfactorily and snapped her fingers. Instantly, the two Coppers stopped moving and crying out. Their faces were still covered in tears, though. It was more than a little scary to see how little Hecate had to do to hurt two powerful Coppers. I did not want to get on this goddess's bad side, that was for sure.

"Now that we had our little fun, I want you to remember what happens to someone complicit in sexual assault." Hecate crouched down until she was right above their faces. She had absolutely no pity for them. Her face was full of disdain and anger. "Are we clear?"

Both Coppers agreed less than a second after she finished her question. I almost laughed at how scared of her they were. After lording their superiority over me, it was ironic that they were now cowering in shame and pain.

The goddess stood up and turned her back on them, a clear sign that she was done. They left so fast that Usain Bolt would have had a run for his money.

Once Hecate finally turned her attention to me, I had a second of intense fear. I had no idea what this Titan wanted. But based on the broad smile that she gave me and her relaxed posture, I was inching toward her not wanting to make me hurt.

"Kalani! It's so good to see you!" she exclaimed with an enthusiasm that was the total opposite of her earlier frozen rage. She started toward me, her arms up as if to hug me before she stopped short. "Oh, put your clothes back on before we catch up."

I had been so focused on monitoring the situation with the Titan and the three Coppers who had assaulted me that my state of undress had been relegated to second-class issues. But now? Now that everything was calming down around me, I was becoming acutely aware of how close to complete nakedness I had been.

Reminders of Alexei's hands on my body and his mouth on mine made me want to throw up.

I was racing against time as I put my clothes back on. They were sweaty, but I didn't care. I wished I had something else to put on me. My towel was somewhere in the arena, but I didn't want to turn my back on the Titan next to me. She had been helpful so far, but I didn't trust the moods of the deities.

"Thank you for helping me." I hoped she could feel my gratefulness for her in my voice. She had saved my life.

"No worries! I have a deep hate for rapists, so this was a great opportunity for me to ensure this bastard learns his lesson. Plus, I had missed cursing people," she added with a sigh and a hand to her heart.

"You, hm… you cursed him?" I knew she was the goddess of magic, necromancy, and the night. But I didn't realize it included curses.

"Oh yes, darling! All three of them! That first one will not be able to even think about someone in a sexual manner without throwing up uncontrollably. And the last two? They will not be able to witness or participate in sexual aggression without feeling like they are being stabbed in their genitals. I am particularly proud of this one. It can be hard to think of good curses on the spot, but I think I did amazing." She put her arms on her hips, looking proud of herself. It was similar to the expression someone would have after getting promoted or getting a semester with straight A's. Except she had just cursed three Coppers.

What world had I landed into?

"But anyway, I was at one of Dionysus's parties, and someone mentioned the presence of a human in the competition. I don't know who spilled the beans – I am banking on Artemis; she holds grudges like no one else, and since last decade's debacle… Well, let's just say we are not the best of friends. My point is that I wanted to let you know that you might get some special attention coming from some of your competitors once they learn that little bit of information. And they will because Olympus is full of gods and goddesses who have nothing better to do with their time than gossip and place bets on who will survive the Tournament."

She went on to muttering something about how she was the only one doing real work here, but I was stuck on the thought of the Coppers learning about my total lack of power. I did not want to know what Elena, Alexei, and Nathan would do in retribution for what had just happened, especially once they learned I was completely human and defenseless compared to their powers.

"I heard you were friends with the twins and little Archer, so you should be fine! I'm sure they will help you; those children are amazing. You might have to stop hanging out at night on your own." Did she seriously call Archer 'little'? What part of him was little? And how did she seem to know the three of them so well? I thought the Coppers participating in the Tournament went directly from Earth to here.

"Thank you for the advice Hecate. I really appreciate it." I meant it. She might have had ulterior motives; she might not. Either way, I was now aware of a critical piece of information to continue ensuring my safety.

"It is my pleasure, dear Kalani." Hecate snapped her fingers, and an antique-looking timepiece appeared out of nowhere. She checked the time, and the timepiece disappeared. "I am sorry to have to leave so soon, but I want you to know I bet on you. And not just because I want to suck it to Artemis. I do think you can make it." And then she was gone. Pouf. Disappeared into thin glittery air.

And I was left standing there, alone in the Pit, wondering how I had gone from practicing gymnastics on my own to having a goddess tell me I was the horse she had placed a bet on.

Chapter Eighteen

"Give me a second to wrap my head around all this." Sadie started massaging her temples in an attempt to comprehend everything.

We had been in her room for the past hour or so. She and I sat on her bed while Søren and Archer were on her cozy little rug. How the hell she had gotten a carpet, I had no idea. My room was as bare as a prison cell.

I had gathered everyone after breakfast for a crisis meeting. It had taken me a while to recount everything, and I had glossed over the details of my time under Alexei's control. I was still embarrassed about how easily he had been able to go through my mental blocks. After weeks of working on them with Archer, I felt like a failure. And it stung. My pride was bruised, my body was hurt, and my self-confidence was shattered. I didn't need pitying glances on top of that.

I had also decided not to mention the dream. Because it was just that, a dream. I didn't want things to get weird between Archer and me — or any stranger than they currently were. And the whole doubt spiral I had fallen into after the nightmare was ridiculous. Based on everything that had happened afterward, I had no choice but to continue to place my trust in these three Coppers' hands.

The two guys had been uncharacteristically quiet throughout my whole monologue. Sadie had only asked a couple of questions.

Overall, it had just been me talking. It had been hard to keep talking at some points, but I had powered through because I knew they needed to know everything if we were to work together.

However, now that I was done and everyone was dead silent, I felt very uncomfortable. I didn't know how they would react to everything I had just dumped on them. And now that they knew that, soon enough, the information that I was human would spread like wildfire through the competitors, would they decide that helping me was too much of a hassle?

"I'm going to go roast some vermin," Søren hissed. He stood up and cracked his knuckles quite aggressively. His whole face, usually always mischievous, was somber and bloodthirsty. He was halfway to the door before Sadie called him.

"I want to kill them as much as you do, brother. But we need to think about this carefully. We can't risk making this situation worse than it already is."

Søren closed his fists, and I could see the muscles in his neck contracting. He did not want to sit back down, but he did so under his sister's commanding gaze. I had to say I felt warm inside to witness that Søren cared enough that he wanted to enact revenge on my behalf.

"Why are you thinking?" I asked Sadie as Søren sat down.

"I think we need to show everyone what the consequences are of hurting you; otherwise, more people will get ideas. But we need to ensure that we don't get in trouble either." She gave a meaningful look to both of the guys. "You both know we can't afford that."

I wasn't sure what she meant, but they must have known because Søren reluctantly nodded. Archer was still immobile, looking impassive. I felt a pinch in my chest at the lack of concern on his face. But it was good. It reminded me that Archer did not have any romantic feelings for me. None. I had to get over myself and fast.

"Why?" I asked the question without realizing it, but I wasn't mad about it. I hadn't asked anything too personal of the three Coppers that they hadn't offered themselves. I hadn't wanted to impose. But now it started to feel like they knew everything about me, and I only had a trailer version of their lives. I wanted more. I needed more.

I needed to feel like an actual member of the group. Not just the outsider they kept around like a pet.

The three Coppers exchanged a long look before Sadie made an approving sound. "We physically can't tell you everything, but the important part is that we are here because of a slight misunderstanding with the gods. And we are on probation – we are not supposed to make any waves. If we do, we could be forced to do a second Tournament. Or worse."

What could be worse than going through this twice? And while this explanation was still way too vague for my taste, it gave me a piece of information. If they were here because of a 'misunderstanding with the gods,' then it meant that they had been on Mount Olympus before becoming participants in the Tournament. And that correlated with Hecate telling me that she liked them yesterday. But if they had already earned their place on Olympus and lived there, why were they back here?

"But that's not important right now. We need to focus on our next steps." Sadie paused for a beat before turning toward me. "You need extra protection at all times. Elena and Alexei will want revenge; there's no question about it. You can't remain alone. Anytime."

"I mean, sure, I can stay glued to your sides all day, but there will always be times when I am alone. Even at night, I am alone."

"That's where I was going. You need to switch rooms and stay with one of us. I wouldn't be surprised if those bastards tried to get into your room when you sleep, so it would be better if you could have extra protection at night."

My room was the only place I could recharge on my own. However, I could see where Sadie was coming from. I was sure Alexei and Elena would want to make me pay for the way last night had ended for them. And I didn't doubt that they could be conniving enough to try to kill me in my sleep. So, even though I had no desire to become someone's roommate, I knew it was the best decision.

"Okay," I nodded after a while of debating this decision. "I'll get my stuff to move in here tonight."

"Oh no, I didn't mean my room!" Sadie exclaimed. "I could go hunt for a couple of corpses to stock in the room, but even then, my power wouldn't be the best help if someone were to break in at night. You can't stay with Søren – it would be strange since he is with Mei. It only makes sense that you would go with Archer. He had the strongest power level out of us three, and you are already supposed to be dating. People will even consider this a sign that your relationship is progressing. It will show that you are still under our protection."

This had to be a joke. It had to. I was desperately trying to put some emotional distance from Archer, and now Sadie wanted me to go and live with him. The logical part of my brain understood why this was the best choice – plus, the two guys had gotten one of the only double rooms in the whole compound, so I would have a bed to sleep on. But the emotional part of me was freaking out.

I turned my gaze towards the man in question, trying to see if he was going to refuse the new living arrangement. He hadn't said anything so far, so I assumed he would. Except he was acquiescing.

"Sure. Works for me."

Søren was next on the yes train. "Cool. I'll go and spend some time with Mei. She only has a twin bed, but she's been wanting to get cozy with me for a while. She won't complain." Based on the look on his face, he was pretty excited about that prospect too.

I wanted to say no. I really did. But I didn't want to be *that* girl who refused to do something completely logical because of stupid reasons and ended up dying a horrible death. I had too much to live for. And I could survive sleeping in the same room as Archer. I had more self-control than that, dammit.

"All right. I'll move my stuff later today."

Sadie clapped her hands together in satisfaction. "Good. Now that this is all figured out, let's brainstorm on how we are going to show dear Elena, Alexei, and Nathan that they messed with the wrong people."

"There is no question about it. I know exactly what we are going to do. And it will be extremely painful for them," Archer declared with venom.

Damn, was it getting hotter in here?

Half an hour later, we entered the Pit during one of the group training sessions. I was more than uncomfortable walking on the sand of the arena. It was way too soon. I hadn't slept at all the rest of the night, too keyed up and terrified of what I would see behind my closed eyelids.

Walking into the arena next to where I had been assaulted was a lot to handle. I just hoped I could get through the whole afternoon without throwing up or needing to leave. I had to show those scumbags I was still standing and would not break for them. I had to prove to everyone – myself included – that I was stronger than that.

Xander, the trainer that had not been the most helpful on my first day, was standing in the center of the arena, observing his trainees doing one-on-one sparring exercises. Hands in the pockets of his leather pants, he still looked just as menacing and intimidating as before. I had to thank him for pitting me against Elena on that very first day on Olympus – if we hadn't sparred then, she might not have been as determined to kill me before the Tournament even started.

From what I understood, Xander was one of the two Golden recruited to teach the Coppers how to defend themselves before the start of the Tournament. Based on how well our first session had gone, I was immensely grateful to have the twins and Archer helping me instead.

Some of the Coppers training noticed us walking in and turned their attention to us. We were an unusual sight at a group training session. The twins and Archer did not believe that Xander or the other trainer could teach them anything substantial. I hadn't seen much of this world but was tempted to believe them, especially if they had the respect of a goddess like Hecate.

Xander must have realized that an increasing number of his students were getting distracted because he turned around. His eyebrows shot up toward his hairline when he saw us. Or my companions, I didn't think he was particularly impressed to see me.

"What a surprise! Have the Aska twins and the grand Archer Vasilias finally decided to grace us with their presence?" I didn't need to know this man very well to see that he was mocking me.

"We are here for a challenge, actually." Archer's tone was very much matter of fact, as if a challenge was something that he did every Sunday after brunch and mimosas.

"Finally, something interesting is happening in this hell-hole of a place!" The mountain of a man exclaimed with a little too much excitement. Having a little bit of deity blood in one's veins must make one very excited at the thought of fighting. I didn't get it. "Step forward and indicate the name of your opponent."

Everyone had fallen deadly silent in the Pit, holding their breaths. Archer stepped forward and called out Alexei's name while staring him down. The other guy looked ready to shit his pants, but he still advanced until he was standing within the circle the Coppers had formed around us. Everyone started chattering, and Xander was about to start talking again when Søren stepped forward and called for Elena. Her eyes widened as if she was surprised to be called out. She should have known. On the sidelines, I heard Mei gasp in shock at seeing her boyfriend issue a duel.

This time, as Elena walked forward, no one started talking. People around us wondered if we were done or if more challenges would be sent out. Sadie took her sweet time, letting the tension go up. Then she stepped forward and stared directly at Nathan. He didn't need her to say his name to know he was being challenged. Then all three of my friends were lined up in front of my three assailants from last night. It was hard for me to look at *them* at first, but once I did, I refused to look away and back down. I wanted to see them afraid. Just as much as I had been.

It took a while for me to realize that everyone was still waiting. Xander was staring at me, his eyes questioning me. It took me a beat to register what he was waiting for.

"Oh no, I am just here as a spectator."

"Hmm, I thought so." Xander then turned dismissively. Rude much? I didn't need him to point out how unlikely I would be to issue a challenge to someone else. I didn't linger too much on it because the trainer was talking again.

"Alright, before we start with the rules, do all three of you agree to participate in the challenge?"

The three scumbags that had attacked me the night before did not seem as confident now. Alexei still looked like he was going to be sick, and Nathan was glancing around as if to determine whether he could flee. Elena was the only one who seemed relatively okay — she was a little paler than usual but had a definite fighting stance. All the same, all three of them nodded their agreement. From what Søren had explained earlier, refusing to answer a challenge was one of the most shameful things a Copper could do. I guessed the three of them still had enough pride to continue.

"Good. Now let's go over the rules. As we are still in the preparation phase of the Tournament, this challenge will not be to the death. Winners will be determined by knock-out or surrender. You cannot remove limbs or hurt the eyes of your opponents. No outside help and no weapons allowed. Any questions?" Xander looked at all six Coppers, ensuring they understood the rules of the fight.

No one answered, but Xander must have taken it for agreement. In the next second, an unseen force pushed me and all of the bystanders back until we were behind an invisible sideline. It happened so fast that I didn't even have time to freak out. Reaching out, my hand came into contact with an invisible dome. And all three of my friends were inside with the three Coppers that had tried to kill me.

From the outside, Xander yelled for them to start. My breath caught. Was it the right solution? I must have started caring more about all three of my friends than I thought because I was scared for them.

Then all hell broke loose.

The first place my gaze got attracted to was Søren. He was facing Elena, who had already shifted into a polar bear. An excited and bloodthirsty grin bloomed on his face. Elena charged at him. A second later, fire exploded out of the blond Copper. He was surrounded by fire tentacles that lashed out at Elena like whips. She tried avoiding them, but the closer she got to my friend, the more she got hit. Soon enough, her white fur was burned in multiple places, and she was limping. With a roar, she came forward again and swiped her front paw at Søren's chest. Her huge claws sliced at his shirt but didn't pierce his skin. With a laugh that made me worry for his mental health, Søren commanded his fiery tentacles to wrap around one of her hind legs. He tugged. She fell. The tentacle holding her leg tightened. She roared in pain.

Søren kneeled next to her and put a flaming hand on her throat. I could see his lips move but couldn't hear his words. However, a few seconds later, he released her and stood back up. None of us needed Xander to announce it to know that Søren had won. Easily so. He had only one scratch on his chest, which hadn't even broken the skin. It was almost annoying how easy it had been for him.

From farther down the sideline, Mei cheered for Søren, screaming that her boyfriend was the best and sexiest man alive. I couldn't suppress a smile when Søren answered by making a heart with his hands in her direction and gracing all the spectators with a bow. Finding my eyes in the sea of people, Søren gave me a thumbs up and a wink. It made me feel a little better.

Next, I turned my attention to the fight happening to my right. Sadie was facing off a buffed-up Nathan. The twins had told me earlier that Nathan was a descendant of Ares, the god of War, and had ended up being a real-life version of the Hulk. He was incredibly strong and could probably break someone in half or crack a tree trunk with one punch. It made me more than a little nervous for Sadie.

I had never seen Sadie use her powers before. I had imagined it a few times, but her raising the dead didn't look like anything I could have come up with. She must have started summoning the dead right at the start of the fight because there were already three mostly whole skeletons fighting off against Nathan. And based on the mounds of upturned sand and earth, they were coming from straight beneath the arena. They had died here. Were these old Tournament competitors? That was not reassuring.

Nathan tried his hardest to crush the skeletons to death, but he was unsuccessful. You couldn't very well kill something already dead. And Sadie could make the skeletons move even when their bones were broken in multiple places and partially crushed. Those things were unstoppable. Invincible. And they had a mission – hurt Nathan. When the Copper broke their bones, the skeletons used the sharp ends as blades. They cut, hit, grabbed, and distracted – Sadie's good, obedient little soldiers. I could only try to imagine what would happen if she had a thousand of those skeletons.

The farthest fight from me was Archer's. He and Alexei were physically fighting without using their powers – as far as I could tell, anyways. Alexei had a broken nose, a bleeding eyebrow, and bruises already blooming everywhere on his jaw and ribs. The guy had coppery blood all over the bottom of his face. Archer was also bleeding, but only from his knuckles. It must have been how the light hit, but his blood seemed to shine like gold.

In a lightning-fast attack, Archer kicked Alexei's knee. I could almost hear the crack from here – how his knee bent unnaturally made me shiver. Alexei dropped to the ground, and I thought that Archer would finish him with a kick or a punch to the head. But he didn't.

He did much worse.

His eyes started glowing. Bright. Much brighter than they ever had in my presence before. Alexei tensed up. And then he started screaming. In pain. So much pain.

I looked away one second to see Nathan yielding to Sadie, a skeleton fighter holding a sharp-as-fuck humerus to his throat. But I couldn't focus on them any longer.

Without my consent, my attention shifted back to Alexei. He was still screaming, constricting, and convulsing on the floor under the weight of Archer's power. The arena had gotten quiet, not even a whisper exchanged between the spectators. And it was blood-chilling to hear those screams echo in the arena and resonate in my bones.

Then the screams stopped. Alexei either didn't have enough strength or enough air to continue making sounds. He was still seizing on the ground, his mouth wide open but silent. And Archer was still standing there. Staring. Hunting.

It felt like forever before Xander dissolved the protective dome and advanced to signify to Archer that it was over.

All of it was over.

It was very anticlimactic how easily they had won. How effortless it had been for them to crush the three Coppers under their heels.

Everyone agreed with me based on the heavy silence that blanketed the Pit.

These three Coppers were so incredibly powerful that it was terrifying.

I was damn glad they were my friends.

Chapter Nineteen

It was awkward. Really awkward. For me. For him. Even for the neighbors – I was sure the awkwardness could be felt through the walls.

I was still holding Sadie's box of clothes with my phone sitting on top – my only belongings. And I was frozen at the door, my eyes wandering across the room. The room was decently big, with a bed, dresser, and desk on each side. They also had a window between the two beds, with a beautiful view of the sea of clouds. Søren had moved most of his stuff to boxes under his bed so I'd have space. And Archer's side was… unexpectedly clean. His bed was made with dark blue sheets perfectly laid out and straightened. He had two books on his bedside table and a whole pile at the foot of his bed. His clothes were all neatly folded or put on wooden hangers. It looked so classy but also so normal, as if I were looking into a contemporary interior design magazine.

It was the first time I had entered Archer and Søren's room. Or maybe Archer and my room, I guessed. It felt like imposing onto Archer's privacy, like crossing an invisible boundary between us. As if my seeing his bed and his dresser full of clothes was something deeply intimate.

I was overthinking this.

"Are you going to get in or just stay at the door all night?"

He was standing to the side, leaning on the doorframe to their private bathroom. He was dressed in comfy-looking clothes, and his hair was still wet from his shower. One eyebrow raised, he crossed his arms on his chest and looked at me as if to say that I was ridiculous standing there. I knew that. I didn't need him to point it out. But moving into his room and closing the door behind me… it was like moving a step forward in our non-existent relationship.

"Just assessing your man cave," I replied, hoping it sounded flippant.

Stepping fully into the room, I let the door close behind me. The soft click echoed between my ears. Trying to showcase casualness and confidence, I walked until I had reached Søren's bed. My bed.

I put the box on the floor by the foot of the bed. Brought my hands together. Clasped them. I took my time turning around as if I could avoid having to look at *him*.

"What's your assessment then? Will the 'man cave' be good enough for her majesty Kalani Mayfield?" His mocking tone made me want to strangle him, which was entirely out of character for me.

"I guess it'll be good enough. Might have to tidy it up a bit, though. Those wrinkles on your sheets look very messy."

Archer had a knee-jerk reaction, his head shifting slightly so he could look at his bed. Ah! Point for Kalani! I couldn't suppress a laugh at seeing him dive headfirst at my words.

"Hilarious, Mayfield. I already miss Søren."

"You are a bundle of joy, aren't you, Sunshine?" I taunted him, smiling at how grumpy he had sounded.

"Only to you, Mayfield."

While Archer wanted to pretend like he was annoyed, he wasn't fooling me. That dimple on his left cheek was peeking its head out. He was amused, and surprisingly, this little banter had relaxed me. Maybe this would be fine.

A comfortable silence settled in the room as I started organizing my things, and Archer lay in his bed, reading his book. Neither of us was really talkative, so it didn't feel strange not to fill the silence. It was relaxing, like two friends who knew each other well enough to enjoy quiet time together. Side by side.

I took my time putting all my clothes away in the spaces that Søren had opened up for me. I put my phone on my nightstand for easy access – old habits die hard. And then, once I didn't have anything else to do, I sat down on my mattress and looked over at Archer for the first time in close to an hour. He was still reading his book. Now that I was paying attention to it, the title was in a language I couldn't read – I couldn't even tell what language it was precisely.

"I didn't realize you read." Just as I said it, I realized it might have sounded rude. Shit. "Not in a mean or weird way. I guess I just didn't know it was something that you liked."

Archer didn't close his book – he brought it down just enough that our eyes could meet. "There's a lot you don't know about me, Mayfield."

Fair point. He put the book back up, indicating that he wanted to keep reading without distractions. I waited for a few seconds while watching him. I must have wanted trouble because I decided to ask another question.

"What language is that?"

The book moved down an inch. His eyes bore into mine. He raised an eyebrow, his signature move to ask me if I *really* wanted to continue annoying him. And I guessed I did because I didn't back down from our staring contest. I was about to explain that I just wanted to get to know him better, seeing as we would be roommates for a while, but he finally decided to answer.

"It's ancient Greek. The language that gods and goddesses speak most often."

"Where did you even learn that?" Maybe this conversation would be a sneaky way for me to learn more about his upbringing.

"Let's say my dad ensured I had access to all the best professors. I had intensive training in ancient Greek and Latin until I turned twenty. Lots of fun, believe me."

"Damn. How many languages do you speak?"

"Quite a few."

"And what's your first language?"

"Not ancient Greek, that's for sure."

"Are you ever going to give me a straight-up answer?"

Archer didn't answer right away. Instead, he closed his book, sat up, and rotated until he was on the side of his bed, facing me.

"Have you ever wondered why everyone speaks the same language as you do here? Even though some Coppers come from countries where English is not the first language?"

That was a weird Segway into a new topic, but sure. If he wanted to talk about that, then that was fine. I'd go for it. Let's see where he was going with it.

"I guess it crossed my mind a few times, but I usually have more pressing matters to focus on."

"Well, Mount Olympus is under various spells that help everyone get along slightly better. One of those magic tricks is that everyone can understand everyone else. You can see it as your words being translated into every Copper's native language. Or it might be something closer to translating your words into a common language. You might have to ask Hecate for the details since it's her handy work. Either way, it takes significant willpower to speak outside of the spell. My point is that it doesn't matter what my native tongue is – it got ripped from me when my feet touched the ground on Olympus. Just like yours did."

I was speechless for a minute because it was wild to think I had been talking with people who had never spoken a word of English before. And I could understand their native language as if it were the same as mine. One more thing that made me realize how much Olympus differed from the Earth.

But what really shocked me in Archer's words was the contempt in his voice at the end. The resentment he had. He was always so stoic and strong, so determined to be the best, that I had never really stopped to think about how he felt about being here in the first place. It was easy to forget that even the strongest people could sometimes have difficulty accepting things.

"Do you miss it? Your life from before the Tournament, I mean." I knew that Archer probably wouldn't answer my question, but I still wanted to show him that I wanted to learn. I wanted to know more about him. That was what friends did.

Archer frowned as if he hadn't asked himself that question in a long time.

"Yes, I do. Everyday." He stopped for a second, debating whether to stop there or continue. "I miss a time when I didn't have to hide who I am all the time."

"I get that." I didn't add anything else because I could tell Archer had reached a sharing limit. And that was fine. Maybe he would feel comfortable sharing more in a few days or weeks.

A long time went by of us just sitting there in silence. My gaze turned to the window where the sun was going down, coloring the clouds in beautiful orange and pink tints. I wished I could have had my camera to take pictures of the mesmerizing view and immortalize it. I could have taken a picture with my phone, but it wouldn't have looked the same, and I didn't want to waste the battery. So, instead, I tried to take pictures with my mind.

"What about you?" Archer's voice broke the silence so suddenly that I jerked in surprise. It had been so long since we had stopped talking that I had to remind myself of our last words before I could answer.

"I miss it too. Especially my little brother, Makaio. He is the light in my life." I had to stop for a beat to rein in my emotions. I wouldn't cry in front of Archer. "But I also miss my classes and teaching gymnastics and surfing. Being here has made me realize just how important some things are. I knew they mattered before but didn't quite grasp how much."

"What about your parents?"

A scoff escaped me at Archer's question. My parents? I wasn't sure they entered in the category of things I missed. "My dad died two months before I was born in a car accident, so I've never met him. I have heard a ton of stories, though, and he seemed like an amazing guy. And my mom," I trailed off, my gaze going unfocused as I pictured her – dark circles under her sad eyes, hair a mess, too tired to even smile. "She hasn't had an easy life. But she loves us, even if, most of the time, she doesn't know how to show it."

Archer nodded as if he understood what I meant. Maybe he did. For all I knew, his parents had been just as emotionally unavailable as my mom. I hoped not. And I sure hoped that my mom was finding it within herself to be there for Makaio now that I wasn't here anymore.

"Wanna watch TV?"

"Wait, there's TV here? I thought there wasn't any electricity or technology from Earth on Olympus!"

Archer laughed at my excitement and pushed a button on his nightstand. The lights turned off, and a hologram appeared near the door. "Hecate is a fan of the Earth, and she likes to magic things for the inhabitants of Olympus that appreciate them. But there's no electricity. It's all magic."

I would thank Hecate for that the next time I saw her. A show started, something I had never seen before. But based on the décor and the costumes – all looking very much Olympus-like – I thought they had a mini-Hollywood here.

Archer didn't add anything, and neither did I. We sat in silence, watching the TV scientists on Earth were still working very hard to create. I didn't get everything that happened between the characters, missing some context, but it didn't matter. It was a way to escape my reality. A way to feel normal again, as if I were back at home, watching a show on my couch.

I fell asleep listening to the actors and Archer's soft laughs when they made an inside joke. And I didn't have any unwanted dreams. Just the dark.

Chapter Twenty

The days passed and transformed into weeks. Weeks that were punctuated by physical training, sparring, and mental training. I didn't have much time to breathe, but I liked it that way. It helped me forget that the beginning of the Tournament was coming much faster than I wanted it. We were only four days out now, and the tension was mounting – both in myself and among the other participants of the Tournament.

I was getting much better at hand-on-hand combat and sword fighting – good enough to hold my own against the twins and even Archer on good days. I was far from being the best at any form of fighting, but I was good enough now that I hoped it would work out during the Trials. Mental training against Archer's magic was also going very well. I could now remove myself from his mental illusions in under twenty seconds. I was still struggling with preventing Archer from controlling my mind altogether, but I could sense when he was coming in and slow him down enough that I could prevent most of the harm from happening. I had been taking our training sessions more seriously after my brush with death courtesy of Elena, Alexei, and Nathan. And I could tell that it was paying off.

Speaking of Elena and her goons, they had not tried anything else against me. I could feel their hateful glances every so often, but they had stayed far away, which suited me just fine. If I could fly under the radar for the next however long until the end of the Tournament, I'd be fucking ecstatic.

Even though my three archnemeses had stopped bothering me, they hadn't slowed down in their descent toward hatred. Charlie – the kid that Elena threatened almost a month ago – arrived with a broken arm and a seriously bruised face at breakfast a few days ago. And based on the proud smirk on Elena's face, it was her handiwork. I tried to and talk with Charlie once most people had left the room, but the young Copper refused my help, stating that he "wasn't weak and didn't need anyone, especially a coward who hid behind others." It stung, but I tried not to take it too personally since the guy was clearly hurting.

And Charlie hadn't been the only person they had been violent with. A few other Coppers had been beaten up by the extremist group they were forming. No one had been killed so far, but I heard it came close to it with a girl – the nurse had arrived and saved her before the worst could happen. The girl hadn't been back to the cafeteria or group training since. Side note, it looked like being a medical professional on Mount Olympus was much more relaxing than on Earth, seeing as they only showed up in cases of grave emergency and did not help otherwise.

Some things had changed for the best in the past two weeks. First of all, my rooming situation had become a lot less stressful. I had spent the first couple of days shoving every hint of more-than-friendly feelings and fantasies I had on Archer behind a heavy-duty security door in the deepest recess of my mind. And it was working. I didn't stare at his chest when he was shirtless in the room or the Pit anymore. I didn't let myself get lost in his eyes. And I sure didn't allow myself to daydream – or worse, actually dream – about kissing him. I was becoming good at being his friend. And only his friend.

But the weirdest thing that had happened in the past two weeks? I had gotten closer to Mei. Pretty incredible. We weren't BBFs or anything, but I had started to… appreciate her. She was fun when she wanted to be, and her endless source of gossip was more than entertaining. Somehow, she knew everything about everyone. And now that I was Archer's fake girlfriend, I had access to all the best insights. I had to admit that it was fun. And I started to see why Søren was attracted to her – she could be nice when she wanted to. Although, she only considered powerful people worthy of her attention.

She was still somewhat of an asshole. Just not an asshole to me anymore.

"Are you listening to me, Lane?" Mei's voice brought me out of my thoughts, and I shifted to look at her. I had told her multiple times that Lane wasn't my nickname, but she insisted I didn't get to choose my nickname. I had abandoned the battle since then.

We were together in the main gardens of the compound. The twins and Archer had had to leave for a "family emergency," and Mei had offered to teach me some yoga. So here I was, trying to imitate her every move and seriously wondering how people could find this relaxing.

"Yeah. Sorry, I was daydreaming for a second, but I'm back."

Mei didn't seem bothered at all and nodded firmly before continuing. "Good. I was saying we should coordinate our outfits."

"Our outfits?"

"Yeah, for the party."

"What party?" I started to feel like a parrot, but I was extremely confused. Were we partying before the beginning of the Tournament? It seemed more logical to party afterward. Once we were sure we would remain alive for a while.

"The opening ceremony, of course!"

Of course. Right. I wasn't aware there would be an opening ceremony. Would it be like the ceremonies at the start of the Olympics? I had always wished I could have seen one in real life. Although seeing as the deities on Olympus had interesting tastes, I wasn't sure the ceremony would be enjoyable for us participants.

"Remind me again what that opening ceremony entails exactly?"

Mei looked at me from where she was doing a complicated yoga pose – neck and arms on the ground, she had her back in a vertical position, legs straight before going back down at an angle to the ground. I was trying to imitate her, and even though I was really flexible, I didn't feel the most confident putting so much pressure on my neck.

"You need to pay more attention to our social gathering calendar, honey. You have a social standing now! You can't just spend your days fighting and not take care of your reputation." She said it with a graceful smile, moving into another one of her complicated poses. Soon enough, her legs were straight up in the air, and she was in a weird handstand where only her head, neck, and upper shoulders touched the ground.

Coming from most people, I would have been annoyed at the patronizing comment. But I knew that she didn't mean it in a demeaning way. She was just unaware that some people didn't share her interests. And, in her own way, I guessed she cared about me. A little.

"But anyways. It's the party the gods and goddesses throw in our honor! It is happening the night before the first Trial so in three days. Formal attire is heavily recommended, although I'm sure my baby will wear an armor, per usual. I keep telling him that leather armors are so old-fashioned nowadays, but he's a little stubborn like that. It's okay; I still love him. But my point stands – I won't have anyone to match with. And let's be real; your boo will probably wear some awfully practical armor too. Therefore, I think us girlies should match!" She almost squealed in excitement at the end, and I shuddered.

Great idea. Superb, really. Just what I wanted to hear on such a beautiful afternoon. Mei's fashion style was very out there. She liked short and sexy dresses, glittery tops, and short shorts. She wanted to feel pretty and didn't mind if it attracted people's looks simultaneously. She used clothes and make-up as a weapon – if a sexy outfit could aid her in reaching her goals, then she would wear it without questions.

I respected that.

However, I didn't feel comfortable when too much of my body showed. Stereotypes and biases arose in sports such as gymnastics, and while I had never been overweight, I also hadn't been the leanest of all my teammates. Underhanded comments and jokes left a mark, even when people claimed they didn't mean it. So, sure, I'd wear shorts and dresses. But I didn't feel comfortable showing off more of my body than was necessary.

Plus, she loved glitters, ruffles, and all the shades of pink possible. I was scared of what the matching looks would be.

"I don't even have any fancy dresses, Mei. I don't think I'll be wearing anything different from the usual."

Mei shook her head, which was a feat, as she was still in the weird handstand pose. "Don't worry about that! We are not allowed to leave the compound to prevent people from trying to flee, but some sewists and clothes sellers are coming over tomorrow. They'll be here to make sure we have the proper clothes to meet the gods. And best of all, it's free for us! A gift before we start the Tournament."

How exciting. And how generous the gods and goddesses were to offer us a cute dress to wear the night before we started fighting for our lives. The worse thing was that I didn't have any argument to use to say no to Mei. Resigned, I shrugged and gave her a tight smile – the kind I gave when I made awkwardly long eye contact with a stranger on the street.

"Great! I can't wait! We are going to have such a great time together!"

I knew I wouldn't be convincing if I tried pretending to be excited too, so I remained quiet. Instead, I focused on trying to imitate Mei's fancy yoga movements. She had told me we would take it slow, but I doubted she remembered what she had looked like when she had done yoga for the first time.

When we *finally* reached the last sun salutation, I was *that* close to feigning a muscle tear to make it stop. Fortunately, I could do a sun salutation decently well, so it made me end this "beginner" yoga session on a semi-high note.

"Ah," Mei gushed, looking rejuvenated. "That felt so nice! I am glad we were able to share this together. Yoga brings people together, you know?"

My knee-jerk reaction was to give her a thumbs-up. Gods, a thumbs-up. Mei thankfully didn't comment on my weirdness – or didn't even see it, which was more likely.

We grabbed our stuff and headed to the cafeteria. Mei made most of the conversation along the way, and she only required that I nod or make an empathetic sound at the right times to keep going. And, trust me, I greatly appreciated that because I was too drained by my day to hold the level of endless conversation that Mei liked.

We were about halfway down the hall leading to the cafeteria when I started to hear the commotion. At first, it sounded like loud conversations, but it quickly morphed into screams and sounds of flesh hitting flesh. Mei and I exchanged a concerned look, wondering what was happening.

I wasn't usually the type to run into danger. A month ago, I would have heard the screams and probably hid or fled. I liked to remain alive and whole way too much to make stupid decisions, especially knowing that I didn't have any martial art training. But four weeks here had changed me in many ways. Knowing that my three friends were supposed to meet us in the mess hall, my first instinct was to run toward it to see if they were okay.

Mei and I ran toward the huge double doors. They were slightly ajar, and we just had to push them a few inches to face a surreal sight. Most of the Coppers within the room were fighting. Like, a full-on street fight where hair was pulled, teeth were knocked, and knees were shoved into men's reproductive organs. Coming from highly trained fighters, it was almost comical.

"What in the stars is going on?" Mei's words mirrored my complete confusion very well. The fight probably only included about a third of the participants – the others must have been on their way to eat or still training – but it was incredibly chaotic and impressive.

The first thing I did after the shock of the situation faded was check for my friends. From where I stood, I couldn't see any of them. The relief that coursed through me was visceral. I didn't even know why I had worried, seeing as the twins and Archer were lethal.

But it looked like I had gotten more attached to the three idiots than I had initially anticipated.

"I don't know, but it doesn't seem good." I took a step forward, debating whether or not I should attempt to stop the fight. I wasn't sure how I would even go about it, though. The room had gotten too loud for me to shout over them, and I couldn't separate people one by one. And after careful consideration, I decided I didn't care enough to try. Mei must have reached the same conclusion because we both leaned against the wall near the door. I just needed popcorn and a Coke, and it would have been like going to the movies.

Soon enough, the Coppers started using their powers. Between the punches, kicks, and various other wrestling moves, some combatants started using human-sized tornadoes, vines that wrapped around their enemies' limbs, or giant carnivorous flowers. It was both disturbing and amazing to see all of the different powers at play. And, for a while, it remained entertaining because I could tell that no one was going for the kill. It seemed like most Coppers were letting out some steam – which was a completely unhealthy way to do it, but it seemed like therapy wasn't big on Olympus.

I even had the pleasure of witnessing Alexei throw up all over himself after he had stared for a little too long at the girl he had just wrestled to the floor. His mind must have slipped. I had a grateful thought for Hecate and her imaginative thinking regarding curses.

However, the fight became much less entertaining when I spotted the glint of metal. Shifting my attention there, I saw a girl retrieve a dagger from her boot. We usually didn't have access to weapons outside of the training area – there was some spell on the entrance that prevented anyone from leaving the arena with a weapon. And our knives for lunch and dinner weren't sharp enough to do severe damage. So, I had no idea how that girl had been able to get a foot-long dagger.

The girl wasn't currently fighting anyone, just standing on the outskirts of the pile of Coppers, looking around. I didn't know her name, but I could remember her hanging out with Elena, looking at her with stars in her eyes as if she were her own personal goddess.

Based on the look that the girl sported – bloodthirsty anticipation – she wasn't up to any good.

I saw the shift in her eyes the moment she found her prey. The girl flashed her teeth as her gaze zeroed in on the back of a guy heaving on the sideline after knocking out one of Alexei's buddies. One look and I recognized Charlie. And he was completely unaware of the danger he was in. The girl advanced behind him, the dagger in hand, her eyes wide with excitement.

I tried to call for Charlie to look out. I screamed his name, but the room was too loud for him to hear me. My legs started running in his direction before I could realize I wasn't next to Mei anymore. I ran as fast as I could. But he was far. Too far from me.

And I saw the moment the girl stabbed Charlie in the back. She must have been lucky to go right through the ribs because the move was clean, her dagger going in smoothly. A scream ripped from the kid's throat – I couldn't hear it, but I saw it on his face, and it resonated through my whole body, ringing in my bones as if I had been right next to him. I saw the moment his eyes turned wild with panic. His hand came to his chest, where the tip of the dagger had pierced through. He fell to his knees. The girl removed the blade and stabbed him a second time. Copper-colored blood poured from the first wound. His eyes turned glassy. And I was still too far.

The whole world had turned hazy around me as I ran toward Charlie. I cursed the size of the room because he was still so far. Too far. There was no way I could reach him before… before it would be too late. Still, I pushed my body to its limits, zigzagging between stray fighters and explosions of power.

I was still fifteen yards away when I saw the light disappear from Charlie's eyes. The girl was standing above him with blood splattered all over her body. And she smiled.

I hadn't been close to Charlie. We hadn't been friends. Not even friendly acquaintances. But I had felt a connection to him. We had been two outcasts here, two people who hadn't been handed the right cards in life. I had seen the desperate hope in his eyes, twin to mine. And I respected that, even at his young age, he had dared to decide to fight anyways.

Thus, seeing him lying on the floor, a pool of blood forming on the tile around his body, was heartbreaking. It made me want to make that coward girl pay for killing him without giving him a chance to fight back. She had used the unfair advantages of being armed and coming from behind to strike. And she was going to pay for it.

To be clear, I had no plan at all.

I ran until I came face to face with the girl who had taken Charlie's life. The only thing I could think to do was ram into her. I had accumulated a lot of momentum, and we both went flying. I landed on her, far enough away from Charlie's body that she couldn't reach for the weapon in his back. And then I punched her. Straight in the face. Based on the crunch and her yell, I broke her nose.

Then I punched her again. And again. She took a few seconds to recover from the shock of my attack before she started fighting back. She punched me in the ribs from below, ripping the air out of my lungs. Fighting to breathe, I pressed my left forearm on her throat and moved my weight up and to the left so that my body prevented her from using her right arm to hit me. With my right hand, I grabbed her free wrist and immobilized it to the ground. She buckled, trying to breathe and escape. But I held as strong as I could.

I had no idea how far I was ready to take this. But I knew I had to knock her out fast if I wanted to avoid meeting her power. Now that I was headed on this path, I might as well go for it.

Except the girl wasn't going to take it lying down. Because, of course, that would be way too easy. Instead, she shimmied her hands out of mine and put them on either side of me. She pushed and thrust her hips up, which made me lose my balance. I had to put my hands out to catch myself, which allowed the cold-blooded killer to escape my hold.

Suddenly I was on my back, and she was on top of me, punching me straight in the jaw. I raised my hands to protect my face, leaving my ribs open for her to hit me again. I groaned as I was forced to exhale with force. Shit. That was a terrible situation to be stuck in.

But if I had thought that it couldn't be worse, I was wrong. Because I quickly discovered that Charlie's killer had a nifty trick up her sleeve. She had freezing hands. Quite literally. Ice Queen girl put one of her hands on my chest, and it was so cold that it *burned*. In seconds, my respiratory muscles slowed down until breathing became a struggle. Panic crept in because the stream of air I could force into my lungs was becoming so small that I was getting dizzy.

I had to fight back. I couldn't just give up now. My first instincts were to fight dirty, so I went for the eyes. It must have been painful because Ice Queen screamed and released me. The cold let up just long enough for me to get her into a desperate chokehold.

And I squeezed.

I felt the moment her body became loose and unresponsive. I didn't know how long I held on, but I was terrified of letting her go, only for her to attack me again. I didn't want to kill her. But I knew damn well that if I gave her the opening to hurt me again, I wouldn't be able to defend myself anymore. By that point, pure survival instincts helped me hold on.

After some time, the cold that was still seeping from her into me depleted my strength. Soon enough, my arms couldn't keep the sustained force up, and I had to let go. I expected Ice Queen to hit me immediately, but she didn't. Instead, she laid limp on me, unconscious.

Or dead.

Gods, I hoped not. I despised and hated her for committing cold-blooded murder on Charlie, but I didn't want her dead. I didn't want to kill her. I wouldn't be able to live with myself if I did.

Still, she remained unmoving, and the only indication I had that she was – probably – still alive was the cold diffusing from her body to mine. I was slowly falling into a state of quiet panic. I knew things were not going well for me, and my body was slowly shutting down from hypothermia. Freezing to death was unavoidable if I didn't quickly move Ice Queen away from me.

Fighting against my overly stiff muscles to push Ice Queen off me took every drop of strength I had left. By the time I was done, relief was instantaneous – no more coldness was seeping into me. However, I knew I wasn't safe either.

I wasn't getting warm quickly enough.

The fighting sounded far away from me, muted by thick walls. Slowly, my vision turned dark and hazy. I couldn't prevent feeling disappointed in myself. After all, I had spent the past month training my ass off to become a skilled fighter. First real fight, and here I was. About to die. Not even during one of the trials but in the middle of the fucking cafeteria.

What a stupid way to die it'd be – frozen to death in a land that was always nicely warm.

Soon, my body was so exhausted from fighting for my life on a limited oxygen supply that I couldn't quite grasp what was happening around me anymore. For a second, I thought Makaio was right there, next to me. His eyes shone with happiness, just like every time I went skateboarding with him. And I apologized to him, even though I knew he couldn't hear me. He couldn't even remember me.

And then, right as what remained of my conscious mind wondered how long it took someone to lose consciousness from sustained hypothermia, I felt a warmth against me. I felt light, like I was flying, and heat was spreading to my side from the unknown presence.

It felt so, so nice. Like I was melting in the sun.

Until the pain came back. Sharp, terrible pain. My ribs, lungs, and jaw were burning from the hits I had taken. My whole body was in pain from the lack of oxygen and the accumulation of carbon dioxide in my muscles and tissues. And my throat was sore from being squeezed by the girl I'd somehow beaten, but not before she'd turned me into an ice cube.

After a long time, I regained enough body awareness to realize I wasn't floating. I was in someone's arms. That someone was walking. And that someone was also the source of the heat that had felt so nice.

It took me a hell of a lot of strength to open my eyelids. And when I did, I found myself face to face – or face to neck, really – with Archer Vasilias. Somehow, he must have felt my gaze on him because he looked down. He didn't smile. He didn't break our eye contact. His arms flexed so that I came closer to him. I blamed the injuries as the reason why I cuddled deeper into him.

"Why is it that whenever I leave you alone, you get beat up, Mayfield?"

"I don't know, Sunshine. I guess I like the danger." My words were a painful croak.

Archer chuckled softly at his nickname. He always said he didn't like it, but I thought it was oddly fitting. And I knew that, deep down, he enjoyed it. "I might have to look over you more closely then."

"Looking forward to it," I deadpanned before closing my eyes again.

Chapter Twenty-One

I was in a ton of pain the following day. It felt like a freight train had driven over me multiple times. Sleep hadn't come easily, so I also felt like I hadn't slept in years. And I was still very much ashamed of how I'd barely won and almost died.

My mood thus wasn't the best when I walked out for the dress fitting.

Mei and Sadie had shown up in my room too early for my taste and dragged me to where the clothing torture would happen. Mei had somehow managed to book a seamstress for two hours and was extra giddy, talking my ear off with what outfits she hoped for.

As for me? I was too busy shuffling around on sore baby giraffe legs to think about which color would fit my skin tone best.

"Archer whisked you away before I could check on you last night. How are you feeling?" Sadie asked, concern lacing her words.

I couldn't help thinking about the night before. About Archer. About being in his arms. He had cleaned up the blood on my face with a damp towel. He had been so gentle. It had made my bruised heart beat a little too hard. The whole thing had been a silent affair. He hadn't said anything or scolded me for being so dumb. I hadn't uttered a word either, still too raw from everything that had happened.

Archer had closed his eyes as he helped me change into fresh clothes. Then he had put me to bed, ensuring I was tucked under the covers. And I had spent the following hours listening to his regular and soft breaths as he slept. I hadn't fallen asleep for a long time, stuck somewhere between awake and reliving the evening events.

"I've been better. But I'll make it through. Nothing's broken."

Sadie nodded softly. "I'm sorry we couldn't be here earlier."

"It's not your fault. I'm the one who made the stupid decision to attack someone armed and had lethal power. I'm just glad you guys could help me out at the end there."

"I mean, I didn't do much. Archer took care of Maeve, and Søren helped heat you back up."

Her name was Maeve then. I expected something a little more dangerous sounding. "Is she still…" I didn't finish my question, but Sadie understood.

"No. But it wasn't because of you. She woke up as Søren was warming you up and then tried to attack us. Archer dealt with her and might have gone a little overboard with the pain. There were four other casualties, though. No one paid much attention to us, so we shouldn't get into too much trouble."

Five people had died. Five. From something that had started out looking like a fight in a sitcom. I couldn't believe that it had been so deadly. One of them had been Charlie. And I could easily have been a sixth body.

It took me a while to process that new information. There were only thirty-five of us left. Thirty-four Coppers were still alive. And me. We were already killing each other off and were still three days out from the first Trial.

Before I could ask for any information on who exactly had died, Mei stopped us before a door richly decorated and clapped her hands in excitement. "Here we are, besties! Let's rock and roll!"

Praying to the gods that I would survive with my sanity intact, I followed in Mei and Sadie's footsteps. Inside, the room had become a full-out dressing room. There were racks and racks of clothes, colorful garments everywhere my eye could see. A whole wall was dedicated, floor to ceiling, to hundreds of shoes. It was quite impressive. I had never seen so many clothes in one place.

A petite woman stood in the middle of the room next to a round pedestal. She was smaller than me. Which was a feat, seeing as most people on Olympus had at least a foot on me. But this lady was very short and had strong curves. She also seemed to be in her mid to late fifties – strange seeing as many deities and Golden decided to stop aging much younger. She looked like a mini version of the fairy godmother in Cinderella – how fitting for her job.

"Hello, ladies! My name is Honora, daughter of Hestia, goddess of the home, earth, and domestic life. I will be your seamstress this morning to prepare you for the Opening Ceremony." Honora had a melodic voice, full of enthusiasm. I could already tell that she and Mei would get along just fine.

We each introduced ourselves, albeit without sharing our parentage. I didn't because she probably didn't care that my parents were Nicole Mayfield, waitress, and Keanu Hale, deceased surfer. And my two friends decided not to share either, although I wasn't sure why.

"Great, now who wants to start?" Honora had barely finished that Mei was jumping forward onto the pedestal. Ensued an eternity watching Mei try on dress after dress. She had decided on a "gold for victory" theme for us to follow, so the dresses she tried on were waterfall after waterfall of varying golden materials.

I had imagined something like those exclusive Galas where celebrities wore extravagant outfits. The dresses that Honora presented to Mei were different from the type of outfits that high-end actresses would wear on a red carpet. The dresses were modern versions of the robes the Goddesses wore millennia ago.

The dress that Mei decided upon was a beautiful gold, with threads of silver peeking through. It had a mermaid cut, one-shouldered, with a solid gold pin holding the right shoulder. A slit ran through the side, allowing her leg to slide out all the way to her thigh as she moved.

Honora spent surprisingly little time fitting the dress to fit Mei's body perfectly. It was impressive because she didn't even touch the needles. They floated around her, zipping where she wanted them to go in a complicated dance.

Then it was Sadie's turn. The blond Copper decided on a dark blue dress with a thick golden strip around the waist that complimented her eyes. The shape looked amazing on her endless legs, and the color suited her tan skin tone and light hair very well. She looked radiant in it.

When it was finally my turn to step onto the pedestal, I was both ready to be done and nervous. I had never really worn the fancy dresses that Honora had brought today. Mom had never had the kind of money that could afford a fancy dress for prom or homecoming. I had gone thrift shopping for dresses and had used some old outfits that one of our neighbors, Mrs. Lopez, had used for her older daughters. They were cute but not tailored to my body or made of the most beautiful silks.

I was also nervous because I had no idea what I wanted. No idea what color would be best. Would wearing a specific color be rude to the gods? Should I get an outfit that made me look like more of a Copper, or should I go for something that could be passed as human? Something that screamed fierce or something that was subdued so I would be lost in the crowd? Did it matter?

The rumors about me being a mortal had not spread to the participants yet, which was extremely strange. The twins, Archer, and I had expected that at least some Coppers would have contacts with their parents, who would have learned this information from their connections throughout Olympus. But no. No one had even breathed a word to me about my parentage. To everyone, I was still the empath that barely had any power.

But now that we were going to a party where all the gods and goddesses would be present, I was scared that the information would come out. And I was worried about the other participants' reactions, especially after what had happened in the cafeteria the night before.

I didn't want to attract attention. But at the same time, if I lost control of the narrative, if everyone found out that I wasn't one of them, then I wanted to be able to control everything else. I wanted people to know that I wasn't afraid.

Thus, a lot was potentially riding on this outfit.

Honora stared at me for a minute, slowly walking around me and examining my body from every angle. It took so long that I had to control myself not to squirm uncomfortably under her gaze.

"I am thinking something light and airy, like the breeze over the ocean and the soft brilliance of a winter sun." Honora moved her hands in big gestures as if she could see said breeze. I was confused. What kind of dress represented the wind and the light of the sun? Not something I had ever worn, that was for sure.

"Hm... sure? What does that look like exactly?"

"My dear, prepare to be amazed! Enchanted! Dare I say, flabbergasted!"

Oh. Well, then. I was getting more curious by the second to see what the small but mighty Golden lady had in store for me.

She had barely finished speaking that she was already whipping around the room, sing to herself as she searched for what I assumed were dresses that fit her very abstract vision. All the while, I expected her to start singing 'Bibbidi bobbidi boo' any second.

She returned to me with only one dress on her arm. Surprising, seeing as Mei and Sadie had tried on at least fifteen and ten dresses, respectively.

"I have the perfect garment for you, young lady." Without waiting for my comment, Honora flicked her hands, and a glittery mist floated around me, blocking my body from view as tiny fabric butterflies floated the dress over to me and forcibly helped me put it on. The whole process looked cool from the outside, but it was unbelievable how strong those little things were as they brought my arms up and down, removed my clothes, and put on the dress.

As fast as it had started, the mist and fabric butterflies disappeared. There was a mirror right in front of the pedestal, and as I looked, I almost couldn't recognize myself. The girl in the mirror looked regal. The dress was white, with an ombre going to light blue toward the bottom of the dress. It went to the ground, falling in soft waves away from my body. The bust was tighter, with gold tresses outlining the bottom of my breasts and the bottom of my ribs. The fabric, white and soft silk, bunched to come over my shoulders before turning into a drape that came around my waist on the right and over my front before it attached to my left shoulder using a beautiful gold pin. I couldn't see it very well from its position next to my neck, but the pin looked like a sun. The rest of the material draped over my bare back, tingling against my skin.

It was beautiful. And I could see what Honora had meant about the whole breeze and sunlight metaphor. The dress was airy and feathery light around my legs, moving with my body but never clinging too hard on my skin. And the white to light blue ombre showed off the vibrant but cold colors of the wintery mornings when there weren't any clouds and the sun was out – illuminating the world but not warming it up.

The longer I stared at myself, the more I felt like a powerful and fierce woman. Maybe not a Copper, but this outfit made me feel proud of myself and my journey – proud of my ruby-red blood.

"It's gorgeous, K. You're gorgeous," Sadie exclaimed softly, a hand over her heart.

Mei agreed and added something about how Archer would fall over himself when he saw it. But I couldn't rip my eyes away from the mirror image of myself. How could a simple dress – however amazing – make me look so different from my usual self?

"What do you think? Does your heart sing and fly in this dress?"

I looked at Honora, ripping my gaze from the mirror, and nodded. It did. My heart did soar in this dress. I felt beautiful and sexy and capable of anything. I felt strong in a way that I had been hunting for since I had landed on Olympus.

"It's the one." It felt like saying yes to a wedding dress with how my heartbeat accelerated at the words. But it might be just as important as a wedding dress was to most people – the Opening Ceremony would be the symbol of the start of a new life. This dress would be my armor when confronting the beginning of the rest of my life.

Chapter Twenty-Two

Today was the day. The big day, when all the training and weeks of getting myself ready would end. Tonight was the Opening Ceremony for a Tournament I had minimal odds of surviving. A Tournament that would be determining for the rest of my life – quite literally.

And, tonight, I had to impress. I had to prove I was a part of this world even though most people on Olympus would never accept my kind – mortals – anywhere close to them.

I was putting on a show tonight. I was going to pretend like I had become a Copper. Pretend I was just as strong and confident as any of the other participants, no matter what information came out. The color of my blood didn't dictate my worth.

Perhaps if I repeated it enough, it would become true.

Sadie and Mei were getting ready behind me, ranting about what Søren and Archer had decided to wear – the leather armor, of course. Both were annoyed at the lack of fashion sense the guys had and wondered why they kept refusing to wear nice clothes.

Besides making the right noises at the right times, I was focused on perfecting my outfit. I had never spent so much time getting ready before, but today felt important. I wanted my appearance to be perfect, to not show any cracks or chinks. The dress would definitely help, but I still had to work on the make-up. Thankfully,

Sadie had somehow managed to get me some make-up items from Earth.

Thank the gods for that because I had no idea how to use the weird color-changing powders and animated brushes.

Foundation. Concealer. Bronzer. Highlighter. Blush. Eyeshadow. Lipstick. I had gone all out and was currently slightly fighting off my eyeliner. Managing to get both sides even was always a struggle.

"What are you doing, K?" Sadie asked when I finally let out a satisfied sound.

"As the queen said, I'm trying to 'draw the cat eye sharp enough to kill a man.'"

"The Queen of England?"

I laughed at the image that Sadie's words conjured in my mind. I'd pay money to see the Queen of England put on eyeliner. "No, I don't think Elizabeth II wears eyeliner or makes poetry about it."

"Then who is the queen?"

I raised an eyebrow at her. "Taylor Swift, of course."

Mei started to sing one of Taylor Swift's most famous songs, and I joined in with a laugh. Sadie smiled, but she didn't even hum along, and not for the first time, I wondered how she couldn't know some of the most famous pop songs of the past few years. She loved old rock, sure, but no one could grow up in the twenty-first century and ignore Taylor Swift's biggest hits.

We were still laughing and in as high of a mood as possible when we stepped out of the room. I had managed to draw my eyeliner sharp as hell, and with the final touch of mascara, I felt ready to fend off all of my enemies. Mostly.

"Damn, you girls are on fire!" Søren even catcalled his girlfriend, and she squealed in delight as she almost ran to him. He tried to kiss her, but she tutted and turned his face until he kissed her cheek instead.

"You can't kiss me! You'll ruin my make-up!"

I didn't focus too much on the happy couple, though. Instead, my eyes were attracted like a magnet to Archer. I had been expecting an ugly armor, but the outfit that Archer wore was nothing if not good-looking. His body was covered in leather from shoulders to ankles, and the material was tight enough to show off his lean muscles. Metal parts were woven on his torso to protect the most vital organs, and multiple daggers were strapped around his waist and thighs.

He looked mouthwateringly good.

And I was having a really hard time removing my attention from how strong his body looked in the leathery outfit.

"You clean up nice, Mayfield." His voice brought chills to my entire body. Based on the self-assured smirk that appeared on his face, he must have seen it.

"Careful, Sunshine. It almost sounds like you are complimenting me."

"Stars, I love that nickname, right Sunshine?" Sadie taunted with a laugh in Archer's direction. He gave her the middle finger, prompting her to laugh harder.

The sibling-like argument they started had at least one good point – it gave me time to get myself under control. I spent almost a minute reminding myself that Archer was not for me to drool over. He was my friend. My fake boyfriend. And that's all he would ever be. He and I made no sense. And he didn't like me that way – I knew that all too well.

I just needed my body to understand that critical piece of information.

"Are we ready to go?" Søren looked at me curiously, making me realize that everyone had started walking already, and I had remained frozen in place.

Shaking my head in the hopes that it would help clear it of all of the unwanted thoughts that lived within it, I followed in the steps of my friends.

We all had this weird, electric energy flowing through us. Part of it was excitation at the prospect of the party – meeting the gods and goddesses was no small feat – part of it was nervous anticipation of the Tournament starting tomorrow, and the rest was worrying over everything that could go wrong during this party. And there was a lot of the latter.

One of those potential bombs was that Mei still didn't know about my non-existent powers and very human parents. It wasn't per se that I or the others didn't trust her, more that she loved to gossip, and we didn't want the information to slip out without her even noticing it. Plus, it had been so long already that it would be awkward to broach the topic now.

But the fact was that she would probably learn that information tonight, along with dozens of Coppers that I was meant to fight against in the Tournament.

I didn't know how she would react. I wished I had dared to tell her before the party, but I had been a coward and preferred to spend the past few days having as much fun as possible.

Now that we were approaching the party, I felt a lump in my throat growing and growing. I had gotten to like Mei and her quirks and her infectious smiles. She was fun. I had gotten to know her well in the past couple of weeks, and I didn't want our friendship to end on a bad note.

"You seem stressed, Mayfield. It's unbecoming of you."

I gave Archer an annoyed glance. This was a really constructive comment, thank you very much. And, per usual, he looked cool as a cucumber, which exasperated me – a lot.

"Oh, come on, I didn't mean it like that. You seem a lot tenser than usual. It's not going to be as bad as you think."

"I don't need empty reassurances, Archer."

"I don't deal in empty promises. You know that. I'll make sure everything ends up fine." Then he gave a pointed look and added, "I promise."

I stared into his eyes for a few seconds, long enough to see that he was dead serious. Knowing that I had Archer Vasilias in my corner was nice, there was no denying that. But I'd be damned if I let him see how grateful I was for his words and presence. So, I nodded stiffly and turned back to focus on the walk.

We were heading to a portal that would transport us to the party's site. It was a similar process to what the Hunter-guy had done to take me from my front door on Earth to Olympus, just more stable and capable of transporting more people. I was slightly nervous about the whole travel-through-space thing, but the twins had assured me it was 'a lot of fun.' Obviously, it hadn't helped.

The portal had been opened by one of Hermes's daughters in the Pit. When we arrived at the arena, I couldn't help but be completely amazed by the ten-foot-high swirling mass of purple and blue floating silently above the sand. Some Coppers walked straight in and disappeared. Poof. Just like that, they were gone. It was like watching one of those fantasy or superhero movies – it looked completely impossible and otherworldly.

Mei and Søren were still talking excitedly as we stepped into the line. A few groups of Coppers were before us, and I had plenty of time to observe the process. It was quite simple. You just had to walk straight into the portal. Who wouldn't have wanted to experience what platform 9 ¾ was like? But still, as the line dwindled to nothing and we were next, I had to take deep breaths to calm my galloping heart.

Sadie went right through, followed by Søren and Mei. And then the portal was right before me, looking imposing and intimidating.

"It's going to be alright, Mayfield. You just walk in and don't stop. Stop thinking about it too much; you're giving me a headache."

"Archer Vasilias, ever the great teacher, aren't y-" I stopped short because he stepped through with a chuckle, and I was left alone.

Someone grumbled behind me about it taking too long. And, yeah, I was holding up the line. Sure. But I needed a couple more seconds.

I took one step forward, the portal only a few feet away. The swirling colors within were almost hypnotizing. So beautiful. One step. A soft sound came from the portal, as if someone was inside, singing a lullaby and calling for me.

One step. There was static electricity coming from the moving mass. I could feel it on my skin, on my hair.

One step. I was so close that barely a few inches separated me from the unknown.

One step.

My leg went right through the portal, followed by the rest of my body. I didn't stop. I didn't slow. I just kept going forward. Going through the portal felt like getting into a perfectly warm bath, followed by the feeling of being on a roller-coaster right as it first accelerated.

And then it was over.

The portal spat me out, and I stumbled, barely managing to remain upright.

Once I had my balance under control, I looked up to find the most beautiful place I had ever been to. We were in the middle of what looked like an exotic garden. The clearing was surrounded by thick trees with big leaves, vines falling from their branches, and colorful flowers. I could see bright-colored birds and small animals in the trees and bushes – none of them looked anything like what we had on Earth. Above us, the sky was the beautiful blue of a clear summer day.

And the party itself did not disappoint either. There was a small orchestra in one corner, playing a captivating melody. Servers walked through the crowd with platters full of small appetizers and flutes filled with a golden liquid – ambrosia. There were fairy lights all around the place, floating above the guests' heads and making the scene look enchanted.

And the guests.

The guests were some of the most beautiful people I had ever seen. Coppers were usually gorgeous. But deities? Gods and goddesses were something else, with perfect bodies and an inside glow that rendered them magnetic. Their clothes were like spun moonlight and sunlight, shining like jewels. Their outfits were extravagant, luxurious, and, sometimes, more revealing than propriety would allow on Earth. It was almost impossible to look away from them.

I had forgotten how impressive Zeus, Artemis, and Athena had been when I first met them. Or maybe I had been too out of it to really pay attention. But being surrounded by all of these deities in their nicest clothes made me feel small and insignificant. And I understood why the Ancient Greeks had worshipped them.

They were the perfect versions of humans. Or humans were flawed versions of these gods. Either way, I almost felt uncomfortable while staring dumbfounded at them. They were so impressive that I thought I shouldn't be allowed to look at them for this long.

My poor little human mind was overwhelmed by the view. How was it even possible that I was standing in the same place as literal gods and goddesses? How were we breathing the same air? And how in the world had my life changed this much?

"They might look impressive but trust me; the gods are closer to mortals than you probably imagine." Archer's deep voice was like an electroshock, bringing me out of my amazement.

"Archer! You can't say that!" Sadie gave Archer a meaningful look as if he should have known better. Was Olympus a regime where citizens couldn't criticize their leaders?

"It's not like I am screaming blasphemy around; you can calm down, Aska. I'm just saying that where it matters most, the gods aren't the perfect beings they portray here."

I raised my eyebrow in surprise at Archer's use of Sadie's last name. He meant business. Sadie shook her head, clearly not happy with Archer's words. He raised an eyebrow, daring her to contradict him. She didn't, but she gave him a look that said to shut up quickly. Shrugging, Archer put a hand over my shoulders and drove me away from the fuming Sadie.

"Anyways, as I was saying, this is all a show to intimidate us before the Tournament. To put stars in our eyes and prompt us to fight to our death to reach their world." He was whispering in my ear as he drove us through the people. "It's all manipulation if you ask me."

A waiter passed us, and Archer grabbed two flutes, giving one to me. "Don't drink this too fast. It'll taste like your favorite drink, whether alcoholic or not. But they usually spike it with alcohol, so it'll get you drunk very fast."

Good advice, for once. Curious about the famous drink, I took a tiny sip. Immediately, the taste of Coke filled my mouth. The bubbly drink had always been a favorite for the whole Mayfield household, and we would celebrate significant accomplishments with a can. We didn't have it often, but I'd used some of my tips several times to buy a pack of six cans. Tasting it now filled me with hundreds of good memories, and I closed my eyes to appreciate it.

I could understand why ambrosia was so coveted — it tasted exactly like my favorite memories.

Eyes closed, I took a second to take it all in. Archer's arm on my shoulders. The taste of perfectly fresh Coke in my mouth. The heady scent of the flowers surrounding the clearing and the stormy scent that Archer always carried with him. The melody surrounding us was so beautiful it brought tears to my eyes if I focused too long on it — as if the music reached into my chest and squeezed all of my repressed emotions out of me.

It felt like I was living someone else's life. Someone who went to fancy parties and wore luxurious dresses and drank expensive drinks. Someone who could walk with a handsome man on their arm without questions. Someone who was someone. Someone important and someone who fit in.

I liked it a little too much.

Because I knew that none of this was real — at least not my reality. I'd never be the kind of girl who could fit in with a crowd of Coppers, Goldens, and Deities.

But, for one night, I could pretend.

Chapter Twenty-Three

The beginning of the party went well, so much so that I started to think the worries that had plagued me for the past few days had been entirely unwarranted.

I drank ambrosia. I ate the fancy little appetizers – I couldn't recognize any of them, but they were better than anything I had eaten before, as would food suitable for the gods be. I even danced with Sadie and Mei to one of the more upbeat songs.

It was fun. The most fun I'd had in weeks, months, maybe years.

By the time I had a nice buzz, I had forgotten everything that had worried me before I had stepped through the portal. I forgot about the five Coppers who had been killed days ago. I forgot about the first Trial starting the next day. I forgot about someone revealing I was human during the party. I forgot about the risk that Mei might discover I had lied to her for weeks, along with her boyfriend and friends. I forgot about my almost death. I forgot about Elena, Alexei, and Nathan almost abusing and killing me. I even forgot about Makaio and whether he was doing okay.

I forgot everything. Ambrosia made me stupidly happy, and it felt glorious.

So, when Zeus stood, looking regal as ever, on a raised platform and asked for our attention, I didn't worry. I was too far past that already.

"Fellow Olympians, gods, goddesses, Goldens, resident Coppers, and of course, Tournament participants, welcome to yet another edition of the Tournament Opening Ceremony." Zeus's voice boomed through the space as if we were in an amphitheater, not in the middle of the forest. Polite claps came from all around me, but neither I nor my friends joined in. Not necessarily because I didn't want to, but I didn't know the proper etiquette, and by the time I got ready to join the movement, Zeus was speaking again.

"Thank you all for coming tonight to participate in the celebration of another community event starting tomorrow. I also want to extend my appreciation to Dionysus, who never ceases to amaze us with his soirees."

There was more clapping, even a couple of whoops, but I was too busy looking at the god in question to join in. Standing to the stage's side, he accepted the thanks with apparent grace. Dionysus was an average-height guy – at least by godly standards – with a hippie look. Long brown hair, fashionably unkempt beard, baggy clothes including a shirt with a flower print, and round yellow-tinted glasses. He was probably the least intimidating of the gods and goddesses I had met so far, but that could have been because I was waiting for him to whip out a "peace and love" sign any second.

"Before we continue the celebrations, I would like to say a word of wisdom dedicated to our dear children and grandchildren who are set to start the one hundred and forty-sixth edition of the Tournament tomorrow." He paused dramatically, his gaze going through the crowd until he found where most participants had gathered. "Dear Coppers, remember that by proving your worth in the arena, you are making us proud and strengthening our community. Whether you are chosen to walk our sacred mountain or not, your hard work and sacrifices will be honored for generations."

The crowd cheered as if the Tournament was a sports competition. As if we weren't about to risk our lives because some deities and Goldens couldn't keep it in their pants.

"Now, I would like to invite my dear daughter Artemis, as the main sponsor and gamemaster of this year's event, to come up and say a word of encouragement." Zeus moved back a step, his white toga and golden sash swooshing around him and glimmering in the light. Under yet more applause, Artemis walked up the steps to join the king of the gods on stage.

Just like the first time I had seen her, Artemis was a study in gold – everything about her, from her hair to her skin, to her eyes and clothes, was in shades of gold. It even made Mei's dress look bland. She didn't look strange, though. She was glowing in both appearance and power. Compared to last time, she had a huge wooden bow and a quiver full of red feathered arrows strapped to her back.

"Good evening. I am honored to sponsor this year's one hundred and forty-sixth edition of the Tournament." Artemis sounded anything but honored, her voice showing as much enthusiasm as someone going to get their wisdom teeth removed. "I believe this edition will be filled with spectacle, feats of magic, and strength and will reveal some of the best Coppers we have had in generations."

The goddess stopped for a beat, letting the people cheer. I was too busy holding my breath in apprehension as Hecate's warnings cycled in my mind. She had said that Artemis had revealed my very human heritage during a previous semi-private gathering. I hoped she had gotten tired of her feud with Hecate since then.

"I am also very proud to be sponsoring the first completely inclusive edition of the Tournament. Indeed, this year we are pleased to welcome a courageous human who has decided to throw her lot in to earn a spot among the gods and goddesses of Olympus." With a hand pointing in my direction and a winning look, she exclaimed, "Please throw a round of applause for Kalani Mayfield."

Fuck.

The crowd had been trigger-happy on the claps so far, but now the clearing was dead silent. I could feel hundreds of eyes on me, burning my skin with the intensity of their glares. Suddenly the armor of my dress and make-up seemed like a flimsy sheet of paper against their anger. I also wished my friends and I had happened to be farther away from the rest of the Coppers, who would be our adversaries.

As they were grasping the meaning of the bomb that Artemis had just launched, I could tell my competitors were going from incomprehension to pure anger. I knew the line of thought they were going through – if I managed to survive, I would take the spot of a Copper meant to live on Olympus amongst deities and their descendants. A mere human did not deserve the consideration or honor of being in the Tournament. I was lesser than them. Thus, I deserved to go back with my people or die.

I had spent long enough dreading this announcement that I had gone through dozens of different scenarios. Artemis telling everyone straight up and naming me so blatantly was not one of them. Now I felt supremely unprepared.

"Wait, Lane," Mei touched my shoulder so that I'd look at her. The crowd was starting to get loud with chatter and hollering about how this – me – was unacceptable. But everything faded when I saw the look of betrayal on Mei's face. "This isn't true, right? You're an empath. You even used your powers on me a few times."

I didn't know what to say. I didn't know how to make it better. Because my "powers" had only been simple body language and facial expression analyses. I'd made a few lucky guesses. I'd played the part in this little game that the twins, Archer, and I had concocted.

And I had lied, lied, and lied some more. By the time I felt like I trusted Mei, it had already been over a month. I had chickened out on telling her because I was scared of her reaction. Søren must have felt the same because he didn't insist we tell his girlfriend. Somehow, I had hoped that I would be able to fake it till the end. That our little charade would never be uncovered.

Here I was, though.

The only human in the middle of a party filled with gods and their descendants. And now they knew. Everybody knew.

Including Mei.

I had nothing to say to defend myself. Because it was true. I had kept it hidden as well as I could over the past six weeks, but my blood was pure crimson. Not a drop of ichor there.

I opened my mouth to say something, anything, but nothing came out. My mouth was dry as a desert, and no words would form on my tongue. Mei saw it. She knew, without hearing the confirmation, that everything was true.

She turned to Søren, who was standing next to her. He had gone unnaturally still, knowing full well that it was coming for him too. The betrayal, the anger, the denial. "Did you know?" Her voice shook, barely a whisper. But we heard, even among the increasingly loud voices around us.

"I… Mei, look, we had to, we needed to pro-"

"Did all of you know?" Mei didn't even let her boyfriend finish before she asked Sadie and Archer. They didn't answer, visibly uncomfortable, but their silence was answer enough.

Søren opened his mouth to say something, but Mei cut him short with a hand up. She had a low laugh, but it was everything if not joyous. It translated into a mixture of shock and disbelief, of pain and sadness. Of mistrust.

"I don't even want to hear it, Søren." Her voice was sharp, nothing of her usual excitedness present. And hearing his real name – not the sweet nicknames she usually gave him – was like a slap to Søren. "Were you ever going to tell me?"

The question was directed at me. I wished it hadn't been. I might have been a coward, but I wished she could have asked the question to anyone else but me. I had to take responsibility for my actions, though.

"I almost did, I promise. But I was scared of hurting you." This was as much truth as I could give her. It didn't help.

Mei scoffed at my answer. I didn't need to be an empath to feel how deep the betrayal and disappointment ran. "I think you all did pretty well to make sure that I would get hurt. Great job." Then she turned around and left.

We all stood there for a couple of seconds, unsure of how everything had gone to shit so fast. Then the clock started running again. Søren left with a rapid excuse, running after his girlfriend. Then it was just me, Sadie, and Archer. And a party full of people who had clearly decided I didn't belong there.

From somewhere behind me, I could hear Hecate — and was it Athena? — try to reason with the more vocal gods, goddesses, and Goldens. I couldn't quite hear what they were saying over the commotion, but I hoped they were able to get things back under control.

On the side of the Coppers, though, things were tense as hell. After all, it was one of their spots on Mount Olympus that I was going for. Something that they had no choice but to fight for. The thing was, I didn't have much of a choice either. It was either fight in the Tournament or be executed because of someone else's mistake. And, on top of terribly missing my family, I wanted to reach the age where I could legally get drunk in America.

I didn't know what grabbed my attention, but I shifted slightly to the right to find Elena looking straight at me. And the look she had on her face? It was the look of a predator seeing its prey helpless and ready to be eaten.

One sentence from Artemis and I had become a meal.

"Come on. We should go back to the compound." Archer's voice didn't have its usual effect on me. I was too frazzled, too ungrounded to get distracted by him.

"I'll go first. You watch her back," Sadie said with what was probably meant to be a reassuring tone. She didn't fool anyone, though. There were many people to go through if we wanted to reach the portal, which meant plenty of opportunities for the situation to continue to go south.

We started walking, and while no one became physically violent toward me, there were plenty of insults thrown my way. I also knew that the mob mentality could make people say and do things they wouldn't usually say or do. I did my best to ignore them — I knew I wasn't the less-than-nothing they were painting me as. But still, it hurt. I hadn't been friends with all of these Coppers, far from it, but I had never been mean to them. I had always tried to be cordial, gave out a smile when we made eye contact, and never made fun of someone for their powers or combat abilities.

But things changed. Fast.

I had lost control of the narrative. Lost control over my image.

And all of that the day before the first Trial.

Going through the portal was a relief. My feet hitting the sand of the Pit almost brought tears to my eyes. And the happy buzz was decidedly gone.

"It'll be alright, Mayfield. We'll figure it out."

I nodded at Archer's words even though I didn't believe him. Now that everyone knew I was human, my position in the Tournament had gone from shaky to insanely precarious. I knew damn well that the other participants would no longer hesitate to go for the kill. The pure anger and disdain they felt for me, the entitlement they had over us mere humans… it would certainly overthrow any fear they had of Archer or the twins beating them up.

I wasn't Archer Vasilias's weak girlfriend anymore.

I was the human who dared to play in the world of the gods. The human they had to squash down and exterminate.

Chapter Twenty-Four

The early morning had been silent. I remained in the room until the very last moment. I hadn't eaten breakfast, but my stomach was so knotted up that I was sure I would throw up if I tried to eat anything.

Archer didn't say a word either as we got ready. There wasn't much to say anyway. Shit had hit the fan during the party. Hard. Like we thought it would. And now I debated whether I should hide in the bedroom until the end of time.

None of us knew what the first Trial would be, so I opted to wear something I could fight in easily but would still protect me from the elements. I had heard from Søren that, a couple of editions ago, one of the Trials had consisted of surviving in a frozen tundra without water, food, or shelter for forty-eight hours. With my luck, we would probably have to do something like that. So, to prepare to the best of my abilities, I wore black leggings with a tight thermal shirt and a grey zip-up sweatshirt. I didn't have anything that could be used as a protective piece of armor, so I hoped that I would at least get a shield if we were to fight each other or mythical beasts.

"How are you?" Archer's voice sliced the dense silence after so long that I almost jumped in surprise. I finished lacing the sneakers Sadie had given me – I had to wear two pairs of socks to make them fit – before answering.

"I'm up. Not crying or freaking out. It'll have to be good enough."

It was true. All things considered, I was surprisingly calm in the wake of the first Trial. We were not even half an hour away from the start, and while my stomach was clenched, my breathing was still steady, my mind crystal clear. Either my body hadn't quite realized what was coming yet, or my training had done its job.

I looked up in my roommate's direction for the first time since I had gone to the bathroom after waking up. He wore an outfit similar to the one from the night before, without the fancy gold belts and accessories. He looked like he was going to the battlefield, while I could've gone to Target in my outfit. Oh well. Can't win them all.

I didn't allow my eyes to wander on his body – I needed to stay focused, and looking at him for too long would be counterproductive. Instead, I brought my eyes up to meet his. The blue of his irises looked darker than usual, almost like the deep ocean below a stormy sky.

"You're going to be alright, Mayfield."

I raised an eyebrow at his words. "Did you get in the business of empty promises overnight, Sunshine?"

"Stop being a smartass." He took a couple of steps forward until he was close enough to put one of his gigantic hands on my shoulder. He squeezed once. "The twins and I will do everything we can to make sure you survive. And you have trained harder than all of these idiots. You're ready."

It was surprisingly pleasant to hear these words from him. He had been a good teacher in the past six weeks but wasn't the most generous with compliments. The simple "you're ready" meant a lot – it said he had faith in me.

I didn't answer – there was a lump of emotion in my throat – but I nodded my thanks. Those thanks were not only for the words of encouragement but also for all the weeks when he had believed in me and trained me to survive. I might have hated most of our practice sessions, but I knew damn well that they had changed me.

And if I had a chance of surviving today and the next two weeks, it was because of them. Because of him.

Seemingly happy with what he could see on my face, Archer decreed that it was time to go. As I passed through the door, I gave one last look at the room. I refused to think it could be the last time I'd see it. I had to remain positive, not think of all the things that could go wrong. For that same reason, I refused to allow myself to look at pictures of Makaio. I did not need photos because I'd see him again. I would. And today was the first step in doing just that.

Walking through the compound was mostly a blur. When we arrived in the side room next to the Pit, there were already dozens of Coppers waiting. Most were silent, deep in thought, or fighting off anxiety. I heard a couple of people talking animatedly about something random – a debate over their favorite superhero movie, maybe – but I could tell they were trying to distract themselves from the thought of what was coming.

Sadie and Søren were already there, waiting for us in one corner of the room. As we crossed through, I looked around for any sign or hint of what the Trial would be like. There was nothing apparent. The room was big enough to fit all forty of us – thirty-five now – but was dreadfully bare. Just rocks and the smell of fear.

I felt the looks that the other participants gave me as I walked behind Archer. I could feel their hostility and hatred. It felt like dozens of needles prickling and burning my skin. I didn't cower, though. So what if I was a human? I hadn't had any more choice in coming here than they did. And I would fight just like them. May the best win.

The twins looked awfully relaxed for people who would have to fight for their lives in the next half hour. I wasn't surprised; the Askas always had that chill and confident attitude that made them so captivating.

"How are the lovebirds doing on this beautiful morning?" Søren exclaimed with too much glee for how early it was – and for the first day of the Tournament. Plus, I didn't want to be reminded of the whole fake dating game we played together. Archer and I's PDA hadn't been anything more than holding hands and some light cuddles since the almost-kiss incident a few weeks back. Still, I didn't want to be reminded of the pretense we had going on. I needed to focus on the trial, not how Archer's lips had felt next to mine.

I rolled my eyes at Søren's self-satisfied grin. From the corner of my eyes, I caught the tail end of Archer giving a cold, hard look of disapproval and annoyance in his friend's direction. See, even he was annoyed at the reminder that he was fake dating me.

"Ignore Søren. Battles get him excited. That worries me sometimes." Sadie came up and gave me a one-armed hug. "Are you ready to kick some ass?"

"I was born ready!" This was a bit of a stretch, but pretending I was overly confident seemed the best course of action.

Sadie laughed but didn't comment on my very obviously feigned confidence. I was going for a "fake it till you make it" type strategy where – if I reminded myself enough times that I could make it, then I would.

From behind me, I heard the very distinct "you're dead, dirty whore" thrown my way. I tensed but didn't turn around. I recognized the voice of Nathan, Alexei's friend. If the hateful group of Coppers wanted to rattle me and bring me down, they'd need more than a cheap insult – especially one I had heard more than once while bartending.

When I looked up, I found Archer glaring at a point behind my head. I didn't have to turn to know he was staring Nathan down. And Archer's facial expression was downright chilling. Murderous. I wasn't at the end of the look and still felt slightly uncomfortable like I should apologize or scurry away in fear.

"Archer, it's fine," I whispered while putting a hand on his forearm. I didn't need a knight in shining armor – at least not at that very moment. "I've heard worse before. Just ignore him."

That little muscle kept popping in my fake boyfriend's cheek as he ground his jaws together. I thought he wouldn't listen to me – Archer had become oddly protective sometimes, increasingly so as the weeks went by. But he broke eye contact and turned his back on me to talk with Søren without saying a word to me.

"He's worried about the impact Artemis' speech might have." Sadie's tone was apologetic as if she could feel the tiny crunch my heart felt when he didn't acknowledge me.

"It's fine. I know he only wants what's best for me. You all do." Crossing my arms over my chest, I tried my best to show that I didn't care. And I didn't. I really didn't. I had way more important things to think about than Archer being protective and blatantly ignoring me. "And I am sure it'll be fine. People will forget about the color of my blood once we are all deep in the Trial."

Sadie acquiesced with a hum, probably not wanting to tell me that it was highly improbable that the other competitors wouldn't put a target on my back. We both needed to believe things would go okay.

I was about to ask Sadie if she knew when things would start when a hologram image of Artemis appeared above our heads in the center of the room. The goddess wore her usual golden apparel, but she had added a thin crown of golden leaves on top of her braided hair. With her beautifully decorated hunting bow strapped across her back, she truly looked the part of the queen of the wilderness.

"Welcome to the first Trial of the one hundred and forty-sixth edition of the Tournament!" Her voice resonated in the room, but it was soon drowned by the tsunami of the crowd's cheers. We could hear them through whatever sound system transmitted the image as well as through the wall separating us from the Pit. There were at least forty thousand seats there – were they all full? My breath hitched at the thought of so many people watching me. This was indeed a show for the people of Olympus.

"I am honored to present the rules for the first Trial." She paused for some suspense. The lady sure knew how to work a crowd. "It will be a fan favorite… capture the flag!"

Based on the crowd's reaction, it was an exciting prospect. The only time I'd seen 'capture the flags' was while watching that movie about the kid who discovered he was Poseidon's son. But I had no idea what the rules were or how far things could go in this version of the game. Sadie didn't seem too worried – she had a relieved look on her face.

"Although I am sure all of you are familiar with this popular game, let me reiterate the rules. The participants have been randomly separated into four teams, each with a flag to protect. The first three teams to capture another team's flag will be saved. The losing team will be transported off the compound for termination." A chill ran through me at the last words. I knew termination was a euphemism for death. Execution.

At least eight Coppers would die today.

Cheers and clapping resonated through the arena. How could these people cheer for the death of kids? None of us here were older than twenty-five. We all had so much of our lives yet to live. Hearing the crowd's reaction made me sick.

"As a reminder, exterior weapons are prohibited. Thus, the competitors will battle using only their gods-given powers and strength. This will be the perfect opportunity for you all to witness the abilities of our young Coppers and decide who you want to bet on. Of course, any fights that might happen between individuals within the Trials are not meant to be to the death, but killing blows are not forbidden." The smile Artemis gave the crowd – and us – made me want to punch her in her perfect teeth.

"As a final point, before I let my assistant announce the teams, I will remind you, dear spectators, that you can place bets on who you believe will survive all four Trials and earn their place on Mount Olympus. If you win, you will receive substantial monetary rewards, and the opportunity to go on a month-long vacation in your place of choice on Earth. Good luck to all of you, and make your godly ancestors proud!"

With that, she waved at the crowd and stepped back, allowing a young woman to come to the mic. She was about my age, with beautiful brown skin and amber eyes. Her body was both svelte and powerful, made to hunt next to her mistress. I vaguely remembered that Artemis surrounded herself with a group of loyal warrior female nymphs, so this must have been one of them.

After a brief salutation, the nymph started announcing the names of the members of each team. She began with team blue. She named each Copper, followed by which deity they were descended from. As their names were called, the Coppers walked up to the corridor leading to the Pit, passing through a thin layer of glittery mist that changed their shirt's color to match their team's.

Soon enough, the blue team, composed of Nathan and seven other Coppers I didn't particularly know, was gone from the room. As the nymph started listing out the red team, my heart beat faster as I hoped to be placed with at least one of my friends.

Looking around the room to assess who was left, my eyes met Mei's on the other side of the hologram. She stared at me expressionless for a while before shifting her gaze to Søren's next to me. He had an involuntary shift forward as if to join her. He didn't. She had made it clear the night before that she didn't want to talk to either of us. It broke my heart to see how sad it made Søren, especially as I felt it was my fault.

"Amara Mendez, descendant of Morpheus. Sadie Aska, descendant of Thanatos. And, finally, Archer Vasilias, descendant of Zeus."

It took me a few seconds to realize that my two friends had been called. Sadie and Archer. To the red team. Without me.

It must have been a subconscious move because, suddenly, I was hugging Sadie. Hard. This felt like a goodbye. "Stay safe," Sadie whispered in my ear. "I'll see you on the other side."

We separated, and I smiled at her, hoping it conveyed confidence. "You too, Aska. Have fun out there." Because I knew she would. She made fun of her brother for getting excited before battles, but she didn't have ichor flowing through her veins – however diluted – for nothing.

With a chuckle and a mock salute, she turned and strode for the hallway. I stared after her for a beat, wondering if I'd ever see her again. My heart squeezed painfully at the thought. This girl had quickly become my best friend here. I couldn't imagine a world without Sadie in it.

"Are you going to say goodbye?"

"I don't know, Sunshine. I thought we were ignoring each other."

I didn't need to look at him to know that Archer was rolling his eyes. He moved a couple of steps to stand in front of me. Sighing because I knew damn well that I wouldn't continue to ignore him – and he knew it too – I shifted to look at his face. He was staring into my eyes, searching for something.

"Remember your training, all right? And don't pick unnecessary fights." I scoffed at his words – as if I went looking for most of the fights I ended up in.

Okay, maybe I had been asking for trouble with Maeve. But, in my defense, she had just killed a fifteen-year-old boy in cold blood, and it had made me lose my mind a little bit.

"Are those actually your last parting words before we head into a deadly battle? 'Don't pick unnecessary fights'? You really know how to make a girl feel special." I might have sounded like a brat, but his hot-and-cold attitude hurt sometimes. And right then? I needed to feel like I mattered to him and he believed I could survive this. And even though I kept trying to convince myself that everything would be fine, seeing him leave made everything too real.

Archer sighed like I exasperated him. I expected him to shake his head and leave, as that was what he usually did nowadays. He gave me those secret smiles, those nice hugs, and that undivided attention that made me hope. And then, right as my frantically beating heart started telling my brain that maybe, just maybe, he had feelings too, he left. Or ignored me. Or became colder than an iceberg.

It had become quite a persistent pattern.

Today must have been pretty special because Archer didn't do any of those things. Instead, he swooped me into a hug, bringing me up until my head was in the crook of his neck, my legs awkwardly hanging down. It was nice – a full-bodied, extra-tight, and very well-executed hug.

All of my previous anger melted like snow under the sun. I didn't think of the other Coppers' eyes on us or their insistent murmurs. The only thing I could think about was how amazing it felt to be held by Archer, how warm he was, and how stupidly nice he smelled. I didn't even feel bad when I took a small whiff, his heady stormy scent filling my lungs.

"Is that better?" His voice rumbled in his chest, and I felt the vibrations against mine.

"Yes. Much better."

He laughed softly, and I felt it everywhere within me. "Good. Now my 'last parting words' are that you better survive this because I've gotten fond of my roommate and want her back in one piece."

"Okay." Why did I suddenly feel shy? And did someone turn the heater on? "Make sure you survive too."

"Oh, why, thank you, Mayfield. I can feel your care warm my bones."

A second later, I was back on my feet, and Archer was striding for the door. I felt cold. And alone, even in a room still full of people.

Someone put a hand on my shoulder. Søren. "It's gonna be alright, K. They will make it out. All of us will."

I appreciated the sentiment, even though some part of me knew there were no guarantees in this world. One day you could be standing in your kitchen, wondering how you would be able to fix your beat-up car, and then, minutes later, you could end up signing away your life in a Tournament with the grandchildren of the mythical Greek gods and goddesses. Who could predict what could happen next? No one.

The nymph had already started naming the people who were part of the green team. I vaguely registered that Elena and Alexei were called. I didn't know most of the people who were also named. Soon enough, seven people had left – one more. And I prayed anything, anyone, that neither Søren nor I would get called. That we'd be on the same team.

The gods, the stars, the fates… they must have had a good laugh because the last name of team green was Søren Aska, descendant of Thanatos.

There was a ringing in my ears. I felt Søren's hand squeeze my shoulders. I heard his words that I would be okay on my own, that

I needed not to show weaknesses. I heard it all, but it didn't quite register. Through it all, I had hoped I would have been able to have one of my friends with me.

But this would be like jumping at the deep end of the pool without floaties.

Søren left, and then there were only nine of us left. I guessed they had decided to put me in the only team of nine. It probably seemed fairer than to have a team of nine Coppers.

The nymph started listing out the names of my team members, and I looked around to see who I would have to fight alongside with. I didn't know most of them; they were the kind of Coppers that hadn't been searching for trouble since the beginning. Training and working hard, but never showing off or using their powers to assert their dominance. I was relieved to see that none of my teammates were obvious supporters of Elena's ideas. Thank goodness.

But what made me feel a little better was seeing Mei's face opposite where I stood. She was already observing me when I looked in her direction. She was pensive and not angry, which was a win. Sure, maybe we weren't on the best of terms. She still resented me for lying to her for weeks – as she should. But I could tell from her facial expression that she was calculating our odds and thinking of the best winning strategies. Mei might have worn the mask of the careless and excessively girly girl, but she wasn't dumb. She knew as well as anyone that we would have to work together to survive.

All of us.

And she might not have trusted me anymore, but I trusted her.

She gave me a nod. Curt, small, and sharp. Not a friendly nod. But a 'let's have a truce' type of nod.

I nodded back just as the nymph was finishing.

"Mei Lee, descendant of Pan. And, finally, Kalani Mayfield, mortal."

I took a deep breath.

I had this. I did. I had prepared for this very instant for the past six weeks. I could survive anything they threw at me.

Following in Mei's footsteps, I crossed the threshold.

Chapter Twenty-Five

The Pit looked nothing like the sandy arena it usually was. We were in the forest. With trees so big and high, I couldn't see the crowd in the stands. I could hear them, though. Cheers and excitement coming from above me in waves. How the hell was this whole scenery possible? I had no idea.

The portal at the end of the short hallway had landed us somewhere deep within the forest. All nine of us were seemingly alone in the woods, standing in a small clearing around a bright yellow flag planted in the ground, the top peaking higher than my height. There was no way to hide that big ass flag. Which was probably the point. How fun would it be if the teams could hide their stupid banner during the game? No, watching kids fight to protect said flag was way more entertaining.

I wasn't entirely sure how we were supposed to know when things started. Had the Trial begun already? Were members of the other teams already running toward us? Jeez, Artemis could have gone into more detail regarding the Trial process.

"Alright, team yellow, we only have a little time to organize, so let's be quick about it." The girl who took the lead was average-sized, with a gorgeous afro, deep dark skin, and the bluest eyes I had ever seen. If I remembered correctly, she was Nafula and a descendant of Poseidon, so she must have a power somewhat related to water, which might not be the most useful when in the middle of the forest.

"I say we should just go and attack another team for their flag; make this quick." The guy who was seemingly seconds away from running into a fight was a bulky, dangerous-looking young man. He and his brother, the slightly smaller version of a gladiator next to him, were grandsons of Ares, the god of war. Cassian and… was it Rory? It might have been Ryan. Either way, both of them had come in bloodthirsty and looking for war.

"A good way to ensure we don't lose is to prevent other teams from getting our flag. We can't just all leave it to go hunt for someone else's." My words were met with an annoyed glance from Ryan – Riley?

"Don't you know your place, mortal? I don't think we've asked for your opinion."

"She's not wrong. You might want to think for a second – if we keep our flag, then we make sure we don't end up in fourth place." Mei gave the brothers a look – one that said, 'Are you dumb?' – before turning her attention to Nafula. "We should split up into three teams. And most of us should stay here to guard the flag."

Nafula nodded her assent and assessed each of us in turn. "I agree, and I think we should keep our strongest fighters here to protect the flag. Then we could have two teams of two that go and hunt for the other teams' flags."

"But what if the other teams also leave their strongest fighters at their flags?" The guy who spoke was a dangly kid who was clearly the youngest of us all. I thought his name was Valentin, and he was a descendant of Hephaestus, the god of metalworking and forges. I had vague memories of paintings and sculptures of his grandfather, and the kid had unfortunately not inherited the muscles.

"We'll need to be smarter than them. We can easily take advantage of other teams attacking a flag and the distraction that would provide to come in and steal the flag." Mei shrugged as if this was obvious. I had never seen this side of her – calculating and methodical – but I liked it.

"Let the other teams fight it out and sneak behind them. Nice." Nafula then turned to the group and pointed at the brothers. "You two will stay here with me." Then she looked at two girls and a boy who had stayed silent. "Sarah and Aria, you're mindreading and telekinesis, right? And Alejandro, you can shapeshift?"

The two girls nodded, and the guy specified he could change into a tiger. Impressive. I would have enjoyed that kind of power.

"All right, I think we should send Aria and Sarah as a team and Mei and Kalani as another."

There were many complains then, most of them revolving around me being powerless, defenseless, and useless in fights. I didn't focus too much on that because I was very intrigued by Valentin. I had no idea what his powers were, but it must have been better than telekinesis. That kid was hiding his game pretty well.

"Rhett, if you say one more word, I promise I'll strangle you!" Mei's voice cut through the two brothers' complaints. I guessed it was Rhett then and not Riley. "Kalani may not have powers, but she's far from useless. We're both small. We will work in the shadows and bring back the red flag."

"Why the red?" Alejandro asked.

"Because Archer Vasilias will be guarding it," Nafula said with a conniving smile in Mei's direction.

Nafula was barely done speaking that a loud gong resonated through the arena. The Trial was starting.

Immediately, Sarah and Aria told us they were going for the blue flag, and then they were running. Mei looked at me expectantly as I stood there, as if I should have started running already. "How the hell are we supposed to know in which direction the red flag is?"

"The conventions want that the red flag is on the east side of the arena, which is opposite from us, in the west. Blue is north, and green is south." And with that, Mei took off.

We ran in silence for a while. Time slipped by, and I had no idea how long we'd been running before we heard the first screams in the distance. I flinched at the sound, but Mei kept going as if nothing had happened. I almost asked her how she could remain so stoic in this situation, but I refrained. First, I could tell she didn't want to talk to me. And second, I had no idea how close we were to members of another team – I didn't want to attempt a conversation and give our location away.

We kept running as silently as we could, zigzagging between the massive tree trunks. Mei had used her power right as we left to ask a few wild birds to go and act as scouts. When a small crow came back, Mei stopped abruptly. The bird circled above her head a few times, making small caw sounds and calling out. I had absolutely no idea what was going on – since I had taken Spanish in high school, not bird language – but Mei seemed to understand what the crow what telling her.

"We are about a hundred yards away from the red flag. It is on a small island in between two small rivers. And there is only Archer guarding it. Good news though, three people from blue are on their way too."

I nodded, listening intently for signs of the blue team. We wanted to use them as a distraction, so we needed to ensure that neither they nor Archer knew we were there. Until the right time, at least.

And I especially needed to stop worrying that Archer's team might lose if we successfully stole his flag. I couldn't afford to think about that. And I needed to remind myself that Sadie and Archer were good enough to win on their own – they would get another team's flag. They had to.

Mei and I didn't exchange any more words as we moved toward the red flag. The closer we got, the louder we could hear the rivers burbling along. Soon enough, we could see a sliver of water and a small island between the bushes and trees. I caught a glimpse of Archer patrolling around the bottom of the island.

As we were going around a tree trunk so big it would need three people to go around, I heard voices coming from our left. I held a hand up, and Mei stopped short, listening to the voices. They were way closer to us than was safe – we needed them to engage in combat with Archer, not us.

I signaled Mei to crouch down in the small cavity formed by a bush next to the tree. We both squeezed in, trying to move into the bush as quietly as possible. I tried to ignore the fact that I didn't know what kind of bush we were currently getting cozy with – knowing the gods, they could have decided to make sure the forest itself would provide to the show by being poisonous or giving us rashes or something. I also didn't know if there was anything living within that bush – I didn't want to come anywhere close to some deadly animal's burrow.

As the voices grew closer, though, neither of us relented to hiding out. I was so scared of moving or making a sound that I held my breath as the trio of Coppers walked past. They didn't seem worried about being discreet – they were not paying attention to where they were walking, crushing branches and kicking rocks as they went, and were talking openly about what they had planned. It didn't seem like the blue team had sent the brightest of their members here.

Soon enough, the three Coppers were past us and heading straight for Archer. It took less than a minute before we heard the sounds of a battle. Mei and I exchanged a look and got up as silently as possible. We moved in a semi-circle around the battle, trying to get behind Archer. I was worried that he would get rid of his three assailants before we even had time to get close enough to the flag, but it seemed like he wanted to play with them. I didn't look – I couldn't let myself get distracted or worry about him – but I could hear the sounds of flesh hitting flesh, and various groans of pain. If Archer had wanted, he could have already had them writhing on the ground, incapable of defending themselves.

Trying to remain focused, I followed in Mei's footsteps until we reached the end of the tree line, on the other side of the island from the four Coppers fighting. The only issue now was the water. The river didn't seem particularly deep – Archer and the three members of the blue team were currently fighting while thigh-deep in one of the two rivers – but walking through would take us longer than we wanted and be loud enough that the four of them would realize we were here. It would take us at least five or six seconds to run from the water to the flag, thus increasing the risk of one of the four Coppers having the time to prevent us from getting the flag.

Mei seemed to have reached the same conclusion because she was observing our surroundings, trying to determine the best course of action. "Can you use one of your birds to take the flag?" My voice was barely a whisper, but Mei heard it.

"No. I tested our flag before we left, and it is pushed too far down into the earth for any bird to be able to take it out. If we manage to remove it from the ground, I have an eagle that can fly it up to our camp."

Good, but that didn't solve our immediate problem. We still had to get to the flag. And decently fast if the slowing sounds of the battle to our left were anything to go by. Desperate to find a solution, I looked up, and my gaze locked onto the tree next to us. While it wasn't the biggest tree we had come across in the forest, it was old and big enough that its branches were a decent size. Branches that went far enough out to go above the water. Branches that were approximately the size of a beam.

I knew how to walk on a beam.

"Wait here and be ready with your eagle. I'm going in from above." I pointed to the branch, and Mei's eyes gleamed at the realization.

I had never been a huge climber. As a kid, I was all for flipping and tumbling, but climbing trees? It hadn't been one of my favorite pastimes. However, I had no choice but to climb this tree, so I didn't think too hard about it and just went for it.

It wasn't an easy climb, as the few holds that I could find were slippery due to the moss covering the bark. It took me longer than I would have liked to reach the stupidly high branch I was going to use. I didn't have time to breathe once I wrapped my arms around the branch – we were on a time crunch.

Pulling on my arms, I muscled my way up onto the branch. Thankfully, the bark covering it wasn't covered in moss, which should make it easier for me to walk on. I barely heard the screams of pain coming from below. I took a long inhale, trying to calm my heart. I knew I had to hurry, but I also couldn't afford to fall in the middle of the trip – I was high enough that an uncontrolled fall would hurt. A lot.

My first few steps were hesitant, testing to see if the branch was as sturdy as it had looked from the ground. When I felt somewhat confident that the branch wouldn't break in half from my weight, I moved a little faster.

From somewhere below, I heard Archer taunt whoever was still standing that they should just give up trying to get the flag. The smug and condescending tone he used was so *him* that I had to contain a laugh. It was a lot funnier when those remarks were directed at someone else.

A few steps, and I was above the river. It was gurgling happily, but I could easily imagine that sharp rocks were hiding in the currents. Avoiding looking below, I kept my focus on the island. I had to make it there.

A few more steps and the branch started the tremble a little. Shit. I still had at least eight feet to go. Maybe a little less if I managed to do a decent dismount away from the branch.

At least two team blue members must have managed to stand back up because the fighting had started again. A movement above my head caught my eye – Mei's eagle was circling in the sky, ready to descend at any moment.

Four feet out. The branch was becoming very narrow, so much so that I felt my ankles work extra hard to ensure my feet didn't slip. As I took one more step, the branch shook, and I felt my left foot slip. Thankfully, years of hard work kicked in. I put my weight on my right foot and used my arms and core to bring myself back before I fell. It all happened so fast that I didn't immediately register that something had changed.

The branch was cracking. Full-on breaking at the proximal end.

However, the most concerning part was that the fighting had stopped on the other side of the small island.

And Archer was staring right at me.

I didn't know how he would react to seeing me here, trying to steal his team's flag. Sure, he had trained me for weeks, and we had gotten close. But being faced with death could change people. Therefore, I didn't wait around to see if he would attack. I pulled my mental shields up higher, keeping them tight against his potential attack. And I ran.

The branch broke right as I was pushing off of my right foot to jump. I still had a little bit of distance to cover to steer clear of the river, so I jumped forward and moved my body into a tight ball, flipping into the air. My legs slammed into the ground, and I took a couple of steps to avoid falling over. My left knee hurt from the landing – the old injury had healed, but sometimes, rough landings would cause the pain to flare up – but I kept going.

From the corner of my eyes, I saw that Archer was also running toward the flag. I pushed myself harder, pumping my legs up the hill, my lungs desperate for air. The eagle was flying above our heads, so low that I could feel the air moving from its powerful wings beating.

And then I was there, so close that I could almost reach it.

Archer was almost at the flag too. Close enough that I could see the sweat dripping down his forehead and neck, and the dark blue ring surrounding his irises. Close enough that he could stop me from getting that freaking flag.

I grabbed the pole, yanking it up, hoping to rip it out of the ground before Archer arrived. Wishful thoughts because the thing was planted so deep that it felt like I had to pull it out of the middle of the Earth, and Archer was already there.

His hands closed around the pole, close enough to my hands that his thumbs brushed mine.

I expected him to pull it back down.

But he tugged it up.

In seconds, the flag was out of its rocky prison and in my hands. The eagle swooped down and took it before flying at high speeds toward our base camp. A flurry of other birds joined it, and they flew in a complicated formation to protect the flag.

"Good job, Mayfield." Archer's face was impassive, but he had smiling eyes.

"Thanks, Sunshine." Then, because I couldn't help but tease him, "I was starting to think you'd need help to get rid of those three over there."

"Says the girl who hid in the bushes for over ten minutes."

Touché.

Chapter Twenty-Six

The rest of the day was filled with relief, joy, and sadness. I was relieved to be alive – my team had finished second, behind Søren's team. Sadie and Archer's team had come in close thirds, with team blue finishing last. The utter joy of reuniting with all my friends and knowing that we were all going to continue this adventure together was incredible. But then came the realization that eight people would not spend another night sleeping in the compound.

It had been a crazy end of the Trial. A gong had sounded, and, in the next second, the whole forest had disappeared. We had ended up back on the sandy arena, feeling slightly disoriented and dizzy from the illusion.

The crowd cheered like we were at the Olympics. The nymph who had announced our names took the mic back and revealed the rankings. Teams green, yellow, and red received standing ovations. We were escorted by black-armored warriors toward the big entrance of the Pit as flower petals and confetti rained upon us.

It had felt exhilarating.

For a second, at least. Then, I looked back to see the eight members of team blue forced into blue fluorescent shackles. Some of them cried. Others just stood there, eyes in the haze. A couple of them tried to fight off the warriors that were restraining them, but a few well-placed hits had them kneeling, helpless on the ground.

I didn't particularly like any of them. Nathan, silent tears streaming down his face, was even a part of the team. I hated him for what he had tried to do to me. But still. These people had been unlucky enough to get their flag last. Now they were going to die for it.

It had broken my heart.

I stopped dead in my tracks for a second. I didn't know what I could have done. Probably nothing. But it had felt wrong to be walked out like heroes when these eight Coppers were going to the execution block.

Sadie had taken my arm and tugged me toward the exit. Her face had said it all – there was nothing we could do. So, I went along.

Hours later, I still felt sick to my stomach.

The only good thing about this day was that we were allowed to go and see the nurse. Before the beginning of the Tournament, the nurse had been reserved for emergency-only situations. Mostly when people were on the verge of dying. But today, we had the opportunity to go and get even our minor injuries healed.

The nurse was one of Asclepius' daughters – the god of medicine and physicians. Going to her office was a bit surreal for a human like me. She had only needed to place her hands over my chest for her healing magic to leak out of her palms and fill my entire body. It had felt like the best bath ever, mixed with the longest and most relaxing night of sleep of my life. I had left her office feeling rejuvenated, and all of my cuts, bruises, and such were completely healed. Even my left knee felt better than even since the injury almost four years ago.

Incredible.

A few hours later, the relaxing effects of the healing magic were gone, and I was back to feeling nauseous.

"Are you going to eat your cake?"

I shook my head, and Søren took the piece of cake. He was undoubtedly eating his feelings since Mei hadn't talked to him after the Trial. The poor guy was hurting, and it only added to the guilt I was currently swimming in.

I must have been an open book because Sadie put her hand on mine and patted it gently. "It's not your fault, K. There is nothing you could have done to save these people aside from throwing your team under the bus and dying yourself. The gods and goddesses have designed this Tournament as a population control measure for Coppers – they want most of us to die, and there is nothing we can do about it. We can only try our best to survive so we can try to make a difference on the outside."

I knew she was right. I knew it, but some part of me kept telling me I could have tried to do something. It felt like that whole moving sidewalk metaphor for systemic racism – you had to be actively doing something against inequalities; otherwise, if you went with the flow, you ended up in the same place as the ones who agreed with racism, just slower. I felt like I was standing on the moving sidewalk and had no idea how to start walking against the flow.

My lips twitched, but I couldn't find it in me to smile, even to express gratitude for her caring words. I didn't know how to express my feelings to my friends, especially as it sometimes felt like they didn't have the same threshold for injustice.

"I get it. I do. I don't have to like it, though."

Sadie said nothing else, but I could tell she didn't fully understand where I came from. I wasn't sure if it was the godly blood flowing in their veins or how they had been raised, knowing they might end up living on Olympus. Still, most of the Coppers here, including my friends, had a very different view of social justice from mine and that of a whole generation of Californian kids. It was pretty alarming sometimes. Like when no one seemed to find it cruel and deeply unjust that the hierarchy on Olympus was based on power levels, ancestry, and how gold one's blood was – all characteristics that people had literally no control over.

I knew there was no changing their way of thinking at that instant. I didn't even have the energy to try. Instead, I had to focus on the next steps. There was still a nine-year-old little boy who was waiting for me.

"What are we doing now?" I didn't expand more, but my friends seemed to figure out precisely what I meant. It wasn't like we had a lot of things happening in our lives outside of the Tournament.

"Now we train."

I could have bet my whole bank account – which was, admittedly, not that hefty – on that being Archer's answer. The odds hadn't been crazy high, though, so I probably wouldn't have won much.

"First, we are going to relax and celebrate being alive." Søren stood up abruptly. "And I am going to get my girl back." And then he was gone, striding confidently toward the table where Mei was sitting with Nafula and a couple of other Coppers.

Mei's eyes widened as Søren forcibly turned her around on her bench. I couldn't hear what he said to her, but it seemed like a long sentimental monologue on his part if her teary eyes were anything to go by. They exchanged a few sentences before remaining silent for a while. Søren was about half a second away from begging her on his knees – I could see his legs trembling – when she nodded. He wrapped her up in a bear hug, probably close to crushing her bones, and then kissed her like it was the end of days.

Sadie cooed, a hand on her chest. "Aw, baby brother has finally worked up the courage to apologize. I'm so proud." She made a show of wiping a tear away from beneath her eye, but I could tell she was proud of him. Honestly, I wouldn't have thought this couple would make it far, but it was great to see them get closer and Søren put effort into getting her back. I was sure that she would still make him grovel a little bit, but it was nice to see both of them smiling at each other like this. They deserved love and happiness, especially after the day we had just had.

Instinctively, my gaze slid to Archer's hand, sitting on the table. Flashbacks of his thumbs brushing mine as he put his hands on the flagpole zapped in my mind. His gentle eyes as he had yanked it up and out of the ground. I had been expecting him to fight me off – the memories of the nightmare I had had about him stabbing me in the back coming to the forefront of my mind. But he hadn't. He had helped me, even though his team hadn't gotten their flag yet. He had chosen me over victory.

It meant a lot to me. More than it should.

The issue was that now, among the gratefulness and relief I felt, my heart also had a hard time remembering that his help hadn't come from a place of love. At least, not the kind of love some part of me still hoped for. I had been so good about putting my growing feelings for this man under lock and key, and that one moment had burst through all of my barriers.

And now my heart fluttered, and I was blushing from just looking at his hand like a stupid, hormone-ridden schoolgirl.

How embarrassing.

At least, the man was too concentrated on eating his cake and hadn't realized – he would have made sure to let me know otherwise.

I did my best to ignore Archer's presence for the rest of the meal, which was decently fast, seeing as Søren remained with his girlfriend and my last two tablemates were halfway done with their desserts. The cake did look amazing – the Olympus version of cheesecake – but even after our conversation, I was still too frayed to think about eating a celebratory dessert.

The rest of the afternoon went in a weird limbo where we didn't really train – Sadie and Søren convinced Archer that we needed time to rest our bodies – but we hadn't ever hung out as a group and not trained. So, we went for a walk around the compound, pretending we were just a group of friends living a normal life. We played dodgeball – with a real ball, not one of Søren's fireballs. And then we went to watch the sunset on the roof.

It was a strange day, to say the least.

I was almost relieved when we finally left from dinner to go to our rooms. I needed time to myself to come to terms with everything that had happened during the day – and the past six weeks. Everything was catching up to me, and I was struggling to cope. Until then, I had trained my ass off to prepare myself for the Tournament, knowing full well that I would be playing for my life. But the whole life-or-death situation had remained sort of an abstract concept. Seeing eight of the people I had lived next to for the past month and a half be taken in chains away, not seeing them at dinner, and knowing they were going to 'termination'… it made it all so *real*.

It was scary as hell.

So yeah, I wasn't particularly ashamed to say I needed time to process. Time to come to terms with the fact that the gods and goddesses weren't kidding when they said their grandchildren would die if they didn't prove themselves to be the best. This was a whole other level of family issues. It made my rocky relationship with my mom seem like a cruise in comparison.

Archer and I each got ready after the other without saying much. He had reached his daily word quota with all the small talk we had in the afternoon. You can thus imagine how surprised I was when he asked me, "Do you want to talk about it?"

Laying on my bed, I stopped turning my phone in my hands – I had been feeling homesick and was debating whether or not to turn it on to watch a couple of pictures – to turn my head his way. The lights were all off in the room, the TV hologram playing an episode of an Olympus drama show – something about the gods and the Trojan War – that I'd already seen in the past couple of weeks. The bluish glow from the hologram partially lit up Archer's face, reflecting off his eyes.

"Are you hiding your therapist diploma somewhere, Sunshine?"

Archer rolled his eyes in exasperation at my poor attempt at a joke. He already sat on his bed, back against the wall to face me, and brought a knee up to rest his folded arms. "I'm serious. I can tell you're feeling off, and I am here if you need to talk to someone."

The seriousness on his face, his words, the way he knew me well enough to tell I wasn't feeling my best… it all meant a lot more than I could express. It was easy to feel alone or inadequate here, easy to become overwhelmed and forget for a second that I had friends who cared about me just as much as I cared about them. Hearing the sincerity in Archer's words caused my chest to warm up.

I debated saying that I would be fine, that I was just tired. An easy excuse that had worked plenty of times before. But in this dark room, alone with him, I wanted to be real.

I wanted to make this moment count.

It took me a long time to decide how exactly I wanted to be honest with Archer, but when the words left my mouth, I felt the most genuine I'd been in a while. "I am scared. Until today, I hadn't fully realized that people would die. I knew that if I wasn't good enough, I could die, but I guess I hadn't quite grasped that my actions during the Trials could cost other people their lives. It's like-" I paused, trying to find the right words. "I *know* that it's not my fault, but some part of me keeps thinking that if I hadn't removed that flag from the ground, then all eight of them would still be alive."

"And you'd be dead."

That was the cold hard truth, wasn't it? That there was no way to win this. Either way, eight people – or nine – would have died. There was no getting around that. Still, that didn't remove the irrational thought that I had killed them. That I'd been selfish and decided that my life was more important than someone else's. And, when I stood in front of the red flag, I hadn't even hesitated. I hadn't thought about whose lives I could be sacrificing for my team's survival. That scared me. It terrified me, actually, because I didn't want to be the kind of person who thought she could decide who deserved to live – I had no right to determine whose life was worth more.

"If it makes you feel better, I would have done it for you." I frowned at Archer, unsure what he meant. "I would have yanked that stupid flag out of the ground and given it to you even if you had suddenly gotten second thoughts and decided you didn't want to live over someone else." He held my eyes for a long time, ensuring I knew he was genuine. "I would have saved your life over theirs. No questions."

It should have scared me that Archer was so unafraid of making these kinds of choices.

It didn't, though.

It made me feel warm and tingly everywhere. And it made my eyes tear up for no reason.

I gave myself a few seconds to get myself back together – I even looked over at the hologram, the show still playing on mute, to avoid his eyes – before looking back at him. He was staring at me intensely as if a fire was burning inside him.

"How do you manage to feel okay with this?"

"You have to think of your reason why. That's how you survive this with your sanity intact." He raised his chin in my direction to tell me to go ahead. "Tell me about your why."

The answer came instinctively. "My brother. Makaio."

"Why?"

"He's the best part of my life. He has so much good inside of him, so much light that sometimes I-" I swallowed hard. "Sometimes I wonder how we can even be related. He makes me happy. He is in all of my best memories. Most of my worst ones too."

I briefly crushed my phone to my chest, wishing I could see his face. "My mom hasn't had the easiest of lives. My dad was the love of her life, that one-in-a-lifetime kind of love. The kind that changes lives and breaks hearts."

Archer didn't say anything but listened intently, as if all of my words were precious. Important.

"He died two months before I was born. Mom hasn't been the same ever since. I know she loves us in her own way. But I guess I look a lot like him, and it's hard for her. It doesn't excuse some of her behaviors; I know that. And I also know she has relied too heavily on me to raise Makaio – it shouldn't have been my role. Don't get me wrong, I love caring for Makaio, but I should have been able to be a kid too." I was rambling; I knew it. But now that I had started talking about my family and how hard it had been to be responsible for a child when I was still a teenager, I couldn't stop. "He's my why because I don't know if my mom will be able to take care of him if I'm gone. He deserves so much more than a mom whose best is often not enough. And I love him so much that I would go through hell to get back to him."

There was a long silence after those words. A pregnant pause when both of us just sat there, thinking of those words I had thrown at Archer. He had wanted to know who I was fighting for, and instead of giving him a straight-up answer, I had laid all of our family issues out in the open.

I should have felt embarrassed. I usually would have. Those thoughts were private, the kind that I kept for times I was alone in my room, lying in the dark and wondering why I couldn't have a mom that cared more.

But I didn't feel embarrassed. I felt relieved. Because, for the first time, I had expressed how I felt. I could have gone on and on about my home situation, but these five minutes had already lifted a weight off my chest.

"Good," Archer nodded. "That's what you have to remember every time we have a Trial. You're doing it for him."

"And you?" I asked before I could stop myself. "What's your why?"

Archer remained silent for so long that I thought he wouldn't answer at all. I wouldn't have minded; it was private, and it wasn't because I had shared that he should feel obligated to do the same. I was almost ready to fall asleep when he finally answered.

"My mom. The twins." He paused for a beat. "You."

Chapter Twenty-Seven

The next three days flew by quickly. Too quickly. We started training again, harder than ever. I worked so hard on my physical skills and mental barriers that, by the time night came, I slept so hard I didn't even dream. Which was nice because I didn't want to imagine what the blue team had gone through.

We hadn't heard from anyone about their whereabouts.

We didn't know if they were still alive or had been killed already.

I didn't particularly want to know; that way, I could still pretend they were still alive. It was my own kind of Schrödinger's cat experiment – as long as I didn't ask questions, they could remain whole in my head.

I spent these past four days working hard to remind myself that I wasn't a killer and there was nothing to do here other than try my best and survive – as long as I played fair, there was nothing to feel guilty about. I thought of Makaio – my why – at least twenty times a day. It helped with the whole not-guilting-myself thing.

I also thought a lot about *Archer's* why. One of his, at least. Namely, me.

As you can imagine, that one word – 'you' – did not help me control my heart and emotions. I did my best to put all of these unwanted thoughts and feelings under lock again, but the more time went on, the less it felt like it worked. The seals and joints on my heavy-duty safe were leaky. Which really sucked because Archer had returned to being friendly with me, only acting like more than a friend when other people were around us. Each time he looked at a group of Coppers and took my hand in his before letting it go once we were out of sight… I felt like tiny needles were puncturing my heart. I must have been a masochist because I started taking advantage of the times when we were in public to be closer to him and touch him – even if I knew damn well it was all pretend for him.

The end of the Tournament couldn't come fast enough so I could bail from this whole place and get some much-needed space between Archer and me. I would need at least an entire universe between us to get my heart and brain to forget about him.

Today was, thankfully, one of those days when I didn't have the time or mental headspace to think about my unsustainable and unreciprocated crush on a god's grandchild. Indeed, I was too busy going over thousands of scenarios for the next Trial to have time to think about something else.

We were back in the room off to the side of the Pit, waiting for our turn to go into the second Trial. Chairs had been lined up in neat rows, and all of us had been assigned seats in seemingly random order. I wasn't anywhere close to any of my friends, but at least I wasn't close to Elena or Alexei either – small mercies. I was between Nafula and some guy I didn't know who didn't seem to want to talk.

Nafula sighed loudly before crossing her arms over her chest and half-slumping in her chair. "I hate when they take this long. We've been waiting here for almost an hour, and we're no closer to being done."

She wasn't wrong. We had been given instructions to be in this room by nine in the morning. And then, after sitting in our assigned seats, the nymph's voice from last time resonated in the room and the arena, stating that this second Trial would be a test of the mind and each participant would face it alone. Since then, she had been calling a new Copper every twenty or so minutes. Nafula and I were in the back of the room, in the very last row. If they continued to loosely follow the seating arrangement, up to twenty people could be left before us.

That was a long time to brew in stress and fear.

The worst part wasn't even the wait; it was hearing the crowd occasionally cheer and scream without knowing whether the Copper who had gone in last had made it out.

"I know, this whole set-up seems unnecessary."

Nafula huffed her agreement and looked back to stare daggers at the door. I hadn't had the time to properly pay attention during the first Trial, but the Copper was a real sight. She seemed to be around my age and always looked well put together. Her afro was beautiful, her dark skin glowed under the harsh lights of the room, and her eyes popped with lashes so big that she must have a stash of really good waterproof mascara in her room. Her lips were also covered in lipstick in a lovely coral shade, making her face glow. She was beautiful, and I wouldn't have been surprised if she could have been a model on Earth.

Were models somewhat related to the Greek deities? All of the Coppers around were beautiful, so the question was valid. I'd have to ask Sadie.

Applauses and whistles rose in the arena, and we all tensed. We knew what was coming. The last Copper was done with the second Trial – however that had gone for them. And whoever went in next would be called in the next minute.

So far, the nymph hadn't followed the seating arrangement to the letter, but she had been calling people seated in the front half of the room. Archer, Mei, and the twins were still sitting in the first three rows, looking all relaxed and almost happy to be here – although Mei was holding onto Søren's hand, seated behind her, pretty hard. I wished I could be this relaxed, but as time passed, the scenarios my brain was coming up with became more unhinged and terrifying.

What did 'trial of the mind' even mean?

Knowing the gods – and Artemis especially – it couldn't mean anything good or fun. Fun for us, at least. I was sure the bloodthirsty crowd was having the time of its life.

A few participants had been quietly talking, but they all stopped. The room became so silent that I doubted anyone dared breathe anymore.

A couple of heartbeats.

And then-

"Thank you for this great show, Amara. Time for the next player!" I would have scoffer if my chest wasn't so tight in apprehension. She made it seem like we were players of a stupid game in a late-night show. "Let's all welcome… Sadie Aska, descendent of Thanatos!"

There were claps and whooping outside. As if she were a celebrity. As if this was all fun and games.

My gaze whipped to my friend fast enough to see her gracefully get up from her third-row chair. She nodded to her brother and Archer before turning my way and giving me a reassuring smile. She even threw my way a wink. Then she walked toward the door with an excited pep to her steps.

And she disappeared in the shadows of the hallway.

The next ten minutes were nerve-wracking. I listened intently to every sound I could hear from the arena, desperately trying to get information from the crowd on how Sadie was doing. The scraps I was getting weren't very useful, though. I had no way to know whether the various *ooohs* and *aaahs* were good. No way to tell if she was crushing it or getting crushed.

I kept reminding myself that she had to be fine. She was Sadie Aska. There was no other option but for her to make it out. Easily.

Nothing could stop Sadie.

Still, when the next name was called – Elena Schmidt, descendent of Ares – I still felt like a weight was on my chest. The not knowing… yeah, I wasn't doing great. And the more time went on, the more the incertitude gnawed at me.

You can imagine how terrible I started to feel as my other friends got called in. Mei, then Søren, and then Archer. I watched them walk through the door as if they were going to the beach or some shit.

By the time everyone had left from the first four rows, my right knee was bouncing so fast that I was slightly worried it would start cramping soon. Nafula wasn't fairing any better. She was getting to new grumpiness heights and staring so hard at the door that it was a wonder there wasn't a hole there yet.

There were only seven of us left now, all kids I barely knew. It was strange how we had lived together for almost seven weeks but didn't know each other at all. Weird paradox, wasn't it? We stayed in our little bubbles, surrounding ourselves with as few people as possible. I wasn't sure if it was the fear of losing people or the fear of being betrayed that motivated those choices. Either way, I wished I knew more about the Coppers around me. Not just because they were my competitors but because I couldn't stop thinking that maybe we could have banded together instead of letting our group fracture into a million pieces under the pressure of survival.

It was a little late for that now.

Desperately trying to think of something other than the Trial and my friends' fates, I used the Coppers still present around me to keep my mind busy. From our location in the very back of the room, I could scan the other Coppers discreetly in a way that would have been awkward – and potentially a declaration of war – in the cafeteria or the Pit.

People watching had always been a fun game for Makaio and me – we'd go to the park and, between two of his skateboarding sessions, we would sit on the burnt grass and eat PB&J sandwiches while imagining what kind of lives the other people had. It had been entertaining and an excellent way to bond with my brother. So, it almost came back naturally when I looked around me, analyzing my competitors from the corners of my eyes.

Questions popped up – where had they lived before coming here? How were their lives back home? Did they have a Golden parent waiting for them here? What was their power? Did they regret their lives on Earth? Did they have passions? Siblings? Hopes? Dreams? Loves? The questions were endless, and because I often had no idea who they were, my imagination was doing all the work.

And imagining that Grumpy Boy, on my right, had been raised within a circus, working shows as a clown and making children cry, helped prevent my thoughts from wandering toward unwanted topics.

This technique worked decently well until I was the only one left in the room. It was starting to be a pattern that I'd be announced last for the Trials. I was sure Artemis wanted it that way to ensure that the best show happened at the end – the grand finale of the human with the hubris to compete with deities.

Once I was left alone in the big, empty, and cold room, there was nothing to distract myself with. My only option to remain sane and not end up in a fetal position on the ground, completely freaking out, was meditation.

Don't get me wrong; I wasn't a big meditation girl. Just like I hadn't been into yoga. Or all those fancy 'clear your mind and clear your body' trends. I always had too much to worry about to empty my mind.

But my high school gymnastics coach had been big into visualization and meditation and *being a master of your own mind* or whatever. We had done his exercises so often that it was surprisingly easy to spring back into them.

Eyes closed, breathing controlled, I focused on imagining a safe space. At the time, my safe space had been the gym. However, a lot had happened since then, so I went for the ocean instead. Surfing had been a way to escape reality for me. I had taken it from my dad. He used to be a professional surfer and came to California to train with a new coach. That's where he met my mom. And, somehow, he must have given me the genetic predisposition to love riding waves on my board – his board. Imagining that I was seated on a board, looking at the horizon over the water, ready to ride a fantastic wave and have the time of my life, helped calm the frantic beating of my heart down.

This whole meditation thing worked so well that I almost missed the moment the nymph announcer called my name. *Kalani Mayfield, mortal.*

I had no hesitation or fear gripping me when I stood up. Or, at least, whatever apprehension I still felt had been hidden under a growing layer of calmness and confidence. I knew I was at a significant disadvantage compared to Coppers in almost all instances. But my mind? I had faith in it. And, while my confidence had been knocked down after Alexei's invasion, the weeks I had spent tirelessly working with Archer had shown me that my mind was strong.

I just had to believe it would be strong enough to survive whatever awaited me on the other side.

Chapter Twenty-Eight

Whoever was in charge of the arena's illusions had been busy again because the Pit did not look like its usual self. I was in a black box, so dark that I could barely see a few feet in front of me. It felt like being thrown into the emptiness of deep space, far from any stars or planets. I couldn't hear or smell anything. And I was alone.

Alone in the dark.

What the hell was this Trial supposed to be?

Time passed, and nothing happened. I was just standing there, looking around in case something jumped at me from the shadows. The dark wasn't a deep fear of mine, but it often made me uncomfortable. I liked to be prepared, and this space – almost like a sensory deprivation room – made me feel vulnerable. I didn't like it.

It could have been seconds or minutes since I had walked into the dark, and I wouldn't have known. I was in a timeless space. With no direction or purpose. Just waiting. Waiting to see what I was supposed to do.

I was about to start wandering – I had to do *something* – when I heard a voice. It started as a low murmur, so low that I couldn't tell where it came from or what it said. I could only look around me, trying to prepare myself because I had no idea whether this voice was a friend or a foe.

Knowing Artemis, I would have bet on the latter.

Seconds flew by, and the murmur became a whisper. Then a soft-speaking voice, words loud enough that I could start recognizing words. Or I would have been able to, had I known the language. But the voice didn't speak in English or Spanish – not that I knew much Spanish anymore. The words themselves sounded like a melody, beautiful and light. But the sentences? The sentences sounded wrong, as if the words' concatenation made them clash. As if whoever was speaking – the voice was androgynous, sounding both female and male simultaneously – was cursing at me. This person did not sound friendly. At all. And I had no idea where they were.

Great.

I loved knowing there was someone out there that seemed aggressive without being able to see them.

Just great.

Unable to do anything else, I made sure my mental blocks were strong and continued to turn slowly on myself, changing directions every so often in the hopes of seeing the unknown person before they came at me.

Except, as the voice turned so loud that it was almost screaming, everything stopped. The space was dead silent again outside of my ragged breaths. Immediately, I knew something was coming – this was the calm before the storm. And the storm would no doubt be a class five on the Saffir-Simpson Hurricane Wind Scale.

I expected a terrifying beast to jump at me from the dark, but I blinked, and everything changed.

I was back in the magical forest, with fairies flying like magical lights above my head, walking toward the gazebo where I had dreamt about that first dance with Archer. Where the dream had turned into a nightmare.

I was alone this time, no Archer in sight. Yet. Because it looked like we were going to go through my nightmare again. And it didn't seem like I could remove myself from the hallucination as I did with Archer's – there were none of the elements I had come to recognize as patterns for mental manipulations. For all intents and purposes, the world had been altered around me – this wasn't a hallucination or vision but more likely an illusion.

Instinctively, I knew what I had to do. I walked up to the gazebo while keeping an eye on my surrounding. Once I got up there, I didn't take the time to look in amazement around myself like I had done while asleep. I didn't dance either. Instead, I turned toward the direction where I knew Makaio would appear.

Sure enough, he was here. My gaze landed on him right as he screamed my name. My heart fractured at the sound, at hearing his desperation, his fear.

"Lani! Please, save me!" His cries were loud in the quiet forest. And, like in my dream, the masked person was holding a knife to Makaio's neck. Ruby-red blood dripped down his neck, drop by drop.

I wanted to run his way, just like I had done then. Except, this time, I froze. More accurately, I was frozen in place, prevented from moving by an unseen force that restrained all of my limbs. I wanted to scream to Makaio, to reassure him, tell him I would make it all okay. But the force was also preventing me from making any sound.

I was utterly helpless. Powerless to help my little brother.

Tears welled in my eyes when the shadowed attacker pressed the knife harder on Makaio's tiny neck. I blinked them away. Suddenly, the twins, Mei, and Archer were there. Kneeling on the ground, restrained with chains, they were held at knifepoint by more people shrouded in shadows.

"This is all your fault, Kalani Mayfield. This is all because of you." The voice came from all around me, the same person as before the forest, but this time, they spoke English.

I wanted to answer that I had no idea what was happening and wanted to help. But my throat was stuck in a silent scream, incapable of saying anything to my friend or brother. I tried to convey how desperately I wanted to help and save them through my eyes.

Except then, the shadow people started cutting and stabbing them. Not deep enough to kill them, but more than enough to hurt and make them scream in pain. And through the tears streaming down their cheeks, they all looked at me as they got tortured. They held me responsible for their pain.

It seemed endless. The stabs, the blood running down their bodies, their screams, and the looks they gave me. Looks that said that I hadn't done enough. I hadn't done enough to prevent this from happening. And I wasn't doing enough to save them. But even as I fought against my invisible bindings, I couldn't move.

I was completely, utterly helpless.

But the worst was the voice. That terrible, terrible voice. It kept whispering in my ears that I was the reason they were in pain. That I was causing their suffering. That I was the reason why they were bleeding to death before my eyes.

Mei was the first one to slump to the ground. Boneless. Lifeless. A pool of coppery blood spread around her small body. Her skin was so pale that she looked almost translucid. And her eyes… her eyes looked up at the night sky, glassy and unseeing.

I choked on a sob, wishing I could go to her. Wishing I could do something, anything, to save her.

"This is all your fault, Kalani Mayfield. You are killing them. Your worthlessness just killed her. It will kill them all." The voice was insistent, insidious, and always present. And the words wormed their way inside my head.

A blood-curdling scream resonated through the clearing as a shadow person stabbed Søren straight through the chest. Time slowed as I watched, helpless, my friend fall to the ground, wheezing in pain. The shadow shifted his face so that it could face mine. And I saw everything as he died – the pain, the fear, and the accusation. The resentment right before the light inside of him went off. The voice must have seen it, too, because it decided to taunt me. "Even your friend knows it is all your fault, little mortal."

Fighting against the invisible force restraining my whole body, I tried to find a solution. Was there something I could offer these people so they would stop hurting the people I loved? Was there anything I could do to stop this madness?

There wasn't anything to do but look, though. And as I did so, I met Sadie's burning gaze. She was angry – so furious and resentful that it was overshadowing the pain she must have been feeling from her multiple wounds. Even without the voice pointing it out, I knew those emotions were aimed at me.

She blamed me.

I couldn't resent her. I was starting to blame myself too.

"Lani! Please! I can't take it anymore!" Makaio's voice was broken and raw from screaming and crying. I felt my heart break apart as I couldn't do anything but watch him in pain. I had always been my brother's protector, and this was my biggest fear – being the reason he got hurt to the point of no return.

I wanted to answer him. Tell him I was trying my best to come to him. Tell him he was strong. Tell him I was sorry. Tell him I loved him more than anyone else.

But my vocal cords were as frozen as the rest of my body. And not being able to comfort my little brother was torture – mental if not physical.

The shadow behind my brother sliced at his chest, so close to his throat that I feared for the worst. Although I could only try to imagine how much pain he must have been in – death might be a blessing. "Look at his tiny body. Who knew a kid could have this much blood inside of him? How long do you think he will keep fighting before the blood loss takes him?" The voice laughed at that as if this was all a game. As if I wasn't stuck watching my brother die before my eyes.

Except Makaio wasn't the next one who had to go. Sadie was. The shadow attacker slashed her throat slowly, and she screamed until she couldn't anymore. And I cried. Tears streamed down my face, blurring my vision, but whoever held me down made sure I could continue watching the show by forcing me to blink fast.

So, I saw it all. The betrayal on Sadie's face. The look full of rage she gave me as she drowned in her blood – full of anger and disdain. I couldn't see my best friend anywhere. Her bright personality, her love, and her care for me had been snuffed out like blowing on a flame.

"See the hate on your friend's face? This is because you killed her. Just like you are responsible for what your boyfriend and brother are undergoing." The voice was having fun with this – it was taunting me gleefully, making sure I knew that they had all of the control over the situation and I had none.

Desperation was *this close* to submerging me. I didn't want to keep watching, but there was no keeping my eyelids closed. I had no choice but to keep silently watching the horror unfolding before me.

One look in his direction told me that Archer wasn't in a better position than Makaio. Rust-colored blood covered his whole body, oozing from dozens of wounds. The shadow behind him held onto his hair, forcing his head back. His eyes, usually either annoyed, amused, or self-assured, were now empty of fight. They glowed with unshed tears under the moonlight, breaking my heart some more. I could tell he was giving up. On himself. On life. On me.

There were so many things I wanted to tell Archer. So many things to admit. To ask forgiveness for. But no sounds would come out. Not even cries of despair that I felt bubbling within my core.

"Lani!" Makaio's scream and my attention snapped to him. He was crying so much that he couldn't speak any more in between the frantic hiccups. I could see why right away. The shadow restraining him had its knife tip pressed against my brother's chest. It should have been an awkward position for the torturer – what with having to hold on to my brother at the same time and having to reach around – but Makaio was so small compared to them that it wasn't. And I could imagine how easy it'd be for the shadow to plunge the knife into the little boy's chest.

It was easy. Too easy. The knife went in like butter.

There wasn't even a scream. The knife must have hit the heart because it only took a few seconds. A few seconds of agony for him, his mouth open in a silent scream, looking at the blade. Agony for me, too, because, even though I didn't feel the physical pain, the way my chest split open at the sight was almost physical.

Makaio then looked up, his eyes locking with mine. He mouthed my name as tears streamed down his baby cheeks. I knew he was asking for help. *My* help. I had always helped him. I had always done my best to protect him. Always.

And now I was failing miserably.

Instead of protecting him from harm, I watched him die. I witnessed his joyful and bright soul disappear from his body. And even with all my strength fighting against my restraints, I could do nothing.

"What a useless sister you are, mortal. Incapable of saving such a pure soul. Helpless to do anything," the voice whispered in my ear. "You should be ashamed."

I was. I was so ashamed and mad at myself. I had lost Mei, Søren, Sadie, and now Makaio. Archer was the last one standing, and he wouldn't be making it long based on how much blood he had lost already.

I didn't want to look at him. I didn't want to see him hurt. I didn't want to witness more suffering, more death. The voice didn't leave me much of a choice, though. The force controlling me ensured I had nothing else to look at except Archer. Archer bleeding out. Archer on his knees, at the mercy of a guy who was destroying him little by little.

I didn't want to see him look at me like I'd betrayed him.

"It's okay, baby, it's okay." His voice was strained, his eyes teary. We both knew it wasn't okay. But if he could pretend for my sake, then I could pretend for his.

I tried to smile at him, but I didn't think the force holding me allowed for more than a slight curving of the corners of my lips. Archer started smiling back slowly, the muscles of his face ticking and jerking from his pain.

The voice was murmuring that he was wrong, that it wouldn't be fine. I didn't listen, though. I focused on Archer's eyes, the deep ocean blue of his irises. I was too far to lose myself within their depth, but I held eye contact all the same.

I held his gaze as he shivered and swayed on his knees from blood loss.

I held his gaze as his body shook from the pain of the many wounds on his body.

I held his gaze as the shadow put both hands around his head.

And I held his gaze as the shadow broke his neck.

The voice laughed so loud that my ears started ringing. I felt like I couldn't breathe anymore as I stared at the five people I cared for the most lying lifeless on the ground.

"How does it feel to be the reason everyone you love dies?" The voice jeered, mocking me. "Was there ever a chance you'd have a worthy life?"

Looking at my friends and family lying on the cold grass in their blood, I had to admit that perhaps not. Perhaps I hadn't ever had a chance. Perhaps all my efforts had appointed to nothing except putting everyone I loved in danger.

"There is a way to save them. Great sacrifices can work miracles."

I didn't want to listen to the voice because I knew they wanted something from me. But those words – "save them" – called to the desperate hope I had to make this right.

Some part of me knew there was a catch. How could anyone revive five people after they had died? But the voice kept on taunting me, telling me that it was all my fault, that I'd forever be alone in the world because of my inaction.

I didn't know how long I remained there, watching the corpse of the people I loved, incapable of moving or looking away, before I cracked. "What is it? What can I do?" The voice must have known I would break because I didn't even have to strain to speak.

There was a second of silence, and I could almost feel the satisfaction this invisible scumbag felt. "It's easy little mortal." There was a ghost of a breath along my neck and cheek as if the voice was right next to me. I dropped my eyes and saw a blade dripping with coppery blood in my hand. "A life for a life."

The voice stopped whispering to me, and the clearing became eerily calm. All of the shadow attackers had disappeared. It was just me standing, surrounded by an invisible presence and five dead people. Within the blanket of silence, the words echoed in my head.

A life for a life.

I knew what it meant. I could save one of them by sacrificing my own life. And maybe the voice was right – perhaps I was only a plight in this world and on the people I love. Maybe it'd be better for everyone if I did give my life to save someone else's. Maybe that was the best I could ever hope to accomplish.

"That's right, little Kalani. This is the best you can offer them. You just have to choose now."

The whispers were constant, telling me to choose, choose, *choose*. And I was starting to panic, my chest constricting because I didn't want to choose. Or, to be fully honest, I knew I would choose Makaio, but I didn't want to say it aloud. I didn't want to abandon the others. I didn't want to have to decide that I cared about my friends less. Because I didn't. I loved them in a different way than I did Makaio. But Mei, Sadie, Søren, and Archer…

It's okay, baby, it's okay.

I could almost see him repeating those words. The man that I had come to love – I couldn't lie to myself anymore – in the past six weeks. The man who had shown me I was strong and capable, even when I didn't believe in myself. I could almost see him telling me it was okay to decide.

It's okay, baby, it's okay.

I wished I could tell him that it wasn't. That I shouldn't have to make a choice like this. That I didn't want to be the reason he died and didn't come back. That he deserved more. And-

Wait.

Baby. Not Mayfield. Archer had never called me 'baby' before. Ever. He despised cutesy nicknames like 'baby,' 'honey,' or 'my love.' He would have never said this, especially at a time like this – a time that wasn't a joke. He would have said my last name.

My eyes whipped to his body, lying at odd angles on the ground. Even though my eyes couldn't pick out anything that wasn't Archer,

I knew it wasn't him. I knew this body wasn't him like I knew the back of my hand.

And then everything fell like dominoes.

I had flashbacks of sitting in the waiting room for hours, of entering the Pit and being in a dark room. Of this being part of the Tournament.

This was the second Trial.

A trial of the mind.

None of this was real. Somehow, the illusion had wormed its way into my mind and made me forget that I was in a Trial. But now I knew. It was still hard to convince myself that none of this was a reality since I could see their bodies on the grass. But I repeated it in my head like a mantra – *none of this is real, none of this is real.*

"So, who have you chosen, little mortal?" The voice was still whispering, trying to convince me that it would be best to sacrifice myself to save one of them.

"No one. This is not real. None of them are actually dead. This is an illusion, and I refuse to participate anymore."

I dropped the blade on the ground. It thudded against the wood of the gazebo at my feet. My voice was steel, with confidence I wasn't sure I felt dripping from every word. I wouldn't let myself get played anymore.

I wouldn't let whichever deity had planned this win.

My words must have been enough to win the Trial because the forest and all the horrors it contained disappeared like the fog lifting over the countryside. The sandy arena returned with its sounds – the deafening cheers and boos of the crowd watching the Trials. And the dagger, glinting in the sun at my feet.

I was disoriented for a second, swaying on my feet as I looked around, fighting the blinding sun to find the box where the gods and goddesses sat. Specifically, I searched for Artemis.

Even from a distance, I could tell from the frown on her face that she was disappointed in my success. I had to refrain myself from giving her a massive middle finger. I knew she was rooting for my defeat, on me proving that she was right in her elitist views. She wanted to show everyone that humans were dirt beneath their feet. That we couldn't fight on their turf. That we shouldn't even be allowed to breathe the same air.

I wouldn't let her win.

And, just because I wanted to make sure she knew I wouldn't back down, I gave her the most sarcastic smile and bow I could manage.

I had just survived two out of the four Trials. I was well on my way to survival – we both knew that.

So, when I stood back up, I locked eyes with her and raised an eyebrow in challenge. *Game on, Artemis.*

Chapter Twenty-Nine

Coming out of the Pit and seeing my friends waiting for me in the hallway was surreal. Sadie and Archer were deep in conversation, seated on a bench near the wall, and the two lovebirds were busy cuddling next to them. For a second, none of them saw me, and I could bask in the knowledge that they were still here. Alive.

It only lasted a second because Mei saw me between two kisses and jumped from Søren's lap. Then all of them stood up, and I couldn't move. I was frozen in place because some part of me was terrified – I had just seen them die horribly, and I was scared that this was just a continuation of the mental torture.

So, I stood awkwardly, tears welling in my eyes as I looked frantically over their bodies. Checking for injuries I knew weren't there. Checking for blood I knew hadn't been spilled.

"K, finally, you're back! You took your time over there!" Søren was all smiles, his bright white teeth on display as he gently made fun of me. He had an arm around Mei's back, holding her to him. And he looked so chill. They all seemed so relaxed and so… normal.

How could I feel normal after what I had just seen and lived through?

"Are you okay?" Sadie took a couple of steps toward me, seeming to sense that, no, I wasn't okay. Shit had gone down in that arena, and even though I had played it tough in front of Artemis, I felt like

I was fraying at the seams. Like my emotions were too big for my body.

Seeing them here was making everything – the fear, the sadness, the agony, the terror – bubble up from my chest, and the bowl was seconds away from overflowing.

I could only shake my head, trying to hold on to the tears and remain as composed as I could. I saw concerned gazes from Archer and Mei, but then Sadie was there. She hugged me, an anchor to my aimless and lost boat. That hug felt amazing because it was the best proof that she was alive and well. That everything had been a terrifying and cruel illusion.

I didn't know how long I remained in her arms, but it took a while before I stopped shaking. The tears didn't fall. I almost wished they did – it might have been a cleansing moment. Instead, all of the adrenaline left my body through uncontrollable shakes and ragged breaths, and when they finally stopped, I felt completely drained.

When Sadie moved back, her frown conveyed all the worry she must have felt. She didn't prod into what had happened, though. She just asked if I was feeling better. I nodded, and it wasn't a lie. The hug had helped, and seeing my friends standing just a few feet behind Sadie made me feel better. I had just needed a moment to make sure that everything was fine.

"Well! It must have been one hell of a Trial, huh?" Søren said brightly, tapping me on the shoulder.

Sadie gave him an annoyed glare, but I smiled at her reassuringly – at least, I hoped it came out that way.

"Yeah, it was intense, to say the least." My voice was a little shakier than I would have liked but oh well. Can't win 'em all. "I'm glad to see all of you. I imagine you all made it?"

Mei nodded emphatically, leaning more on her boyfriend's side. "Yes, it wasn't the easiest, but we all made it!"

I couldn't find it in myself to answer Mei's enthusiastic smile. I didn't know what she had seen out there, but I doubted it had been the same thing I had gotten. Or if it had, then all of them were much more insensitive and coldhearted than I had thought before.

Before I could figure out what to say to that, Sadie offered for us to walk to the cafeteria to get an early dinner. The Trial had taken so long that the whole day had gone by. Now that Sadie had mentioned food, I realized that I was terribly hungry – the stress and anticipation had hidden the hunger until now, but it came back with a vengeance.

Right away, everybody started walking toward the mess hall. They were probably just as famished as I was. Unsurprisingly, Søren was dragging Mei ahead in front of everybody else – that man was always starving, no matter how much he ate. Somehow, he still looked like one of those ancient Greek statues. Gods, I wished I could have the metabolism that godly parentage gave these kids.

I started walking behind the lovebirds and Sadie when fingers intertwined with mine. I knew right away that it was Archer – I could recognize his calloused but gentle hand, the heat coming from his skin, and the way he held my hand tight enough that I felt grounded. From the corner of my eyes, I looked around to see who else was with us in the hallway, who we were pretending for.

Except it was just us.

No one was there to watch us.

Knowing that he had chosen to hold my hand warmed me from the inside. Like a marshmallow melting in hot chocolate.

Neither I nor Archer spoke during the walk. Holding hands that way, in almost empty hallways, felt already too intimate. So, of course, by the time we reached the cafeteria, I had a solid blush going on.

Entering the cafeteria was a surprising affair for two reasons. The first was that only a little over a dozen Coppers were sitting there – had all of the others failed? Or were there people who were done eating already? How many had failed the second Trial? Seeing so many empty tables was troubling. But what really surprised me was that Archer dropped my hand as soon as we were in view of the other competitors.

Why did the ridiculous thought that he cared – that he wanted this moment to be just for us – make my heart flutter so hard?

I was thankful for the line and choice of food for the distraction they provided me from… well, from too many things.

I took my time serving myself, choosing dishes whose names I didn't know but had tried and liked. To be fair, most of the food items I had encountered on Olympus I still couldn't name. I never asked anymore; I just tried, and usually, they were much better than most Earthly dishes. Yet one more advantage of living on this piece of rock.

Once we were all seated at our usual table in our corner of the room, I tried to ignore how close Archer sat to me. His presence was like a magnetic field next to me, causing all my atoms to line up in his direction.

Søren raised his glass of water and exclaimed loudly, "Skål!"

"What does that mean?" I asked, confused because it was the first time in eight weeks that someone had said a word I didn't understand.

"It means 'cheers' in Danish," Sadie answered while clinking her glass against her twin's.

"And what are we celebrating exactly?" Archer had a frown on, which was his usual response to most things fun.

"Archer, come on! We're celebrating being alive, silly!" Mei laughed and clinked her glass on Archer's before turning to say sweet nothings to Søren. She didn't see it, but Archer threw her a dark glare. Watching Mei and Archer interact was always funny – they were often polar opposites, and her joyful, sometimes slightly clueless comments annoyed Archer to no end.

Even though I didn't feel like celebrating and having fun after the day I'd just had, I still played along. After all, we had done a pretty incredible thing today by getting one step closer to earning our place on Olympus. Still, as everyone started eating and talking animatedly, I felt the emptiness inside my chest that wouldn't disappear. I couldn't focus on anything else outside of it – how long would it take for me to feel normal again after such a traumatic experience?

"Mayfield?" Archer's voice snapped me out of my thoughts and back to reality. He and Sadie were watching me with concerned expressions. "Do you want to go over your Trial?"

"We've already started debriefing while waiting for you, but we'd love to hear what happened to you." Sadie had her mom face on, the one she put on every time she wanted to take care of one of us.

Did I want to talk about what had happened? Not really. But I knew the therapist I'd seen for a couple of sessions after my gymnastics accident in high school would have said that it was essential to express my feelings and be vulnerable with the people I trusted. So, I'd do it, but first, I wanted to know if what I'd seen during the Trial was on par with everybody else's experiences.

"What did you guys see during the Trial?"

Both of my friends must have seen that I wanted to delay the inevitable, but I was glad they agreed to play along. "From what we gathered, the Trial was about facing one's fears, seeing through illusions, and showing strength of will," Sadie explained while cutting her meat into tiny bits. "We all saw a version of a strong fear we have. For instance, I ended up surrounded by thousands of huge spiders. It was quite terrifying."

I actually had to scoff a little because I always found it funny that Sadie, the girl who could literally raise the dead, was terrified of spiders.

"I ended up on the roof of a skyscraper and had to jump across to another building to escape someone chasing me. The jump itself wasn't even that far. It was just getting close enough to the ledge that was a challenge." Mei's fear of heights was not something I thought had such a significant impact on her. After all, we had gone to the training compound's roof as a group a few times, and she hadn't freaked out. But I guessed the building wasn't that high, so she might have been able to trick her body into not panicking.

My eyes landed on Søren since he was right next to Mei, and he sighed dramatically. "Well, if we're sharing our dirty laundry... I got thrown into a frozen desert without my powers. Freezing to death didn't appeal to me so I quickly pierced through that ridiculous illusion."

Our eyes shifted to Archer, who sat ramrod straight on the bench, staring in the distance. He didn't speak for a while, and I wondered if he would ever tell us what had happened to him. I was about to start talking about my own experience when he cleared his throat.

"Let's just say I had a nice encounter with my stepmother." I had never heard him speak with so much hatred for someone before – not even when he had been livid at Elena, Alexei, and Nathan for cornering me in the Pit. His tone was so chilling that I didn't even ask for more information. I knew that he wouldn't give me anything else.

And now that everyone had shared their part, I had no way to delay this any longer. I swallowed the nerves that had taken residency in my throat and cleared my throat, feeling weirdly apprehensive around my friends.

"I… I saw all four of you and my brother get tortured and then killed. Through it all, some invisible psychopathic person restrained me, and I was forced to watch without being able to intervene. And then-" I had to stop for a second because I could feel the weight of the blade in my right hand again. *A life for a life.* "And then, the voice gave me a knife and convinced me to sacrifice myself to save one of you."

Somehow, I managed to get through this whole monologue without breaking down in the middle of the cafeteria. I wasn't sure how I wasn't crying right now. Reliving the trial… well, I was glad I'd had the sense to put my hands beneath my thighs so they would stop shaking. And I was suddenly grateful for the capacity to bottle up my emotions – I couldn't break down here, not when I was surrounded by sharks who would love to see me bleed.

There was a long silence. All of my friends were digesting the news. The Trial I had gone through seemed so different from theirs, although being responsible for the death of the people I love and ending up alone in the world was one of my fears. Potentially my worst fear.

"You didn't, though, right?" Sadie's voice was tight as if she were repressing her emotions to remain calm.

"No. I almost did. But Archer actually saved me." A wry laugh escaped me as I remembered the tiny detail that gave the masquerade away. "It's a good thing you always call me Mayfield. The illusion of you calling me 'baby' is the only reason I didn't go through with it."

As I finished, I glanced toward Archer and found him staring at me, his eyes glimmering with an emotion I couldn't name. Oh, how I wished for those empath powers right now. It would have been helpful to know not only how Archer was feeling but also what emotions the others were going through. I felt terribly vulnerable, revealing my deepest fear, and I wanted to know if their perception of me had changed.

No one peeped a word for so long that it felt like forever. Sadie and Archer were having a mental conversation thanks to his gifts. Those were incredibly annoying.

"Damn, K. That was a lot more hardcore than what we ended up with. None of us were at risk of dying from our illusions. We just had to see through them before a timer went off." Søren was saying aloud what they must have been thinking because Sadie winced.

"Was the blade real?" Archer's sudden words caused me to jump a little in surprise.

I nodded, remembering how it had been at my feet as the real arena returned to focus around me. It was the only thing present in the illusion and real life. Now that I actually thought about it, if the dagger had been real, then I would have probably really killed myself.

How unfortunate.

My mind was spinning with the implications of Søren's words. If none of them had ever been in danger of dying during that second Trial, why had I been given an actual blade and manipulated into sacrificing myself for the greater good? Was it against me? Against my human status? Or was it because I had been the last competitor to go, and the organizers had wanted to spice it up at the end?

Either way, I was both scared and furious about this special treatment I'd been offered.

"But why would they try to make her kill herself that way?" Mei asked, more serious than she'd been in days.

"Maybe to show that humans are much weaker when faced with mental control? Or maybe because some people on Olympus despise humans and would do anything in their power to ensure that none of them get to earn their place to live among them as anything other than slaves."

"Archer!" Sadie whisper-shouted with indignation, the same way she had during the Opening Ceremony when Archer had also made controversial comments.

"What? We're all thinking it, Sadie. Grow a pair and stop being so damn afraid of saying anything less than loving about those assholes we call gods."

The staring contest that Archer and Sadie were in was glacial at best. Jeez, this had gotten tense really fast.

"Should we be talking about this in public?" I asked, looking around nervously. We were at a table decently far from any other Coppers. Still, you couldn't always tell who was listening and whether their parents or family members were trading in advantages for information. What Archer had said was true, but his words could easily be relayed as blasphemous to the wrong people.

Based on the day's events, I already had enough enemies, as it were. I didn't need any more.

However, Sadie and Archer didn't want to stop staring daggers at each other. I had never seen them angry at each other. Ever. Witnessing a disagreement like this, when neither of them would back down, was worrying.

"Sunshine," I murmured, putting a hand softly on his biceps. His gaze snapped to mine for a hot second before he looked down at my hand. I almost removed it but realized I didn't want to. I wanted to be the one he could count on to bring him back, to ground him when his emotions got the best of him.

I didn't add anything else, but he brought his eyes back up, and we stared into each other's eyes – each other's souls – for what felt like years. Everything slowed down, including my heart rate. It felt like we were in our bubble, away from the world. And by the time we came back to the real world, the lines between Archer's eyebrows had disappeared, his face calm and collected one again. Even his whole posture had relaxed.

Removing my hand from his biceps was like leaving a warm house in the middle of a freezing winter day – I suddenly felt so cold. I didn't let myself dwell on that, though. I shifted on the bench and brought my attention back to the conversation.

"… need to figure out whether this is an attack against Kalani herself or against the idea of having a human live on Olympus."

Mei acquiesced at Søren's words. Somehow, she had fit in just right with our group since she had been made aware of my… unusual circumstances.

"Agreed. I'll reach out to our outside connections for intel," Sadie announced as if nothing had happened.

"Who are those connections?" I hadn't ever questioned much who the twins and Archer went out to see every so often. I knew they weren't supposed to leave, but I guessed they were good enough at sneaking around to make it out and back in without being seen.

"Our dad has a soft spot for us," Søren answered with a proud smile.

"And Hecate likes me for some reason." Archer started eating again, focusing on his food to avoid looking at Sadie in front of him. "We'll get answers fast enough."

And that was that for this conversation. For the remainder of the meal, they chatted about random things, all of them avoiding mentions of the Trial or how I'd almost died. And I tried my best to smile and nod at the correct times. But my mind was stuck in a moonlit clearing where blood ran on the damp earth and stained the delicate white flowers on the grass. I couldn't escape the desperation I'd felt an hour before. The second Trial had branded my soul, and I didn't know how to heal from that.

A few hours later, when I left the bathroom after showering and getting ready for bed, I felt a little more settled. Not fully okay yet –

I'd probably never get to be okay again, not the way I'd been before – but slowly getting closer to that point.

Archer was sitting on his bed, shirtless, reading another one of his books in ancient Greek. He seemed hyper-focused on whatever was written on the page, so I moved around the room silently, hoping this night wouldn't be too bad.

"Thank you for earlier."

I frowned in confusion. "What for?"

He turned one more page, his gaze never leaving the paper. "With Sadie. I lost control. I shouldn't have."

"You know, you don't have to always be the one in control of your emotions, right? You can let go sometimes. The world won't fall apart."

This time, he closed the book and sat up to face me. "Yeah? And what happens when something terrible happens to one of you because I wasn't at my best?"

"That's awfully conceited of you to think that we can't function without you, Sunshine." I chuckled at the way his eyes narrowed. "But, just to reassure you, I'd be there and support you in trying to save us all from doom."

"Really?" He leaned forward, his elbows resting on his knees.

I swallowed thickly because his gaze had gotten intense, and I wasn't sure we were talking about him being vulnerable anymore. "I'll always be by your side."

"Good. I'll stick by you too, Mayfield. Until the end."

Chapter Thirty

The cake was drop-dead delicious. Somehow even better than the one we'd had a few days ago. The chocolate melted in my mouth, and I felt like I had reached culinary heaven. I must have released a moan of delight because Mei snorted a laugh before me. I could have felt embarrassed about my expressive reaction to the food, but she was also having the time of her life with said cake – so much so that she wasn't even wasting time breathing between bites.

For a second, I wondered why the twins and Archer weren't back yet. They'd left us to do one of their secret things and Mei had given me a yoga session. The cake made up for the terribly boring and uncomfortable afternoon.

I was in the process of taking the biggest bite of cake I could manage somewhat safely when a scream resonated in the cafeteria. It was bone-chilling and echoed in the otherwise silent room, making the hair on the back of my neck rise.

Before I even turned to look at the source of the scream, I knew it would be bad. My chest tightened in fear, and my heart beat frantically.

Still, the anticipation hadn't quite prepared me for the sight that greeted me when I turned around and faced a ghost. Not a literal ghost, but a ghost of my past that had lived in my nightmares for weeks now.

Charlie.

He was lying there; body contorted in a pain-inducing angle, coppery blood staining the white floors and the corners of his mouth. But the worst was his eyes. Glassy, unseeing, they still somehow managed to stare straight at me as if piercing my soul.

And once I made eye contact, there was no escaping the pull of him.

It felt like being sucked into a black hole – Charlie was exerting so much gravitational pull on my soul that I felt myself get closer and closer. And my body wouldn't hear the desperate pleas echoing in my head to get as far from him as possible.

I didn't have control anymore.

None at all.

My feet stopped when I was standing in a puddle of blood. White shoes in bronze blood. I almost felt Charlie's life force draining from his body and surrounding me. I must have started crying because everything was blurry except for his eyes, staring directly into the deepest recesses of my soul.

I could feel his judgment. He was dead, but I could hear his voice accusing me of not helping. Of not having done enough to save him.

And I had nothing to say to defend myself.

Coward. Good-for-nothing human. You left me. You left me to die.

Charlie's voice was loud in my head, loud enough to drown my thoughts. But then other voices joined in. At first, they were whispers, but they grew in intensity until I could recognize Makaio's voice. Mei. The twins. Archer.

Charlie's gaze finally released mine, and my eyes snapped up, desperate to escape his pull, only to meet five more dead bodies.

We weren't in the cafeteria anymore.

I was standing in a clearing lit by the purest moonlight and twinkling with fairy lights. And I was surrounded by everyone I cared for. Dead.

The voices were now shouting in my head, and I couldn't escape them. I couldn't escape their words. I couldn't escape the lifeless eyes surrounding me, accusing me of the deaths of everyone I loved.

I couldn't escape the pain their screams caused me – a physical pain that tore my mind apart. And I sure couldn't escape the truth in their words.

Everything was spinning out of control. Reality was warping and bending, and I was in so much pain. Sobs racked my body. Tears streamed down my face, but I could still see so clearly. I could see the pain on Sadie's face. I could see the terror in Makaio's dead eyes. I could see the judgment in Søren's body, frozen in time.

And everything was too much.

Too much pain.

Too much grief.

I screamed, desperate to escape the view, and the words, and the world. I screamed until my throat was as painful as my head and heart. I screamed until I had no air anymore.

I fell to the ground, knees splashing in Charlie's ever-flowing blood. I didn't have air anymore. I didn't have a voice, either. But still, I kept silently screaming and screaming and-

A hand touched my shoulder, and everything stopped. I blinked, and my eyes opened to pitch black dark. There weren't any voices in my head anymore – everything was deadly silent, too silent – and no bodies were around me anymore. But something – someone – was holding onto my shoulder, and I didn't know who it was.

My first instinct was to fight. I had to defend myself from whoever this was, even if I couldn't see the assailant. I thrashed and readied myself to scream when hands grabbed my wrists and pinned them down next to my body.

"Stop it, Mayfield. You're going to hurt yourself."

Archer's voice – gentle if a little annoyed – was so jarring that I stopped dead in my tracks. What-

"You were having a nightmare. I brought you out of it."

His hands were still around my wrists. Tight enough to hold me in place but not so much that it'd hurt. His skin was warm, and the calluses on his fingers scratched my skin in soothing motions. Somehow, his calm words and the physical contact were enough to get my body to press pause for a second and assess the situation.

Archer was here – alive and well. I was lying in my bed, covers tangled around my legs. And my eyes were getting used to the dark – I could see the vague outline of Archer's body next to me.

It was a dream.

It was just a dream.

Acknowledging that I wasn't stuck in the clearing anymore and that everything I'd seen had been a nightmare helped. My chest inflated all the way for the first time in what felt like hours – it felt like a boulder had been removed from my shoulders. But, while my heartbeat was slowly returning to normal, I still felt unsettled. It was hard to banish what I'd seen from my mind.

"Can I let go? Will you stop fighting me off like a wild cat?"

I couldn't see Archer's face, but I could imagine the mocking grin on his face. I'd usually snap back at him – bantering with him always made me smile – but I wasn't anywhere close to my normal mindset. So, instead, I hummed a noncommittal sound and remained immobile.

After a few seconds, Archer's fingers relaxed and moved away from my wrists. I also reached for his hands – my skin felt too cold without his warming it up.

"Thank you, Archer." My voice was weak and still shaking. I didn't particularly want him to hear the trembles in my voice, but I needed to thank him, even if there wasn't a way for me to tell him just how grateful I was. That nightmare had been awful, especially after the traumatic Trial I'd just survived a few hours ago.

"No worries, Mayfield. Happy to help." His words were soft, and I could almost see the worry in his eyes. He touched me like I was delicate porcelain ready to break at any point. Archer wasn't that gentle with me. Ever.

He remained silent for a while, and I was like frozen in place. The silence and the cold from where my skin wasn't touching Archer's anymore provided plenty of space for my mind to think. And my thoughts were hovering way too close to everyone I loved dying.

Still in the dark, I heard the moment Archer started moving away. His shorts rustled, and he sighed softly. "I'll let you sleep."

"No," the word spilled from my lips. I was suddenly sitting up, my body desperately reaching for his. "Please."

I hated the way I sounded – desperate and scared. Especially in front of Archer. I didn't want him to think I was any more helpless than he already believed. But here, in the dark, alone together... well, there was no hiding the emotions close to overwhelming me. Being this vulnerable was not something I usually did. It made me feel very uncomfortable.

"I don't want to be alone."

There was a lot hidden in that sentence, but I instinctively knew Archer understood the hidden layers behind my words. I was terrified of being left alone with my thoughts and emotions. For weeks, I'd fought against the world I'd been thrown into while enduring emotional lashings from the trials and the ruthlessness around me. One could only bottle up emotions so far until they overflowed.

Today was the tipping point.

Archer remained silent for a second, and my chest – already tight with the vulnerability of showing my fears to him – squeezed painfully. I didn't know how I was going to react to rejection. I painfully needed a friend right then. Someone to help me ride the wave of despair and fear. Someone to hold my hand until I felt okay again.

Just the thought of having to lay in my bed, alone, all night, without anyone to help remind me that my friends and brother were fine... my hands started shaking, and my breathing quickened.

"Okay." Archer cleared his throat. "I'll stay with you."

I was relieved. So, so relieved. I couldn't say anything, though, because there was a lump of emotions stuck in my throat.

"Scoot over."

I obeyed without questions and shifted until Archer could sit next to me, his back against the headrest. For a second, I was frozen in place, wondering how I had ended up sitting in bed with Archer. But the thought was only fleeting, barely there. My mind was already overwhelmed with the fear and hopelessness that the nightmare had brought back. There wasn't much space left for thoughts about the man beside me. At least, not in the way I usually thought about him.

"Are you going to remain in this weird position for a long time, Mayfield?" Archer patted the mattress next to him. "Come here. You'll be more comfortable."

He was right. Once I scooted back and sat next to him, our shoulders touching, I felt better. The light physical touch was just enough to ground me into reality and stop my imagination from going back to those places. The cafeteria, with Charlie's dying gaze pleading with me for help. The clearing in the woods, with Makaio's cries and my friends' screams.

Archer's presence didn't stop the wave of uncontrollable emotions but took it down from a tsunami to a strong wave.

For a while, neither of us spoke. I tried to concentrate on my breathing, on my shaking limbs. I tried to calm my beating heart down to a normal level. And Archer's calm, even breaths were a metronome in the storm, helping me gather myself.

I still struggled, though. The nightmare had brought to the surface of my mind many things I'd buried in the past few weeks. Being kidnapped and thrown into a whole new world. Being separated from my family. Fighting and training every day until my body couldn't move anymore. Making sure I never showed a weakness because I was surrounded by ruthless Coppers. Witnessing Charlie's death. Being forced to watch my friends and little brother being tortured and executed in cold blood. It was a lot. It was too much. And, while I somewhat managed to stop the panic I'd fallen into from the nightmare, the fear was slowly turning into an endless pit of sadness and grief.

Grief for who I used to be.

Grief for the girl who'd sung "Single Ladies" while doing the dishes. The girl who had her life all planned out. The girl who would never be again.

I must have started crying because a tear fell on my hand. For a second, I was shocked at that realization. I hadn't cried in so long. Way too long.

It should have felt nice – crying was usually cathartic in a cleansing sort of way. But the tears kept falling silently and didn't make me feel better. I just felt sad, and so, *so* lonely.

I must have made a sound because Archer's hand grabbed mine. He squeezed my hand, just tight enough that I could *feel* that he was here, holding onto me. It was nice, but it wasn't quite enough. Somehow, he felt it because, the next thing I knew, I was snuggled into his chest, and both of his arms were around me.

The hug was warm. Archer's arms were like bands of steel around me – an armor to protect me against the rest of the world. And there, breathing his scent and feeling his heartbeat against my cheek, I felt safe.

Safe enough to completely break down.

One second I was silently crying, and the next, I was sobbing uncontrollably, my tears staining Archer's soft t-shirt. The mental barriers I'd built to contain my emotions and continue to push on were crumbling down. There was no stopping them. The only I could do was ride the wave of grief, anger, fear, and loneliness.

And hope I'd make it to the other side.

I didn't know how long I stayed that way – buried in Archer's chest, sobbing – but Archer was here through it all. His arms held me together as I fell apart. His thumbs drew small circles on my back to soothe my bleeding heart. And he murmured reassuring words every so often – just to let me know that I wasn't alone in this, that he would always be here with me.

After what felt like forever, my tears dried up. My body stopped shaking. My breath evened out. And my mind quieted down.

I wasn't feeling great – I wasn't sure I'd ever feel that way after everything I'd been through. But letting myself feel my emotions allowed me to drain down the anxiety and grief caused by the nightmare and the events of the past few weeks. I was still scared for my friends and brother, still worried about myself, and still angry about the injustice of my situation. But I wasn't terrified or drowning in pain and sadness anymore. My feelings felt more level, like the calm ocean after a nasty storm.

"Are you feeling better?"

Hearing Archer's voice after all of this was a shock. I'd been in his arms for a long time, but the dark room — how it prevented us from seeing each other — had made being vulnerable easier. Being reminded that he'd witnessed my breakdown was uncomfortable.

"Yeah." I swallowed nervously and tried moving away, only to be stopped by his arms tightening around me. "Sorry about that."

"Don't be. It happens to everyone."

I wasn't sure whether that was supposed to help or not. How could it be considered normal to force young adults and kids into a Tournament that broke them mentally? Was it supposed to make us stronger? It sure didn't feel that way. Forcing me to witness my friends and brother be tortured and killed, even if it had been an illusion, was monstrous. Forcing all of us to compete here and survive through violence was inhumane. None of it was okay. None of it was normal.

"Do you trust me?" Archer's words were hesitant, almost shy. What was happening?

"In theory."

That made him laugh, the sound warming up my chest. I was so glad he'd been there — even if being this open with him made me slightly self-conscious. I'd needed someone to help me through the night, and Archer had been there. Without questions. At least this forsaken Tournament had brought me amazing friends.

"Let's test that theory then," he chuckled.

In the next breath, the room had disappeared. I had to blink against tears from the blinding light all around me. But the smell… I would have recognized the beach anywhere.

Sure enough, once I managed to open my eyes without crying, I was met with a postcard-worthy view. White sand surrounded us, with palm trees in the background behind Archer. The only sounds came from the gentle waves that brought clear cater onto the warm sand. And it smelled like home.

"Why… why are we here? Where are we?" I was so confused that I didn't even realize it was now very bright around, and I was still almost sprawled onto Archer's chest. But the moment I turned to look into his face, the realization that his face was dangerously close hit me like a brick wall.

Shit.

I almost jumped out of the way and looked away at the ocean. I'd woken him with screams in the middle of the night, then proceeded to spend however-long sobbing in his arms, plastered all over his chest. I didn't particularly want to see what he thought about that now that we were both somewhat calm and in broad daylight. I tried my hardest not to be self-conscious, but it was hard.

"I thought it'd be nice for you to get away, even if it's not quite real."

"That's… thoughtful." This considerate version of Archer was almost scary. "Why the beach, though?"

Archer cleared his throat before answering, almost as if he was uncomfortable. "You mentioned you like surfing. I figured that must mean you enjoy the beach."

A slow smile grew on my face because this was sweet. I couldn't even remember that conversation. It must have been a passing comment, something I'd said after Søren had asked one of those really untactful questions about what *little humans* could possibly have for hobbies. Knowing he'd listened and remembered…

"I'm surprised you paid attention." I wasn't sure why I said that, but it seemed like I was on a 'let's be open and honest' roll tonight and didn't have the energy for a filter anymore.

"What do you think I do? Spend every waking second thinking about sparring and training?"

"Yeah, actually. I bet your fun thoughts revolve around your favorite chokehold position or that fencing combo you love to use against the twins. Thrilling stuff."

He scoffed in false offense, and the small laugh I released surprised me. He playfully shouldered me, and, this time, the smile remained on my lips. I felt a little lighter.

"Do you want to talk about it? I won't judge, I promise." His words were serious and barely loud enough to be heard above the gentle sounds of the waves.

For a minute, I stared at the horizon, where the ocean met the sky. I wished I could take a board and swim straight into the unknown, far enough that no land would be in sight anymore. Being alone, far from Olympus and its endless sea of clouds, sounded nice.

I couldn't escape, though. Maybe talking to Archer would help instead. And then, in the morning, I would return to being the determined human doing everything in her power to survive. For now, though, I would allow myself more time to be vulnerable.

"Everything that happened since I arrived on Olympus has finally caught up to me, I guess. Charlie, the second trial… all of the deaths have been too much. I don't know how I am supposed to deal with the terror I feel every time I close my eyes or let my mind wander because all of the horrors I've seen haunt me. Am I expected to be fine with all of it?"

Hands on the warm sand, I focused on the ground and how solid it was beneath me. Then, I focused on the breeze that blew strands of dark hair away from my face. I'd just opened up, and the world – however fake and given to me by Archer's gift – kept spinning. The world hadn't imploded. Talking about it, putting my feeling out there for the wind to take away felt freeing. My old therapist would have been proud.

"You're not expected to be fine. *No one* should be okay with what you've been through, especially after being ripped out of your life without any knowledge of this world." Archer paused for a second, and his pinky finger brushed mine. "I'm glad you are not giving up. Because those huge feelings that you have? The way you look at the world and see its beauty and flaws but still decide to love it? Those things make you so much worthier of living than any of us."

My chest was tight again, but not because of anxiety anymore. Archer validating my feelings was liberating and reassuring but painful too. It hurt to hear him acknowledge the traumatizing events that all of us were forced to participate in. But I needed it. I needed to know that I wasn't crazy, that those things I was feeling and experiencing weren't just underwhelming little offenses.

"I am scared of going back to bed. I keep seeing all of you dying, and I don't know how to stop my thoughts from going there." My voice cracked at the end, and I inhaled quickly to stop the tears gathering in my eyes.

"I know, Mayfield. I know."

I didn't turn, but I could imagine the soft lines on Archer's face. He'd been in my nightmare at the end, bringing me out of it. How much had he seen?

"I promise I will bring you out of every single nightmare you have. No matter how many times I have to bring you to the beach, I'll be there."

I believed that.

Neither of us talked afterward. We sat in comfortable silence for a long time, watching the movement of the ocean and listening to the birds chirping away. Our pinkies still touched, and we didn't move away.

When I finally fell asleep, I didn't dream.

Chapter Thirty-One

There was a coppery taste in my mouth. Blood. It might have been from the cut inside my cheek, from the way my teeth had bitten in. Sadie's right hook was a little too powerful for my taste.

"That's going to bruise," I complained while spitting bloody saliva on the sand.

Sadie grinned and went for a body hit. I dodged and kicked behind her left knee, causing her to lose her balance and fall to her knees. Then I reached around and wrapped my arms around her neck in a chokehold. She wrapped her hands around my forearms and tried to get me to let go. After a few seconds of me holding on for dear life, she changed methods. I saw her move a knee up too late and didn't have time to prepare myself when she pushed up and back. Suddenly, I was flat on the ground, and the shock of my body hitting the ground caused my arms to relax for a second. Sadie used that tiny crack in my defenses to push my arms up and flip us so that I was the one being held on the ground.

"Nice try," Sadie taunted as she blocked both of my wrists above my head with one hand and punched me in the ribs with her other hand. The air rushed out of my lungs, and I fought to catch my breath before Sadie hit again. I had to find a way out of this and fast.

I couldn't get any traction from my arms, seeing as they were stuck above my head, but Sadie hadn't done the best job at holding my legs to the ground. My right leg was mostly free to move. Sadie punched me again in the ribs – why did she like this spot so much? – and I lost all of my air. But the hit gave me a good distraction to move my right foot closer to my butt and push up in a one-legged glute bridge. Sadie fell forward and to the side, leaving an opening for me to push her the rest of the way off me and stand back up.

Sadie got back up, too, and we circled each other, panting and trying to get our breathing back under control.

"Can't believe the human is still standing. You're losing your touch, little sister."

"Shut it, Søren." Sadie's eyes didn't stray from me even as she berated her brother. "And I was born two minutes after you. That gives you hardly any ground to call yourself the older sibling."

I heard Søren laugh in the background, always happy to annoy his sister, followed by Mei, who shushed him and told him to let us focus on the sparring.

I wasn't sure how long we'd been at it, but it must have been longer than usual because I felt like my lungs were one hit away from giving up. It was good – not the lung situation in itself, but the length of time. It meant I finally held my own in one-to-one combat against a well-trained Copper. Better late than never, right?

"Let's just call it a day?" Archer's offer was so unexpected – and out-of-character – that we all stopped and stared dumbly at him.

"What do you mean? You want us to end on a *tie*?" I was slightly breathless and totally confused. Archer had once told me that 'there is no tie in real life, just winners and corpses.' Which was a tad extreme but, I had to admit, worked in the context we were in. Either way, I felt inclined to go and check whether he had a fever and was losing his mind. Could Coppers become sick? Or did their diluted ichor blood help their immune system become invincible? That would sure be nice and convenient.

"Stop looking at me like I am losing my mind. The Third Trial is tomorrow. We don't need to exhaust either of you before then. And I want a shower." He then proceeded to ignore all of our concerned glances and started walking toward the door.

"O-kay then," Sadie exclaimed, drawing out the two syllables and clapping her hands. "Great job, Kalani. You had me worried there for a second with the chokehold."

I chuckled because, let's face it, she could have resorted to a number of methods to get rid of me, including her power. In actual combat, my adversary would probably do so without remorse. But I still appreciated that she played by the rules, and I had to admit it was nice for the ego to have been 'close enough' to hurt a Copper.

It was a great boost in confidence before tomorrow.

"You too, Sadie! Great job on the ribs there." I put a hand over the spot she had decided to hit multiple times in a row. It was more painful than I would have liked to admit. I had gotten used to always being sore and bruised lately, though. That came with the territory of fighting every day. I knew I'd be fine.

Sadie only smiled and pushed her shoulder against mine playfully. That hurt. Oh well. I sure hoped a good night of sleep would help.

The worst thing was knowing that the hits I'd worked really hard to put on Sadie wouldn't be remembered on her skin like hers would be on mine. Like most Coppers, Sadie's bruises didn't even have time to fully bloom before they disappeared – she healed soreness, hits, and cuts in minutes. Oh, the perks of being a deity's grandchild.

Mei and Søren had already started walking out, so we followed them, albeit a little slower. We passed by a few groups of Coppers who were training in preparation for our next Trial. Most people had somber faces on – there were only twenty of us left, and we had no idea how many people would make it past the next step. Many alliances had also been broken during that second Trial, so a few people had to find new people to train with – or choose to train alone.

"How are you feeling about tomorrow?" Sadie asked as we entered the main hallway.

We had taken care not to talk about the upcoming Trial too much in the past four days. We had discussed the past Trial a bit – especially when Archer returned from a solo excursion out of the compound with information from Hecate. The goddess had told him that, from what she knew, Artemis was the head person of a group of deities and Golden who didn't want Olympus' purity to be destroyed by a human. Basically, the special treatment I'd been lucky to receive in the Second Trial had been a way to eliminate the threat my very red blood posed on the whole community living on this mountain. Plus, Hecate had added that because she had been the one to sponsor me entering the Tournament in the first place, it had placed a target on my back – by killing me, Artemis would give a petty middle finger to Hecate. Overall, I didn't know if I should be grateful that none of this was personal or horrified that beings with so much power could have such exclusive and radical thoughts.

Anyway, my point was that while we had talked about how terrible the last Trial had been, we hadn't discussed the new one coming as a group. Here again, I wasn't sure why everyone had tiptoed around the topic as if it were taboo. For me, it had been because I wanted to live in denial for a little bit longer – I didn't want to hear any statistics or other non-helpful information on how deadly the Third Trial usually was.

"Honestly, I don't know how I feel about it. I've been trying to ignore the fact that we still have two other Trials to go through, so I haven't let myself think about it much."

Sadie hummed and nodded slowly a few times, debating what to say. We walked by Elena and Alexei, who were coming from a separate hallway. I avoided looking at them, not because I was scared – the more days went by and the less emprise that night in the Pit held on me – but because I wanted to remain in that weird truce we had going on. They hadn't tried to do anything to me since the twins and Archer had kicked their butt and humiliated them in front of everyone. I wanted to keep it that way for as long as possible. I had enough issues with the resident gods and Goldens without having to worry about those two weasels.

"Usually, the Third Trial isn't as… personal as the second one. It's supposed to be something physical that tests your strength, agility, and overall fitness level." Sadie wiped the sweat off her forehead with her wrist, huffing to remove a hair stuck to her mouth. "Ugh, I hate sweat; it's so annoyingly sticky and gross."

I raised an eyebrow in question. "Is that really what you're most worried about at the moment? Sweat?"

"I know, I know… I should focus on the important stuff. Anyway, my point is that I don't think Artemis or the others will have as much wiggle room to make your Trial harder or deadlier than ours."

It should have relieved me, but I was still very much aware that even a regular Trial could kill me. I didn't have the Coppers' superpowers or supernatural healing. But at least a standard Trial could give me a fighting chance.

"That's great news." My deadpan tone made Sadie smirk. She could read me as easily as a book sometimes.

"I'm glad I could be of help. Now go take a shower. You have some blood on your neck." She shooed me away, and I rolled my eyes at her antics. We both knew the blood came from the sharp hook she had lovingly given me, leading me to bite my cheek so hard that it opened the skin pretty badly. I'd be wincing when eating and drinking for a while.

I didn't bother saying anything else to Sadie and put my hand on the door handle to my and Archer's room and waited for the magic to recognize me before entering. Sadie waited until I was in the room before leaving to go to hers.

When I got in, Archer was already in the bathroom, the distinctive sound of the shower running. He liked long showers, so hot that the steam was usually thick when I came in afterward. How long he took to get ready always made me laugh – I wouldn't have expected it from such a surly, grumpy guy.

I liked it, though.

Smiling to myself, I took my time choosing clothes from the box that Sadie had kept adding stuff to over the past few weeks. It wasn't ever cold here, but I wanted to wear something cozy and comfortable tonight. I was humming one of my favorite Taylor Swift songs and debating between two pairs of sweatpants when the door to the bathroom opened. I turned my head, surprised that Archer was done already, to find him with only a towel around his hips. He was wiping his hair with another small towel, beads of water dripping down his neck and torso.

"You got a bit of drool there, Mayfield." He pointed to the side of his mouth. His arrogant, self-assured smirk made me want to strangle him.

"You wish I paid that kind of attention to you, Sunshine." I must not have been very convincing because his smirk widened, clearly enjoying himself.

I really wanted to say something that would make him regret his words, but his bare chest and his attitude were too distracting, and, to my defense, I was tired. So, instead of risking giving him more ammo to make fun of me, I rolled my eyes at him, grabbed my clothes, and almost sprinted toward the bathroom.

I hoped the shower would let me clear my head and regain my composure. It didn't. What the shower did do was cleanse my body and make me feel nice and refreshed. But even after brushing and braiding my hair, getting dressed, and wasting as much time as possible, I still couldn't get Archer out of my head. It sucked and annoyed me to no end. I wished I could give my rebellious heart a stern talking to about having crushes on unattainable men.

When I walked back into the room, Archer was thankfully fully dressed in grey sweatpants and hoodie combo. We both had the same idea of dressing comfortably for our last dinner together before the Third Trial.

Had I ever mentioned how sexy grey sweatpants could be? No? Well, I should have.

It took a lot of concentration for me to ignore him and walk straight to my dresser. I could *feel* his gaze on me as I busied my hands with making my bed and arranging my single pillow. We both knew I was gaining time and avoiding him – I could feel Archer's smugness from the other side of the room.

"Are you feeling better, Mayfield?" His tone conveyed very clearly that he wasn't asking about my overall state of being but how flustered I'd been earlier.

Deciding that continuing to fluff the thin pillow would only give him more ammunition to play with me, I turned around, stared him down, and crossed my arms over my chest defiantly. "Slight moment of confusion. Stress and fatigue will do that to you. But we're all good now. My body remembers how there's absolutely nothing to be attracted to here."

Archer chuckled darkly before standing up from his bed and taking a few steps toward me. Hands in his pockets, he appeared relaxed, but the way he stalked forward… it was like he was chasing prey.

"Oh, really?"

I nodded and fought to keep my head high even as he kept advancing. He was only two steps away now, closer than we usually were in this room. "Yes, I-" I stopped short because, suddenly, he was right there. Close enough that I could smell him – like a storm that was coming over the ocean. Close enough that I could *feel* him. The goosebumps that spread on my arms and legs were thankfully mostly hidden by my clothes. But the blush that crept up my neck and my face? Oh, Archer saw it.

"What is it, Mayfield?" He raised his hand and traced his fingers against my cheek. "Is it the stress again?"

I wanted to answer, but I couldn't. My throat was tight, my skin flushed, and I couldn't move my eyes away from his. He was the Sun, and I was a planet orbiting around him, closer and closer, incapable of escaping his gravitational force.

His fingers traced circles on my jaw, moving lower to my neck. Shivers ran through my whole body at the touch, and my breath caught. I couldn't feel the soreness or the sting on the inside of my mouth anymore. Everything I could feel was aligned on *him*.

Archer bent a little closer so I could feel his breath on my skin. The pad of his fingers – slightly calloused from holding weapons and fighting so often – landed on my neck, right on my pulse.

"Why is your heart rate so fast?" He hummed approvingly, caressing that little part of my neck. It felt so intimate. And I couldn't stop myself from thinking that we were alone. There was no one here. No one we had to pretend for. *No one but us.*

"Is your little heart overwhelmed, Mayfield?" His voice was husky. "Would it be because of me?"

I wanted to say no. To say that I wasn't into him at all – it would have been a lie, but it would have been the safest bet for my heart. Instead, my hand gripped his wrist and pressed his whole palm against my neck and upper chest. My breath hitched. His eyes flared with something that looked a whole lot like hunger.

I wasn't sure whether he leaned down or I went up, but suddenly our mouths were so close that we breathed the same air. I was lost in his eyes, completely mystified by his aura and his presence and *him.*

And I wanted to push on my tiptoes so our lips would touch so damn bad. His fingers had splayed on my chest, almost burning my skin. And I felt this thread linking my chest to his as if he was pulling on some rope inside my chest.

We were so close I could almost feel his light stubble on my skin and his lips on mine – a ghost of a kiss. I was slightly ashamed to say it, but I'd thought about what a real kiss with Archer would feel like. A lot. I knew it'd be like fireworks. It had to be, after what the half-kiss in the cafeteria had been like. But I wanted to know for sure. I *needed* to experience it.

Archer's hand moved down half an inch. His other hand went to the back of my head, fingers threading in my hair around the base of my braid. My eyes fluttered shut, tingles spreading through my scalp. And then-

Someone banged on the door. "Hurry up, guys! I'm starving!"

Archer and I almost jumped apart. He went to open the door for Søren, and I turned around, frantically looking for something to busy my hands – myself – with. My heart was pumping like crazy, and I could feel the skin of my face burn with a mix of embarrassment, guilt, and… and desire so potent I felt ashamed.

"Was I interrupting something?" Søren asked. I could feel his suspicious gaze as I looked around for my sneakers.

My mouth was desperately dry as I bent over to put on my shoes. He had been interrupting something. But now that the moment had shattered like glass, I wasn't sure what any of it had been. Were we actually going to kiss? Would it have meant anything other than a game?

"No, all good, man. Let's go." Archer's words were nonchalant, and they cracked something in me. What had I been expecting? For him to say that there had been something between us? That we had been half a second away from kissing?

Maybe this moment hadn't been as special for Archer as it had been for me.

And I had to accept that as truth instead of torturing myself with what-ifs.

Chapter Thirty-Two

I should have brought one of Archer's books over. Sure, I couldn't read most of them since they were in old, primarily dead languages. But he might have had one in plain, ordinary English, and no matter the topic, I was sure it would have been more entertaining than whatever my brain could come up with on its own after two hours of waiting.

You knew what they say — two are a coincidence, three is a pattern. Well, it seemed like my being picked last was a pattern for whoever chose the order the competitors were going in for the Trials. How exciting, right?

Anyways, I was back in that stupid room, waiting on my uncomfortably rigid chair and watching everyone go in one after the other. I didn't have a watch or phone, but I knew it had been at least two hours since I'd first sat down. Since then, everyone had gone, including my four friends.

I was starting to get used to the whole maybe-walk-to-our-deaths thing, which meant I didn't feel sick to my stomach watching my friends walk out to the Pit. I was still worried, but I knew they'd be fine. I didn't need special powers to know they were better than any other Coppers competing here.

Amara Mendez, the girl with the nice and cozy gift of making one's worst fears come to life in one's mind, had been the last to leave the room. I'd been alone for a little while, probably over ten minutes. The nymph would say my name any second now. I was both scared and excited.

Excited to finally have a way to burn my frustration away.

Archer and I had dutifully ignored the whole almost-kiss incident that had happened before dinner. All night and even this morning before coming here, we had tiptoed around the topic, pretending that everything was fine and that we hadn't almost kissed in an empty bedroom.

So, overall, I was mad. And annoyed. At him for instigating the whole thing last night and at me for being unable to control my emotions better.

From what I'd seen so far, many deities and their descendants had very different visions of relationships than we had at home. Commitment was often a loose concept. Being immortal might do that to people – you got bored with vanilla monogamic relationships. Maybe Archer had been raised in this mindset and wanted to play around.

Either way, I was annoyed and trying to forget about it. The Third Trial would undoubtedly help to clear my mind from those unwanted emotions.

I was almost impatient.

The crowd had been reacting intermittently throughout the whole morning, and I knew Amara was done when the wave of cheers grew to new heights. Anticipation heightened my senses, and I stood up before the nymph even started speaking.

Sure enough, a few seconds later, the sweet voice of the nymph filled the room. "What a great show we have had so far! The crop this year is amazing, don't you think?" She paused for a second to let the spectators cheer, clap, and act like they were watching a basketball game instead of a sick version of the Olympics. "And now, to end this beautiful day, let's all welcome Kalani Mayfield, our very own mortal!"

I tried not to be hurt that the crowd gave equal parts cheers and boos at my name. I wouldn't win popularity contests any time soon, that was for sure.

I took my time walking to the door, readying my nerves and my body for what was sure to be an interesting Trial. At the start of the morning, the nymph, whose name I still didn't know, had explained that today's Trial would be an obstacle course and that everyone who made it through successfully would advance to the next round. It should have been great news, except that meant the course would be so challenging that enough of us wouldn't make it. My main consolation was that the skills and strength I'd gotten from gymnastics usually made me decent at Ninja Warrior type things.

As I entered the Pit, I was once again impressed by whoever was in charge of transforming the arena for these Trials. Mei had told me that a few Goldens were gifted with strong enough illusions that their creations were tangible for as long as they put power into them. That seemed like one of the coolest and most useful powers I'd seen. And these Goldens were pretty creative because their version of Ninja Warrior was very different from what I'd seen on TV or tried once at the big gym close to my university. None of them had had a flaming ground below the flywheels or – were those crocodiles? – in the pool we had to cross on what looked like an unstable bridge.

Swallowing down my nerves – I needed to appear strong and determined, which meant I couldn't show how scary this obstacle course was – I strolled toward a black line drawn on the sand. I tried my best to ignore the crowd looking down at me, but it was hard. During the past two Trials, we couldn't watch the stands. It had been just us and whatever we had to face. But today? Oh, today I had the joy of seeing every single person that had come to the Tournament to watch the show with popcorn and free refills of soda. And there were a lot of them. I wasn't sure how many people the Pit could sit, but it felt like standing alone in the middle of the field at a big football stadium. And, sure, I'd competed at gymnastics meets where we had a lot of spectators, but never anywhere close to this.

Forcing myself to refocus on the critical part – the course itself – I looked around for clues and information to help me through. From where I stood, I couldn't see considerable amounts of blood or solitary limbs, so I was guessing that many people had made it through.

The course was extensive, with four – no, five – different parts to it. And, of course, each section was much longer and deadlier than regular obstacle courses. It wouldn't be fun otherwise.

Makaio was a great fan of Ninja Warrior, so I'd watched it often enough to recognize most of the versions of obstacles in the Pit. The first obstacle was one of those unstable bridges over the pool with what, upon a closer look, looked like a mix between a rhinoceros and a crocodile. How fun. Then we went right into the whole flywheels-over-fire section. There were eight wheels, staggered at a few feet of distance and at least eight feet over the ground – which was nice and high because the flames below looked very aggressive.

I couldn't see clearly behind those first two obstacles, but I could glimpse a huge warped wall at the very back. Way to end this great course, with a wall taller than a fucking building.

I must have taken a little too long to get myself on the starting line because someone cleared their throats on the mic. I didn't need to look over to know it had been Artemis – that lady had cockiness radiating from every pore. I did look over to the balcony after a couple of seconds, though, and my gaze snagged on Hecate, sitting to the side of the balcony near a few deities I didn't know. She had this intense look on her face, staring at me with her deep purple eyes – I didn't know what it meant, but I hoped she was still on my side.

As soon as the very edge of my shoes hit the black line, a countdown started resonating in the arena. A giant hologram appeared over the course in the middle of the Pit, counting down from ten. How dramatic.

My heart rate did go up as the numbers went down, though. I took deep breaths, trying to calm my nerves. And when the hologram hit zero, I ran. I ran hard and fast because I didn't want to let myself think about the risks or how crazy this was for too long. I had to get started.

A little too quickly for my taste, I reached the platform before the pool filled with weird hybrids. I knew from watching all those show episodes with Makaio that the best way to go about the unstable bridge was to go for it and never slow down until the end. As long as I kept my feet perpendicular to the length of the cylinder, I should have enough traction to keep my balance. Hopefully.

Following my semi-plan of action, I slowed down to a brisk walk but didn't stop when I arrived at the beginning of the cylinder. I didn't look at the hybrids that had gathered around the bridge. I didn't listen to the crowd cheering for me to fall. I didn't even pay attention to my own doubts. I just started speed walking down the bridge.

Unsurprisingly, the bridge rotated along its axis, making it treacherous. Years of balance training had their perks, though. I knew how to walk on a beam like it was normal ground. Of course, the bridge was moving, which made it much more complex than a beam. But my body knew how to regain its balance under stress and unexpected circumstances, skills that would probably save my life today.

I wasn't sure how long I was on that cylinder. It felt like forever. Forever of me feeling like I'd fall any second. I almost did fall multiple times, barely saving myself. When my left foot reached solid ground, I felt like I'd aged ten years. I hadn't had timed to properly feel the strain on my body during the crossing, but now that I was standing without the threat of falling into a pool filled with monsters? Yeah, I could feel how shaky my whole body was just fine – from both exertion and adrenaline.

"Holy shit," I huffed, hands on my hips to try and catch my breath. This would be a killer – hopefully just in the metaphorical sense.

For a second, I stood there, watching the crocodile -rhinos look at me like I'd disappointed them. I didn't feel bad at all. I was sure they had lunch with at least one person before I arrived here.

Once I had mostly caught my breath, I turned on my heels and stared ahead at the next obstacle. There was a short length of sand before the ground gave way, and flames appeared. Even from where I stood, I could feel their warmth and hear them roar and crackle.

Those flames were as real as they came – or at least they felt like it. I was sure they'd burn like real fire too.

Looking up, I analyzed the flywheels. They were scattered too far for me to reach out and grab the next one – I'd have to throw myself from wheel to wheel. From what I could see, the ledge I would have to hold on to was small, about the size of my first two knuckles. There would be no margin of error.

I took a deep breath, clenching and unclenching my fingers repeatedly. I had to believe in myself. I had to believe that I would make it. I closed my eyes. Breathed in. Deep. Controlled. And then breathed out, expelling all of my doubts with it.

Then I ran, gaining as much momentum as I could. My right foot slammed on the very edge of the hole, and I pushed up, jumping higher than I ever had before. I reached up, up, up. I was desperately trying to get to the wheels. I could feel the heat from the flames licking the bottom of my soles and calves. And then, right as I started to be scared that I hadn't jumped high enough, my fingers latched onto the ledge of the first wheel.

Relief was short-lived because I didn't have time to waste. Gravity did its job as soon as I gripped the wheel, and the tension on my shoulders and fingers increased. Uneven bar work had given me excellent grip strength, but this was a different position than the one I usually had – both hands turned in, holding a thin disk. I could feel sweat gliding down my forehead, neck, and back – from the exercise, the heat, and the stress. I needed to hurry before my fingers became so slippery that they wouldn't hold onto anything anymore.

As soon as I had a good grip on the ledges, I started swinging my body back and forth, storing energy to make the jump. Back and forth, back and forth. Four times. And then I threw myself. It was a leap of faith. One that paid off. My fingers grabbed the next wheel, my shoulders straining as my body fell. I had no time to relax because I was only two down, six more to go before I could reach the ground.

The rest of the section was a repetition of the same moves. Swinging, jumping, holding on for dear life, repeat. When I reached the last wheel, my arms were burning, and my fingers were cramping up from holding on so tightly and fighting off the sweat that made them slide little by little. I had to make it through. I had only one more jump. One more.

Using my core and back muscles, I swung my body one last time. It took more swings to get the momentum I had accumulated so quickly at the beginning. But I didn't give up – I swung, and then threw myself off the wheel. It was the worst throw I'd done so far, but by some miracle, I landed roughly on the ground. After tumbling a few times, I landed on my back, staring at the bright blue sky.

Thank the stars.

And not 'thank the gods' because they were the reason I was stuck here.

I remained there for almost a minute, trying to catch my breath and wondering whether my arms would make it through the whole course. I had gained substantial muscle strength from the constant training I'd had over the past seven weeks, and I'd already been strong beforehand. But this course was going to be more challenging than anything I'd ever done before, and I wouldn't have any second chances. Either way, I didn't have much of a choice.

Resigned to continue, I slowly pushed myself up and sighed when my shoulders protested the movement. This was going to be fun.

From where I sat on the ground, I could see the next section very well. It was a mix of two obstacles – a pool frozen over with what I could only imagine were underwater obstacles, followed by a vertical wall with… were those throttle pegs holds? If so, I'd have to sink pegs into holes in the wall to create the holds for me to climb up. And I'd be completely wet to do so, which meant slippery fingers. Very slippery.

The pool wasn't the longest, only about twenty yards long, but I had no idea how many obstacles I'd have to go through below. I could hold my breath for a decent amount of time, but I'd have to make sure I didn't waste oxygen down there – I would have to ensure I remained as efficient as possible.

I didn't let myself panic. I didn't have the luxury of hyperventilating and losing my mind – I needed to prepare myself for potentially the longest and most important game of holding my breath ever.

Analyzing the obstacle as thoroughly as possible from up here, I started breathing deeply and slowly. The more I breathed, the longer I inhaled for, increasing my lungs' size and capacity to hold air. Once I felt like I had as good a control of my lungs as I'd get, I slowly advanced toward the pool's edge. The water surface was a few yards down from the edge, completely frozen over except for two holes, one at each side of the pool.

Inhale. Exhale. Inhale. Exhale. Inhale.

Jump.

The water was so cold that my whole body contracted right away. The cold was a painful vice around my head. I had to actively tell my muscles to relax so that I'd be able to move. Looking ahead – the water was surprisingly clear and easy to see through – I saw a transparent wall with a small hole, just tight enough for a body to fit through, to the very right side of the pool. Immediately, I pushed against the bottom of the pool and swam toward the hole, trying my best to glide through the water and use as little energy as possible. Unsurprisingly, as I went through the hole, I faced another wall with a hole on the other side of the pool.

For a quick second, I looked up at the faint light that came through the thick layer of ice. It was almost eerie, like something you'd see in a movie or a documentary about the wonders of the ocean. It was beautiful, the light moving and changing in the water. I could have looked at the show for hours. I didn't allow myself to remain distracted, though. My lungs were not burning yet, but they would soon enough.

The next minute was both the quickest and longest of my life. I swam from hole to hole, trying my best to control my burning lungs. After a while, I started blowing small amounts of air periodically, tricking my body into thinking everything was fine and I was breathing normally. It worked at first. But by the time I pushed off of the fifth wall, my respiratory muscles were seizing. Hard.

As I reached the sixth wall, I saw the hole in the ice. Less than ten feet away. So close and so far away at the same time. But I could get to it. I would.

Rallying my strength and doing my best to ignore how my vision was blurring at the edges, I pushed off the last wall with as much strength as possible. I had tried my hardest not to use my legs too much – leg muscles were the biggest in the body, after all, so they used the most oxygen – but now that I was so close, I kicked as hard as I could. This was a fight for my life. A fight I had to win.

The swim felt endless, as if I were sludging through Jell-O instead of water. I was halfway up when I had no more air to exhale, and my vision was so dark that I could barely see the pit of light coming from the hole.

I had almost lost hope when my hands touched the edge of the ice – sharp and so cold that it hurt. My face broke through the water.

Then air was everywhere. On my face. In my lungs.

And tears were in my eyes. Of relief. Of pain, so intense that I was worried my body would crack and break and shatter into tiny pieces.

For a second, I wasn't sure if I'd be able to get myself out of the water. My muscles had been so deprived of oxygen, my body so full of carbon dioxide, that I wasn't sure I had the physical means to crawl out of the frozen water and onto the ice.

For a short instant, so quick that it barely even existed, I imagined how easy it would be to let it go. To stop clawing at the ice to remain afloat. To stop fighting. To just let myself go and float into nothingness. It would be easy. So much easier than continuing to fight.

But I couldn't. Makaio's round face was stamped into my mind's eye, pleading with me to come back and be with him. I also saw Archer, his face so close, his lips almost kissing mine, his hands on my skin. I saw Sadie – hugging me when I almost broke down, being the best friend that I had ever had. I saw Søren – joking around with me and bringing light to our worst days. I even saw Mei and her wry humor.

I couldn't just give up on them. Or on myself.

So, I pulled. Hard. So hard that my fingers hurt, and I worried my fingernails would break off. But they didn't. And, after long, excruciating seconds of battle with the ice and my own body, I was out. I still had to crawl some more, but then I was lying on the ice, staring at the sky.

It was almost ironic, really. Was I going to end up in this position after every obstacle on this course?

It took me a long time of hyperventilating and lying still to regain enough body awareness to know I had to move. Not because I wanted to finish this course. No, I didn't particularly want to continue this Ninja Warrior thing on steroids. But I had just spent time in freezing cold water and was now lying on the ice. My body had been shivering this whole time. If I stayed much longer on the ice without moving, I was worried my body would go into hypothermia, and I wouldn't survive.

I had to move. Moving would warm me up. Moving would give me a chance.

Chapter Thirty-Three

Getting up was almost impossible. Taking the first step toward the wall was terribly hard. The second step was hard. The third was difficult. By the time I reached the wall, I was still in pain but didn't feel like my joints would break and my heart would give out.

A win was a win.

There were two pegs on the ground. They were a mix of wood and metal, thick enough to safely wrap my hands around them. The only issue was that my fingers were still half frozen and completely wet. The day was warm, but the air around this icy pool must have been spelled to remain cold. Cold enough that my body wouldn't warm up, and the water on my skin wouldn't dry until I finished this section of the course.

Breathing was more manageable now that I had brought my body under control after the prolonged hypoxia. I started moving my fingers to warm my muscles up. At the same time, I looked up to the top of the wall. It was about fifteen feet high – not crazy high, but not easy either after this freezing underwater thing.

From all around me, I could hear the spectators' frustration at me taking my sweet time. No one had said we had to hurry through the course, though. Rushing through the sections would only cause me to make mistakes and die what was sure to be a horrible death.

Still, I knew I had to get up that wall quickly so my body would stop shivering and tensing up in shock from the cold. Taking one last deep breath, I grabbed the pegs and planted them into the lower holds. They fit in like gloves, gliding in but remaining firmly planted within the rock. I briefly tested their strength for a second before forcing myself to pull on my arms and heave myself up.

In case you wondered, rope climbing hadn't been my favorite part of practice. I was proficient at it, but it was a pain. So, had I continued to train it regularly once I had been on my own? Nope. Not at all. So, I was clearing up cobwebs and hoping muscle memory would kick in.

It took a few seconds, but surprisingly, my body did seem to remember how to climb things up using only my arms. Soon enough, I was halfway up the wall, my arms shaking slightly from the strain. It was a repetitive sequence of steps I'd known by heart. Secure the grip. Put weight on my top arm. Hang on one arm long enough for my free arm to plant the peg into a higher hold. Use the new grip combinations to move my body up the wall. Repeat.

It was actually quite anticlimactic how fast I climbed. I would have expected that my arms or frozen fingers would have given up halfway through the climb, but they hadn't. Somehow, I'd made it to the top. Reaching the top felt like standing on top of Mount Everest – as if I'd achieved the feat of climbing the highest mountain in the world.

As I'd expected, the cold dissipated as soon as I reached the top of the wall. Suddenly, it was nice and warm again. I felt like an ice cube melting in the sun. It was glorious.

The top of the wall was wide, at least ten yards. The rocky surface was smooth, the perfect surface to run onto. And I would need to run because behind the wall was a big hole separating me from the next wall. The distance across was a few yards long. Not terribly long, I guessed. Still longer than I would have liked. I knew I could usually jump that distance. But that was when I was in good physical condition and not half frozen and completely exhausted.

Oh well. We'd have to see.

Still slightly shaking from the whole ordeal I'd just gone through, I slowly walked toward the edge of the wall. I knew I should refrain, but I still went to see what was at the bottom of the trench. Spikes, sharp and deadly. How fun. I was sure those would feel great if I failed and fell onto them.

"Gosh Kalani, you know better," I chided myself as I moved back a few steps until I couldn't see the spikes anymore. That was rule one of extreme climbing, wasn't it? Never look down.

Swallowing down the nerves, I did my best to erase from my mind the sight of what awaited me in the space below. My steps were slow as I backed down until I reached the far edge. I knew my body could make that jump. I just had to believe that I could do it in my situation.

"I can do this. I can do this. I can do this." My murmurs were a mantra to raise the confidence I needed to do this. As good a motivational speech as I could give myself under the stress and exhaustion of the day.

I could hear whistles in the background. How fast had the others gotten through this? If my taking a minute to rest after almost drowning and freezing to death annoyed the crowd, then had the other competitors just run through the whole course? I suddenly imagined Archer powering through the obstacles, looking relaxed as ever, and I couldn't suppress a small smile at the thought.

Shaking my head – as if it would help me eliminate any unwanted thoughts I had – I took one last steadying breath. *I could do it.*

And then I started running.

I could only take a few strides, which was enough to build speed and momentum. I didn't hesitate when I jumped. I pushed harder on my right leg than I'd ever done before, launching my body forward. The jump seemed endless, the seconds elongating into forever, my body weightless and not bothered by gravity. It was exhilarating and made me understand why people did extreme sports.

Then, for another endless second, I worried I wouldn't make it. Gravity took hold of my body, and I started going down, down,

down. My heart started beating wildly as the fear of falling took hold. And then, right as I felt hope leave me, my body crashed into the wall. Only half of my body landed on the top, the rest hanging down. The next few seconds were a frantic fight to bring my body up and out of danger.

I made it up, but in my desperate fight to avoid falling to my death, I opened my left forearm on the rocks, blood streaming down to my skin. Ruby red, glistening in the sunlight, my blood dripped, dripped, dripped down my fingers.

Great, just what I needed. Hopefully, I wouldn't have to escape sharks or another predator that hunts bleeding prey. That would be extremely unlucky on my part. Not surprising given how this whole Tournament was going for me so far, but unfortunate for sure.

Hissing at the sting of the wound, I stood up and stared at the last part of the course. I could see the finish line from where I was – so close and so far away at the same time. I couldn't suppress a ragged breath intake at the sight. I needed to get there.

There was still a section to go through. And it looked – dare I say easy? First, I had to get down from the wall I was standing on. The ground wasn't as low as the spiky hole or the pool, though – both had been indentations in the ground and were lower than the rest of the arena. This was good news because I wouldn't break something while dropping down. Then, I would have to run the length of half a football field before going up a warped wall.

A classic.

I'd tried this type of obstacle a few times, and it all came down to gaining enough speed, not decelerating, and putting as much of my feet' surface area as possible in contact with the wall at all times. It was far from the hardest obstacle the bloodthirsty deities in charge could have come up with. Especially to end this whole debacle of an obstacle course.

It made me wary. Suspicious.

It was the same feeling I got when faced with a multiple-choice question on an exam that seemed way too obvious. You know, that feeling of second-guessing yourself so hard that, after a while, you couldn't tell if you even knew what the question was about anymore? That's what I felt like while looking at that empty expanse of sand.

Like someone was playing a trick on me.

I knew I had to get going – I wasn't frozen cold anymore, but my body was still slowly losing strength and blood. However, before I jumped, I shifted to look toward the balcony. Most of the gods and goddesses sitting up there looked bored as hell, but two of them were watching me with rapt attention. Hecate was leaning forward, elbows on her knees. I couldn't see her facial expression clearly, but I hoped it was one of confidence in my abilities. And, unsurprisingly, Artemis was glaring daggers at me. I didn't need to be a mind reader to know that she wished for me to *finally* die and stop being a pain in her elitist ass.

After sending her a quick smile – I couldn't stop myself from antagonizing her because, damn it, I wasn't about to take discrimination lying down – I turned back around and faced the very last part of this course. I shook my arms and legs out one last time – hoping it would help me wake them up after the paralyzing cold – and then jumped. I had learned to fall in gymnastics, so I instinctively moved my body into a tuck and roll, absorbing the shock smoothly. I was pretty proud of myself for making this jump so nicely and almost gave myself a pat on the shoulder.

Wincing at my sore muscles, I took a few steps forward, looking around for obstacles I hadn't seen from above. I couldn't see anything, though, no weird reflection of light or subtle change in the ground surface or-

A growl came from behind me, chilling my bones and causing me to shudder. I froze for a second, my fight-or-flight instincts confused about what the situation required. My body didn't remain confused for long because the *thing* behind me moved just enough that I could see it from the corner of my eye. Black fur, blood-red eyes, a hint of long and sharp teeth.

Fuck.

I knew this was too good to be true.

I didn't wait for the beast to move to start running. If I thought I had run fast before, this was like using every single drop of energy I had to power my leg muscles and go fast, fast, faster. I knew the beast was chasing me – I could hear its panting breaths, its growls. I could feel it behind me, closing in. I wished I had something, anything, to slow that beast down. A rock, some godly given power, anything would be better than the nothing I currently had.

There wasn't much time to dwell on how unlucky I was because I barely had enough time to breathe or think about anything other than how I was going to reach the warped wall before the beast.

I could vaguely hear the crowd cheering – for me or the beast; I wasn't sure and didn't particularly want to know. Either way, the sounds from the spectators and the beast made my blood pump harder with the adrenaline. It helped with the full-speed run I was on – I had never run this fast for this long.

The growls were getting closer. I didn't look back to see how close the beast was. I knew it was too close, and I had no time to waste. My feet were battering the hardpacked earth and kicking up sand behind me. My arms pumped back and forth, back and forth, helping to build up speed. And the warped wall was coming. I was getting closer, only a couple dozen yards away.

So close.

And still so far away.

The beast barked aggressively, and I had to suppress a whimper at the sound. I was terrified. There was no point in denying it – I was terrified by this raging beast that was hot on my heels and determined to tear into me and eat me and hurt me. I didn't want to die, and after everything that I had gone through in the past seven weeks and during this whole obstacle course, I couldn't comprehend that I was close to losing it all because of a fucking monster chasing me like it had been starved for months and I was a tasty dinner.

I didn't want to be anybody's dinner.

So, I kept running. I didn't have a choice. I couldn't do anything but run, hoping I would make it to the top and the beast wouldn't follow me.

The beginning of the slope was coming, only a few yards away now. One good thing about this whole chase was that it would force me not not slow down when getting up the warped wall. However, I wouldn't have a second chance of making it up – if I fell during the ascension, there was no doubt that the beast would attack.

I wouldn't fall. There was no other option.

I *wouldn't* fall.

When my foot touched the start of the incline, I felt a pinch of relief. However, the terror mixed with deep concentration prevented the relief from taking hold. There was still so much to do.

The beast was so close that I could hear every breath, growl, and paw hitting the ground. I could even smell it – sulfur, smoke, and blood.

I could feel its hunger.

Focusing on what I had to do was hard, but I did my best to pay attention. At least, being chased was a great incentive not to slow down. As I started climbing the wall, I consciously reminded myself to put my whole foot on the slope. My calves and thighs were throbbing from the effort, but I didn't let myself slow down. I kept going up, up, up.

Until the slope became so steep that I couldn't take steps anymore.

I jumped.

The beast was right there, at the bottom of the slope, growling and ready to pounce.

My heart was beating so hard that I was sure it would explode out of my chest.

My fingers barely grasped onto the ledge, but it was enough. I held on for dear life, acutely aware of the beast prowling beneath me. My arm was in pain, the wound throbbing. My grip was losing strength gradually, like an hourglass dripping sand.

I had to get up to the top. *I had to.*

Ensued the longest and hardest muscle up I'd ever done. Inch by inch, I fought against gravity, against my exhausted body and the doubts filling my mind, to bring my body up. I was in tears by the time my body was safely on top of the wall.

Tears streamed down my face in silence, pain battering my body, and the relief of being alive mixed with sheer exhaustion. I didn't have the strength to move anymore, not even to turn onto my back or move my ankles and feet onto the solid surface.

The adrenaline flooding my body dropped, and there was nothing left. My limbs were like lead, so heavy that I couldn't move them. The world around me was slowly becoming fuzzy and blurred until everything was far, far away. Soon, the sounds from the crowd were only a faint whisper, unintelligible and drowning out. And then my vision became dark until everything faded away.

Chapter Thirty-Four

The world came back piece by piece. First, I heard faint whispers – multiple voices, none of them that I could remember or identify. I couldn't tell what the voices were saying. The words were still muddled, spinning around my mind but never settling down long enough for me to analyze them.

Then, after what felt like forever, I smelled the scent of storms brewing over rolling waves. It came from very close to me – from the deepest and closest voice. I knew that smell, it came from someone I loved. What was his name? I couldn't remember – my body and brain were submerged in a deep, deep ocean.

After a while, I became aware of a soft material against most of my skin. Soft and warm. And I was lying down on a comfortable surface. A bed. I was in a bed. Mine, based on how familiar it felt. How had I gotten in my bed?

My last memories were of a terrifying monster chasing me and me running, running, running away. And then me hanging from my fingers, high in the air. Everything else was a fuzzy mess. So how had I ended up in my bed?

What had happened?

The thoughts were getting clearer, and the voices increasingly louder until I finally could recognize the speakers. Sadie and Archer. That made sense because we must have been in Archer and I's room. I still couldn't quite catch what they were saying.

Slowly, I started to be able to move my fingers and toes. From the memories that were gradually coming back to me, I would have expected to be sore from head to toes. I didn't, though. I felt strange, a little stiff, but there was no pain.

"I know you're awake, Mayfield. Open your eyes." The mattress dipped as Archer spoke directly next to my ear, so close that I had no choice but to understand. No choice but no obey.

The light was so blinding that I had to close my eyes for a few seconds before I could open them again. As my vision was getting used to the brightness, I heard light steps approaching my bed.

Once I could finally keep my eyes open for longer than a couple of seconds, I was faced with my two friends. They were both next to the bed – Archer sitting on a chair, his elbows on the mattress, and Sadie standing beside him. They wore matching looks of worry.

"How does the sleeping beauty feel?" Sadie tried giving me her signature reassuring smile, but I could see right through it. She had been worried about me. And seeing her, the positive caregiver of the group, clearly anxious about me was concerning.

"Strangely… fine. I don't feel sore at all and," I looked over at my left forearm, "don't have any wounds anymore. I'm guessing the nurse helped?" My voice was a croak, and I cleared my throat to help. "How long did I sleep for?"

My two friends exchanged a meaningful look and didn't answer right away. Raising an eyebrow in surprise, I threw a questioning look their way.

"A little over a day." Archer paused for a second before adding, "Thirty hours, to be specific."

Holy shit. I was shocked for a few seconds, unsure how to react. I had always loved to sleep, but thirty hours? How was that even possible?

"What happened?"

Sadie leaned in a little so she could put her hand over mine. "You lost consciousness after reaching the finish line of the course. Archer had to go in and get you out. The nurse came over and healed you, but it appears that human bodies don't deal with hypothermia, blood loss, and such intense effort the same way our bodies do. She had to put you into a healing sleep so that you'd survive without any lingering issues."

No kidding. Ichor, even diluted down, must have been really helpful in making it through all of those deadly obstacles. My human body, with its regular red blood cells, couldn't withstand freezing water and blood loss on top of exercise so intense that even world-class athletes would suffer. Still, hearing it from Sadie's mouth was a striking realization that I'd almost died.

I'd been so close to it that even a magical healer had struggled to save me.

That was scarier than it had a right to be.

Sadie must have interpreted my silence as tiredness because she squeezed my hand and bent her head slightly forward. "I was waiting for you to wake up, but now that you are, I'll let you rest. I'm glad you're alright. And I'll let Søren know – he had to leave earlier because he wanted to check on Mei, she has also been hurt during the Trial, but she's better now."

Then, without giving me time to answer, she turned around and left. And then it was just Archer and me. Without my consent, my brain brought back flashes of us embracing, so close that our lips barely brushed against each other. I had no business thinking of this – there were many more important things to care about than my attraction for this man. But the way his eyes bore into mine as he sat there, waiting on my bedside… stars, it made my heart flutter.

I cleared my throat nervously and broke eye contact with him – my eyes landed on his longer-than-usual facial hair. Not quite a beard, but longer than a five o'clock shadow. "Thank you for coming to get me."

He waited for a second, a muscle in his jaw clenching and relaxing a few times. "You scared me."

"Really?" I wasn't sure why I sounded so breathless.

His eyes snagged mine back, and I couldn't escape his magnetic aura this time. I couldn't quite decrypt his facial expression – it looked like fear and some sort of longing. But it couldn't be.

"Watching you go through the course was torture. I almost walked in multiple times." He stopped for a bit. "I should have."

"We all had to go through the Trial on our own. There was nothing you could do." What I wanted to ask, though, was if he'd really watched me. And why.

"I know. It doesn't mean I didn't want to run in there and get you from under the ice. Or kill that hybrid monster. Even if it meant I had to kill all the guards on my path."

I shivered, but not from the fear that those words should have brought to me. I shivered from the intensity in his eyes, the way his face broke open to reveal his sincerity, and his genuine care and affection for me. And the fury that he had felt during the Trial. The fury he had felt for me. Because he cared.

And that gave me way too much hope.

"You're here now. That's all that matters." The words were almost a whisper, revealing too many of the confusing emotions I felt.

I expected him to nod and move away, which he usually did. We were both professionals at dancing around the situation, and he was not the type to be vulnerable and openly display his feelings. But he didn't turn away or give me one of his signature arrogant remarks. Instead, his eyes went down, and he clasped his hands so tight that his fingers turned white.

"I-" he stopped to swallow; his eyebrows crunched as if in pain. "I should have done more. Seeing you faint and not knowing if you were still alive," he shook his head. "I was so scared."

I didn't know how to respond to that. It was the first time I saw him so open. It was incredibly destabilizing.

Instead of saying anything, my hand landed on both of his. They felt warm and solid – grounding – under my touch. His eyes snapped up to meet mine. He opened his mouth to say something, but no sound came out. We were frozen in time, staring at each other, with my hand on his clasped ones.

And then, suddenly, he moved at the speed of light, and his lips landed on mine.

My first reaction was surprise. Utter shock. But I wasn't dreaming. His lips were there, they were real, and they were touching mine. They were surprisingly soft and warm and firm and gentle. And he was kissing me. And he had made the first move.

I sensed the moment he started pulling away – he must have felt I was completely still. But I woke up from the shock right then and followed him. My eyes had closed on their own, but I didn't need to see him to know the moment we both realized that we wanted this kiss. He pushed back into me, his hands coming around my head and neck, mine grasping at the front of his shirt.

The next moments went from a gentle peck to frantically trying to get closer, closer, closer. Close enough that nothing could come between us. This kiss contained all the restrained passion and pent-up frustration of the past seven weeks of living in this space together but not allowing ourselves to explore this attraction.

It wasn't a pretty kiss, not the type you'd see in romance movies when the two main characters declare their feelings to each other and kiss under the rain. No, our lips were learning the shape of each other, clashing and dancing in perfect harmony. This kiss was messy and raw and full of so many different emotions. And it felt like us. Like we were colliding and exploding into stars and energy and the most intense experience ever. Like we had no tomorrow and had to make the most out of every single second. I didn't even feel like I needed air – Archer's lips on mine, his hands in my hair and my hip, and the passion I felt from him were all I needed.

Except, after what felt like forever, I physically had to breathe. Moving slightly back, I put my forehead against his, our ragged breaths mingling together. His left hand cradled my jaw, his thumb caressing my skin and giving me shivers. And the stiffness in my body was gone, replaced with a fire that burned within my chest and wouldn't die out.

My hands were clenched on the smooth fabric of his shirt, clinging to him like he was my rock in the middle of a storm, and I needed to bring him ever closer. I could feel the faint echoes of his heartbeats under my hands – boom, boom, boom. A war drum playing a frantic rhythm.

"Kalani." His voice was hoarse and oh so sexy. It made my brain tingle in time with my swollen lips.

I didn't answer with words but leaned forward to kiss him again. And he didn't protest – his lips were hungry and passionate, fighting with mine in an intricate dance that I had never known before him. I didn't know kissing someone could be like this. I didn't think it could be like merging two souls, like drinking the elixir of life and communing with something bigger than myself. Kissing Archer was all of that and more. And I couldn't get enough.

I didn't know how long we stayed like this, but it felt like both forever and not long enough when we finally stopped kissing each other for longer than ten seconds. We had ended up lying on my bed, on our sides, facing each other. We stared into each other's eyes for a long time, our hands always on each other as if we were both scared of cutting physical contact.

"Do you regret it?"

"No." The word left my mouth faster than I could think, but it was true. Some part of me was scared of rejection or of being played with. But no part of me regretted kissing Archer like my life depended on it. I had almost died multiple times. It was still possible that I would not make it past the end of the week. And I was tired of playing it safe and hoping for the best without taking unnecessary risks. I was tired of being the responsible one who thought about every outcome and always made sensible decisions.

I wanted to feel reckless and brave and… and loved. I wanted to feel loved more than anything else.

"Do you?" I had to wrench the words out of my mouth because the answer terrified me. What would happen if he said yes? How would I ever be able to continue to live with him after that? But I had to know. I had to know if this was a fleeting moment or something more.

I waited with bated breath for him to say or do anything. He must have stayed silent for only a few seconds, but it felt so long that I started to fear the worst was to come. I closed my eyes, unable to see my hopes and dreams crushed beneath me. I couldn't watch the disaster that was surely coming. I wouldn't be strong enough to hide the pain that his words would bring.

Archer's thumb moved up my neck and cheek until it caressed right below my eye, removing a tear I hadn't realized I had shed. "I dreamt about this moment for weeks. I would never regret being with you, Mayfield. Ever." His voice was a gentle balm on my battered soul. This time, the tear that fell wasn't from pain.

When I opened my eyes again, Archer had moved our faces closer to each other. His eyes were gentle and warm. He put a small, light kiss on my lips. It was not a passionate kiss, and it only lasted for barely a second, but it fully cemented his words in my head. He didn't regret this. He didn't regret me.

It felt amazing.

"I like you, Mayfield. A little too much for my own good, seeing as you attract trouble like a magnet." And there it was, his mocking grin. This time, though, I knew deep in my soul that he cared about me and wanted to make me laugh. It worked. I couldn't suppress a small laugh and a dumb smile.

"I like you a lot, too, Sunshine."

"I know." Cue the self-sufficient half-smile.

I gave him a light tap on his chest, and he laughed. I'd never seen him so relaxed. Actually, I'd never been so relaxed myself – or at least not in so long that I couldn't remember it. A tight knot that had lived in my chest for years slowly unraveled. And I felt light. Lighter than ever. As if I could suddenly float up and fly among the clouds.

Some part of my brain gnawed at me, though, reminding me that a relationship between the two of us was forbidden. The gods had made a law decades ago that Goldens and Coppers weren't allowed to have children with humans anymore to prevent the overpopulation of Olympus. The different colors of our blood were the perfect visual representation of everything that separated us.

"Don't worry about it. No one here will care about us being together. We have pretended to be together for weeks, and no one has cared."

"Did you just read my mind?" Archer had promised he wouldn't ever use his power on me without my consent, and I trusted him, but it was suspiciously close to what I'd just been thinking.

He raised an eyebrow and tapped my nose with his index finger. "I don't need it. Your face is as open as a book. And I was serious; we'll be fine."

"As long as we're here, sure. But I don't think the gods will see it that way once we get out of here. I don't think they'll let a very red-blooded human live on Olympus and be with their stronger Copper."

He didn't deny it. We both knew that my being a part of this Tournament was already causing issues. What would happen when the part of Olympus that thought humans were dirt beneath their feet discovered that I had the hubris of thinking I could be good enough for someone with ichor in his blood? The gold in Archer's veins was as much a barrier between us as any of the spells that kept us contained within the compound and Olympus.

"We will figure it out when we cross that bridge," Archer said reassuringly.

"And what happens until then?"

Archer propped himself on his elbow and bent his head so his lips could graze my neck. Once. Twice. Until I had shivers all over my body. My hand went to his back, and I wished I could feel his skin instead of his shirt. "I don't want to pretend anymore."

"Me neither," I answered on a breath, eyes fluttering shut. "I want to be with you."

A husky laugh escaped him, his chest vibrating against mine. "For once, we're in agreement, Mayfield."

The next three days went by in a whirlwind of Archer. It felt like we were back in high school, sneaking around to be together every chance we got. We were two young people who flew through life high on our newly formed relationship. Any time we were alone, we ended up stuck to each other, always reaching for physical contact – even if it was holding hands or sitting flush next to each other. Our beds somehow ended up pushed together, and we slept close, seeking comfort even in our dreams.

Those three days were incredible. I loved every second I spent with Archer as something more than friends. We kissed and hugged and talked until the deep of the night. He didn't tell me much about his dad or stepmother, but he told me many stories about his mom and childhood. I could imagine it all vividly now, his mom working as a stylist and making baby Archer the cutest – and most impractical, his words, not mine – clothes ever. I could imagine him running around their house playing basketball or reading thrillers and mysteries. When he told me about the time his mom bought him a kit to solve a made-up murder mystery – so that he could be like his favorite book characters – I saw him, a kid with dimples and hair long enough to get in his eyes, playing the part of a grand detective and taping photos of the made-up murder all over their living room.

Every day, every hour we spent together, I could fit a new piece into the intricate puzzle that was Archer. I loved it. Learning about his hobbies, dreams, and family was like discovering a new facet of him, making me appreciate him even more.

We were getting our fill of each other as if our days were counted – which they probably were. And while our friends had found out easily enough, we had both come to the unspoken conclusion not to change our behavior around the other competitors. There weren't a lot of them left – we were twelve survivors after the third Trial – and they probably wouldn't care if we suddenly started to kiss in public. But, other than the fact that neither of us was huge on PDA, I believed we both wanted to put a separation between our previous fake dating scheme and what we had now. For weeks we had pretended and put on a show. But what we had now? It was real, and I didn't want to make it look like the game we had played before.

Overall, these three days would have been like a great vacation if not for the apparent black cloud on the horizon. The fourth and final Trial. The last hurdle we had to go over before we could relax and finally let ourselves fully live.

That last Trial was the reason why we were here, lying on our double bed in the dark, pushing back against the urge to sleep. It must have been the middle of the night, but neither of us wanted to close our eyes yet. The Trial would be first thing in the morning. This night could be the last we had together. I didn't want to waste a second of it.

"What happened here?"

I couldn't suppress a laugh at Archer's horrified words. "Makaio can be reckless when he skates. That day, he tried a new trick and landed so hard on the ground that he opened both knees and knocked three front baby teeth out. His smiles were horrible for weeks afterward." Remembering these moments was cathartic.

"Damn. It looks like that kid inherited all the good genes for fun and bravery." In the faint light from the phone screen, I could see Archer's half smile, popping a dimple and gently making fun of me. We both knew I was a rule follower at heart, the perfect balance with Makaio's love for wreaking havoc.

We had gone over dozens of pictures of Makaio and me, even a couple I had of all three of us with Mom. I had decided to use the last eighteen percent of battery I had left to show them to Archer before... before whatever would happen in the morning. I hadn't realized how much I needed to talk about them and show him pictures until we had started. Telling Archer about my brother and my life before I landed on Olympus was the closest thing I had to introducing him to the person I loved most. And he was invested, asking questions like he'd never seen the world I had lived in. He had told me he had lived in the middle of nowhere in Canada, which might have been, admittedly, very different from a big city in Northern California.

A quick look at the top of my screen told me I had two percent left in my battery life. That was minutes at most. That phone wasn't new; most days, those last couple of percent were gone in a flash.

I swiped to another picture of us making silly faces at the camera. I had my tongue out, and he had his fingers in his mouth, deforming his lips into what was probably intended to be a scary face. "I wish you could meet him."

"I will. You'll introduce me to him, and he'll love me."

He would. Makaio would absolutely love Archer. I had no doubts about that.

And the phone died.

Chapter Thirty-Five

For once, we weren't sitting in that cold and empty room. Instead, we had been given fancy seats on a raised platform near the center of the Pit. I wasn't sure I liked it. I certainly didn't enjoy feeling like a monkey in a cage under the watchful eyes of over forty thousand people. They were all waiting for us to do our tricks and put on a show to entertain them – it made me feel very sorry for the zoo animals.

I wasn't the only one who was uncomfortable with this whole setup. Sitting on my right, Mei bounced her leg up and down at the speed of a full-on galloping horse. She had broken her right wrist and a few ribs during the last Trial, and after seeing the nurse, she still needed a little time to mentally recover from an almost-deadly fight with whatever hybrid had chased us. Mei had been strange in the past few days, distancing herself from us little by little. It was a behavior I recognized – I had experienced it myself after I lost everything related to gymnastics – and I saw the signs accumulating as the days went on. She isolated herself in her room. She didn't speak as often or laugh much anymore. Her smiles became fake, the ones used to pretend everything was fine and make sure no one asked questions. I was a little worried about her, but I also knew that people reacted differently to stress. And she was sitting next to me, which meant she hadn't given up.

I was glad she was still here. And Søren, seated on her other side, was also relieved she had made it. He'd been scared, though, so he hadn't left her side for the past four days. Even right now, he held her hand discreetly in between their seats.

I was glad we were allowed to sit wherever we wanted today. Not just because I got to bask in Archer's calm confidence from where he sat to my left – although that was a pretty nice advantage. No, I was thrilled that we weren't seated next to random people because, out of the remaining competitors, there would have been a high probability that I'd have ended up next to either Elena or Alexei. To say that I wasn't happy they were still here was a euphemism.

Out of the forty competitors that had started this Tournament, only twelve of us had made it to the last Trial. And, based on what Søren had felt necessary to share at dinner two nights ago, the last Trial was usually one-on-one fighting with only one winner per fight. Therefore, six of us were expected to make it out. That was some pretty bad odds overall.

From where she was seated on Archer's other side, Sadie muttered something, but the crowd drowned it as they cheered the appearance of the gods and goddesses in their very private and fancy balcony. I felt nauseous when they arrived and waved graciously at the crowd like the good and benevolent leaders they weren't. I wanted to force them off their pedestal, especially Artemis, who so clearly wanted to crush me and all of my fellow humans under her heel.

"Relax, Mayfield, the best revenge you can have on her is winning this." Archer must have leaned really close to my ear because I heard him loud and clear. We had agreed we wouldn't appear too close to each other during the Trial, so I threw him a warning look. Per usual, he didn't seem intimidated by my glare and grinned like this was all fun and games. Good for him if he thought this was amusing.

The announcer nymph waited until the crowd calmed down before starting her little welcoming speech. "Hello, Olympus, and welcome to the very last Trial of this one hundred and forty-sixth edition of the Tournament!" Clapping ensued, right on cue with the nymph's tilt of the head forward. I almost wondered if they had rehearsals to ensure the spectators could clap and cheer at the right times. This was timed better than spectators on talk shows.

"I am pleased to announce that today's Trial is the epitome of the Tournament, where the very best of our competitors will be fighting against each other to determine who deserves to live on our esteemed Mount Olympus." She paused for a few seconds, letting the emotion heighten. "Today, our competitors will fight to the death, and only the strongest, most determined will survive."

Wait up. To the death? What the hell? That got really intense, really fast. I must have tensed up quite noticeably because Archer brushed his fingers against the side of my leg – the barest of brushes but enough for me to know he was here. That it was going to be okay. I had trained for that, after all. I hadn't gotten my ass kicked for days on end during eight weeks to start doubting myself before we even started the real fight.

"The competitors have been paired into duos that we believe will provide for fair and entertaining fights. The fights will happen in the ring at the center of the arena." Right as she said so, a ring looking very much like an MMA cage, only twice as big, appeared in front of us, right smack in the middle of the Pit. "No weapons or outside help are allowed. Of course, the competitors will be allowed to yield if they so choose, although such a cowardly decision will only be rewarded by termination."

Alright. That was pretty explicit. And, while my stomach was twisting at the words, the crowd seemed highly excited at the prospect. Disgusting.

"Don't forget that today is the final day to place your bets on who will win this Tournament. If you have placed bets earlier in this competition and your Coppers are still in contention, your potential wins will still be calculated from the earlier odds. For those of you who wish to place new bets today…" and she kept going about the bets as if we were horses running at the racecourse.

I zoned out a little, focusing instead on the remaining competitors. Outside of me and my four friends, there were, of course, my two archnemeses, Elena and Alexei. When I'd seen the latter before entering the Pit earlier, he had looked at me, made an obscene gesture, and then ended up dry heaving over a flowerpot in the hallway. It had been incredibly satisfying.

Nafula, who had been on my team during the first Trial, as well as Amara Mendez, who could make your worst fears come to life within your mind and quite literally paralyze you in fear, had also made it. Surprisingly, Cassian, who was the Ares descendant who had been my reluctant teammate during the first Trial, had made it too – he hadn't seemed like the brightest bulb in the house, but I guessed he had a powerful gift and was physically strong, which must have made up for the rest. The last two survivors were Ibrahim Khan, a descendant of Apollo who could manipulate light, and Binh Nguyen, one of Hermes's grandchildren with some sort of teleportation gift.

Everyone here was powerful – the most powerful Coppers out of all who had started this Tournament with us. There was no doubt that the fights would be impressive, especially because of the stakes. No one would back down. Including myself. I had no special powers, but I wouldn't give up easily.

However, something was gnawing at my mind. The fear that I would be placed against one of my friends. I wanted to think we'd both refuse to engage in the fight. That we'd fight against the system to find another way. But I wasn't sure what would actually happen. Fear and survival instincts could change people. They could make people do things they wouldn't normally do.

Including killing a friend if it could save them.

Fortunately, the first tandem to be called was Nafula and Ibrahim. Since that first Trial, I'd learned that Nafula had inherited from her grandfather, Poseidon, the ability to remove water from things and move that water wherever she wanted. Neat, right? Causing sudden dehydration in her enemies to the point that their tissues shrank, and they died slowly must have been convenient in the Tournament. I wasn't sure what Ibrahim could do exactly – maybe blind people?

Or make optic illusions? – but I wasn't sure he'd be able to prevent Nafula from wringing every single drop of water from his body.

Both Coppers stood stiffly under a tsunami of applause from the spectators. None of us, down on the dais, clapped. None of us felt any joy or excitement seeing them enter the cage. Although Alexei had a wicked look on his face, as if watching people fight to the death made his insides flutter in happiness. The guy had probably tortured animals for fun as a child. Gods, I hated him.

As soon as the two Coppers entered the ring, the door they had come through closed with a clang, and a faint bluish light emanated from the metal. I didn't need explanations to know instinctively that the light came from a spell used to ensure that none of the combatants escaped from the cage. It was the magical version of barbed wire.

There was a loud gong coming from everywhere at once. Nothing happened for one long second. And then both Coppers were running at each other. Everything happened really fast. They exchanged a few powerful hits with their fists and feet. But then something unexpected happened – Nafula went for what looked like a very powerful hook to Ibrahim's head, but he had disappeared before her hit could land. Quite literally. Based on the surprised gasps around the arena, none of us could see him anymore.

Neither could Nafula.

She was turning slowly on her heels, holding a defensive position and waiting for Ibrahim to attack. Because he would. And since he had used his power to bend the light around him until none touched him anymore and he became virtually invisible, she could not prepare for the attack. Although… maybe she didn't need her eyes.

We must have reached the same conclusion at the same time because she suddenly stopped moving and closed her eyes. Her hands started glowing a faint blue, so dark it looked almost black. I could see the reluctance on her face – she did not want to use her powers in such as deadly way. She wasn't like Alexei. Hurting others – killing them – did not excite her. But she knew she had to do it.

A gargled scream came from behind her. Ibrahim's hold on the light dropped, and he was back in our view in the blink of an eye. He was kneeling on the ground, hands grasping at his throat and chest, desperately clawing at his skin. What the-

The answer came to me like a bomb.

She was drowning him. She must have gathered enough water from his body and moved it within his lungs. Drowning him even as he was standing on a barren expanse of sand and dried earth.

How ironic.

It lasted forever. Or at least it seemed like it. Ibrahim struggled and fought, convulsing on the ground and clawing at his chest until he had bloody gashes all over his skin.

He didn't tap out.

When he finally died, the arena remained silent for one long moment. Nafula had tears in her eyes but didn't let them fall. Instead, she stood tall and proud as she received a standing ovation. But I could see the way her hands shook and how she had to blink rapidly to prevent the tears from falling.

One had fallen down my cheek. Bending my head down to hide, I hurriedly wiped it away.

"What a great fight!" the nymph exclaimed with a joyous tone that would have been better suited for a boxing announcer. "Nafula Mwangi, you have proven your worth and are welcome to take your due place on the dais beneath the gods and goddesses of Olympus."

I hadn't realized it, but six ornate chairs had appeared on a grand stage beneath the balcony where the deities lounged under the sun. Nafula walked out of the cage – the door had reappeared – and to her chair. Her steps were stiff but hurried as if she wanted to get out of the spotlight as fast as possible. I understood that. I wanted to go and hide in the world's deepest hole and hadn't had to go in the cage yet.

No one came in to take care of Ibrahim's body. It just disappeared. There one second and gone the next. As if he'd never even existed.

I didn't have time to dwell on how unjust it all felt – that Ibrahim didn't even get an acknowledgment or a word, that no loved one had come down to be with him, that he'd been treated like a disposable toy to play with and discard when useless – because the nymph was back at it. Søren was called, followed by Cassian.

Mei gave a small whimper when her boyfriend's name was called. He squeezed her hand tight, gave her a movie-worthy kiss, and left to walk confidently to the cage. We all knew Søren was strong – he'd shown it when he'd humiliated Elena a few weeks ago. But still, seeing a loved one enter this cage of death was brutal.

The last time I'd seen Søren fight, he'd played around with Elena, hurting her slowly and making sure she had plenty of time to know, deep in her soul, that she would lose. Today, though, he didn't play. How he dispatched Cassian – who had initially been confident with his fight-centered power – was nothing if not clinical. Cassian did not even stand a chance.

Søren used multiple fire vines to snatch all four of his limbs and tackled him to the ground. The vines were tight, and the other Copper, screaming in pain from the burns, could not move for the life of him. Søren asked if he wanted to stop three times. When Cassian shook her head for the third time, the blond Copper snapped his neck.

The whole thing lasted less than a minute. The spectators were clearly disappointed – they must have expected more of a show – because they didn't cheer nearly as hard as they had for Nafula. Even the nymph seemed less excited when she thanked Søren and invited him to join Nafula on the winners' dais.

Next up was Archer with my dear friend Alexei. The latter looked like he almost pissed his pants when the nymph called his name after Archer's. It was satisfying – or it should have felt that way. But knowing he would die didn't make the revenge feel sweet.

Before he stood up, I turned to look at Archer, and his pinky finger grabbed mine. I could read it all in his eyes – how much he cared and the promise that he'd be fine. I knew he would. That man was the strongest and most powerful Copper within this

Tournament – maybe even ever. But still, it felt nice to see the determination, confidence, and care in his eyes.

When they both entered the cage, Archer said something to Alexei. I saw his lips move but couldn't hear the words under the ambient noise. Based on how his face became paler than it already was, Alexei must not have enjoyed the comment.

My breath caught in my chest when the gong echoed in the arena. Alexei tried to charge Archer – probably thinking he'd have more of a chance in hand-to-hand combat than magical fighting. Except Archer didn't want to play either. His eyes glowed for a second, and Alexei stopped short, his eyes widening and staring at something only he could see. A few seconds passed, and he started cowering in fear, whimpers coming from his lips. For a moment, I wondered if Archer would make it last.

But then Alexei dropped like a rock to the ground, screaming in pain so loudly that it made me wince. His body was convulsing on the sand, incapable of doing anything but taking it. Archer asked something coolly, probably if the scumbag wanted to submit. Honestly, I wasn't sure he could have tapped out even if he wanted to. Archer didn't even ask again – he stood there, above the Copper drowning in pain, and closed his fists. Alexei's body heaved up, his scream dying in a strangled sound, and then his body fell back down, limp and lifeless.

The nausea I felt was almost enough to make me throw up. I'd just witnessed three deaths without doing anything to stop them. It made me want to puke and cry and flee at the same time. If I survived today, how was I supposed to live with myself? How was I supposed to be able to look at myself in the mirror?

My gaze kept locking back onto Alexei's body. His limbs were at odd angles – not broken but not in positions that people would ever voluntarily put themselves into. His face was turned our way, glossy eyes unseeing. I had hated the guy – despised and feared him equally. But seeing him like this? I didn't feel any satisfaction or relief.

Seeing his body disappear as if he'd never existed was a relief. I wanted to forget about him – about Ibrahim and Cassian, too – but his lifeless body was burned into my mind. Like a permanent tattoo I wished I could remove.

A hand took mine, making me jump in surprise. Turning my head, I met Mei's eyes. She was scared; it was clear as day. She had been so confident in her abilities during the first three Trials. She'd been badass Mei, showing how strong and capable she was – more than earning her place here. But now that we were faced with a Trial where our acts would directly cause someone else's death or lead to our own… well, that was very different from capturing another team's flag or running an obstacle course.

I felt that too. This Trial was a whole other level, and I didn't know how anyone could go through it without freaking out.

Søren and Archer had, though. They'd both gone through the motions like they had done this a hundred times before. That was scary because the Søren and Archer that I knew weren't cold-blooded murderers. At the same time, however, I was glad they were still alive. Glad that they hadn't been the ones to die.

Did that make me a terrible person?

"We're going to be okay, Mei." The words left my mouth without my consent. I knew I couldn't make that promise – there was no way to know that either of us would make it out. She knew that as well as I did. But she nodded and smiled. Not her usual bright smile, which she gave without counting to her friends. But a smile nonetheless, one that conveyed too many emotions for me to process.

And I didn't have time to think about it more because the nymph announced the next two fighters. "Our next two adversaries will be Binh Nguyen and Amara Mendez!"

The crowd cheered, but I didn't hear them. A loud ringing echoed in my head from the shock. If Binh and Amara were to fight now, then… then it left only four of us here and, outside of Elena, the last two were my friends.

Sadie and Mei must have realized it at the same time because Mei's hand tightened in mine, and Sadie turned to look at us with wide eyes. All three of us knew what was coming. At least one of us wouldn't make it. There was no other way.

Sadie moved down a chair so she could be seated next to me, and we stared at each other for a second, speechless and terrified.

"It wasn't supposed to happen," her voice broke on the last word. "Archer and I had talked with Hecate. She said none of us would fight against each other. I don't-" She was interrupted by the gong.

On the other side of the arena, where the winners were seated, both Archer and Søren were standing and yelling something at the gods in the balcony above. I couldn't tell what they were saying. I didn't care much anyways. I was falling into a downward spiral of panic, wondering what I would do if I ended up against either Sadie or Mei.

"I don't understand." Sadie was choking on tears, her words heavy, and Mei had completely frozen next to me.

None of us watched the fight. It must have lasted a while – longer than the other ones – because the spectators sounded like they were having fun. But I couldn't get my mind to wrap around the situation. The worst-case situation.

We had come so far as a group, helping each other, and it would end today. There wouldn't be five of us anymore.

As I shifted to look back at the guys, my gaze briefly met Elena's. She had a satisfied smirk, telling me without doubts that she had had a hand in this. Maybe this was her revenge for being cursed by Hecate and humiliated by Søren after trying to mess with me. Perhaps this was just her hating on humans and spreading her hate to my friends. Either way, she was enjoying the way all of us were stuck in a state of incomprehension and barely restrained panic.

My head was still like cotton, eyes unfocused and teary when the screams stopped from the cage and the applause thundered. I was still slightly shaking, my hands gripping my friends so tightly that it hurt, when the nymph thanked Amara.

I stopped breathing when the silence grew thick. The world had stopped spinning, and we were all waiting for the other shoe to drop.

"And now, for our second to last fight, please welcome Mei Lee, descendent of Pan, who will compete against Sadie Aska, descendent of Thanatos."

Chapter Thirty-Six

Everything stopped for a moment. Like my body and mind had pressed pause on life. Like the world needed a second to recover from the earthquake these words had caused. I just sat there, a weight on my chest so big that I couldn't breathe or move. I couldn't process the words for a while, hoping I'd just misheard. Maybe it was all a misunderstanding.

Except it wasn't.

It couldn't be.

The Tournament was supposed to be hard and cruel and unfair. We'd all been lucky so far, my friends and I. We'd beaten the odds, and it looked like it was finally time to pay it all back.

My awareness of the world returned with a view of the guys in the distance. Archer was slumped in his chair, looking both anxious and relieved. And Søren? Søren was standing, a hand on his mouth, looking ready to either break down in tears or destroy the whole arena with the gods and spectators inside. I could understand that — he knew very well that either his twin sister or his girlfriend wouldn't make it. That was enough to break someone.

Next, I felt the bone-breaking grip of Mei's hand. She had frozen and stared at the cage, fear written on her face. On my other side, Sadie whispered 'no' in an endless mantra, slowly shaking her head.

I wasn't sure what I was supposed to do. What was I supposed to say when my two female friends were forced to go into a cage and fight to the death? Were there words that could even help them? I wasn't sure they existed.

"I can't do it." Mei's voice was barely loud enough to be heard above the spectators' growing annoyance at their lack of action. "I knew coming in that it would be hard for me to fight. But against you?" She gave Sadie the saddest, most resigned look I had ever seen.

"No, Mei. We can refuse to fight. We can force them to do something else. We can-"

"It has to be you, Sadie. We both know that if we hadn't been friends, if we had had to fight for real, you would have decimated me. There is no question about who would have won."

That was true. All three of us knew it. Mei's gift with birds was handy in most situations – including during the first and third Trials – but it was useless in a cage where no birds could help her. And even then, Sadie was as strong as Søren, both twins only second in power strength to Archer. Under normal circumstances, this would not have been a fair fight.

"Still, I can't do that to you. I can't-" Sadie stopped and swallowed, tears welling in her eyes and seconds away from falling. "I can't do that to Søren."

I knew Sadie and Mei were close but nowhere near best friends. But it wasn't the point. She was still part of the family. None of us had thought she and Søren would become anything remotely strong. Neither Sadie nor I could stand her at first. But the thing with Mei was that once she decided you were worthy of her attention and friendship, she opened up and grew on you like the most resilient and prolific weed ever. One day I had been exasperated at her attitude, and then the next, we were joking around together and bonding over our love of pop songs. And I knew that Mei had grown on Sadie too.

And that was without even considering how much Søren now cared about Mei. I didn't think they had called it love or anything so serious – neither of them was the type to put important words on something like that. But it was plain as day – in the way they held each other and looked at each other. There was no other word for it than love.

"We both know you'll do great things on Olympus, Sadie. I don't have the power level or network to do a tenth of the change and good you will bring to the mountain."

Sadie shook her head vehemently. How was she supposed to agree to that? How was she supposed to say that she'd sentence her twin's girlfriend to death? How was she supposed to go with that when her brother was pacing back and forth like a lion in a cage not even sixty yards away from us? I was sure he'd be here with us if not for the dozen guards that appeared to keep all four winners away from us.

And what was I supposed to do? I was still in the middle of this horrible conversation, unsure how anything I said could help. I didn't want Mei to sacrifice herself. But I also didn't want Sadie to die. Agreeing to this beforehand seemed cruel. But I knew that it'd be even more destructor if they fought.

"I can't kill you, Mei. I won't. You're my friend. You can't ask me to do it."

"Then let me yield."

The nymph announced that Mei and Sadie had to get in the cage in the next minute, or they would both be disqualified. We all knew what disqualification meant.

Both girls were still looking into each other's eyes, not moving an inch at the announcement. Then Sadie nodded slowly.

"We'll fight for you. We'll do everything we can to change it." It was the best she could offer and not quite a promise that she'd save Mei, but I knew she meant it. Sadie and Søren would for sure fight for the gods to change the rules. There was little hope, but a little was better than nothing.

Tears were falling down Mei's cheeks as she wrapped me in a hug. I must have started crying, too, because my cheeks were wet. We hugged for a while, and I hated that it felt like goodbye. Mei whispered in my ear that she had loved getting to know me and hoped I'd have the life I wanted after all this was over. I wasn't even sure what I answered. Everything was happening as if I were in a dream. I wanted to scream and tear into someone – anything to make someone pay for what was going to happen. I didn't do anything, though. I remained in my spot like a coward and watched my friend walk to her death.

Sadie didn't follow right away. She wrapped her arms around me, too, and squeezed. I squeezed back as hard as I could. I knew she needed someone to ground her and remind herself that she was only doing what she had to do. If nothing else, I could be that person for her.

"Please, Kalani, please make it out. I need you to survive this. I can't lose both of you."

I couldn't physically answer – there was a huge mass in my throat that wouldn't go away and wouldn't let me talk. But I nodded and then watched her enter the cage. I had to force myself to watch them in there. Had to force myself *not* to look away.

I watched as the door disappeared, and the metal glowed bright blue.

I watched as the gong echoed in the arena.

I watched as neither of them moved.

I watched as Mei yielded, her voice sounding like thunder in the Pit.

I watched Søren fall to his knees in tears, restrained by two guards.

And I watched more guards come in and put magical cuffs on Mei's dainty wrists.

By the time she was walked out of the Pit and Sadie arrived in the winners' area – where Søren refused to look at her – I was crying silent tears. And my heart was broken in half, white-hot pain radiating in my chest.

But the anger I felt was slowly overpowering the pain and devastating sadness. My tears dried up, and my body became numb. I was angry at the people in the stands, cheering like we didn't deserve basic human decency, like they were watching a show and not real people – real *kids* – having to fight and die in the hope of earning a spot in Olympus. I was angry at the gods and goddesses for being the ones responsible for this. They had been the ones going to Earth to have fun with humans. They had been the ones who had birthed so many children that their grandchildren were too numerous to be able to all fit on this stupid mountain. And they had been the ones who had decided that starting this Tournament was the only way this situation could be resolved.

And then they had the audacity to watch us fight and bleed and die from their balcony up above. All for something that none of us had control over.

The anger was bubbling in my chest, growing and feeding itself. Soon enough, it was the only thing I could feel. This rage was swirling and mounting. It was a tsunami, building and building, until the moment when it became so big that the wave destroyed everything in its path.

I knew that anger wasn't the solution to my current problems. But it sure helped mask any fear I had, knowing I'd have to enter the cage with Elena in the next minute. She had beaten me once before, but the rage was erasing all of the doubts that the usual me would have had.

When the nymph called our names, I didn't hesitate to get up. I wanted to hit something. Elena would be a great punching bag.

I didn't look in my friends' direction. I didn't look at the gods' balcony either. My steps took me to the cage door, and I entered, my eyes focused on the back of Elena's head.

Mayfield, don't let your emotions rule you. I jumped in confusion, my anger breaking for a second. The voice sounded exactly like Archer, but it was in my head. One quick look told me he was still sitting in his chair, leaning forward and elbows resting on his knees, looking anxious. How-

Oh, I was going to strangle him.

He had dared to use his damn intrusive power against me. After repeatedly telling him that I never wanted to have him – or anyone else – in my mind. I had no idea how to answer him because he was too far, and I didn't know how to do this whole mind-speaking thing. But I wished I could because I wanted to scream at him that it wasn't okay to walk all over my boundaries just because we were now something more than friends.

Archer must have sensed that my anger was now directed at him – probably using the power he shouldn't be using on me in the first place – because his voice echoed in my head again. *I know I promised I wouldn't use my power on you. I am sorry. But I can tell that you are mad, and you need to calm down a little bit. You can channel your anger during the fight, but you can't let it control you. If you do, she will take advantage of it, and you won't… you won't make it out.*

That was a sucky apology. But I wasn't reckless enough to not listen to Archer when he was giving me fighting advice. After all, he could hold his own and beat both of the twins at once and hadn't even had to move to best Alexei. He knew what he was talking about, and I would have been very dumb to choose not to listen and heed his advice.

Still, I didn't enjoy having to reflect on my emotions. After working through a couple of deep breaths, I could reluctantly see his point. The wave of my anger and rage was this close to overflowing and overwhelming me. And I knew that anger made people do stupid things.

I wouldn't be allowed to make any stupid mistake, though. Elena wouldn't let me.

Archer raised an eyebrow at me, and I had to contain myself to stop my anger from taking the best of me. Gods, I hated when he gave me those self-assured and borderline conceited looks. But I didn't let myself get pissed at his attitude and gave him a sharp nod instead.

Good. Now show Elena and everyone else how incredible my girl is.

His confidence in my abilities was reassuring and bled into me. Knowing that he thought I could do it… well, it reinforced my own confidence and determination.

Elena was standing about ten feet away from me, feet shoulder-wide, knees slightly bent, and hands half-clenched at her sides. She was ready to pounce. With a deep breath to further control my rushing emotions, I positioned myself in my fighting stance. It felt natural now, almost as easy as breathing.

"Are you ready to get crushed, little human?"

"Are we trash-talking now? I didn't know we had gotten to that point in our relationship."

Elena sneered, seemingly annoyed that I wasn't cowering in front of her. To be fair, the last time we'd properly fought, she had handed me my ass in a nice little gift package. Since then, though, I had trained and trained and trained some more with the best fighters of the Tournament. I had bled and cried and sweat to become the best fighter I could be. And maybe I still couldn't hope to win against Archer or the twins at their full strength. But Elena? Oh, I wouldn't lose against her. She had taken a lot of things from me during the past eight weeks – my confidence for a while, my ability to feel safe among the other competitors – but she wouldn't take my life.

"You don't have your bodyguards to protect you now, do you? How does that feel?" Her intimidation technique was weak at best. I had trained for weeks specifically to be able to defend myself without the help of anyone else.

I didn't answer verbally. Instead, I gave her an amused look and a raised eyebrow – because I knew showing her that I wasn't scared would enrage her. And while I was doing my best to control my emotions, I wouldn't mind if she lost control of hers.

Elena didn't appreciate my confidence, and she showed it through her squinted eyes and clenched fists. She wanted to make me hurt, and it was reciprocated. I didn't want to think about what kind of person that made me, how different from the old Kalani I had become.

"As this wonderful edition of the Tournament comes to a close, the organizers have decided to make this last fight more memorable." I could feel the excitement working in waves around the arena at the nymph's words. "To ensure the fight is more exciting for all of us, no godly-given powers will be allowed."

I couldn't suppress a smile at those words. I had been trying to ignore the fact that Elena could transform into an eight-foot-tall polar bear. I knew that she wouldn't transform into it right away – she would have wanted to prove that she was stronger and better than me by humiliating me with her fists before she finished me with her foot-long claws. So, I knew I would only have a short window of time to act and defend myself.

But now, the cards had been shuffled around and redistributed. Unfortunately for Elena, her hand had become significantly worse while my odds had improved. I knew it, and she did too.

Based on the chatter coming from the stands – it sounded like a huge beehive – most spectators were unsure how to feel about the announcement. Preventing Elena from using her power meant the fight would be less impressive and showy. But it also meant that it would last longer, which would be a change compared to the past battle during which Sadie and Mei hadn't even exchanged one blow. Either way, for once, one of the gods' decisions was in my favor, and I wouldn't be ungrateful.

The gong reverberated in the arena. My heart skipped a beat. This was it.

Elena didn't even wait for a second before pouncing on me. She must have expected that I would let her do whatever she wanted with me like last time. I didn't. Sidestepping her, I moved in a semicircle around while she struggled to stop herself and turn around – one disadvantage of being a tall and very imposing person was more momentum, I guessed.

She wasn't a bad fighter, though, so it wasn't long before she attacked again, her fist aiming for my head. I ducked below her arm and sent a hook to her ribs. She grunted but didn't relent and rammed her knee into my stomach. The air got shoved out of my chest, and I moved back a couple of steps to catch my breath.

"Are you yielding already, little human?" Elena taunted me as we circled each other.

"In your dreams, Schmidt." I gave her what I hoped was a chilly and intimidating smile. Being intimidating as a petite woman was hard, but I did my best.

There was something to say about how determined Elena was. She charged again, and, this time, I only barely managed to evade her hit. The plan I had designed with the twins and Archer was for me to spend the first couple minutes tiring my adversary. I'd pretend to be too scared to go on the offensive and let the other Copper waste their energy. The key was to avoid getting hit during those first two minutes. However, Elena was very determined to hurt me, and fast. She wouldn't make it easy on me.

Trying to destabilize me after focusing on upper-body hits for a while, Elena swiped her left leg under my feet. I jumped, but the bottom of my feet still grazed her shin, partially making me lose my balance. I managed to land back on my feet, but the second it took me to use my core to regain my balance was enough for Elena to gain the advantage. She lunged forward, and her right fist hit me square in the jaw. Pain bloomed, and I tasted the iron of blood already. Shit.

Bringing my guard back up, I feinted to the left before sidestepping Elena on her other side. In the split second it took her to adapt, I kicked behind her knee hard enough to cause her leg to buckle. There was no audible crack, but she yelled in pain. Without waiting for her to recover, I punched her in the back of the ribs.

Elena didn't let me have more time to hit her because she straightened – although most of her weight was on her right foot – and rapidly shuffled away from me. Her retreat gave me a few seconds to take inventory of my body. The knuckles on my right hand were open and bleeding. My jaw was in a lot of pain, and I was worried I had a loose tooth, but I would make it past that. Losing a tooth would suck, but it would mean I'd made it out alive.

"I guess the rumors you trained were true then," Elena said as she spat on the ground.

"Does that scare you?"

She snorted as if that was the most ridiculous thought ever. "A mortal like you could never get to my level."

I didn't even deign to answer because I knew damn well that people who thought that other groups of people were less worthy than them could not be reasoned with. Instead, I advanced on her, deciding to start taking matters into my own hands.

Elena saw me coming but didn't back down. She kept her guard up and pared my first jab. My second jab landed on her jaw, but she used my attack to punch me in the chest, thankfully a little off from my throat. Again, the air got smashed out of my lungs, but I didn't retreat because I saw it. A real opening.

Because Elena was having fun trying to hit my face, she had left her right side slightly open. And, since I was much smaller than her, I had the perfect angle for a liver shot.

There would only be one shot like this, and I knew I had to make it count. So, I waited until Elena was distracted by a hook I feinted before putting all of my strength behind a jab right in her liver. Right away, the Copper folded in half under the pain, and I had the crazy thought of doing one of Søren's Brazilian jiu-jitsu choke hold tricks he had taught me for fun.

The thing was, I knew that, with her size and strength, Elena would destroy me if we came to wrestle on the ground. Therefore, I had done my best to remain upright. But she was in so much pain that she left me free rein for a few seconds. And Søren's trick, which had seemed impossible to put into place when he'd showed it to me a week ago, was the type of floor move that could work. Maybe. If I remembered it correctly and didn't mess up.

Determined to make it work, I pushed Elena hard enough to make her fall on her side. Then, I slid to the ground, and right as she started breathing a tiny bit easier, I put my left leg around her neck, grasped her right arm over her head, and linked my left foot around my left leg. Then I squeezed.

At first, Elena didn't react. But, after a few seconds, the pain from her throat and lungs became worse than her pain from the liver shot, and she started struggling. She tried to grip my legs to part them, but I held as hard as I could. How I locked her arm straight over her head also prevented her from sitting up or having a wide range of motion. She was stuck.

I could feel her resistance slowly fading but didn't relax. I had to make sure she wasn't playing me and pretending to be beaten. But I didn't want to kill her. Even after all of the things she had done to me and many of the weaker Coppers during the weeks preceding the Tournament, and even as I held her at my mercy, I didn't want to do it. I couldn't do it.

I wasn't a killer.

"Elena," I grunted, keeping my body locked to prevent her from evading. "Yield. You have to yield."

She didn't, though. She kept trying to untie my legs, and I used every muscle in my body to resist her efforts. Then her hand was only barely tugging at my leg. And after a few seconds, she wasn't even trying anymore.

"Elena!" I was pleading for her to stop this. I might have been a coward or hypocritical, but I didn't want to end her life. I didn't want to be a part of the problem, and I didn't want to become the kind of person who could kill another human being – or as human as a Copper could be. But I also wouldn't let her kill me.

Archer had told me to always remember my why, always remember why I was fighting. Makaio's smiling face was there, in a corner of my mind, reminding me that he was waiting for me. Reminding me that I couldn't give up.

So, I kept squeezing, panic swelling in me but not letting myself relax. And I started losing hope that Elena would yield. I didn't fully understand how these Coppers had been raised, but it seemed like many of them had been taught that dying during a fight in the Tournament would be more honorable than submitting to someone else. That made me sick, but there was little I could do about it now.

I was losing hope. Losing hope that Elena would say that word I was hoping for. Until I felt two little taps on my thigh. A universal sign for yielding. One that said loud and clear that I could let her go.

I had won.

I had made it.

I was going to live.

Under a massive wave of cheers – the first I'd received since that terrible Tournament had started – I relaxed my legs and arms. Tears were suddenly running down my cheeks, I was shaking, and I wasn't sure I'd be able to move. The adrenaline I'd had running through my veins for ten minutes was crashing down, and I was cold and trembling and shaken to my core.

The nymph reluctantly announced my victory, and I just lay there, unsure whether my legs would support my weight. Elena rolled off me, and I saw the blue light emanating from the cage's metal fade.

I couldn't quite believe it was over.

The shock of it all – of still being alive against all odds – was so immense that I had to fight back a full-on breakdown. I was happy, ecstatic, and relieved, but also sad and slightly terrified of the *after*. What was I going to do? Could I just go back to my life? Would the gods reverse the enchantment that had erased my existence from my family and friends' memories? And if they did that, would I even manage to get back to my old life? I wasn't sure the new me would manage to slip back into the mold of the old Kalani. I'd have to try, though.

From the corner of my eyes, I saw a couple of guards walk up to the cage – they were coming for Elena, who was also still lying on the ground close to me. Suddenly, I felt the need to leave this cage – it was burning my body and clawing at my insides.

I almost jumped to my feet. I had to stop for a second because my head was spinning, and I took that time to look at the winners' platform. All three of my friends were standing, and Archer had the biggest smile I'd ever seen on his face. That smile and the way it lit up his face warmed my heart. Without even realizing it, I smiled back at him, and it felt like we were the only people in the world.

"Hey!"

Surprised, I turned around. Elena was standing there, right next to me, her eyes full of revenge and burning hatred. I opened my mouth to say something to her, but I had no time.

She moved, and I saw the dagger in her hand. For a second, I was confused – we weren't allowed to use weapons. But then, before I could realize what was happening, her hand moved to my body.

Thud.

The dagger sank into my stomach. At first, I didn't feel anything. Just the shock of seeing the dagger pushed to the hilt in me, mixed with incredulity because, after everything that had happened these past eight weeks, after surviving so many things I shouldn't have, after all of this… it was the end.

I was going to die. Right here. In the middle of the arena.

Then, the pain came. It was like a tsunami, exploding from my chest and devastating everything in its path. I was drowning and burning alive at the same time.

After the pain, I felt numbness and weakness in my limbs – I fell to the ground without being able to help myself. My chest was in white-hot pain, and my heart was beating fast and irregularly like it couldn't quite keep up. My brain was becoming muffled like I was swimming in cotton, but I knew something was wrong. Other than the obvious knife in my abdomen.

Among the debilitating pain, the muffled screams and shouts in the background, and my body desperately grasping for air, for life, I had the very clear thought that the dagger must have been poisoned. Why would my body respond this way to a stab wound otherwise?

Seconds by seconds, the rest of the world slowly disappeared, leaving only me and the burning fire in my abdomen and chest. I could hear my name in the distance. It started as Archer's voice but changed to my dad's. Which was weird because my dad wasn't there. Or was he?

Everything blurred, and my thoughts were too thick to move through. Somewhere, it felt like someone was putting their arms around me. It smelled like the beginning of a storm, like thunder clouds over the middle of the ocean. Archer.

"You have to fight Kalani. You can't leave me like this. Fight, darling. Please, stay with me. Keep your eyes open. Help is coming.

I promise, everything is going to be okay. I love you, Kalani. Stay with me."

And then, there was a slight pressure on my lips. Did Archer kiss me? That didn't sound right, though. I was always Mayfield to him. We didn't do sweet nicknames.

I was losing my mind. That was the only logical answer.

My cheeks were wet. Was I crying?

Everything turned black. And I was sucked into it like a meteor past the event line of a black hole. Like I was in nothing. Nowhere. Alone.

And surprisingly, the last thing I remembered before everything disappeared was Mom's voice: "Big girls don't cry, Kalani."

Chapter Thirty-Seven

Archer

Some moments in life changed one's perception of the world forever. I had experienced plenty of those. Or, at least, I thought I had.

My life had been a succession of unfortunate experiences, most of them due to other people's choices. Namely, my dear old dad and his lovely wife. They had been a thorn in my side since the day I was born. I couldn't blame everything on them, though. I had made bad choices too, and they had led me here as a part of this archaic tradition the gods liked to call the Tournament. As if Coppers had to be honored to fight for something they should be owed. No one asked to be born. Somehow, though, the consequences of birth always fell on the children.

My point was that there had been plenty of times during my twenty-five long years of life when I had experienced things that had forever changed the trajectory of my life. I hadn't realized that something could be worse than discovering my dad's identity or being shipped off to the Tournament twice.

Living on Olympus should have taught me that there was something worse.

There was always worse.

And this, watching Kalani Mayfield close her eyes and bleed out? Well, it was worse than anything I'd experienced before. Watching her fall had moved the planet on its axis until my body, soul, and the whole universe had been altered.

"No, Mayfield, you can't leave me. You can't leave me." My hands were pressed against her wound, surrounding the dagger, trying to stop the blood from leaving her body. It was useless. Her red blood was staining the sand beneath us, draining into the ground. Still, I couldn't give up on her. "Please open your eyes. Please, Mayfield."

My heart was pounding in my ears, but I still felt the hand on my shoulder and heard someone telling me to move back. I couldn't move back. I had to be there and watch her chest move slower and slower. So, I continued compressing around the wound and pleading with her to open her beautiful green eyes, which had tiny golden flecks when the light hit them just right. The eyes that squinted a little when she smiled at me. The eyes that held a whole universe of emotions and love within them.

"Archer, stop." This time, I knew it was Sadie. She grasped my shoulders and forcefully pulled me back. "Don't be an idiot, Arch. The nurse is here."

Removing my hands from Kalani's body was like wrenching myself away from a piece of myself. Who knew I'd get so attached to this little spitfire? I had sworn off humans as soon as I'd learned who I was, but she had broken down every single one of my barriers. And now that my heart was utterly bare and vulnerable for her, she was leaving me. How fair was that?

Still, I moved back and allowed the nurse to move closer to Kalani's prone body. She was so, so still now. She was usually so full of life – always moving, fighting, and annoying me – that seeing her so lifeless was heartbreaking.

I should have been there. I should have rushed to her side as soon as she'd won. Nothing would have happened then. Mayfield had trusted me, and I'd let her down.

The nurse started working, but I didn't trust her – she had the lazy attitude that most Golden and gods had on this forsaken piece of rock. I also had the nagging feeling that she had ingrained the whole 'those below my station are unworthy' state of mind.

We needed better. We needed Asclepios.

Getting to my feet and wiping my bloody hands on my pants, I looked to the balcony for the old man. Most of the gods – as well as most of the spectators – were still sitting in their chairs, watching Mayfield fight for her life as if this was all a fucking show. But the god of medicine wasn't lounging up there. Actually, I wasn't sure I'd seen him at all, which wouldn't be surprising as he was always either tinkering away in his lab or sleeping. Old age did that to you.

Fuck. What was I supposed to do without Asclepios?

There was a commotion to my left, and my gaze fell on Elena being removed from the premises by three guards, two others preventing Søren from attacking Elena. I wished I could destroy her myself – I'd make it slow and steady, make it hurt until she begged for the sweet, sweet release of death. She deserved that and so much more for attacking Kalani after winning fairly. Stabbing her with a dagger she wasn't supposed to have, much less use after losing her fight, was as cowardly and despicable as could come. My fists itched to smash every one of her bones to make her pay. But I had to stay close to Mayfield. I had to be there. Just in case she needed me.

"Can you heal her?" My voice sounded weak and even broke at the end. I didn't recognize it or myself anymore. The nurse didn't answer right away, her hands moving frantically over my girl's body. I had never seen her so… unsure. It didn't make me feel confident in her abilities.

I repeated my question, my words stronger than before. The nurse's back tensed, but she continued her work without turning around. "The blade was poisoned. Probably aconite."

My blood froze in my veins. Aconite. Even if I hadn't been raised with every single Greek mythology story, I'd have known those purple flowers were deadly. And if Elena had put poison on her blade, it meant that she had planned to use it. The shot might not have been initially explicitly intended for Kalani, but it still reeked of premeditation, desperation, and wickedness. Poison was a coward's weapon. It fitted Elena well.

"And? What does that mean?" This time it was Sadie asking, her tone uncertain and restrained.

The nurse still didn't look back at us, but I didn't need to use my powers to know she was uncomfortable with her shortcomings. "I am not gifted in poisons. The best I can do is stop the bleeding, repair her tissues, and put her in a healing sleep."

"Will that stop the poison?"

The nurse ignored Sadie's question for a quick second while busying herself on Kalani's still body. But then she answered, and I wished she hadn't. "Not really. It will slow the advancement of the poison in her body, but it won't stop the worsening symptoms. It will delay her death and give you more time to say your goodbyes privately."

Her words chilled my blood. I heard Sadie gasp next to me, followed by a sob. I couldn't move my eyes away from Kalani's face. It was paler than usual, with a nasty bruise on her jaw and blood staining the corners of her mouth. She looked peaceful, though, almost like she had fallen asleep. Her braid had fallen apart, and her chocolate hair was spread around her face, resembling a painting. I would do anything to have her wake up and yell at me for being an arrogant asshole. I would give anything to have her call me 'Sunshine' again and kiss me one more time.

She couldn't die. She had just won. She had beaten all of the odds and proved that she deserved so much more than what those elitist deities thought.

For a long minute, I just stood there, incapable of doing anything, not even able to stop the endless tornado of thoughts I had about her, about all of the times I could have done better, about all of the times I could have had with her if not for my irrational fear of loss and attachment. And now it was too late. Now she was lying in a pool of her blood, and I had so many fucking regrets.

I stood there as Kalani's chest started moving so slowly that I could barely discern her breaths anymore. I watched as the dagger was removed and the wound in her abdomen closed. I watched as two men brought a stretcher and put her on it. And as they started taking her away from the prying eyes of so many of Olympus' inhabitants, something woke up in me.

I wasn't the type to lie down and take it. I had never accepted my fate with a nod and a resigned smile. Ever.

Today wasn't going to be the first time I did so.

A beat later, I was running toward the exit, bypassing the stretcher and everyone else. I didn't let myself look at Kalani because I had to keep going. I had to do something. So, I ran even as the twins called my name.

I knew where to go; that was the perk of having been in this cursed training compound twice. Corner after corner, I headed for the Eastern exit of the compound, the one that was usually less guarded – although I technically didn't need to hide anymore since I had *earned* my right to live. Still, old habits die hard.

No guard was near the entrance, just what I was hoping for. I had no time to waste on small talk. The way through the garden was so ingrained in my brain that I didn't have to think – my feet knew where to go. Five minutes later, after weaving through the nicely arranged garden – an excellent way to show how beautiful and incredible Mount Olympus was and give the competitors something to fight for – I reached the fence that surrounded the entire perimeter of the compound. I always found it funny that this fence and the Golden that guarded it were not visible from the compound's main building. It gave the new Coppers the idea that they were in paradise. You couldn't have a paradise surrounded by a magically charged fence, could you?

Tom, a middle-aged Golden who liked booze more than his job, nodded from his post near the Eastern gate. We didn't say anything to each other – he knew I'd get him his favorite whiskey in the next couple of days – but he didn't need me to tell him what to do. He unlocked the gate, and I walked right through.

Then, it was another fifteen minutes of me climbing this fucking mountain like a fire was catching up to my heels. I had never climbed Olympus this fast, but I'd also never had such strong motivation to go to the top. Usually, going to see my sperm donor was the bane of my existence. Today, I hoped he'd act as a father for once in his life and give me the help I so desperately needed.

I wouldn't leave him a choice but to help. Even if I knew that asking for it would be like swallowing a thousand shards of glass.

Now, you might wonder why I decided to go to dear old Dad instead of the god of medicine. Fair question. The thing was, Asclepios's house was very remote, on the other side of the mountain, and it would have taken me at least an hour to run there. The royal manor was closer, especially for me, who knew all of the back entrances to the royal garden. And after everything that had happened these past twelve years, my genitor owed me.

When I reached the entrance to the manor that I despised with all of my soul, the guards tried to stop me from entering. I didn't even let them speak. With one breath and a look their way, I was inside their heads, firing mental connections and sending neural messages until they moved aside and let me go. I walked in and clenched my jaw at the headache starting to form – controlling minds in such a specific way always hurt.

The palace halls were mostly empty, with most people still returning from the arena. It rendered the building even colder than usual – which was a feat, trust me. I hated the big hallways with fancy high ceilings, white marble floors, and giant columns with statues to the likeness of my father and his family lining the exterior wall. I hated how everything was spotless, expensive-looking, and pure – nothing like me, the bastard of the family that everyone kept hidden from view.

My steps were confident as I strode toward my dad's office. He was always there, partly because he did have stuff to do and partly because it was the only room where my stepmother refused to go. She said she didn't like the atmosphere there. Whatever that meant.

Once I arrived in front of the door – heavy wood with complicated designs in thick gold foiling on its surface, just in case people didn't quite realize he was important – I took a deep breath to calm myself. I had always tried my hardest not to enter this palace or this room. Being here of my own volition was uncomfortable. I wished I could turn around and find another way to save Kalani, but I knew he was my best bet. Unfortunately.

Knocking was easier than it should have been. I didn't even wait for him to answer before entering. He could decide that I was the most impolite of his children, and I wouldn't care at this point.

My father was sitting there, in his ornate chair fit for a king, behind his fancy desk, an even fancier pen in his hand. Looking every bit like the magnanimous and holy leader he was supposed to be.

"Son, I'd say it is a surprise, but it would be a lie." His voice boomed in the room like thunder. Fitting for the king of the sky.

"Let's skip the niceties and get to the point. I want you to save Kalani Mayfield."

Zeus raised an eyebrow in that look I hated, the one that said he found my words immature and lacking whatever he wanted to see in a son. "And why would I do that? You know I don't intervene in Tournament matters."

I scoffed because, ironically, he had been the one to decreet the law that Coppers had to fight for their lives. He was the reason the Tournament had started in the first place. How ironic that he now claimed himself incapable of regulating said Tournament.

"Except she won. Per the rules of the Tournament, she completed all four Trials and earned her right to be a resident of Olympus. Correct me if I'm wrong, but aren't you supposed to protect and rule over all inhabitants of Olympus?"

My father leaned back and crossed his arms over his chest. I could almost see the gears turning in his head. I knew that he had pressures coming from multiple sides. Artemis and all the deities and Goldens that followed her racist train of thought must have been lobbying for him to ensure Mayfield didn't earn her spot on the Mount. And, while I didn't have the easiest relationship with my dad, I knew he respected the rules – even when those rules weren't fair. For once in my life, I had the rules on my side.

"She's a human."

"Yes, and? You agreed to have her compete after one of your hunters messed up. She made it through all four Trials and won. The color of her blood doesn't change any of that." I could feel the pressure of time weighing on my shoulders and chest. I had to hurry this up. Kalani didn't have forever. And I *couldn't* fail. "Elena attacked with a prohibited weapon after it had been officially announced that Mayfield had won. Per your own laws, using aconite poison on a citizen of Olympus is a crime. There is no reason why you couldn't act."

Zeus assessed me with a deep, thoughtful frown. I knew this was the determining moment in our debate. The moment when he decided to forgo tradition and external pressures to make the right decision. It took longer than I would have hoped, to the point that I started thinking of how long it would take me to get to Asclepios' house. Maybe I could stop at Hermes' on the way and beg him for a portal. The guy had always liked me, so maybe-

"I can't do anything directly for her. Based on what I heard, she is already in too bad of a shape for anything I am able to do. Asclepios has gone on a meditative journey, and I could send for him, but she will be gone by the time he makes it to her. But if you convince Death to make an exception, I will look the other way."

That was as good as I would get. It would have to be good enough. Now I just had to find Death. Good thing that he cared about his children more than my father did.

I was halfway out of the door when Zeus called my name. "Have you thought about my offer?"

I clenched my jaw so hard that it hurt. "My answer hasn't changed. I don't want to work as your enforcer and will never do so. I don't care about your political schemes. You can force me to compete in this cursed competition a third time, and I'll give you the exact same answer."

I didn't wait around to hear his answer and left. Someone was counting on me. Mayfield had shown me what love should feel like and what a family looked like. It made me realize – if I still needed it – how toxic my father's self-proclaimed care had been.

I ran faster on the way back down, almost flying down the mountain to get to the training compound faster.

There was only one thought in my head – I had to get to Kalani before anything happened.

Tom was half passed out on his chair when I entered the compound garden, and I didn't even spare him a word. Instead, I kept running, my legs aching and sore from the effort. I couldn't slow down, though. I didn't know aconite poisoning enough to know how long Mayfield had before she… before it was too late.

Hallway after hallway, I sprinted through the compound, pushing through throngs of random people who were touring the training compound as if they were in a museum. If I weren't so focused on life-and-death matters, I'd probably have to restrain myself from punching these idiots in the face.

Panic was building up in my chest for every second that separated me from the infirmary. I couldn't stop myself from wondering if I'd been too long and if Kalani was already-

No. She couldn't be gone yet. She couldn't be. I'd go and get her back from literal Hell. We barely had any time together, and I couldn't accept that we would have no more time.

"Archer!" My heart skipped a beat at the sound of my mother's voice. She stood at the end of the hallway, next to the infirmary door.

Seeing my mom there made me feel so much better. I knew she'd help me save Mayfield, just like I knew she would understand the way my world had shifted after meeting the fiery human. I loved my mom. She had always been there for me, loving me and raising me to be the best version of myself. She was everything my father wasn't, and I didn't know how I could have survived everything that had happened these past twelve years and remained sane without her support. And seeing her in front of me after months of forced separation, some part of me wanted to hug her so badly and ask her to make it all okay.

"Oh baby," she exclaimed as I got closer to her. "It's so good to see you!" She had tears in her eyes, and even though the need to see Mayfield was like a living, breathing thing in my chest, I had to stop and hug my mom. She deserved that and so much more.

Having her in my arms, even for a few seconds, was like getting a breath of fresh air. Her gentle and loving presence was a calming balm on my soul. It didn't slow my frantic heart rate or make the panic in my head disappear, but it made me feel supported. I knew she had my back. She always did, and she always would.

"Thank you for being here, Mom." I wasn't sure why I sounded so choked up.

"I'll always be here." She moved back and held me at arm's length, her knowing gaze checking over my body for injuries before returning to my face. "The twins told me about her. She's in there, fighting. Go and be with her."

I opened my mouth to tell her I still had to find someone to save her life. But she tutted and held her index finger up. Priya Vasilias had the kind of presence that made people – me included – stop and wait with bated breath for her words.

"Tell me what to do and go hold her hand. She needs you, and you need her."

I almost contradicted her – I'd never been the kind of guy to *need* a girl. I'd never needed anyone outside of my mom. But she was right. Mayfield had wormed her way inside of my heart like a bug in an apple, and now that she was in, I would never be able to remove her. It was high time that I stopped pretending otherwise.

"Okay." I swallowed nervously. "I need you to find Death."

She nodded, and with a squeeze of my hand, she left. And then I had nothing left to busy myself with. I physically needed to see Mayfield to make sure she was still breathing and still alive. But, at the same time, I was terrified of the state I would find her in once I stepped into the infirmary. I was terrified of seeing her lying on a bed, still and pale and unmoving and empty.

I didn't know how I'd react if she died, and all I could do was hold her hand.

But not being there if something happened would be worse.

So, I opened the door and forced myself to walk in. The room was small because the nurse never had any patients. Coppers could usually heal themselves decently fast, and the nurse only ever intervened after Trials. It was all a ploy to see which Coppers could undergo pain and injuries without giving up.

The room was small, with only two beds inside, separated from each other with a screen. The twins were sitting on chairs next to the bed on the right side of the room, their shoulders slumped and tense, faces drawn. I could feel the tension coming off them in waves – not just from being forced to watch Kalani fade away, but from everything that had happened in the arena before that. I'd never seen them angry at each other – not like this, not for real.

I didn't spend much time pondering whether Søren would forgive his twin for condemning his girlfriend to death because my eyes glued themselves onto Mayfield.

She still had that angel-like appearance, especially with her abdomen wound closed and the white sheets laid above her. She looked peaceful and calm in a way I hadn't seen before. But the way her lips had taken on a blue sheen, the little beads of sweat forming on her hairline, her usually sun-kissed, tan skin turned porcelain-white… there was no doubt that she wasn't well.

"How is she?" I could barely recognize my own voice. It was a hoarse whisper that betrayed how scared I was of the answer.

"Somewhat stable. She's still breathing." Søren didn't look up to me as he spoke. He was staring at his clasped hands intensely. "Her skin is growing colder, though."

"The nurse left a while back and hasn't come back." Søren visibly tensed up at Sadie's words, and, seeing it, she folded in on herself.

We were fucked. Going through this Tournament was supposed to be annoyingly boring. This – our friend group broken, distant, and staring at one of our new friends dying while another was waiting for execution – hadn't been in the plans.

I nodded and moved until I was right next to Kalani's bed. I hesitated for a second before taking her hand in mine – it was cold and clammy, unlike her usual warm hold. My fingers tightened on hers, and, of course, she didn't squeeze back. She didn't open her eyes, didn't smile at me, didn't tease me on my overly serious face. That broke something in me. Something that I hadn't even known I had but now took all of the space in my soul.

Watching her like this, I had this terrible feeling that I had wasted so much time with her. For weeks I'd known she was attracted to me – I hadn't even needed to use my power to know that. Kalani Mayfield was an open book when it came to emotions, especially to me. She blushed whenever I touched or looked at her for too long. She couldn't stop herself from teasing me and gravitated toward me even when she very obviously thought she shouldn't.

I knew that she liked me. And I knew that I liked her. There was nothing for me to do but to like her. And I used our fake dating scheme as an excuse to touch her and act like we were more than friends. But I told myself I couldn't do anything more than that because it would be too dangerous for her. The gold that flooded my veins was a visual representation of everything that separated us – my powers, our two different worlds, her family still on Earth, and the people who despised humans here. There was no denying all that, but I decided to be a coward and didn't fight for her.

Until that night, when I couldn't stop myself anymore and kissed her.

It had been glorious. It had been the best decision I'd ever made. The smile on her face, her eyes glowing with joy… stars, making her happy was worth any obstacles we'd have to tackle together.

We'd have three days. Three. Fucking. Days.

And now, here she was, slowly dying from aconite poisoning. And I couldn't stop from wondering if, had I been braver, she would have been safer.

"What did Zeus say?" Søren's words snapped me out of my thoughts.

I blinked away the beginning of tears and looked up into his red-rimmed eyes. "He said that if Death agrees to make an exception and save her, he will look the other way."

Søren's jaw clenched. Instantly, I knew my mistake. His girlfriend was awaiting execution, and mine had been allowed a free pass from death. He didn't say anything, though, and I didn't know what to say to make him feel better. I felt so fucking powerless right then. Powerless to help Kalani. Powerless to help Søren. Powerless to save Mei. Powerless to fix Sadie and Søren's relationship.

I hated feeling powerless.

The door swung open, and I jumped, turning around and ready to defend Kalani from danger. Except it wasn't a threat but my mom with Thanatos, god of Death, on her heels.

"Dad!" Sadie jumped from her seat and ran to her father's arms. Both of them had always been close. Their hug lasted only a couple of seconds, but she already looked better afterward.

Thanatos wore his usual black robe, looking every bit like the reaper he was supposed to be. It was ironic because that man was the nicest and most protective I'd ever met.

"Son," he gave a nod and warm smile to Søren. "And Archer. Your mom told me you needed my help."

Chapter Thirty-Eight

Kalani

Everything had been dark for so long that I didn't even remember what light was. Everything I could remember was the nothingness around me and the numbness that I felt – somewhere very far from whatever remained of my consciousness.

It was strange because I knew something was wrong. I couldn't remember what was wrong, but I knew that something was. The dark was peaceful and cold in a nice way – the good cold that feels great when bundled up under three blankets right before falling asleep. Nothing had ever felt so relaxing before. Somehow, I knew that shouldn't be right.

There had been a time when the dark had started taking me away. I'd felt it slipping over me and dragging me further in its hold. It hadn't been scary. Not really. I wasn't sure there was even a way to feel such strong emotions as fear here. All I felt was a calm embrace, and then my mind started to go. Everything had fallen away, and I felt like I was falling into a deep, deep sleep.

And then something happened, like someone had cut the link that bound me to the force dragging me away. I'd bounced back into the normal darkness, and my brain had started to feel awake again. Since then, I'd felt like I was moving away from the void, floating toward… I wasn't sure where I was heading exactly. I just knew there was a destination waiting for me.

I had no consciousness of time, so a small eternity could have passed when I started feeling warmer. It wasn't anything close to a nice warm bath, but I had the vague sensation that my limbs were slowly defrosting. Another eternity passed before the dark started to fade away and let tiny rays of light through. It was like that moment when the very first rays of dawn appeared and broke the night's hold on the world. And as the light fought off the void, my mind became more awake.

To the point when I heard voices.

Okay, that sounded weird. I wasn't having hallucinations – at least, I didn't think so – but I was hearing whispers as if people were talking in the background, somewhere far away from me.

For another forever, the whispers were so far away that I couldn't understand them or even recognize the voices. But, by the time my limbs felt defrosted enough to attempt movement, I was aware enough of my surroundings to recognize a woman's voice and a man's voice farther away. They seemed to be arguing, and then everything stopped. A heavy blanket of silence fell. The only thing I could hear then was my heartbeat – pounding like a war drum and reminding me that I could feel my body again.

It took an unearthly amount of energy for me to move my fingers. At some point, I felt like my right index and middle fingers moved. I wasn't sure if it had actually worked, but then I felt something – *someone* – move.

"Open your eyes, Kalani Mayfield." The command was given right in my ear, loud enough for my fogged-up brain to hear it clearly. It felt like a scorching brand on my soul.

My eyes opened without my consent, the light blinding me so much that tears streamed down my cheeks. Fluttering my eyelids to blink away the endless tears, it took me almost a minute to be able to see what was around me. And the first thing I saw was a goddess.

Hecate.

The goddess of magic was leaning so far over me that her face was right above mine. If I could, I would have jumped in surprise at the view.

"Hello, little human. You sure took your sweet old time."

I opened my mouth to answer, but my throat was dry as a desert. The only sound that came out was a choked groan. Great.

"What was it? You thought the last Trial was too dull and felt the need to spice it up?" Hecate had a smug grin, as if she was having the time of her life. Maybe immortal life on Olympus lacked excitement. "Either way, you sure did leave an impression."

I wasn't sure how the goddess had concluded that I had been the one to decide to "spice it up" when Elena had been the one wielding the blade. Maybe the view was different from their godly balcony.

Hecate gave me a glass of water, and after I gathered enough force to lift my head, she titled it, letting the water fall down my throat. It felt amazing, hydrating my parched mouth and bringing my whole body back to life. After a few sips, the goddess removed the glass, and I already felt better.

"What-" I stopped for a second, swallowing, before trying again. "What are you doing here?"

Hecate put a hand on her chest dramatically, her purple eyes glimmering with mischief. "Why? Are you not happy to see me, dear child?"

I was terribly confused. The last thing I remembered was Elena stabbing me in the abdomen and then… and then everything was dark. So, really, no one could blame me for being surprised to wake up after being attacked and find a goddess next to me. Everyone would be startled in my situation.

"I'm just-" I shook my head, hoping to scatter the remaining clouds within my mind. "I'm confused about what happened. How am I… How am I still alive? Where am I? And where are my friends?"

"What happened is that you are one lucky human. Your boytoy convinced the big man to make an exception for you, and he was able to get Death to bring your soul back into your body." The goddess nodded like I should have been super grateful, and I wanted to, but honestly? I had no idea what half of her words meant. I guessed my boytoy was Archer. But who the hell was 'the big man'? And did she mean the whole lasso-my-soul-back-into-my-body thing literally? She either didn't see my confusion or decided she didn't care because she kept going as if nothing was wrong.

"You were lucky that happened because that aconite poison? Well, it's a nasty thing that very few people know how to heal, and none of them were around."

"Aconite? As in the purple flower?"

"Yes, that one. I might have had a hand in creating it, but I must have used a little too much magic, and it's become one of the deadliest poisons in the world. Your friend must have really wanted to hurt you if she braved the merpersons to get it from the island down the hill."

I barely even remembered Sadie telling me about the island, the dangerous people that lived in the lake around it, and the deadly purple flower. I wasn't sure if knowing those things would have helped me at all, but it was yet another example of how unprepared I had been for this life and this world.

"But to answer your questions, you are in the infirmary at the training compound, and your friends left a little while ago. Archer had stayed here for the past day, and I had to kick him out so he'd get a shower half an hour ago. Trust me, that was needed." She smiled at me as if we were in on an inside joke. These gods were so, so strange.

I was about to ask her why she was in the infirmary when the door opened, and Archer walked in. His face lit up like a Christmas tree when he saw me awake. His smile was so big, and his eyes glittered like the stars. It made my chest feel like it was filled with champagne, the bubbles popping behind my ribs. Was that happiness?

"Mayfield!" In a beat, he was standing next to me, both of his hands cradling mine. "Are you okay? Do you feel any pain? Do you want me to call the nurse?"

It was surprisingly cute to see him so worried. "I'm fine, Sunshine." And it wasn't a lie. I felt decently well, much better than I should have after being stabbed and poisoned almost to death. And the more seconds went by, the better I felt. I blushed under his gaze, though, mostly because I could remember him saying he loved me before I fainted. However, I didn't bring it up because I might have dreamed it, and even if it had actually happened, it had been a high-strung situation – I wasn't sure if he still felt that way.

Archer nodded, but I could still see his eyes traveling over my body nervously in search of a wound.

"Alright," Hecate drawled with a too-wide smile. "I'll leave you two lovebirds to your reunion. I am glad to see that you, my dear protegee, are doing well." She started walking to the door, her high heels tapping loudly on the tiled ground. She stopped right before the doors and turned halfway our way. "Oh, and Kalani, thank you for proving Artemis wrong. It was a delight to see you win." And then she was gone.

The goddess' words were a great reminder that she was nicer than most deities to me, but most of it came from a place of personal interest. She had used me as a pawn in her petty rivalry against Artemis. My win had been her win, too – it had been proof that Hecate had been right when she'd said I, a human, could survive.

"I am so relieved to see you awake." Archer's voice was rough around the edges as if he'd screamed or cried a lot lately.

"Thank you for saving me. Hecate told me that you convinced some 'big man' to allow for 'Death' – is that Thanatos? – to spare my life."

A strange mix of emotions passed on his face. I couldn't discern every single one but clearly saw embarrassment and worry. Why would he feel that way? Was there something wrong? Had something else happened during the time I'd been asleep? How long had I been asleep anyways?

I was probably overreacting, but still, I was starting to feel tense and uncomfortable. Even more so as Archer gently put my hand back on the bed and moved a small step away. *What was happening?*

"Look, Mayfield. I have something to tell you. I-" he broke off and cracked his knuckles nervously. "I haven't been completely truthful with you."

Oh my gosh. He was going to break up with me. That would undoubtedly top the way Brad had broken up with me in the middle of our college's cafeteria and screamed at me for not bawling my eyes out. This time, I would probably cry. I'd only known Archer for eight weeks, but time and relationships worked differently here. All the experiences we had gone through together had made us closer than I could have hoped to be with anyone else I'd known for years.

But maybe he didn't want to be shackled down with a human, especially now that the Tournament was over. Or perhaps he'd had someone waiting for him outside, and I'd been a nice little intermission.

"I am not a Copper." That was so not what I was expecting that I stared, gobsmacked, my brain fried. Archer still had his head down, shifting uncomfortably from one leg to another. "My mom is a Golden. She was born from Athena after she went to observe the fights during World War One. And my father... well, my dad is Zeus."

"Zeus, as in the king of the gods? As in *the* Zeus? God of Lightning and the Sky and whatever?"

Archer nodded, his face somber.

"And I'm guessing he's the one you convinced to help me?"

"Yes. I am not particularly close to him, but I was able to appeal to him, and he allowed Thanatos to help."

It took me a few seconds to wrap my head around all of this. It explained a lot of things. Archer was significantly stronger than every single Copper in this Tournament. There hadn't even been a competition for him – he could have crushed them in his sleep. Being Zeus's son was sure to give him exceptionally strong powers. And now that I thought about it, one the few times when he had been hurt, Archer had always been cautious to hide his blood, probably to ensure no one saw how different it looked compared to a Copper's blood. Archer must bleed almost pure ichor. Almost as pure as a god.

"Do the twins know?"

Archer shifted once more, face down. "They aren't Coppers either. They're Golden. Thanatos' children."

Oh. Okay. Wow. I wasn't sure exactly how I was supposed to react to that. My three friends had casually omitted to tell me they weren't Coppers for weeks. And I understood lying to protect someone – hell, I'd done it to Mei – but this felt like a lot.

"How come you were in the Tournament then? I thought only Coppers had to prove their worth."

"You're right. Technically only Coppers have to fight. I have been forced to go through it twice, though. My mom hid the truth that I was Zeus's son for years until one day when I accidentally used my magic in front of the wrong person. Hera got terribly pissed at yet another proof of her husband's adultery and forced me to participate in the Tournament. I made it through, and then, six months ago, I refused to obey my father's order to work for him as an enforcer. I would have had to use my powers to torture and extract information from whoever is the latest threat to his reign, and I refused to be a part of that. Except he asked me during one of his parties with the most influential gods, and my refusal became an attack on his ego and political status." Archer stopped for a second, his jaw clenching hard. I could tell he didn't particularly want to relive those moments. "Zeus tried to use the twins against me to force me to accept his offer. They refused and had my back – which was dumb of them. You don't go against the king of the gods like that. Anyways, I'm sure his lovely wife convinced him it'd be a great way to change my mind to force all three of us to participate in the Tournament."

Damn. I was not expecting that at all. And, now, I could understand why Archer had been reluctant to tell me about it. He had been betrayed and hurt after he'd revealed his secret, so it only made sense that he would be hesitant to share it with me. Sure, it hurt a little, but I understood.

I hated seeing him so uncomfortable and worried, so I grabbed his hand and tugged him toward the bed. The stress lines on his face relaxed, and he sat on the edge of the mattress, facing me. The physical touch made me feel better, and I could tell it comforted him, too – his thumb brushing over my skin in soothing motions was a betrayal of his inner feelings.

"I am guessing you three not being Coppers is why you were allowed to leave the training compound before the Tournament started?" I had often wondered what those 'family matters' were that required a couple of them to leave for a few hours while the last one babysat me.

"'Allowed' is a strong word for it, but yes. The twins and I have been meeting with my mom and their dad as often as we could to keep in touch with what was happening on the mountain. They have been trying to help us as much as they could."

I nodded pensively, trying to catch up on all the little details that suddenly made sense. Their odd behaviors sometimes. Why none of them seemed to be well acquainted with the latest Earth news. Their obvious superiority over the Coppers regarding fighting skills and power level. Their references to 'being on probation' more than once. So many things were now making sense.

"How old were you the first time you competed?" My voice was soft because I knew instinctively that he'd been young. Too young.

"Almost thirteen."

The breath got knocked out of my chest. I couldn't even imagine a baby Archer, scared and impressionable, surrounded by young adults who were ready to fight to the death. Pushing myself up with surprising ease, I moved closer to him and leaned my side against his, my head landing in that crook between his shoulder and neck.

"Are the scars from then?" I hadn't asked about them yet, not wanting to hit sore memories. But I knew they were related to this, and at this point, I figured I might as well ask.

"Yeah." He swallowed roughly. "That year, during the fourth Trial, we were allowed weapons. I managed to get my opponent to surrender, but not before he was able to carve things in my back.

Hera was the gamemaster that year and insisted I didn't need a healer." His voice was level, chest lightly rumbling, but I could tell that, under his apparent casualness, he wasn't okay.

How could it be okay for gods to act like this with children? "I'm so sorry this happened to you." And I was. Mount Olympus might be a beautiful place filled with riches and magic, but many things were wrong with it too. The lack of humanity was one of them.

I was grateful that he was sharing all of this. Seeing him so vulnerable and truthful felt terribly intimate.

"It's been a long time. I'm fine now. I do understand if all of this change something for you. This place hasn't been kind to you, and I am more closely related to gods than you might feel comfortable with."

I scoffed because how gold and iridescent his blood was didn't matter to me. And I knew that he was a kind man who cared a lot. I was lucky to be on the short list of people he had a place for in his heart. His parentage didn't change any of that.

Leaning away, I put a hand on his chin and moved his head so he could look into my eyes. Then I gave him a stern look. "Don't be stupid, Sunshine. I'm keeping you."

After I woke up, there was no time for rest or exploration of Mount Olympus. I'd been asleep for a little over a day, and unfortunately, a lot had happened during that time.

While Archer had been working to heal me, the twins had also been pleading for someone's life – Mei's. Based on what Archer had told me, they had argued that Mei had had to fight Sadie, who wasn't a Copper. Since Sadie already had the right to live on Mount Olympus – all Goldens had that right – they had argued that it would only be fair to let Mei live too. The deities on the gamemaster committee had decreed that the rules were there for a reason. Mei had surrendered, and so she didn't deserve to be spared.

She was executed a few hours before I woke up.

I hadn't been able to say goodbye. She must have been terrified. My hurt clenched every time I tried to imagine her facing death in the eyes.

And now I was there, standing next to Archer and Søren as we stared silently at the tombstone. Sadie was standing farther away, tears streaming silently down her cheeks, but not coming any closer to her brother. I wasn't sure if he had talked to her since the Trial.

Thanatos, wearing dark robes and a guilty expression, was standing at the edge of the trees, as far from his children as possible. Before the ceremony had started, he had tried to go and talk to Søren. I hadn't been able to hear the words they exchanged, but it hadn't gone well based on Søren's angry posture and Thanatos's somber face. At all. Truth be told, I wasn't sure there was a good way for Thanatos to explain to his son that he hadn't been able to save his girlfriend – especially with me, the human who had been brought back to life, standing right there.

A woman was sobbing to my right – Mei's mom. She was a small and frail-looking thing too. They looked so alike that I did a double take when I first saw her. Her pain and sorrow were almost physical things, waves crashing over me with each of her sobs.

Mei's name was engraved on the stone. She had insisted on being incinerated, so her ashes were buried with a gold coin under the earth – it was payment for Charon and ensured her soul was ferried to the Underworld. I wished I'd been able to see her before… before she had been killed.

A man was singing a soft and haunting melody on the side, forcing all of my emotions to bubble up to the surface. There was no stopping the tears or the memories of her that played like a movie behind my eyes. I couldn't stop thinking about how much life she still had to live. How much she'd been robbed of.

It was so unfair. She had only been twenty-one years old. She'd barely started living. And because of a little ichor flowing through her veins, she had been cut short.

And all of us were left destroyed in her wake.

The twins weren't even looking at each other. Sadie was so ashamed of what had happened that she isolated herself. Søren avoided looking at me for too long, probably because I'd been saved while Mei hadn't. Archer had stuck to me like glue ever since we'd walked into the clearing and seen Mei's tombstone. And I? Well, I wasn't sure how I'd ever manage to stop crying.

During the fourth Trial, I'd felt all-consuming anger at the thought of Mei being forced to surrender. But here? Staring at the tombstone and what remained of a friend? The anger was gone, and all that remained in its wake was sorrow. Overwhelming and unstoppable grief. A wave of despair so high and rough that I wasn't sure how I'd stop tumbling under the water and come back for air.

The sun died below the sea of clouds, and the beautiful oranges and pinks disappeared. The man stopped singing as the last rays of sunlight vanished, and the silence became an oppressing presence. It was a shadow that reminded me of all that we had lost and everything that we had failed to accomplish. Mei was the epitome of the long list of regrets I had. And the dark gave my mind plenty of opportunities to remember every single second I'd shared with her – from our rocky start to the desperate hug we'd shared right before she entered the cage. I wished I'd been able to tell her how much she had come to mean to me then. I wished I'd been able to express how much I cared for her and how sorry I was that it hadn't been me or anyone else entering that cage instead of her.

Later that night, as Archer and I lay side by side in our two twin beds pushed together, I still couldn't rid myself of the image of Mei's smiling face as we got ready for the Opening Ceremony and sang to Taylor Swift's best songs. How could everything have gone so wrong since then?

"What happens now?" I knew Archer wasn't asleep, but I still whispered because it felt like we were hiding from the world in our room. Sadie was still sleeping in her old room tonight, but everyone else, including Søren, had left. And here, cuddled together in the dark, it felt like we were alone, and the whole world had stopped for a moment.

"I don't know, Mayfield. I guess we learn how to live with this."

I knew what he meant. 'This' meant not only the emotional and physical trauma we had undergone after weeks of fighting for our lives, but also the scars on our souls that we had earned from seeing so many people die around us, witnessing a friend die, and now seeing our support system explode from within.

"It's going to take a while, but things will get better. I promise."

Archer kissed my forehead, and I felt a single tear roll down my cheek. I hoped it would get better. So, I pushed the uncertainties of the future into a dark corner of my brain and nestled closer to the man who had moved mountains to save me. He would say we had saved each other, and that might be true. Either way, the Tournament had brought me a lot of pain but also incredible people I was now lucky enough to call my family.

"I love you, Mayfield." Archer kissed my forehead with such tenderness it brought tears to my eyes. "We will figure everything out. Together."

Warmth spread through my chest. I whispered those words back – I love you – in his chest and listened to the calm beats of his heart.

We'd get back to it. Our family would fix and patch itself back together. I knew we would. And I'd hold onto Archer's hand as we did it.

Chapter Thirty-Nine

Somehow, the world kept spinning. After almost dying and witnessing Mei's funeral, I would have thought that everything would stop. How could things keep going on as usual?

But things did go on as normal. I woke up after a night filled with nightmares, and it was morning. The sun had continued spinning. Time had kept on flowing like sand slipping through my fingers.

I didn't know how to keep going, though.

For over two months, I'd had a definite goal to help me push, train, and fight every waking second of every day. It hadn't been easy. No, it had been awful, and I'd wished for different circumstances so many times. But that goal – surviving, no matter what – had helped me cope with everything I'd witnessed and been forced to do.

Now that I had survived, things had shifted.

Everything I'd endured for months was swinging back in my face like a three-ton boomerang, and I had no way to stop the wreck that was coming.

I had boarded a one-way track to a full-on emotional breakdown two months ago and was fast approaching the terminus.

I wished time would stop and let me take a breath. Oh, how I wished I was a Copper and had powers over time right now. So many things would have been easier if I hadn't been a stupidly weak human with blood as red as rubies.

Perhaps going back to sleep was the solution. It would give me a reprieve from the haunting memories of Mei's death. Charlie's death. My death. So many people had died for so few of us to survive. How was any of it fair? How could I even look at myself in the mirror now?

Angry tears welled up as the self-disgust built up. Sleep would provide a reprieve from that too. From the guilt and the shame.

Except sleep would bring nightmares. And too often, nightmares were just as bad as reality, if not worst.

Frustration was building, and I pressed the heels of my palms on my eyes, desperate for relief from the endless thoughts that plagued me. Was there a way to stop thinking? Meditation might help.

"Mayfield?"

I opened my eyes to find Archer standing in the doorway to the bathroom. Steam was coming out of the shower, and his hair was still dripping wet. He hadn't shaved, so a light stubble covered in cheeks and jaw. He stopped at the threshold and ran his towel over his dark hair.

"How long have you been up for?" My voice was hoarse, probably from last night's tears and the screams from nightmare number three. The night had been rough.

"A couple of hours." He took a few steps toward me, looking at me like I was a flight risk. I might have been. "How are you feeling?"

Deciding that it was too late to attempt to hide from the world, I sighed and pushed myself up on one elbow. "Not great."

I didn't add anything else, but Archer had witnessed my sleepless night and dried my tears. He knew. He understood.

Archer nodded at my words and moved closer until he was standing right above me. He bent down and gently kissed my forehead, his hand cradling my jaw. "It'll get better. I promise."

I wasn't sure that was true. Or, at least, it wouldn't get better anytime soon. To be honest, I didn't want things to feel fine. I didn't want to be better because it would mean forgetting Mei, Charlie, and all the kids killed because of their parents' mistakes. The pain in my heart was the least I could do to honor them.

Still, I didn't argue with him. I knew Archer wanted to reassure me, and I didn't want to worry him. Instead, I watched him put on combat boots over his black cargo pants. He'd worn casual clothes yesterday, and I had only ever seen him wear this black combat attire during training. Was I missing something?

"Where are you going?"

"I need to go report to my boss. I took a few days off after the Tournament ended, but I need to meet with him to ask for couple more vacation days. Just until you're more settled in." He didn't turn around as he explained, focused on tying his boots.

"Your boss?"

"Yeah, the twins and I train the young Goldens on the mountain. We teach martial arts, ensure they become fit, and teach them discipline. We've worked there for five years now. And our boss is a Golden, one of Ares's sons."

How did I not know that? How did I not know which job my boyfriend had? There was this uncomfortable twitch in my chest, and I had to fist the sheets to stop from fidgeting. Why the hell was this bothering me so much?

"I'll be back as soon as I can, okay?" Archer's words were accompanied by a small reassuring smile and a hesitant look. This was all so awkward as if neither of us knew how to interact with each other now that everything was over and done.

I didn't trust myself to speak, so I just nodded. I smiled, or at least tried to. One look and I knew that Archer had seen right through me, but he didn't remark on it. Instead, he opened the door and left.

Long after the door had closed behind him, I was still reeling from the interaction. It was stupid, really. Sure, I hadn't known that Archer was teaching Golden children. But I knew so much about him. I knew he loved reading thrillers and mysteries. I knew he preferred sleeping on the side of the bed closest to the wall because it made him feel like no one could take him by surprise. I knew the hawk tattoo on his left pectoral represented his dreams of freedom from his father's hold. I knew he preferred hand-to-hand combat because he wanted his body to be a weapon and not rely on something else that could be used against him. I knew the way his eyes lit up when he managed to make me smile. I knew the way his body moved to fit mine perfectly.

I knew him.

Right?

Was I overthinking this? There was no way to know everything about a person after only two months. He didn't know everything about me. But then, could I be sure we were meant to be together? Had we gotten close because of the Tournament and the heightened emotions it had brought? Was trauma the only thing that tied us together?

Stop it, Kalani. You know that's not true.

But even then, the intrusive thoughts wouldn't leave me. They mixed in with the haunting memories of the Tournament, creating a perfect storm in my mind.

I wished I could talk to Sadie about it – she'd know what to say to reassure me. She always had the right words.

Unfortunately, Sadie had disappeared after the ceremony the night before. I understood her need for space after everything that had gone down. Still, I wished my best friend was here. I longed for one of her hugs.

Somehow, through the haze of my thoughts, I managed to get up and shower. Every step was painful, but I knew that if I let myself lay in bed for another second, I'd fall into a bottomless pit of despair.

The shower helped me cleanse my body, if not my soul. I didn't want to feel refreshed afterward – it felt like a betrayal to Mei and Charlie to allow myself to feel anything less than terrible – but I did. And putting on fresh clothes helped me feel like things were normal. Like I was getting ready for another training session with the twins, Archer, and Mei. Like I'd walk to the Pit, and all of them would be there, whole and well, bantering and laughing together.

Stop. Don't go there.

Instead, I busied myself with packing my clothes and the few belongings I had to be ready to move. I wasn't sure exactly where we would move, but I knew neither Archer nor I wanted to remain in this place longer than necessary. The walls, the furniture, the air itself, everything here reminded me of all that we'd lost.

I was folding my workout clothes away when a knock sounded at the door. Archer wouldn't knock – it was his room. Søren was usually much louder when knocking – although I doubted he would even come to this room, seeing as he couldn't look at me the day before. For a second, I hoped Sadie would be standing there. However, when I opened the door, it wasn't my best friend waiting but her dad.

Thanatos.

What a surprise.

"Good morning Kalani. Can I come in?" The god's voice was low and smooth, exactly what I imagined death would sound like.

"Hi. Yes, sure," I stammered, surprised, and moved to let him in the room. "Archer isn't here if you want to talk to him."

"No, I actually wanted to speak with you."

His words left me speechless, and my mind immediately went to all of the worst-case scenarios I could imagine. Had there been an issue with the magic the God of Death had used to save my life? Had Zeus changed his mind and decided I wasn't worthy of living on Olympus?

There was a long silence during which the god assessed the room before pointing to the bed, signaling me to sit down. He had a soft smile, but it didn't ease my worries. After all, what pleasant conversations ever required people to sit down?

"First, how are you feeling? I haven't been able to see you since I helped you out to check on you."

'Helped out' meant resuscitate, and I was thrown off by how crazy it was that I was sitting next to the God of Death. Those kinds of things – incredible, fantastical things – were only supposed to happen in movies and books, not in real life.

"I'm good. Alive and as well as I can be, I guess. Thank you for that."

"Good." Thanatos paused, and his gentle eyes searched mine for a few seconds. I could see his daughter in him, in the way his eyes softened and he gave reassuring smiles. "I wanted to have a conversation with you about something I felt when I touched your soul."

"When you touched my soul?"

"Yes. The poison had already killed you when I was called in. Your heart had just stopped beating. I had to forcefully grab your soul and pull it back into your body before it left for the Underworld. That is not something I often do, far from it, but I did feel something… odd."

"Something odd?" Gods, I felt like a parrot, but I was too stunned for anything more sophisticated.

Thanatos folded his hands on his thighs in a very proper way. It was a good reminder that he was old – after all, Death had been there since the beginning of life, hadn't it? – and very much not human. And it made me worry because what would a being like him find odd?

"I am unsure how to breach this topic, but," he cleared his throat uncomfortably, "do you have any information about your lineage?"

"My parents? Well, my mom is very much human and works as a waitress. My dad died before I was born. Car accident."

Thanatos hummed pensively and seemed to weigh his next words carefully.

"Do you have any information about your father's origins?"

"I mean… I know he moved to California from Hawaii, where he grew up. I don't think he had much family there anymore. At least, my mom never mentioned anyone. I don't know much else. My mom didn't like talking about him after the accident."

"Interesting."

There was another pause, and I fought against the urge to start fidgeting. Where was this going? And why the hell was the God of

Death being so evasive? I needed a straight answer and decently soon so my mind would stop wandering to worst-case scenarios.

Finally, Thanatos started speaking again.

"As I mentioned previously, I had to touch your soul in order to save your life. When I did so, I felt a ripple of energy – that is the best way I can describe it. I have not performed this maneuver many times, but I have done it enough to know that human souls don't react this way to my touch."

"What do you mean?"

"It means you are not completely human."

The words felt like a bomb. Like something had exploded inside my head, and nothing would ever be the same anymore.

"But- but it's not possible. My blood is red. Completely red. There isn't even a drop of ichor in it." I sounded frantic and didn't even care. This conversation couldn't be real. Or the god was mistaken. There was no other way.

"I agree with you – you are not descended from the deities of Olympus. However, there is something in you that is not quite human. It might have been locked away before, and your death allowed it to come forth. I am not sure."

"As in, someone would have wanted to keep it hidden?"

"Maybe. Or maybe your heritage was naturally locked up from being surrounded by humans. Either way, I would advise that you look into your father's life. And you might experience some… unexpected events."

"Am I going to wake up next week and start leaking magic uncontrollably? Will I explode with magic? What the hell is going to happen to me?" I might have started to hyperventilate. This was too much.

Thanatos was amused by my poorly hidden panic but refrained from more than a lopsided smile. "No, child, your powers, whichever they might be, will not suddenly explode out of you. However, you might see small signs that you have new abilities over the coming weeks or months. From what I have felt, I believe your hidden abilities will not be extremely powerful. This should grant you the opportunity to decide whether you want to explore your magical heritage more or not. Either way, I strongly recommend that you keep this information private."

This whole conversation was a whirlwind of information, but Thanatos's insistent stare emphasized his last sentence.

"Why?"

"There are many political plays at work on Olympus. Some deities are already tense about your acceptance into our community. I don't believe they would be particularly open to welcoming a human with a magical heritage not born from Olympus. Thus, I encourage you to be very careful who you disclose this information to. Be assured that, for my part, you are the only person I have exchanged this information with, and I won't broach the subject with anyone else, not even my children."

Then, after a quick goodbye, the God of Death was gone.

Still stunned, I stared out the window for a long time, lost in thoughts. Who would have thought that dear old dad might have unknowingly given me a sprinkle of magic? Not me, that was for sure.

Here went my hopes that life would get easier from now on.

Epilogue

The air had a familiar smell that I had associated with home for so long. For twenty years, to be specific. I wasn't sure it was the only place I could call home anymore. A lot of things had happened since I'd left Earth.

Walking through the streets of my city was surreal. The cars and bikes and chatter and kids playing and distant police sirens were a melody I'd been used to once upon a time. But after almost nine weeks of the calm paradise that was Mount Olympus, my senses were slightly overwhelmed.

Archer's hand in mine was grounding, and I was so grateful he'd offered to come. It turned out that coming back to Earth and my family hadn't been as easy as I'd expected. First, Hecate had shown up the afternoon after Mei's funerals to talk with me about the memory enchantment placed on my family and friends after the hunter guy had messed up and brought me to Olympus. After my talk with Thanatos, I expected the worst – I'd been right.

She explained that the memory spell wasn't supposed to be removed. She could try, but she couldn't promise that it would work or that it wouldn't have unexpected side effects such as the partial recovery of memories, distortion of memories, or even the development of mental disorders in the individuals that the spell had impacted. That had been a shock. I'd survived the Tournament by holding onto the belief that I'd be going back to my brother, and I hadn't quite been made aware of the risks inherent to removing the memory-erasing spell.

But outside of that already significant hurdle, I realized I was terrified to go back home. A lot had happened to me during these past two months, and to survive, I had been forced to adapt. The Kalani Mayfield that danced to Beyonce that fateful morning was nothing like the Kalani I was today. And that was scary. Even if my family could remember me, I was terrified they wouldn't recognize me anymore. Would Makaio still be able to love me if he knew I had killed people? I wasn't so sure.

And then, to add even more information onto the already relatively high shit pile, I'd been told that time on Earth moved differently than time on Olympus. I'd spent close to nine weeks on Olympus, but eight months had already passed for my brother and mom. Eight months.

It had taken me three days to gather the courage to finally travel to Earth. I'd asked Archer if he would come because I needed someone to be with me in case something happened. Which was utterly irrational. After all, Hecate hadn't attempted to reverse the memory spell yet. No, I was here today to assess the situation. To see what my family's new life without me was like.

So, here we were. Walking down the street I'd taken almost every day for years to go to high school. Two blocks away from our – their – apartment complex.

Archer's hand in mine was the only thing stopping me from freaking out in the middle of the street.

Muscle memory was driving me to my destination – which was nice because my mind was racing with thoughts and scenarios of what I could find when I'd finally see my mom and brother. In the haze, I barely even registered the Christmas lights hanging around or even Archer's poorly hidden interest in seeing Earth – it was probably disappointing after living almost all of his life on Olympus.

We walked one more crosswalk by the skatepark next to our apartment building. I wasn't sure what made me turn – I hadn't paid much attention to anything since we'd arrived – but here he was.

Makaio.

Not even thirty yards away from us.

He had grown at least an inch, his hair was significantly longer and falling on his eyes, and he was wearing his winter clothes, but I could have recognized him anywhere.

I was stunned, speechless, as I watched him joke around with a kid I didn't know before getting on his board and going for a ramp skill he'd never been able to do. I had a knee-jerk impulse to go to him – he was going way too fast for something that he didn't master – but he executed the skill flawlessly.

That was the first knife to the heart.

I'd been gone long enough that he had probably learned a lot of new skills. Skills that I hadn't helped him with. Skills that he had perfectioned without me giving him pointers or putting Band-Aids on his shins.

That hurt me more than it should have.

"Is that him?" Archer's voice was gentle and just loud enough for me to hear over the incessant background noise.

I couldn't speak because too many emotions were stuck in my throat, but I nodded. It was him. My little brother. The kid who had been the light in my life for nine years. He wasn't nine anymore. His birthday had come and gone without me there.

Second knife to my heart.

Makaio went for another skill – a fancy jump I didn't know – and I tensed as he wobbled on the landing and barely made it out without a fall. I had the urge to go and tell him to be more careful with skills he hadn't mastered yet, but I didn't move. I stayed rooted to the ground in the middle of the sidewalk, incapable of moving my eyes away from him for even a second.

He didn't seem unhappy.

The thought came to mind, and I didn't want to listen to it. There was no denying the truth, though. He still had his chunky cheeks and had new clothes on – not the fancy kind but nice enough for me to know they were either nice vintage or new. Mom had been taking care of him. And he had been taking care of himself too.

I didn't want to believe he had been fine without me for months when I'd cried for days before falling asleep without him. Honestly, I'd hoped that he would be okay without me, but now that I could see him so happy and well, I realized that I still had the selfish hope that not having me would have made a difference.

And now that those thoughts had started coming, they wouldn't go. And it was completely ridiculous. My whole existence had been wiped from his memory, so there was no reason why he would be missing me. There was no reason for me to be sad that he was doing good without his big sister to help. I should have been ecstatic to see him so well.

Still, tears were gathering in my eyes as his friend – a new friend I'd never met before – trash-talked him, and he answered back with a confidence he hadn't had eight months ago.

"Do you want to get closer? We could sit on the bench; it might be less suspicious."

Archer's words made me jump in surprise. Of course. We were standing there watching kids play on the skatepark like creeps. It would be better to remain inconspicuous.

Again, I nodded, and Archer tugged me to the old rickety bench on the side of the park. We sat close, his arm going around my shoulders. Like two lovers who were enjoying a lovely winter afternoon on a Sunday. And I wished it could be the case. Oh, how I wished I could have met Archer and the twins while still being the Kalani that Makaio knew and loved.

We sat there for a long time. There were a lot of kids and teenagers playing around, but my gaze remained glued on Makaio. And I couldn't decide whether I should go and talk to him or not. I wanted to hear his voice and hug him like a starved man would crave food. But I didn't know how I could even introduce myself. I couldn't just come up and say, 'Oh, hi! I'm your sister, Kalani!'

And I thought that it was painful to watch my brother play without recognizing me, but it became worse. Because mom showed up. She had never come to see Makaio skate before. She'd always been either working or sleeping and never made time for that. But here she was. She was still in uniform from her shift at Mikey's Dinner, but she didn't have her usual broken look on her face. She smiled when she saw Makaio, and he smiled back at her. He was at the age when kids didn't want to show affection anymore to their parents, so he didn't hug her or anything, but they talked, and she ruffled his hair with a laugh. Then she opened her purse and gave him a small bag of sweets. His favorites.

My fists tightened on my lap to the point when I could feel a sharp pain from my nails biting deep into my palms. This – a loving mother who cared about her son and did her best to be there for him – was hard to watch.

Again, just as the thought appeared, I wished I could take it back. Because it was good. It was amazing that Mom had been able to pull herself together and become the parent that Makaio deserved. Maybe not having me there anymore had forced her to stop relying on someone else to raise her son. Or perhaps not having a constant reminder of the love of her life she'd lost was good for her mental health. Either way, it was good. It had to be good. And I couldn't be annoyed about it because Makaio deserved to feel loved and cared for and supported. He deserved the world, and I couldn't be resentful of her for not being so generous with me.

Archer's hands took mine, and he gently forced them to relax. There were half circles painted in ruby red blood on my palms from how tights I'd closed my fists. He then put a finger on my jaw and turned my face toward him. He was worried, and I could tell he wasn't sure how to help me.

"What do you want to do?"

"I don't know." I didn't. I was sitting in this terrible spot where I desperately wanted to have my family back, but they seemed good. They seemed happy in their new two-people life. Was it fair for me to risk their sanity and mental health for something they didn't miss? Was the bone-deep loss I felt more important than their happiness?

Would I be able to live with myself if I shattered everything they had built together, and it went wrong? Makaio had a mom now. I couldn't take her away from him.

Maybe doing the right thing now could partially atone for all the selfish decisions I'd made to stay alive.

"Let's go." I had to physically wrench the words out of my body. This was the hardest decision I'd ever made. But, watching Mom stand on the sidelines and cheer Makaio on as he tried his new jump skill again, I knew it was the right thing to do.

"Are you sure?"

I stood up and wiped my bloody palms on my dark jeans. You couldn't see the red on it. The black absorbed my blood and made the too-red stains invisible. Maybe that'd be a good metaphor for the rest of my life. Now that I wasn't moving back with Makaio and Mom, there was nothing waiting for me back on Earth. The only thing I had were my friends – however broken up we were – and a place on a mountain I'd given blood, sweat, and tears to earn. Maybe living on Olympus would be good. Perhaps it would heal the wounds that littered my heart and soul. And maybe living among people with gold in their veins wouldn't be too bad. Maybe we would manage to get to a point where we would learn to accept each other even with all of the differences that separated us.

And I'd still check up on Makaio every so often. To make sure he was okay. Just in case, one day, he needed me.

I turned around and took Archer's hand in mine. It still felt so small compared to his palm. I tugged him up, and although I could not manage to haul his big body all on my own, he obliged and stood up.

I gave him a tight smile, the best I could do in this situation. But I tried to convey how grateful I was for him through my eyes. He was my rock, and all the gold between us wouldn't stop us from figuring everything out.

"Let's go home."

Acknowledgments

Bringing this story to life and sharing it with the world was one of the most fulfilling and exalting adventures I have had. Every step of the way, I was lucky enough to have a village of people helping me and supporting me.

First, this story would not be in your hands right now if my parents and brother hadn't pushed me to believe in myself and publish my work. So, thank you so much to my dad, mom, and Noah, for your unwavering support throughout all of these months and for putting up with me when I needed to vent about the book. More than that, thank for teaching me early on that books are beautiful. (And thank you Tampa, our sweet puppy, for always being a bright light in my day.)

Thank you to Laura, my dear friend, who showed me it was possible to be a successful indie author. Seeing you share your story with the world was inspiring and the push I needed to follow in your footsteps.

A huge thank you to my amazing beta readers: Anneke, Emma, Georgie, Margaret, Sophie, Elsa, and Macy. To all of you, your feedbacks and the hours we spent exchanging ideas together were essential to the development of the story. Your guys were incredible. Thank you so much for being my friends and early readers.

Thank you to Alice Power and Beck Michaels (Whimsy Book Covers) for bringing the cover of 'All the Gold Between Us' to life.

Alice, your art is incredible, and you have managed to represent Kalani exactly how I'd imagined her. Beck, you have worked your magic on the design of the cover and managed to find a way to perfectly complement the art. Thank you to both of you for your amazing work.

And, finally, thank you to all of you readers. I have been dreaming of publishing a book since I was ten years old. All of the people above were essential in helping me publish this book. But you, dear readers, are the ones I get to share this story with. Thank you for giving 'All the Gold Between Us' a chance and for helping me share this story with the world.

Author's Note

Thank you so much for reading *All the Gold Between Us*. Writing this book has been an incredible adventure from start to finish, and I am glad it has found its way to your bookshelf.

The second book of the *Claiming Olympus* series will be released in the spring/summer of 2024.

If you have enjoyed Kalani's story, I would truly appreciate if you could leave a review on Amazon or Goodreads. I can't explain how important reviews are for authors!

If you would like to be informed about new releases or other fun things related to my books, please consider signing up for my newsletter at jadelebrisauthor.com and following me on Instagram. I would love to keep in touch with you all and share my passion for books with you.

About the author

Jade Le Bris is a fantasy author writing novels inspired by Greek mythology. *All the Gold Between Us* is her debut novel. During the day, she is a Doctor of Osteopathic Medicine and Microbiology PhD dual degree student at Michigan State University. Growing up in France, Jade spent twelve years writing stories before finally publishing her first book. In her free time, she enjoys reading fantasy and romance novels and watching shows with a pink drink in hand.